THE TREE OF STORY

THOMAS WHARTON is an award-winning writer for adults and younger readers whose work has been translated into several languages. *The Tree of Story* is the third book in The Perilous Realm series, which began with *The Shadow of Malabron* and *The Fathomless Fire*. The author says of the Perilous Realm, "It is not just a world with stories in it. This world is Story. It is the place that all the tales in our world come from. Whatever you might find in a story, you will find here. Adventures, strange encounters, riddles. Heroes and monsters. Bravery, goodness, and terrible evil. And many other things that have yet no name in our world. And you are here now, and that means you are in a story, too."

The author is a professor of English at the University of Alberta, and lives in Edmonton with his wife and three children.

The Tree of Story

The Perilous Realm
Book Three

THOMAS WHARTON

Doubleday Canada

Doubleday Canada and colophon are registered trademarks of
Random House of Canada Limited

Library and Archives Canada Cataloguing in Publication

Wharton, Thomas, 1963-, author
The tree of story / Thomas Wharton.

(The perilous realm)
Issued in print and electronic formats.
ISBN 978-0-385-66459-2 (bound).—ISBN 978-0-385-68083-7 (epub)

I. Title. II. Series: Wharton, Thomas, 1963- . Perilous realm
series.

PS8635.I249T74 2013   jC813'.54   C2013-903072-7
                                                C2013-903073-5

Jacket illustration © 2013 Jin Jian Xu

Printed and bound in the USA

Published in Canada by Doubleday Canada,
a division of Random House of Canada Limited,
a Penguin Random House Company

www.randomhouse.ca

10 9 8 7 6 5 4 3 2 1

For Mary

Magic and story ... they're really the same thing.

—Nicholas Pendrake, Loremaster

CAST OF CHARACTERS

WILL LIGHTFOOT
A boy from our world whom some in Fable call the Pathfinder.

ROWEN OF BLUE HILL
A girl from Fable, raised by her grandfather, the loremaster Nicholas Pendrake, after the death of her parents at the hands of the Nightbane. She has a powerful gift of storysight.

SHADE
Will's wolf friend, given the power of speech by the Stewards. Once their loyal companion in the war against the Night King.

MALABRON *(also called the Night King, the Storyeater, the Master of Fetches, the Deliverer)*
The lord of the Shadow Realm. The great enemy of all free folk, Malabron wants to devour all stories so that only his own remains.

FINN MADOC
A young knight of the Errantry who has been searching for his outlawed brother, Corr.

BALOR GRUFF
A wildman found as a baby by knights of the Errantry and raised to become one of their greatest scouts and trackers. Over seven feet tall and immensely powerful, Balor has taken Will Lightfoot as his knight-apprentice.

AMMON BRAX
The archmage of the island of Kyning Rore and a former student of Nicholas Pendrake. Brax seeks the hidden power that he suspects Pendrake of concealing.

CORR MADOC *(also called the Sky Lord)*

The master of a fleet of flying ships. Outlawed by the Errantry for a murder he committed years ago, Corr leads his Stormriders in an endless battle against the Nightbane for possession of the powerful ore known as the *gaal*.

FREYA RAGNARSDAUGHTER

A young woman from the city of Skald. A friend of Nicholas Pendrake's, she brought a warning for him from the dragon Whitewing Stonegrinder about the enemy host marching on Fable.

DOCTOR ALAZAR

A healer of the Errantry and the former physician to the King of the Sunlands. Alazar is a good friend of Balor Gruff's.

LORD CALIBURN

Marshal of the Errantry in Fable.

THE MARROWBONE BROTHERS

Two vicious, overly talkative trolls of a kind known as hogmen. Driven from Skald by Pendrake, the Marrowbone brothers were brought to Fable by Freya Ragnarsdaughter as prisoners.

MORRIGAN

A young woman of the Tain Shee. Once enchanted to the form of a raven by Malabron's dreaded servant, the Angel, but saved by her brother, Moth.

THE FAIR FOLK *(also known as the Tain Shee or simply the Shee)*

A wandering, elusive people driven from their home in the first war against Malabron. They are his greatest enemies.

GRATH

One of Corr Madoc's lieutenants. Grath is an exile from his people, the mordog, most of whom serve Malabron and call him the Deliverer.

CAPTAIN EMRIC THORNE

Captain of the Guard in Fable.

EDWETH LITTLE

Nicholas Pendrake's housekeeper, she has cared for Rowen since she was a small child.

MIMLING HAMMERSONG

A dwarf from Stonesthrow Mine. Once a fighter-for-hire on many quests, this friend of Rowen's longs to return to his former life as a miner of precious gems.

MAYA PENDRAKE

Nicholas Pendrake's wife and Rowen's grandmother. Maya disappeared years ago into the Weaving, where Rowen recently found her.

RIDDLE

A shape-shifting being who most often takes feline form. Riddle is a servant of Rowen's grandmother, Maya.

THE STEWARDS *(also known as the First Ones)*

Beings of power and wisdom who wove the Perilous Realm's first stories in ages past. The Stewards vanished after the first war against Malabron.

IN THE FIRST BOOK, *The Shadow of Malabron . . .*

Will Lightfoot, a boy from our world, ran away from his family and stumbled into the Perilous Realm, the world of Story. There he was stalked by terrifying specters called fetches, but was rescued by Rowen, a girl from the city of Fable. Her grandfather, Nicholas Pendrake, a toymaker and master of lore, feared that Will was being hunted by Malabron, the Night King, who wished to destroy all stories but his own. At the library of Fable, Will accidentally awoke Shade, a talking wolf who became Will's protector and loyal friend. Determined to find a way home before Malabron's dread servant, the Angel, tracked him down, Will set out from Fable with Rowen, Pendrake, and Shade, as well as Finn Madoc, a young knight in training, and Moth, a mysterious archer whose companion was a raven named Morrigan. With his new friends, Will travelled far and faced many dangers before he finally found the way back to his own world. In the end, however, it was revealed that the Angel had been sent to capture not Will but Rowen, who discovered she had hidden powers of her own, and a destiny greater than she had ever imagined . . .

IN THE SECOND BOOK, *The Fathomless Fire* . . .

Fearing that Rowen is still being hunted by Malabron, the Night King, Will Lightfoot returns to the Perilous Realm, only to discover that during his absence his adventures have become legend and he is hailed as a hero. No sooner is Will back in the city of Fable when he must set off in search of Shade, his wolf friend, who has gone missing. Will is accompanied on his search by Finn Madoc and Balor Gruff, knights of the Errantry, and the healer Doctor Alazar. They find Shade far in the north, but are taken captive by the Sky Lord and his Stormriders. The Sky Lord turns out to be Finn's outlawed brother Corr Madoc, waging an endless war against the Nightbane for control of a vast lode of the coveted ore known as *gaal*. While Will and his friends are detained in Corr's fortress, the Nightbane unleash an unstoppable army of spirits known as fetches, encased in *gaal* armour. Will is certain the fetch host's purpose is to destroy Fable. Corr Madoc eventually lets Will and Shade go free to warn the Errantry of the approaching threat.

In the meantime, Rowen has a dangerous journey of her own to make. In order to test her gifts as a loremaster, Rowen's grandfather Nicholas Pendrake brings her to the secret "inner realm" known as the Weaving, from which she must find her way back alone. Rowen succeeds, but soon afterward she is attacked by a creature of Malabron known as a thrawl. In defending his granddaughter Pendrake is carried off to the Shadow Realm in her place. To make matters worse, his toyshop is taken over by the mage Ammon Brax who is after the Loremaster's secrets. To elude Brax, Rowen escapes into the Weaving with the shapeshifting creature Riddle. There she meets her grandmother, Maya, who had vanished years before. Maya gives Rowen a mysterious ball of golden thread to help her in the coming struggle against Malabron.

With the help of the ice dragon, Whitewing Stonegrinder, Rowen seeks out Will and Shade. Together they set out to free Pendrake from the Shadow Realm, while the Night King's forces close in around Fable and its defenders prepare to fight the final battle for the freedom of the Perilous Realm . . .

THE YOUNG MAN HAD been walking since sunrise. The day was cold and overcast, and he was hungry. He had met few other travellers on the road, and not for the first time he wondered where his weary steps were taking him. If anywhere at all, he thought. On days like this he felt far older than his twenty-one years.

He came around a bend and there ahead, pulled off to the side of the road, stood an old red stake truck. All sorts of things were piled on the back of it and tied together with rope: pots and pans, cloth bundles, stacked chairs and crates. Nearby, a woman sat in front of a small fire, stirring something in a pot over the flames. A much older woman sat beside her muttering, her face as pinched and sour as a withered crabapple. A girl of fourteen or fifteen stood in the middle of the road with her arms wrapped around herself, looking off into the distance.

Two young children, a boy and a girl, were perched on an over-turned wooden crate, watching the woman cooking at the fire.

The truck's hood was up and a man was hunched under it, his face hidden.

The young man stopped near the truck. He nodded to the woman at the fire and smiled at the little boy and girl, who stared at him without expression. He addressed the man working under the hood.

"Can I help?" he asked.

The man glanced up, a scowl on his grease-smeared face.

"You carrying a spare engine?"

"Not today," the young man said.

"Then *no*, you can't help," the man said, and went back to his work.

"Do you have anything to eat?" the little boy asked.

The young man shook his head and the boy's gaze moved past him as if he were no longer there. The girl standing in the road gave him a brief unwelcoming glance and turned her back.

"I do have something with me that might be useful," the young man said.

"What is it?" the little girl asked.

"Stories."

"Stories," the old woman grumbled, pulling her shawl tighter around her. "A story won't fix a busted motor or fill an empty belly."

"No, but a good one will carry you for a while," the young man said. "And some stories you end up chewing over for a long time."

"No one here needs any fairy tales," the man said without looking up from his work. "It's a hard world and people can't be trusted and that's the end of it. You might as well keep going, boy."

"I know a story about that," the young man said. "About a boy who kept going when he should've stopped. He ran away from home and got into a lot of trouble. But since you're sure you don't need any stories, I should be on my way."

"What happened to him?" the little boy asked.

"Tell us," the little girl demanded.

"Well, I would, but . . ."

He glanced at the woman by the fire. She eyed the children thoughtfully, then faced the young man.

"Go ahead," she said. "But we've got nothing for you in return. Just so you know."

The young man nodded, then gestured to an overturned wooden bucket. The woman shrugged. The young man slipped off his heavy pack, sat down on the bucket and began.

He told them about a boy who stole his father's motorcycle and crashed it. When he woke up, the boy found himself in a strange world that was like no place he had ever been before and yet was somehow familiar, like a place he had read about once in a book. The boy couldn't find how to get home, but what was worse, *things* were after him. Ghostly things that could take the shapes of people he knew in order to trick him.

The young man paused.

"This one's a pretty long story, come to think of it," he said. "Are you sure you want to hear the rest of it?"

"Yes," the little boy and girl said together.

No one else objected, so the young man continued. He told them how the boy was rescued from the ghostly things by a brave and clever girl, and how the two of them became good friends. The girl and her grandfather agreed to help the boy find a way home.

As the story went on, the young man saw that the older girl had moved a bit closer and was listening while pretending not to. Even the man lifted his head from time to time as he worked.

The young man told how the boy and his friends travelled great distances and had many exciting adventures. They crossed a deep dark forest and were nearly lost forever in a treacherous bog of forgetfulness. They battled monsters, met a dragon of ice and were hunted every step of the way by a being of ancient malice.

At last, when all seemed lost, the boy did discover the way home.

"It seemed that he'd found a happy ending," the young man said. "And yet . . ." He looked off into the distance.

"That's not the end," the little boy said. "There's more, isn't there?"

"There has to be," the little girl said.

The young man nodded. "That's just how the boy felt after he got home," he said. "He knew the girl was still in danger. He couldn't forget her." He considered the woman by the fire, still stirring whatever was in the pot. "But I'm sure I've overstayed my welcome."

"You could go on a little longer," the old woman said, her face not quite so pinched and sour. "Since you've got this far."

"Tell us some more," the little girl pleaded.

"I'm at your service," said the young man. "Though . . . it would be a tremendous help if I could wet my throat. That is, if you have anything you might spare."

The woman at the fire glanced at the man, then she ladled out some of what was in the pot into a small bowl. The young man sipped the watery but warm broth and smacked his lips.

"That hits the spot, thank you." He handed back the bowl, took a deep breath and began again.

He told them how the boy returned to that other world, and how he found that much had changed for the worse in the short time he'd been gone. The boy had to make another dangerous journey to rescue his friend the talking wolf and the girl was forced to go on a journey of her own, to a place even stranger than the world she came from. After many adventures the boy, the girl and the wolf were reunited, but then a greater and more terrible task awaited them.

While the young man was speaking, the woman had fed the fire with a bundle of sticks and now she brought out a small sack full of turnips, carrots and cabbage, which she and the older girl began to slice up and drop into the pot. A savoury aroma soon rose with the steam. The old woman sighed, dug into the bag at her feet and produced a small round loaf of bread. She tore off a thick white chunk for the children to share. The man wiped his hands on a rag and went to the back of the truck, where he unstopped a small cask of cider and poured himself a mugful. He was about to bring it to his lips when he paused, frowned and handed the mug to the young man.

They all watched the young man lift the mug and take a long, deep drink. Then he wiped his mouth on his sleeve and gave a satisfied sigh.

"Well, I won't keep you from your dinner," he said. "Thank you for your hospitality and for listening."

"But you didn't finish it," the little girl protested. "There's got to be more."

"She's right," the older girl said. "You have to finish it."

"I want to hear more about knights and dragons," the little boy said.

"Go on, lad," the man said. "Finish it. There'll be no peace until you do."

"Well, I'll tell as much of the rest of it as I know. I was only there for some of it, you see."

"*You* were there," the older girl said doubtfully.

"Were you the hero?" the little boy asked.

"I was there, but no, I wasn't the hero. There *were* heroes. Some of them were my friends. They were very brave and did great deeds that will never be forgotten as long as tales are told. Some sacrificed everything for others, even their lives. I'll need some time to tell the rest of it, but if you like what you hear, I would ask only to share a little of your meal and the warmth of your fire. However, before I start I should warn you—the story hasn't quite ended yet. The truth is, you and I—all of us—are in this story, too, and it's still going on, right here and now."

"Never mind that," the old woman snapped. "Just get on with it."

The young man nodded but did not begin right away. His gaze went to the road that lay ahead, as if he expected to see someone there, someone he had been waiting a very long time to meet again.

The road was as empty as it had been all day.

"All right, then," the young man said, more to himself than the listeners around him. "Let's see where this story takes us."

1

FABLE WAS STILL THERE.

Rowen came out of the woods with Riddle, the cat, at her heels. She halted and took in the welcome sight of her city, as if she'd been away from it for years instead of just days. With all that had happened in those few days, she had feared she would return to find only smouldering ruins. But Fable was still there, though not everything was the way it had been when she left.

Will Lightfoot joined her a moment later, with Shade, the wolf, beside him.

To the south, across a wide, rolling valley, the little walled city stood as always on its terraced hillside. Not far from the main gate lay a long grassy plain used at times by the Errantry as a parade ground, or in the fall by folk who came from all over the Bourne for the harvest festival. To Rowen's surprise this great field, known to everyone as the Course, was now dotted with dozens of patched, grey-green canvas tents, but this was no festival. The tents were gathered around an immense white-and-gold pavilion topped with a bright flag that snapped in the wind. A flag Rowen had never seen before, embroidered with the image of a rampant red bear.

Many people could be seen moving about among the tents. Some were grooming horses, others polishing armour and sharpening weapons. Voices and the ringing of hammers could be heard through the still morning air.

"Are they enemies?" Will asked in alarm.

"No, they're friendly, whoever they are," Rowen said, knowing it was true even as she spoke. "They've travelled here to help defend Fable."

It was all happening too fast, she thought. Only a few days ago she had returned to Fable with her grandfather, Nicholas Pendrake, the Loremaster, after almost a year away. They hadn't been home long before they were attacked by a thrall, a creature woven of words, which had been sent by Malabron, the Night King, to capture Rowen. Grandfather had fought with the creature and it had taken him, instead, to the Night King's domain, the Shadow Realm. Desperate to find him, Rowen had gone with the shapeshifting cat Riddle into the Weaving, that strange dreamlike place that held the threads of every story that ever was or ever might be. There she'd met her grandmother, Maya, who had been lost in the Weaving years before.

It turned out that all this time Grandmother had been changing the weave of the Realm in small, unseen ways. From within the Weaving she could even change the past, and so she had woven ancient prophecies and portents against the day that Malabron ever threatened the Bourne. This was why these tents and pavilions now dotted the Course. Those Storyfolk down there, whoever they were, had heeded the prophecy and answered the call. And this meant that the battle for Fable was at hand.

"It's really happening, just like Grandmother said it would," Rowen breathed. "They are the first. There will be more."

Balor Gruff, the shaggy-headed wildman, lumbered up to Rowen and Will, with Brannon Yates, his fellow knight-errant.

"Friends, you say?" Balor asked. "And more of them on their way?"

Rowen nodded.

"Many more," she said. She could see them at the edges of her inward sight. Long snaking columns of armed men and women, soldiers and warriors, even ordinary folk from many lands, all marching along the Bourne's narrow roads toward Fable.

"They'll be welcome," the wildman said, folding his great hairy arms across his chest.

"Will they be enough?" Will asked, eyeing Rowen. Will knew about her gift for seeing the threads of Story in things. He was hoping, she realized, that she could see into the future to tell whether the city would be saved. Her gift allowed her to see the past much more clearly than what lay ahead, but now one frightening thread of certainty touched her from what was to come: all the defenders, those already here and those on their way, would not hold back the enemy.

But she couldn't tell Will and Balor that.

"I don't know," she said quickly. "I don't know how it will end."

Will nodded and looked away. She saw that he'd guessed she wasn't telling them everything, but he wasn't going to pursue it. He knew as well as she did what was on its way to the Bourne.

Only a few days ago Will had returned to the Realm from his own world because of a warning that Shade was in danger. With Balor and Finn Madoc of the Errantry he'd ridden north in search of the wolf. They had found him alive, but they'd been taken captive by the Stormriders, who ruled those barren lands from their flying ships. The leader of the Stormriders turned out to be Finn's older brother, Corr, who had left the Bourne years before in rebellion against the Errantry and had never returned. Since then Corr Madoc— or the Sky Lord, as he was known—had been at war with an army of Malabron's servants, the Nightbane, over a vast lode of *gaal*, the terrible fever iron that powered Corr's skyships and gave his men berserk strength in battle. Not long after Will and his companions arrived at Corr's fortress, the Nightbane unleashed a great host of fetches, mindless wraiths encased in spell-woven armour and obedient to Malabron's will. To everyone's surprise, the fetch host had marched past Corr's fortress and headed south for the Bourne.

Finn had stayed with his brother, but one of Corr's men, Brannon Yates, had led Will, Balor and Shade south in a skyship powered by *gaal*. The ship had been about to crash when Rowen and Whitewing Stonegrinder, the ice dragon, found them and brought them to Rowen's childhood home, the abandoned farm at Blue Hill. It was from the farm that they'd all set out before dawn this morning, leaving the ailing dragon behind to rest and recover his strength.

They had returned to Fable to warn the Errantry about the fetch host. But Rowen had also come because only here could she find the way to where her grandfather had been taken.

Her grip tightened on the staff she was carrying. It was her grandfather's, left behind when the thrawl captured him. Now more than ever Fable needed its loremaster. She had to find him and bring him back.

Balor's booming voice shook Rowen out of her thoughts.

"Well, let's not stand here taking in the sights," the wild-man said. "You must be eager to get home again, Brannon."

"I doubt the Errantry will be as eager to see me," Yates said quietly.

"Think of your family, man," Balor said. "You told me about your mother and your sister. They've been waiting all these years for word of you."

"I've thought about little else, Balor."

Yates had hardly spoken on the journey from Blue Hill and Rowen's thoughts had been elsewhere, so she hadn't paid him much attention. Now she regarded the man, startled by how pale his face was. Beads of sweat stood out on his brow and he was trying to hide the tremor in his hands by clasping them. It was the *gaal*, Will had told her. The craving for fever iron became a sickness that eventually killed Corr's men or drove them mad. Yates had insisted he was free of his desire for the poisonous metal, but clearly the *gaal*'s ill effects still lingered.

She looked at Shade then, waiting quietly at Will's side, and her heart went out to the wolf. He had been poisoned by the *gaal*, too, when Corr's men took him captive. Shade's silver-grey coat was no longer sleek and shining but stood up in dark hackles. He was larger, as well, Rowen was sure, leaner and bonier, and his eyes, once bright and penetrating, had lost their gleam. The fever iron had caused these frightening changes and its effects didn't appear to be wearing off. Worse, Rowen knew that if Shade went with them into the Shadow Realm, he would change beyond recognition into a creature of that nightmare world. The wolf would become a monster called the Devourer. There was no doubt of it. She had seen it with her story-sight, the gift she had of seeing how things once were or how they would be.

Shade's eyes met hers. The wolf, as always, seemed to know what she was thinking.

Without further talk they started down the hillside and soon reached the road that skirted the Course on its way to the main gate of Fable. As they passed the camp of the foreign army, they could smell freshly baked loaves and frying food and were keenly reminded they hadn't eaten for hours. Many curious looks were exchanged between them and the soldiers they passed, and in the end Balor couldn't resist stopping to talk to one of them, a heavy-set, dark-skinned man almost as large and imposing as the wildman himself. He was sitting against a pile of bedrolls and other gear, plucking the strings of a scuffed and battered lute.

"Where do you hail from, friend?" the wildman asked.

"I might ask you the same question," the man said in a thick, unfamiliar accent. He gave them all a coldly appraising look that included a suspicious scowl at Shade, then went back to playing his lute.

"This is our home," Balor said, clearly struggling to hold in his anger. "We've just returned from a long journey and it's a bit surprising to find all of you camped on our doorstep."

"That it must be," the man said, and his look softened. "Forgive me. We've been on a long and tiring journey, too. I am Jodo Flyte, captain of bowmen and troubadour. We're soldiers of the Red Duke, whom some call Bearskin, from the many-towered city of Tintamarre. Perhaps you've heard of us."

"I've heard of the Red Duke of Tintamarre," Balor exclaimed. "He's said to be a great leader of men. But his city's so far from here. No one I know has ever been there."

"It's far enough, to be sure. We've been on the march for twenty-seven days. Only just arrived late last night and some of us are still waiting for our breakfast."

"I'm sorry to hear that. I'm Balor Gruff, knight-errant of Fable, and these are my friends. But tell me, what brings you here in such numbers? There must be well over four hundred in your party."

"Nearly five hundred," Flyte said. "Not long after we set out we met a company of musketeers from the kingdom of Sarras, our neighbours to the east. They were marching to your country for the same reason we were. To join in the battle."

"What battle would that be?"

"The one that's coming, Balor Gruff. It seems peaceful enough here right now, I realize, but the things we saw on the road. Houses and crops burned, bodies in the ditches. Folk everywhere fleeing their farms and villages. A few of them joined us. Farmers, smiths, carpenters. They were ready to fight, though they had no weapons other than hay-forks and hammers. Nightbane of every foul breed are on the move, massing in great numbers and heading for your peaceful little country, my friends, raiding and burning as they go. I couldn't tell you why, but it will all be decided here—and soon."

Balor looked up at the walls of Fable and then at his friends. "So we've heard," he said.

"Our Duke met with your Marshal last night when we arrived," Flyte went on. "Fortunately Lord Caliburn heeded the Duke's warnings."

"Well, I'm grateful you've come," Balor said, "but how did you learn all of this in time to make such a long march?"

"It's a strange tale," Flyte said. "We have had peace in Tintamarre for many years, but our Duke was still troubled. He was growing old and preparing to pass the rule of our land to younger men, but lately in his dreams he'd seen a city besieged and in flames, its people crying out to him for help. Yet where he might find this city, and when the battle would be, he did not know. Then one night not long ago we were feasting in the great hall of the Duke's castle when a bird flew in through one of the windows. A bloodcrow, it was. A bird of omen. It alighted on the table in front of the Duke, dropped something from its beak, then flew out another window before we had time to do more than marvel at what we had just seen. The crow had dropped a small, white, five-pointed flower. Nobody knew what to make of this. Then one of our oldest comrades, a veteran of many campaigns, spoke up. 'That is the flower of the Errantry,' he said. 'I fought alongside knights of Fable when I was very young, at the battle of Hob's Knock. They were good and valiant men.'

"'Then Fable is the city in my dream,' the Duke announced. He ordered maps brought to him, and the way from Tintamarre to the Bourne was charted out. That night we all pledged ourselves to the defence of a city none of us had ever seen."

"A long and dangerous road to take on the strength of an old man's dream," Balor said.

"We love our Duke," Flyte said, his voice hoarse with emotion. "He came to Tintamarre many years ago from a land across the sea, where he had fought in what he believed would be the war to end all wars. He was wounded near to death and he found healing, but those who healed him foretold that there was yet one more great battle left for him to fight. And so he set off to find it. His wandering steps brought him to Tintamarre. In those days cruel robber barons had carved up our land for themselves, but the Duke gathered those of us who resisted and restored our hope. He made true knights of us and led us to victory. And that is why we have travelled all this way, Balor Gruff, on the strength of an old man's dream."

"Well, I thank you for it," Balor said. "Though you

should know there's a worse threat on its way than bands of Nightbane. But I can't say any more until I've spoken to my own commander."

The crossbowman leaned back slowly on his bale of gear. "Well, then, I won't keep you from delivering your message a moment longer. I hope we'll meet again, Balor Gruff of the Errantry, when this is all over."

"So do I, Jodo Flyte. Perhaps if we both survive this, you will write a ballad about it and I will sing it."

"I look forward to that."

They left Flyte tuning his lute and kept on up the rising road to the gates. As they were about the cross the bridge over the stream that encircled the city, a voice hailed Rowen. She turned to see, hurrying toward her, a burly man with a shaggy red beard. She did not recognize him at first, but then she saw he wore the pleated leather armour of a Skalding and she remembered him.

"You're Freya's friend," the man said when he reached them. "I am Eymund Spearbreaker."

"I remember you," Rowen said. "Is Freya with you?"

Freya Ragnarsdaughter had never been far from Rowen's thoughts on the journey from Blue Hill. Her father was an old friend of Rowen's grandfather. Freya and a party of her fellow Skaldings had arrived in Fable some days ago, bringing a warning from Whitewing Stonegrinder of the battle ahead. The Skaldings had stayed on in Fable, vowing to help the Loremaster defend his home.

Eymund glanced back at the walls of Fable with a scowl. "We were escorted out of the city under guard last night," he said bitterly. "No one told us why, but we aren't welcome in Fable anymore. Freya didn't come with us. She never returned from Appleyard after she went there to ask that we be allowed to remain in the city. We've been waiting here for word of her ever since. The Errantry doesn't seem to mind having us camped out here between them and their enemies, but no one will tell us anything about Freya. I was hoping, young miss, that you might know something."

Rowen recalled her last sight of Freya, when she'd been led away to be questioned by Captain Thorne. The captain was just being cautious, Rowen reasoned. He would have let Freya go as soon as it was obvious she was no threat. So why hadn't she rejoined her people?

Brax, she thought then. *He's done this. Because the Skaldings are friends of Grandfather.*

"The last time I saw Freya was at Appleyard yesterday evening," Rowen said. "I don't know anything more than that, but I'll find out where she is if I can. And if there's some reason she can't join you, I'll send word."

Eymund bowed stiffly.

"You have my thanks," he said. "We're not leaving here until she returns to us. We were ready to help defend Fable when we first arrived, but now this is about Freya. If there's to be a battle, we'll do our part to keep your city standing, for her sake."

Before Rowen could answer, Yates stepped forward.

"I don't know where your friend is," he said to Eymund, "but I'm here to fight for this city, too. My name is Brannon Yates. I would join your company, if you'll have me."

"Brannon, what is this?" Balor exclaimed.

Eymund regarded Yates warily. He seemed to be appraising the knight's pale, hollow-eyed face and not much liking what he saw.

"Isn't this your home?" Eymund said at last. "Why would you stay out here with strangers?"

"I no longer count myself a knight of the Errantry," Yates said to Balor. "I have no right to enter this city in the company of one. I must earn that right. Then I can show my face at Appleyard and in my mother's house."

"You don't have to do this, Brannon," Balor protested.

"Join us if you wish," Eymund said. "We won't say no to another sword . . . if you can wield one."

"I'll do what I can," Yates said, then he turned back to the wildman. "I realize you have a duty to inform the Errantry that I'm here, Balor. If they send someone to arrest me, so be it. But I ask you, say nothing to my mother and sister. Don't let them find out I'm home until after the battle."

"I'll leave that to you, Brannon," Balor said, clapping a hand on his friend's shoulder. "You'll be seeing them yourself soon enough."

Yates nodded, but there was no conviction in his eyes. He turned away then with Eymund, and Balor and the others kept on up the road.

They crossed the bridge over the stream and arrived at the gates, which they were not surprised to find shut and guarded. The number of sentries had been doubled and more were pacing the battlements above. One of the two sentries who stepped forward to bar their way was a grey-bearded older man who recognized the wildman.

"You're back, Balor," he said with a startled look.

"As you see," Balor snapped. "I have much to tell the Marshal. And urgently, I might add. So if you don't mind, Jasper Haws, we'll be on our way."

"Of course, Balor," the sentry said quickly. "But these others . . . This is the girl, Master Pendrake's granddaughter, isn't it? We have orders, Balor, from Master Brax that if the girl was found, she was to be kept under guard until he comes to get her."

"Orders from Brax," Balor muttered, and Rowen feared he was close to erupting in rage. "Well, be that as it may, you're not keeping her, Haws. I'm the one who tracked her down and no one else is getting the credit for it, understand? I'm taking her to Master Brax myself."

He glanced at Rowen then, and to her surprise and delight he winked at her. She knew she had to play her part, so she did her best to appear frightened of the wildman.

The sentry seemed about to protest, then he nodded.

"Very well," he said. "But what about these other two?" He gestured to Will and Shade.

"Haws, surely even you have heard of the Pathfinder, Will Lightfoot."

The younger sentry stepped forward eagerly.

"I have," he said. "And Shade, the wolf."

To Will's discomfort the sentry stared at him with something like wonder. Then the young man's gaze fell on Shade, and Will saw his eyes widen with fear.

"If it wasn't for Shade, we wouldn't have made it home," Will said quickly. "He saved us."

"And Will here has his own important news for the Marshal," Balor added. "So if you don't mind . . ."

Despite the uneasy looks both sentries were giving Shade, they stepped aside at last and let Balor's party pass through the gatehouse. The wildman led the others up into the crowded main street of the city. As they hurried along, they took advantage of the noise and bustle to move close together and talk.

"They have *orders* from Master Brax," Balor growled. "We've only been gone a few days and . . . *hrrnh*, now I've heard everything. Nobody gives orders around here except the Marshal and Captain Thorne, and even Thorne doesn't sneeze without Lord Caliburn's say-so. This Brax moves quickly, doesn't he?"

Rowen could only nod, her thoughts troubled. The mage

Ammon Brax had travelled to Fable claiming he wished to see his former teacher Nicholas Pendrake once again, but it soon became clear he was hoping to ferret out the Loremaster's secrets. After Rowen's grandfather was captured by the thrawl, Brax had convinced the Marshal that Rowen should be taken to Appleyard for her own safety, and then he had moved into the toyshop, her grandfather's own house and the home in which she had grown up.

Something close to panic gripped Rowen at the thought. The mage had been alone in the toyshop for well over a day now, ever since she'd fled Appleyard with the dragon to find Will. In that time Brax had surely been busy searching through her grandfather's things, and her greatest fear was that the mage had already discovered the raincabinet, the secret entrance into the Weaving that had been hidden in the toyshop for many years. What's more, Brax had clearly been busy strengthening his position and influence in Fable. And that would make what she had to do even more difficult.

"Do you have to take us to Appleyard now," she said to Balor, "as you told the sentries?"

The wildman regarded her with his usual glowering expression, which both she and Will had learned could as easily turn to laughter as it could anger.

"I don't understand all this loremasterish stuff," he said, "but it's obvious even to me that you need to get back to the toyshop right quick. And now that I've met you, Rowen of Blue Hill, I know better than to stand in your way. You do what you have to, lass."

"Thank you, Balor," Rowen said, "but won't you get in trouble for letting us go?"

"I'm thinking I should go with you. It sounds to me like you could use a hand with this mage. I'm sure that Shade and I could persuade him to leave."

"No, Balor, you must go to Appleyard and warn the Errantry about the fetches," Rowen said. "That's more important. And while you're there, maybe you can find out what happened to Freya. No, if Brax already has the Marshal on his side, we can't just force him to leave or scare him out of the toyshop. Shade could do that easily, but it wouldn't keep Brax away for long. If we throw him out, he'll just be more convinced we're keeping something from him."

"Then we have to find some way to get him to leave Fable for good," Will said.

Rowen frowned and glanced down at Riddle, who padded along close to her. The cat had not left her side since she'd said goodbye to her grandmother in the Weaving. And now a new thought struck her, an idea so foolish and dangerous and *perfect* that it stopped her in her tracks.

"There is a way," she breathed, as if speaking to herself. "Yes, it could work. The mage would have to leave if Grandfather came back."

"What's that?" Balor said with a frown. In the noise of the street he hadn't caught Rowen's murmured words. But Will had.

"You're right," Will said. "That would change everything. If the Loremaster returned . . ."

The wildman scowled.

"But that's the whole problem—" he began to protest, then he saw that Rowen and Will were both looking at Riddle, and his jaw seemed to become unhinged. On the journey from Blue Hill he had been told a little of Riddle's history and what he was capable of. "You mean, this . . . the cat . . . he could . . ."

"He can," Rowen said firmly, though the truth was that where Riddle was concerned, she was never entirely certain of anything. The cat gazed up at her, its inscrutable eyes giving no hint that it understood what she was planning.

"Balor, no one must know about this," she went on. "If people think Grandfather has come back, they'll want to see him. They'll have questions. We have to be careful. We don't know who Brax already has on his side."

The wildman plucked at his bushy beard.

"It's risky," he said at last. "And I don't like all this secrecy. It's not the Errantry way. But very well, Rowen of Blue Hill, not a word out of me."

The wildman turned to Will then and placed a huge hand on his shoulder.

"I know you're planning to go with Rowen, lad, while she searches for Master Pendrake. From the sounds of it that's going to take you someplace *bad*, and well, I don't approve. As my apprentice, you're bound to obey my orders without question."

Will stared up at the wildman in stunned silence. With all that had happened over the past few days he had nearly forgotten that he had joined the Errantry and become Balor's knight-apprentice. He had taken an oath before the Marshal to serve and protect the Bourne, but if Balor ordered him to stay in Fable, he would be abandoning Rowen and Shade when they most needed him. There was no way he could do that. He needed to break his oath to the Errantry.

He was opening his mouth to tell Balor as much when the wildman waved him to silence.

"You have to obey my orders, Will Lightfoot," he said, "and I'm ordering you to stay with Rowen. Help her do what she must and be safe. Get her and yourself and Shade home. I wouldn't expect anything less of an apprentice of mine."

Will swallowed hard and nodded. "I'll try, Balor," he said.

"This whole business is a few hundred miles over my head," the wildman went on, his voice even lower and rougher than usual. "But there's one thing I do understand, and it's that the three of you need to stay together."

"Thank you, Balor," Rowen said, and she darted forward and wrapped her arms around the wildman. He looked startled for a moment, then cleared his throat and patted her carefully on the back.

"You will find your grandfather, my dear—I'm certain of it," he said huskily, then he turned to Shade.

"I haven't known you long, wolf, and I'm not about to give *you* any orders. Just look after them, you hear? That's all I ask."

"I will do my best, Balor Gruff," Shade said.

"Balor," Will said, finding it hard to speak with the lump that had risen in his throat, "you be careful, too."

"We'll see each other again, my friends," the wildman said, "mark my words, and when we do, we'll have a galloping great story to tell by the fire at the Golden Goose."

In the wildman's eyes Will thought he caught a glimmer that might have been tears, but Balor quickly turned away and headed up the rising street to Appleyard.

2

A SHORT TIME LATER Rowen, Will and Shade were hurrying along Pluvius Lane, followed by a tall figure, hooded and cloaked and leaning heavily on the Loremaster's staff. The lane was busy at this time of day, and more than a few heads turned at the sight of the wolf at Will's side and the silent, cloaked figure behind them. Rowen walked quickly, eyes fixed straight ahead. She was hoping to avoid meeting anyone she knew, with all the delay and awkward questions that would bring.

When they reached the toyshop at the end of the lane, Rowen rapped on the door and stepped back. There was a long silence. Will resisted the urge to look behind him.

Just as Rowen was stepping forward to knock again, they heard the sound of the bolt releasing. The door slowly opened and the mage, Ammon Brax, stood before them. He must have had some means of seeing who was outside the

door before he opened it, because his face was already composed into a look of glad surprise, though Rowen saw a flicker
of fear in his eyes when they fell on Shade. But he masked his
alarm swiftly and opened the door wide.

"Thank the powers you've come home, child," he said to
Rowen. "I was beginning to fear the worst."

"I'm fine, thank you," Rowen said coldly. "And I've
found Grandfather."

The hooded figure standing behind them moved forward
and lifted his head. The mage's mouth dropped open. Clearly
he was face to face with the last person he had expected to
see: Nicholas Pendrake, the Loremaster of Fable.

"Ammon," Pendrake said. His voice was low and strained.

Brax clutched the door frame in a white-knuckled grip.

"Master Pendrake . . ." he breathed. "You're—"

"Grandfather is tired, Master Brax," Rowen said, nodding toward the doorway. "Please . . ."

Brax recovered his wits enough to nod quickly and step out
of the way. The old man strode through the doorway, followed
by Rowen, Will and Shade. Once they were inside, Brax hastily
shut the door, while still staring at Pendrake in disbelief. One
could almost see the mage's thoughts working, scrambling for
some way to turn this unwelcome surprise to his advantage.
Rowen noticed with a pang that the toys on the shelves lining
the front hall had been upended or pushed aside. No doubt by
Brax in his search for her grandfather's secrets.

If Edweth were here . . . she thought. The housekeeper
always kept the shop neat and tidy. But Brax had forced her
out, too, and now she was locked up in Appleyard. Was she
all right? Rowen wondered.

Then she caught sight of the mage's polished ivory staff
leaning near the door, in the place her grandfather always
set his, and a spasm of anger shot through her. She wanted

to knock the mage's staff to the floor and scream at him to get out of her house, but she knew she had to play her part and let Riddle play his.

"Tell me what happened, Nicholas," the mage said. "Where were you captured? How did you escape?"

The old man still had not lifted his hood.

"I escaped," he said heavily. "That is all the answer I can give you for now, Ammon. There is much to do and time is against us."

"I never gave up hope that you'd return," Brax gushed. Rowen saw beads of sweat glistening on his brow. "With all my efforts I could find no trace of where you had been taken. And then your granddaughter disappeared and—"

He darted a suspicious glance at Will.

"This is Will Lightfoot, a good friend," Pendrake said. "And Shade."

Brax nodded quickly to them both. His gaze lingered on the wolf.

"Thank you for all you've done, Master Brax," Rowen said. "But Grandfather is very tired and needs to rest."

"There is much to do," Pendrake said brusquely, still leaning on his staff. "We have little time."

"Yes, yes, of course," Brax said. "We've been aware of the Night King's rise for some time at Kyning Rore, but none of us imagined he would trouble himself with remote places like the Bourne. That is strange indeed. But rest assured, Nicholas, I will stay and do what I can to help. After what you've been through . . ."

He paused and studied Pendrake's hooded face doubtfully.

"Master Nicholas," he said. "Forgive me, but your eyes . . ."

"Yes, my eyes," the Loremaster murmured, lowering his head slightly. "The ordeal I've been through has left its mark on me. It will pass."

"Are you certain everything is all right?" Brax persisted.

"Everything is *not* all right," Pendrake said with a trace of anger in his voice. "Dangers surround us and every moment counts. You must . . ." The old man hesitated and glanced at Rowen. "You must return to Kyning Rore as fast as you can, Ammon. Your fellow mages will have need of your wisdom and guidance in the days to come."

"That may be so, but I do not feel right about leaving you. What if more of those creatures, those thrawls, return? The two us together have a greater chance of fending them off than either of us alone. Besides, Kyning Rore is far away, and the true threat is here." He shook his head as if struggling with himself. "No, Master Pendrake, forgive me, but I must disobey your wishes. The council of mages will have to do without me for the present. What kind of a friend would I be if I left you at such a time?"

Pendrake did not answer. He stared blankly at the mage, then glanced again at Rowen. After a pause she stepped quickly forward.

"Grandfather just needs to rest, Master Brax," she said firmly, and grasped the old man's arm. "We will be fine now, really. We have Shade with us. He can protect us from anything."

The mage darted another uneasy glance at the wolf, who stood watching him with a steady, impassive gaze that gave even Will a shiver. Shade truly was a frightening sight, and this was clearly not lost on Brax.

The mage nodded slowly.

"Yes, I see," he said. "Perhaps you're right. Very well, I will take my leave if that is your wish. I pray that you will not need me. And I hope, Nicholas, it may ease your mind to know I made sure the toyshop was not disturbed by vandals or curiosity seekers while you were gone. I assumed there must be things here that you would not want falling into the wrong hands."

"You have my thanks, Ammon," Pendrake said, placing a hand on the mage's shoulder. "Though there's precious little here worth stealing."

"As you say," Brax said with a slight bow. "Be well, Nicholas. Rest and mend yourself. I hope we'll meet again under happier circumstances."

"As do I, Ammon. Go safely, my friend."

Brax gathered his cloak, staff and travelling bag from beside the door. With one backward glance at Shade, he opened the door and strode out.

Will shut the door firmly behind him and bolted it. When he turned back to the others, Riddle, the cat, was crouched where the Loremaster had been standing. The staff was back in Rowen's hand.

"It worked," Will said, his shoulders sagging with relief. "He's gone."

"You did it, Riddle," Rowen said to the cat. "I almost believed you were Grandfather."

Riddle licked a paw, as if nothing that had happened held any interest for him. He was a cat again and acting like a cat.

"The mage will come back," said Shade, and they all turned in surprise to the wolf.

"How do you know that?" Rowen asked him.

"Before the Stewards granted me speech, I was a hunter," Shade said. "I stalked other animals and learned their ways. Sometimes an animal I hunted would pretend to be injured, then when I neared, it would rear up and strike. The mage is like that now. I could smell it on him. He wants us to believe he has given up, so that we will lower our guard."

Rowen frowned and looked away. She righted one of the fallen toys on the shelf beside her.

"Yes," she said. "He'll be back."

"You're the one he's really afraid of, Shade," Will said. "With you here Brax won't dare set foot in the toyshop."

He had spoken in the hope that he could still prevent Shade from accompanying them to the Shadow Realm. Rowen's dark hints about what might happen to their wolf-friend there had not left his thoughts for a moment.

"I will be not be staying here, Will Lightfoot," Shade said. "I am coming with you."

"You can't do that," Will said quickly. "We need you here. In case the mage—"

"I am coming with you, Will Lightfoot, wherever you go," the wolf repeated, with a rare trace of anger in his voice. "You should understand that by now."

"But what about Brax?" Will said. "Rowen, you know I'm right. Tell him. Shade has to stay in the toyshop. He can't come with us. *Tell him.*"

Rowen gave them both a look of pain and sadness.

"We can't force you to stay here, Shade," she said. "You have to do what you think is right."

"Rowen . . ." Will began, and to his shock she turned on him angrily.

"We have no choice," she said in a choked voice. "None of us."

"I will stay in the toyshop," said Riddle.

Will nearly cried out in shock when he looked in the direction of the small tawny cat and found in his place a huge tiger. Rowen had told him that this was Riddle's original shape, but Will had not yet seen it for himself and he stared in awe. So *this* was Riddle, this magnificent creature even larger than Shade, whose shaggy coat seemed made of rippling flame and shadows. He was from the Weaving, Rowen had said, and the sight of him now gave Will his first inkling of what that strange place might be like.

"You'll have to keep pretending to be Grandfather," Rowen said to the tiger, "no matter who arrives at the door. Just keep Brax and everyone else out as long as you can, no matter what."

"I will keep them out," the tiger said. "But, Rowen, the Weaving is my home. Without me guiding you, you may be lost there."

"I'll have Will with me," Rowen said. "He's the only one who can help me find the Fair Folk. He's the Pathfinder. That's what Grandfather called him. We'll be all right, Riddle."

She turned and hurried along the front hall. They all followed her into the kitchen, where she proceeded to fill a small pack with bread, cheese and whatever else she could find in the cupboards.

"No telling how long we'll be gone," she said.

"Remember what Balor said about Brax moving swiftly?" Will asked. "If he's got powerful friends at the Errantry, they might help him try to force Riddle out of the toyshop."

Rowen had finished gathering supplies and slung the filled pack over her shoulder. Her mind was made up and she was clearly impatient to be going.

"We can't do anything about that now," she said shortly. "Just keep everyone out, Riddle. No matter who they are. No matter what it takes."

"I will do what I can," Riddle said. "But I do not kill. Now that I remember what I am, I will not take the life of any being."

"I know that," Rowen said quickly, her face flushing as though she saw Riddle's words as a rebuke. "But remember when you lived in the forest how you tricked people with voices? You made them lose their way and then played your riddle games with them. Can you still do that?"

"I can still do that," Riddle said, and now it was his turn to sound stung, as if such foolishness was beneath him.

Rowen was heading for the doorway and then stopped.

"If anything goes wrong," she said to Riddle, "if you have to leave here, will you be able to find us?"

"I am a creature of the fire. I can go anywhere it goes. But I have never been beyond the black river. I do not know what would happen if I crossed into the Shadow Realm."

"Well, if you can't find us or you're not able to join us, then return to Grandmother, Riddle. Stay with her, please."

"I will."

It looked to Will as if Rowen was about to throw herself into the tiger's arms. But instead she nodded hastily and hurried from the room.

Will and Shade followed her down the hall and up the winding stairs. They climbed to the top floor, where they found the Loremaster's workshop door wide open. Clearly Brax had moved things around: many of the heaped and piled books had been placed in smaller, neater stacks, each with a scrap of paper sticking from its pages. Will guessed these were Brax's notes to himself about what each book contained.

"He's been cleaning up," Rowen said, then she smiled bitterly. "Grandfather won't be happy to see that when he gets back."

She paused a moment, then picked up a small lantern from the desk. Will remembered that she had carried a lantern like this when he'd first met her, in the Wood outside Fable. It was a called a waylight and it enabled the one who carried it to find hidden refuges called snugs. Rowen opened the little glass-paned door of the waylight and looked inside.

"He's gone," she said, glancing around the room anxiously. "What did Brax do with him?"

Will realized she meant the wisp, Sputter, who lived in the waylight and could be sent to deliver messages. Rowen set down the lantern and looked around the room.

"Sputter," she called. "If you're here, it's all right. You can come out now."

They heard a faint crackling sound that made Will think of the sparklers put on birthday cakes. The sound issued from behind them, from an old clock hanging on the wall above the Loremaster's desk, a clock shaped like an owl. The hands on the clock face in the owl's belly were spinning wildly and the crackling sound was getting louder.

"Sputter, are you in there?" Rowen said, leaning close to the clock.

Without warning the clock face sprang open. A tiny ball of fuzzy blue light shot out and bobbed above Rowen's head.

"Sputter!" Rowen cried. She held out her hand and the wisp descended into her palm, trembling and buzzing like an insect. "I'm so happy you're all right, Sputter. It's good he didn't catch you. But I have to go now. I can't stay. So I want you to leave here and find Edweth at Appleyard. When she sees you, she'll know I sent you and know I'm all right. Go on now."

The wisp buzzed more loudly in Rowen's palm but stayed put there.

"Don't be afraid," Rowen said softly. "You'll be safe with Edweth."

"I think he wants to stay with you," Will said.

"I wish I could take you with me, but where I'm going is worse than staying here."

The wisp's pulsing light flared brightly, casting a pale blue glow over Rowen's features. The tiny creature had no eyes, no face, but there was no doubt it was agitated and frightened. Rowen pulled in a deep breath.

"Come with us, then," she said. "There's no time to argue about it."

She held her hand up toward the open waylight. The wisp bobbed up and down a moment and then sped inside the lantern, where its light dimmed to a paler blue glow. Rowen shut the little door, then lifted the waylight by its wire handle and set it atop the Loremaster's staff. Will thought it would slip off as soon as Rowen moved the staff, but to his surprise the lantern stayed in place. He peered closer and saw that the lantern's handle was now embedded in the wood.

"How did you do that?" he asked.

"Do what?"

Will pointed to the lantern. Rowen looked up.

"Oh," she said, and frowned. "I didn't—it just happened. I didn't even think about it."

She tugged at the wire. It was stuck solidly in the wood of the staff.

"That's just how it needed to be," she said, and gave the staff a gentle shake. The lantern clinked against the wood.

"Is he going to be all right up there?" Will asked. He thought the wisp would be shaken about as Rowen walked with the staff.

"As long as he's in the lantern he's fine," she said. "He's used to being carried on long walks."

Rowen took a final searching look around the workshop, as if reluctant to leave it. She paused in front of a tapestry beside the doorway. It was tall and narrow, hanging nearly from the ceiling to the floor, and on it was an image of a towering tree, its branches spreading to great clouds of green leaves dotted with glittering points of silver like stars.

"Grandmother wove this for Grandfather," Rowen said wistfully. "Before she went into the Weaving."

"I know this tree," Shade said. "It is the tree that stood on the hill where we met at midsummer, in the time before the Storyeater, the one you call Malabron. We met there with the Tain Shee and the First Ones."

"The First Ones?" Will asked.

"The Stewards," Rowen said. "The oldest of all living beings in the Realm, Grandfather says. They spun the very first stories out of the Weaving. They created the tree, too. From a distance, Morrigan of the Shee told me, it looked like a great green cloud. At midsummer the white blossoms would open and scatter seeds throughout the Realm. The seeds were living things, as well. Some carried dreams and tales from the Stewards and returned with news from distant places."

"The messenger wisps," Will said. "So Sputter was one of them? I never knew that's where he came from."

"But then the tree was destroyed, wasn't it, Shade?" Rowen asked. "That's what Grandfather told me."

"Yes, in the war with the Storyeater," the wolf said. "Along with many other things that were good and beautiful."

No one spoke for a while. Will's thoughts were heavy. He knew something he needed to share with Rowen, but so far he hadn't been able to tell her. Before he'd been reunited with her he'd met a man of the Horsefolk, who lived in hide tents on the plains. The man was a Dreamwalker, a seer, and he had seen Rowen in his visions. He knew she would be going to the Shadow Realm long before it happened, but he'd said nothing about her search for the Loremaster. According to the Dreamwalker, Rowen had another task before her, a much greater one that would change the fate of everyone in the Realm.

Will glanced at Rowen and then away again, not wanting her to see the look on his face. How could he tell her about what he knew, when all she wanted was to find her grandfather and bring him home? It would be too heavy a burden for her, he thought. And she might not believe him anyhow. He couldn't even tell her what this greater task was. He hadn't really understood the Dreamwalker's words.

"Well, then," Rowen said heavily. "Let's go."

They left the workshop and hurried down the hall to the rough-hewn door of the raincabinet.

Will hung back with Shade while Rowen stepped forward and opened the door.

Before them was a tiny room, with the same broom, mop and bucket Rowen had seen in it the last time she'd been here. Shade stuck his nose tentatively into the doorway and sniffed.

"It looks undisturbed," Rowen said.

She leaned in and tapped her grandfather's staff against the back wall. From the little room came a smell of damp and a faint scent of soap, and Will remembered when he'd first come to the toyshop. He'd already been confused and frightened by this strange world he found himself in, then he'd opened this odd door and to his terror found pouring rain and an echoing darkness inside. Now it was only an ordinary broom closet and he wondered if he had imagined what he had seen here before or if Rowen had somehow brought them to the wrong door.

"How did you get through it before?" Will asked.

"I didn't," Rowen said. "I mean, whenever I opened the door myself, there was only the broom closet. But when I came here with Grandfather the other day, the closet was gone and there was just the rain. That's what I thought we'd see this time."

"What do you think's happened?"

Rowen frowned.

"The closet is only a disguise, to keep people from seeing what's really here. It's made of the same thing as Riddle. Grandfather calls it the fathomless fire. But *we* know this room's not really here, so we should be able to see through it."

"Then why can't we?"

"I think it's my fault," Rowen said slowly, her brow knitting. "When I left here the last time, all I could think of was

that I needed to keep Brax from finding the Weaving. So I
told the broom closet before I left and—"

"You *told* it?" Will broke in, not sure he had heard right.
"Told it *what*?"

"No, I mean I told it like a story. I *wove* it, out of the fathomless fire. It was the same with the staff and the lantern just now."

Will frowned. "I don't understand. If it's not some magic
spell, then . . ."

"Grandfather always said to me, 'Magic and story—
they're really the same thing.' They're the fathomless fire.
It's in everything. Or everything's made of it. Some stories
are very strong and they hold together longer than others."
She placed a hand against the back wall and pushed. "I suppose I made this one too well."

"So what do we do?"

Rowen stepped back and bit her lip. Will could see her
knuckles whitening as she gripped the staff.

"We don't have time for this," she said, her voice low and
strained. All at once she lifted the staff and with its bottom
end struck the back wall of the closet.

To Will's astonishment the stone shattered and with a
rushing sound the countless tiny bits became a glittering falling curtain of water. As he watched, spellbound, the other
walls swiftly melted into shimmering cascades.

Rowen stood back. "There," she said.

"You made this rain, Rowen of Blue Hill?" Shade asked.

"It was always here," Rowen said. "That's what Grandfather told me. I just helped a little."

Will leaned forward and craned his neck to look up. There
was no ceiling anymore. He saw only bright droplets falling
out of blackness and heard a far-off rumble of thunder. When
he'd first seen this impossible sight, he had wanted to ask
Master Pendrake where the mysterious doorway led, but he

hadn't dared then. Now he was going to find out what lay
beyond the rain, and the thought troubled him. Rowen had
already told him a little about this strange place called the
Weaving. She'd said it was something like the world of one's
dreams, where things were always changing into other things.
It was a tricky, shifting place you could get lost in very easily
and never find the way out again. Rowen's grandmother had
gone into the Weaving years ago and had stayed so long she
was no longer able to get back.

Raising his voice against the rushing din, Will said,
"You're sure we can find the Fair Folk in there?"

"Grandfather told me that the loremasters of old could step
through the Weaving to other places," Rowen said. "To distant
lands or even other worlds. I know it's true because I followed
the thread of the thing that took Grandfather, the thrawl, and
it brought me to the edge of the Shadow Realm." She drew a
deep breath. "I came to the black river that Riddle spoke about,
and I waded across. I was nearly there, Will. In *his* realm. The
water was so cold. I could feel the life leaving my body. I think
if I'd gone all the way across, I would've become a fetch. But
Riddle saved me. He pulled me back in time."

"Riddle must've known what would happen to you."

"He *is* the fathomless fire, Will. It's like he's . . . the oppo-
site of whatever a fetch is. He knew I couldn't go that way to
find Grandfather. But if I could reach the Shadow Realm
through the Weaving, then maybe it can also lead us to wherever the Fair Folk are. They're the only ones who would
know another way, a hidden way into the Shadow Realm.
That's what I'm hoping, anyhow."

"So the Weaving is like one of those knot-paths that take
you from one place to another in the Realm?"

"I suppose so, only it's more like *every* path is there, on
the other side of this door. So there must be one that leads

to the Fair Folk. There must be. We just need to find it. When I give the word, follow me through and stay close. The rain will be over in a moment and then we'll be in the Weaving. Just stay close to me, no matter what."

"Wait—what if Brax gets past Riddle?" Will asked. "If he comes up here and sees this rain, he's sure to find the Weaving."

"I'll put the broom closet back in place," Rowen said. "When we've gone into the Weaving, the closet is all that anyone will see."

"You know that for sure?"

Rowen didn't answer. She was staring into the rain, her whole body tensed and ready.

"Now," she said, and without another word she darted forward into the cabinet. The rain closed over her and she disappeared. Will and Shade shared a glance, then they followed.

3

THE ENEMY BROKE THROUGH the outer wall of Corr Madoc's fortress just before dawn.

All night the catapults of the Nightbane had launched smoking black stones at the walls. Stones that burst into flame when they struck and shook the fortress from its turrets to its foundations. The defenders had struggled to shore up the wall with timbers in the places where it seemed weakest and most likely to give, but they could not work fast enough in the face of the unending barrage. At last, with an avalanche of broken stone, one large section of wall caved inward. When the dust cleared, the Nightbane that had been gathering on the slope below the fortress came charging up to the gap.

Finn Madoc was at the breach with his brother's Stormriders. They'd had just enough warning of the wall's collapse that they'd had time to gather and form a wall of their own, with their long shields overlapping one another. There was no keep to fall back to. The shattered wall opened directly onto one of the lower passageways of the fortress and had to be defended at all costs.

The Nightbane in their hundreds poured through the breach, howling and brandishing their weapons. They broke upon the shields of the Stormriders like a dark wave.

Finn was in the midst of the Stormriders. Behind him he could hear the growls and yips of Corr's vicious hunting wolves, which had been brought up to join the defence. Finn had no shield of his own, so he'd stayed back from the front ranks. The coat of mail and helmet he was wearing he'd taken from a Stormrider killed earlier in the siege. He had his own sword, though, his Errantry blade, and it was at the ready for the moment the defence faltered and the enemy broke through the tight-knit phalanx of the shields.

He didn't have to wait long. The gap in the wall was wide and the Nightbane kept arriving, more than Finn had ever seen. They massed up against the shield wall, hammering and beating at it with their weapons, roaring and shrieking. Through the press of bodies Finn caught glimpses of contorted faces: mordog, creech, awgren and other creatures he had no name for. Finn braced his feet as well as he could on the stone floor of the chamber. He pressed up against the back of the Stormrider in front of him and felt the man behind him pressing against his own back. Like one enormous armoured body, the tightly ranked Stormriders shuddered as the enemy strained and battered against the shields. Soon men began to shift their footing, and some slipped and stumbled and had to scramble to their feet. The defence was being slowly, inexorably, pushed back and sheared apart.

At last spearpoints and blades found gaps in the wall of shields and stabbed home. Men fell, screaming. The gaps widened even further. More Nightbane pressed in, hacking and slashing.

Then all at once the wall collapsed. The Nightbane surged.

Like caged beasts unleashed, Finn and the other Storm-riders that had collected behind the phalanx charged forward with a roar and met the enemy.

There was no time now for fear. No time to think of anything other than what had to be done. The screams and clatter of metal faded in Finn's ears and his attention was trained only on what came at him. He parried and dodged and hacked, and as each opponent went down before him, another took its place. Dimly he was aware that men fell around him, and were carried off. The wolves fought savagely, but before long they were all killed.

The Nightbane kept coming.

At last Finn's sweaty grip on his sword hilt slipped. He lunged to keep it from sliding out of his grasp, and as he did so, something landed hard on his helmet and felled him to the earth. He struggled to rise, his ears ringing, and through the blood obscuring his vision he saw a mordog in spiked armour, raising its mace for another blow. Then someone appeared between him and the mordog and he saw it fall.

A huge hand gripped his shoulder and a voice growled something at him. It sounded like Balor Gruff, his old friend in the Errantry. But Balor had left the fortress hours ago with Will Lightfoot and Shade, in one of Corr's skyships. He couldn't be here.

Finn climbed unsteadily to his feet and stood face to face with Grath, his brother's mordog lieutenant.

"I asked, are you alive?" Grath shouted at him. "Yes, looks like it."

Something had changed, Finn thought. The noise of battle had ceased. He looked around. There were no Nightbane to be seen. Still dazed from the blow to his head, he rubbed his temple and his fingers came away bloody.

"Cut over your eye," Grath said. "From the rim of your helmet."

"Is the battle over?" Finn asked.

"They've fallen back to regroup," Grath said. "We've got a moment to catch a breath, no more."

Finn nodded. He looked down, saw his sword in the dirt and picked it up. The mail coat he was wearing was splattered with blood, the fine weave of links torn in several places. He removed the helmet and saw that it was dinted so badly he had to cast it aside. How long had they been fighting? It seemed only minutes. All at once he realized he was desperately thirsty.

Finn glanced around to see if anyone might have some water. To his surprise he saw Ord, the golem, not far from where he stood. The towering, impassive man of clay was holding up another section of the outer wall that appeared ready to collapse, while around him a party of dwarfs was frantically hammering together a makeshift brace of thick timbers. Finn had wondered if Corr would send the golem down to bolster the defence. Ord was, as far as anyone knew, impervious to harm and never needed rest. He would have been of great use at the breach, but Finn understood it was more vital to have him protect the wall from further collapse. Otherwise the breach would be twice as wide and the defence would be quickly overrun.

Finn glanced at one of the Stormriders standing near him. From a leather pouch at his belt the man took a pinch of small black grains and slipped them into his mouth. He grimaced, then noticed Finn's gaze and broke into a grin.

"Back at it," he said. There was a mad light in his eyes that Finn had seen in many of the other Stormriders. They all had pouches at their belts, even Grath. If the fighters were exhausted or fearful, even if they were wounded, the *gaal* rekindled the fierceness in their hearts and the strength in their limbs.

It was what all this killing was really about, Finn thought. His brother, Corr, in league with the dwarf folk known as the Ironwise, was locked in a deadly struggle with the Nightbane over the precious and deadly ore known as *gaal*.

Fever iron.

The Nightbane had driven the Ironwise from their ancestral city, Adamant, with its vast lodes of unrefined *gaal* ore. Nonn, the Ironwise chieftain, wanted his people's city back and Corr desired more of the *gaal* to keep his flying ships in the air and his men fighting.

Corr was still in his command chamber, as far as Finn knew, high up in a tower of the fortress. He had left the defence of the wall to Grath while he directed his few remaining skyships against the motherworms, bloated flying dragons that spewed their fiery spawn like gobbets of fire.

Finn still found it hard to believe what had happened to his brother in the years since Corr had left the Bourne. He was the Sky Lord now, a title he had taken from a mighty ruler of ancient legend, and his men followed him, nearly worshipped him, as if he was that legendary ruler returned from the dead. This fortress perched on the edge of the barren Valley of Fire, it was said, had been the first Sky Lord's palace. Ages ago it had been raised by the power of the *gaal* into the clouds. Then came the first war against Malabron, and the sky fortress had fallen to the earth and into ruin, until the exiled Ironwise took refuge in it and rebuilt it.

Now the fortress was once again under siege. With the army of Nightbane had come a host of fetches, mindless spectres encased in *gaal* armour. The Nightbane had begun their relentless assault on the fortress while the fetches marched south out of the valley. Will Lightfoot had been certain they were headed for the Bourne. Finn had agreed and had pleaded with Corr to abandon the fortress and fly his skyships south to defend his own country. Corr hadn't listened.

There was a cry just then and Finn looked up to see black-feathered arrows soaring through the gap and falling into their midst. The man he had just watched swallow the grains of *gaal* was already on the ground, an arrow through his neck.

Finn ducked with the others as the arrows whizzed around them. One of the shafts plucked at his sleeve as it shot past him. This was the reason the Nightbane had fallen back, he realized. This time they were starting with a barrage of arrows, to pin the defenders down and thin out their numbers before the second onslaught arrived. And it would arrive all too soon. The defenders could hear the shrieks and metal clamour of the Nightbane horde as it charged back up the slope toward the gap. They would be here any moment.

The remaining shield-bearers were forming another phalanx. Finn fell in behind it, but he stood closer this time to the front line, because there were fewer Stormriders at the breach now and no more reinforcements had appeared.

He gripped his sword hilt and felt a tremor in his hand that he couldn't master. He was exhausted, he knew, and still dazed from the blow to his head. But there was no choice and nowhere else to take refuge. If the defence gave way here, the fortress would be wide open to the enemy.

Then the second assault was upon them. As many Nightbane as before, their numbers seemingly endless, bounded and shrieked through the gap and down the heap of fallen stones.

They crashed against the shield wall, and the shock rippled through the tightly packed defenders. Finn felt it strike him this time as if the blow had fallen directly on his own armour. He felt the strain as the shield-bearers were pushed back, and he lowered his head and pushed forward with all the strength he had left. For what felt a long time that was all he knew: the sight of men's iron-shod feet, slipping and bracing themselves again in the bloody muck, the grunts and growls of effort, the dull bite and ringing of metal on metal, the stench of sweat and fear and death heavy around him.

Then he felt the phalanx straining, buckling, and he looked up again to see Nightbane spearpoints thrusting into the gaps between the densely packed bodies of the defenders ahead of him. One barbed point made right for him and he lopped it away with his sword. He spotted another spearhead jutting from the back of the shield-bearer ahead of him, heard the man's gasp of shock, saw him fall.

Finn darted forward, grabbed the shield as it slipped from the dead man's grasp and lifted it before him. A mordog's axe-blade glanced across it with a clang and Finn staggered back. For an instant he lost his footing, then regained it and pressed ahead between the shield-bearers on either side of him.

The Nightbane before him were like another wall, a seething wall that bristled with sharp metal.

Then a barbed blade thrust out from that wall and drove in under his shoulder. He felt it bite and tear at his flesh. Something crashed into him and he fell.

He found himself on his back in the dust and rubble, looking up at a patch of pale blue sky through the breach. He could hear the clash of metal and the roars and screams, but they seemed to be coming from far away. He tried to rise, but something was holding him down. He lifted his head. Someone had fallen on top of him. Another Stormrider, with an arrow in his neck.

Finn struggled and heaved, and the dead man slid off him. He caught a glimpse of the Stormrider's dust-caked face under a shock of dark hair. He was young. Not much older than Will Lightfoot.

Finn knew he had been wounded, but the pain throbbing in the pit of his arm seemed as far off as the noise of battle. He struggled to his knees, searching for his sword. His arms and legs were shaking and he began to retch. He knew that the fear he had forced down at the start of the battle had broken loose and was taking him over and he could do nothing to stop it. Once he regained his feet he would run. He would flee this place of death in blind panic. All his training as a knight of the Errantry, his oath to protect and defend, none of it would matter. Nothing could hold back this fear.

Then Finn saw the leather pouch hanging from the belt of the dead Stormrider.

Without thinking, he reached out, clutched the pouch and tore it free. His trembling fingers fumbled at the drawstring. Then the pouch was open and he dug in his fingers and took out a pinch of the tiny black grains. An acrid smell like burning tar stung his nostrils. He hesitated a moment, then slipped the grains onto his tongue. The fever iron tasted like ash and metal and something else, a sour *wrongness* that told him this poison did not belong in his body.

But it was too late.

Before he could tell what the *gaal* was doing to him, a shadow fell over him and a huge hand gripped his shoulder.

It was Grath.

"Still alive," the mordog said. "Lucky." Then he spotted the pouch in Finn's hand and he grinned. "Knew you'd see things our way sooner or later."

He held out his hand. Finn accepted it and was hauled to his feet by the mordog as if he weighed nothing. As soon as he was standing, he felt something rushing through him, like a cold fire coursing in his veins. The pain in his shoulder had

vanished, as had his fear and weariness. Everything around
him and everything inside him was as sharp and brilliant as
crystal, as if he had stepped out of a dim room into dazzling
winter daylight.

So this was what fever iron did to you. Finn's hands knotted into fists. He knew he would return to the battle and he
would kill and kill. The beasts had to pay. They would pay
for what they had done to him.

Then he noticed there was no clash of metal, no harsh
cries and screams. The Stormriders were standing at the
breach, their weapons ready, but there were no Nightbane
at all.

"They've fallen back again?" Finn asked. He felt a strange
surge of anger at the thought. He was ready *now* to fight and
kill. He didn't want to wait.

"They've gone this time for good," Grath said. "The look-
outs confirmed it. The Nightbane are retreating to Adamant.
Seems pretty clear it's not a feint to draw us out."

Finn glanced at the men on either side of him, their faces
grim and set. There were so few left. So few.

"No one is left to be drawn out," he said bitterly. The
enemy was gone, but the rage of battle still blazed in him. He
became aware that he was clutching the pouch of *gaal* in his
hand. If he dropped it, the grains would spill onto the ground
uselessly. Maybe he should, he thought, but he could not
open his hand and let it go.

"They mowed into us pretty good, didn't they?" Grath
said, and laughed.

Finn glared at the mordog, startled by the callous tone in
his voice. He took in the deep-set eyes on either side of the
doglike snout, the lipless gash of the mouth. This was a face
that Finn had been taught all his life to hate and fear, the face
of the monster in the dark. The beast *out there*.

The mordog laughed again. "You all do that," he said.

"Do what?" Finn said.

"You *men*. The way you look at us. At my people. Like you've found a dead rat in your ale."

Finn looked away, angry that his thoughts could so easily be read by a creature like Grath.

"My brother ordered you to watch over me in the battle, didn't he?"

Grath confirmed his guess with a nod.

"You're welcome," the mordog said dryly.

"I thank you for . . ." Finn began. "Thank you. But I don't need watching over."

"You're a good fighter," Grath said, scraping the gore off his blade against the sharp edge of one of the fallen stones. "You've been in a few tight corners like this already, that's clear. This is your first war, though, isn't it?"

Finn thought of the boy with the arrow in his throat.

"Is that what this was?" he asked. "Seemed more like slaughter to me."

"Is there a difference?"

"Most of those we killed were mordog," Finn said. "Those are your own people lying dead out there."

To Finn's surprise Grath growled and spat.

"*Shu koth*," he snarled. "Puppets. They still dance to the Deliverer's tune."

"The Deliverer?"

"That is what my people call *him*. The Night King. Malabron."

"So they've hated and killed us all these years because he told them to?"

Grath's mouth twisted in a sneer. "Maybe, a long time ago, one of *you* killed one of us," he said. "Maybe that's how it all started. Have you ever thought of that?"

Finn turned away angrily and the pain in his shoulder blazed up with such sudden fury he had to stifle a cry. The fever iron's effect was already wearing off, and he caught himself wishing for it to come back. He still couldn't let go of the pouch in his hand. Someone else might need this *gaal*, he told himself. He had to keep it for the others, not for himself.

"It wouldn't have happened like that," he breathed. "My people only kill when we have to, to defend ourselves. We're not beasts."

"Of course not," Grath said with a shrug. "We are."

"I didn't say that."

"You believe it."

Finn was silent.

"All my life I was taught that your kind hated us and wished us dead," Grath said. "I never saw anything that proved otherwise. The cunning ones, we called your kind. You were always smaller and weaker than us, but just a little quicker, a little cleverer with tools and plans. We lost everything we had to you, the elders said. They said it was because the true lord of this realm, the one you call the Night King, had been defeated and banished long ago by you and your allies, the Ancient Powers. So we took him as our lord, our god, and fought his battles for him, waiting and hoping for the day he would come again and lead us to victory."

"Malabron only wants power for himself," Finn said. His head was pounding, making it difficult to form his thoughts into words. And his wounded arm was burning and throbbing worse than ever now. "He'll destroy everything to get it, even those who serve him."

"And yet my people still die shouting his name," Grath said. "But I no longer serve the Night King." He gave a dry laugh. "Maybe that means I am no longer mordog."

"How did it happen?" Finn asked. "How did you become an enemy of your own people?"

"When I was still very young, there was a healer in my village who began to preach a strange new idea: that we did not have to make war on your folk, the cunning ones. That we could learn to live in peace with you if we renounced the Deliverer, who was no god but only a weaver of lies. My people thought the healer mad and drove him from the village. For years I wondered what had happened to him. Finally, when I was grown, I went looking for him. I needed to see the healer for myself."

"Why?"

"Because he was my father."

"Did you find him?"

Grath nodded.

"He was living in a cave in the hills like an animal. He knew who I was before I said a word. He had known I would seek him out one day. I told him what had happened in our village since he'd been driven out. His own family—my mother and my sister and I—shunned and spat on by everyone. Living like dogs on the few scraps the others tossed away. And now that I was old enough I had sought him out for one reason. To kill him."

Finn stared at the mordog. "Did you?"

"I raised my blade and he just sat there, not moving, not looking at me. Then he said, 'If it's my time to die, at least I will not die a slave.' And I put down my sword. I asked him why he had spoken against the Deliverer. Why he had slandered our god. He looked at me then, and he said that if I wanted an answer, I would have to stay with him. I stayed with him a long time and he taught me many things. He showed me the truth—that I *was* a slave. That we mordog served a master none of us had ever seen, who cared nothing for us. Our purpose was only to hate and to kill. To be the monster that others feared."

Grath lifted his blade and examined the notched edge.

"It was a very hard thing to do, he told me, to walk away from your own story. But it was the only way to freedom. So I took the path he showed me. I walked away. A few of my people followed me. The rest turned against us."

He looked up at Finn with a bitter smile.

"I walked away, but I didn't get far, did I? I'm still fighting someone else's battles."

A Stormrider approached carrying a water bucket with a ladle hooked to its side. At the sight of the water Finn remembered how thirsty he was. He reached for the ladle, but had to use his left hand because he could no longer lift his sword arm. He drank and the water left a bitter, metallic taste in his mouth. There was *gaal* in the water, too, he realized. A trace of it, anyhow, and he felt a craving for more. He wanted to feel that icy fire surge through him again. To see everything with that sharp, cold clarity.

Finn thought then of Freya Ragnarsdaughter. He had met her on his journey with Will Lightfoot. Before, he had thought the Skaldings were little better than savages, but he'd soon found out how wrong he was. He remembered the soft, warm touch of Freya's hand in his as they danced, her bright blue eyes. Her city was far from the Bourne, a journey of many days through dangerous wilds. At least, he thought, she would be far from Fable when the fetch host arrived there. But if Malabron wasn't stopped, Freya's city would eventually fall, also. There would be no more music and dancing in Skald.

Grath's harsh voice broke into his thoughts. The mordog was standing again, looking out over the valley.

"Your brother walked away from his home, too," he said.

"And you travelled all this way to bring him back. That I don't understand."

"That wasn't why I set out in the first place," Finn said. "But yes, I want him to return home to Fable."

"To face judgment?"

"He has to," Finn said. This was not something he wished to speak of, and his head was spinning now. He needed all his concentration just to stay upright, and his injured arm was a dead weight without feeling. There was no longer any pain and there should have been. He knew vaguely that he had to do something about this.

"Because he killed someone," Grath said.

"Yes," Finn said, struggling to remember what they were talking about. "A young man. A boy, really, who tried to stop Corr's men from stealing Errantry horses. Corr struck him down and rode away. So yes, that's the reason I've been searching for him all these years. He must answer for what he's done."

"So you'd turn your brother in for *one* killing?"

"I swore an oath that I would."

Grath shook his head. "You cunning ones are not so smart after all, are you?" he said. "You know he'll never go back there with you. Why should he? He's the Sky Lord. He didn't become that by sparing those who got in his way."

"He's still my brother. He's still Corr Madoc of the Bourne. He'll do what's right."

"That's what he *is* doing, boy," Grath said, and he shook his head and turned away. Finn was about to reply angrily when a hand fell on his shoulder.

It was Doctor Alazar.

"Finn," the doctor said. "I'm glad to see you." His face was streaked with sweat and the front of his tunic was dark with blood. There were even tiny flecks of red on the lenses of his spectacles. He looked exhausted, and Finn remembered that Alazar had been in the infirmary all this time, working with the dwarf healers to keep Corr's wounded Stormriders alive.

"You, too, Doctor," Finn said warmly. Alazar had accompanied him from Fable on the journey to help Will Lightfoot find Shade. Once Corr had agreed to let Will go, Finn had wanted the doctor, as well, to return to Fable, but Alazar had seen the terrible state of the Stormriders' infirmary. He had chosen to stay and help, even though he detested what Corr had done to his own men by giving them the fever iron.

"Have you seen Corr?" Finn asked. "Is he all right?"

The doctor frowned.

"A motherworm crashed right into the observation platform," he said. "Most of the Stormriders there were killed. Corr was burned, but we got to him in time, Finn. He'll be all right. He sent me to find you. He wants to see you in his command chamber. He wouldn't go to the infirmary, of course. That damned *gaal*. It makes these fools believe they're immortal."

"Thank you for helping him, Doctor," Finn said. "Are you coming back with me?"

"I've got work here," the healer said, looking around at the blood-stained Stormriders still standing guard at the breach.

Finn nodded. He was about to hurry away, but there were black spots bobbing in front of his eyes now and his legs wouldn't obey him. He stumbled and felt the doctor's arm catch him.

"Finn?" Alazar said. "What is it?"

Finn brushed at the black spots in front of him. They wouldn't go away. And now something was roaring in his ears.

"Look at your shoulder," Alazar cried. He'd lifted a torn flap of Finn's blood-soaked wool tunic. "Great sun, why didn't you come find me?"

Finn knew there was an answer to that question, but he

couldn't call it to mind. The black spots were filling his vision, there was nothing else to see—and then he was falling like a cold, hollow thing into the dark.

He woke up in a soft bed in a long, vaulted stone chamber. The room was lit by candles in sconces on the walls. His sword arm was bound tightly with bandages and held in a sling. It felt stiff and the pain had come back, although now it was only a dull throb. And there was something else. Yes, the cold fire was in his veins again. Not as strong as before, but it was there. Someone had given him more of the *gaal*.

He lifted his head and Doctor Alazar appeared beside him, setting a clay jug and goblet on a small table beside his bed.

"Welcome back," the doctor said with a frown of concern. "How do you feel?"

Finn rose unsteadily on his good elbow and with effort managed to move himself into a sitting position, propping his back against the bed's rough headboard. The chamber, which he guessed was the infirmary, was lined with beds like his, though they were all empty.

"Better?" Alazar asked.

Finn tried to speak but his throat was parched. "Could use some water," he managed to croak.

The doctor lifted the goblet. "Here."

Finn greedily gulped down the cold, refreshing water. When he was finished, he looked around the room. "Where are the other wounded? I thought this place would be filled up after the battle."

"It was. You've been here an entire day and then some, Finn. We patched up those we could. Not all of them made it."

Finn heard the exhaustion in Alazar's voice. He had not known the doctor well before they set out from Fable with Will Lightfoot and had thought him dour, even a little odd the way he was forever writing in his journal and collecting plants and stones and other curiosities. Yet since they'd come to the fortress, he'd worked tirelessly to save the wounded Stormriders, even though he condemned their all-consuming war and their enslavement to the *gaal*.

"Where is Corr?" Finn asked. "You said he was burned—"

"Corr is fine. It would seem nothing can kill the man. He came to see you often. You'd lost a lot of blood and your arm was in a bad way. I thought I would have to take it off, Finn."

"Take . . . my arm?" Finn said. A chill slid through him.

"Despite all I did the wound began to mortify. Your entire upper arm was swollen and turning black. I've never seen it happen so quickly. I didn't see any choice but to take off the arm. Then Corr came. He brought his own dwarf healers and they gave you . . . well, something that's keeping the rot in check. I don't know if your arm will ever heal, but for now it isn't getting any worse."

The doctor looked quickly away.

"What did they give me?" Finn asked, though he already knew.

"I argued with him, but Corr insisted," Alazar said. "It was a restorative laced with *gaal*. More than I've ever seen any of the Stormriders have. And the poultice on your arm is of the same concoction. I'm sorry, Finn. It was either that or the arm."

Finn lay back. He could feel the liquid fire rushing through his veins, felt his heart hammering as if he were running up a steep hill. Yet there was something cold at the heart of the fire. A kind of icy rage, pure and savage, that would stay hidden until he chose to unleash it.

"What happens now?" he asked almost indifferently, as though they were talking about someone else.

"You will have to keep taking the *gaal*," Alazar said. "Otherwise the rot will almost certainly return and it will spread quickly. And then I'll have to remove your arm, if it isn't too late already for that. I'm sorry."

For a moment Finn felt something, a hollow sadness that cut through the cold fire inside him. Then it was gone.

"It's not your fault, Doctor," he said. "You did the right thing."

Alazar studied him in silence and then pulled out a small leather pouch from the pocket of his tunic. It was a twin to the one Grath carried on his belt.

"Take only a few grains each day," the doctor said. "That should be enough. It will have to be. Only a few grains, Finn. More than that and . . . well, not all the Stormriders who died in the siege were killed by the enemy. I found some without any wounds. I believe they took too much of the *gaal* and it burned them up from the inside."

Finn nodded. He accepted the pouch from the doctor and closed his hand tightly around it.

"Where is Corr?" he asked.

"I couldn't say. He was here not long ago, sitting at your bedside, but Nonn called him away suddenly. He's probably in his command chamber, making plans for the assault."

"The Nightbane have come back?"

"I mean he's planning his own assault. Corr has been re-pairing his skyships while you've been here. Apparently he and his Stormriders have decided they haven't had enough punishment. They're going to attack the city."

"Adamant? That's madness."

Finn threw back the blanket and began to climb stiffly out of the bed. His arm hung in its bindings like a dead thing. He was wearing only his shirt and breeches, and he looked around for the rest of his gear.

"Wait a moment," Alazar said. "You've just woken up, Finn. You're in no condition to—"

"I'm not staying here, Doctor," Finn said. "There's no point anymore. I have my medicine. It's all I'm going to need now."

Finn found Corr not in his command chamber but on the burned and blackened observation platform, standing at a chart table with another of his lieutenants, a man named Kern. Instead of his usual cloak and mail Corr was wearing a dark, dully gleaming plate armour Finn had never seen before. His neck and part of his jaw was bandaged. Nonn, the ancient-looking leader of Corr's dwarf allies, stood nearby, looking out over the valley with several of his people gathered around him. They were speaking among themselves in low voices and now and then darting glances at Corr.

When he saw Finn, Corr's lined, weathered face buckled with gladness and relief. He beckoned his brother over and stiffly put his arms around him. For the first time since he'd discovered the Sky Lord was his brother, Finn saw that Corr was moved by something other than anger or reckless resolve. For a moment it was just the two of them and all else was forgotten.

"Thank the powers you're all right, brother," Corr said. "The doctor told you . . . ?"

Up close Finn could see the terrible blisters on Corr's face and neck. He should have been in agony, but of course he was taking the *gaal* powder. At last Finn could understand how his brother was able to shrug off such terrible punishment to the body.

As Corr pulled away, Finn looked more closely at the strange armour his brother was wearing.

"We've discovered the fetches aren't indestructible," Corr

said, noticing his glance. "We broke two of them open with the lightning. Once the fetches inside had fled we were able to salvage enough of the armour to make one complete suit."

"You're wearing *fetch armour*?"

"That's one of the lessons of your beloved Errantry, isn't it? In battle you always have two weapons at your disposal: yours and your enemy's. The metal is amazingly light, and there's so much *gaal* in the alloy one no longer needs to consume the fever iron powder."

"Corr, this is *his* armour. He commands the fetches with it."

"His will may be strong enough to control those mindless wraiths, but his realm is far away and here *my* will is stronger. I've tried the suit now and it's safe. I want you to have it. It can help you."

"Many of your people died at the breach," Finn said, ignoring Corr's offer. "Our people. Bournefolk. We would have been overwhelmed if the Nightbane hadn't retreated."

"They didn't retreat," Corr said. "Not exactly. Kern was in the observation skiff. He saw it all."

The lieutenant nodded. Kern was a small man with the quiet, self-effacing manner of a clerk. He had seemed to Finn out of place among the frenzied, battle-hungry Stormriders, yet he had a pouch of *gaal* on his belt like everyone else. Something else he carried was a small book and a pencil, with which he always seemed to be taking notes.

"The host broke into three at the bottom of the slope," Kern said in an expressionless voice, as if reading out a list of supplies. "The smallest group fled back across the valley to Adamant. The other two, at least a thousand in each, marched to the east and west of us. They climbed the valley walls again, on either side of the fortress, and headed south."

"They passed the fortress as if we weren't even here," Corr said.

"That's because they don't care about the fortress, Corr," Finn said. "The Nightbane are leaving the valley to join the fetches. They're all marching to the Bourne. Will Lightfoot was telling the truth. They're marching to destroy Fable."

Corr exchanged a glance with Kern.

"You still believe the boy's wild story," Corr said to Finn. "That a host of armoured fetches and an entire army of Nightbane are needed to conquer one insignificant little town in the middle of nowhere."

"Malabron is moving quickly now, Corr—sooner maybe than even he had planned—because of something that's happened in Fable. I don't know what it is, but I believe Will. Your Stormriders, the Ironwise, this fortress—none of that matters to him anymore, if it ever really did. Probably the dwarf city doesn't, either, now that his fetch army is built. Malabron has staked it all on taking Fable. His forces will crush everything in their path, and then the Bourne will be another dead land, like this one."

He gestured at the map and pain shot through his arm and side. The fever iron that Alazar had given him was wearing off already, he guessed. For a while it had swept aside the fear he'd felt for his friends, but that fear was still there.

There was a map spread out on the chart table and Corr studied it now. He ran his fingers across its rough parchment and he seemed to be weighing what he'd heard. Then he looked up at Kern.

"Take out the skiff," he said. "Make another sweep. Confirm the Nightbane are still on the march, that they haven't stopped or circled back."

"Sir, the scouts just reported in," Kern said quietly, glancing at his little book. "The Nightbane are almost two days' march away and still heading south. There's no need to take the skiff out again so soon."

"Take it out," Corr growled. "Go yourself this time."

Kern nodded, tucked away his book and slipped from the room. Before Finn could speak to his brother again, Nonn, the Ironwise chieftain, appeared at Corr's side.

"My lord," the old dwarf said in his deep, gravelly voice, "the siege has depleted both our numbers and what stores of the *gaal* still remain to us. You know this. Even if you went after the fetches, how far would the ships get and what could they do? Our only hope lies across the valley. If Adamant has truly been abandoned by the Nightbane, then this is the time to launch an assault and take it back. What does it matter where the enemy has gone? We will not get another chance like this."

Corr's finger stopped at the black circle on the map that represented Adamant.

"Without the *gaal*, my lord," Nonn went on, "your men will not fight and the ships will not fly."

And without it I will die or lose my arm, Finn thought.

"We need to make sure about those dragons first," Corr said. "We've spoken of this already."

"There have been no dragon sightings since well before dawn," Nonn said. "We think all the motherworms may already be dead or driven off. And there can only be a small force left at the city, if any at all. My smiths have nearly finished repairing and equipping the remaining skyships. Give the word, my lord."

Finn gripped his brother's arm.

"Corr, you must listen," he said. "Even if Will and Balor made it home already and brought a warning, the Errantry will have no chance against the fetches and the Nightbane. Maybe we can't stop them, but we can slow them down. We can put ourselves in their way and give our people more time."

Corr looked down at his brother's hand on his sleeve. He placed his own scarred hand on Finn's.

"You mustn't strain yourself, brother," he said. Then he faced Nonn. "Can your smiths have the ships ready within the hour?"

The Ironwise chieftain turned to one of his people, a scarred and wizened old dwarf even more ancient looking than Nonn.

"Have the repairs been completed?"

"Almost, my lord. There are only a few calibrations left to be—"

"Get it done," Nonn barked, then he turned back to Corr. "The ships will be ready, my lord, but there isn't enough *gaal* left to take the fleet all the way south to your homeland. You know this."

"We're not going to Fable," Corr said. "We'll be sailing for Adamant. We will recapture your city, Nonn, and once we have the mines we will build a hundred skyships and nothing in this world will stop us, not even fetches in armour."

"No indeed, my lord," Nonn said, his wizened face breaking into the first smile Finn had ever seen from the dwarf chieftain.

Finn turned away. He looked out the observation platform, but all that could be seen now was a curtain of roiling smoke. Fable was so far away and he was bound now to the same deadly metal that held his brother in its grip. If he refused the *gaal*, he would die. But it would surely kill him, and probably all too soon. Either way he had failed his friends. He could no longer help them.

"We must save ourselves first, Finn," Corr said behind him. "We're of no use to anyone else otherwise. Get some rest. I'll send for you when the city has been taken, and then we'll talk again about the Bourne."

Finn faced his brother. He looked at Corr's scars and terrible burns, and it seemed to him he was looking at a truer map of the Valley of Fire than the one spread out on the table.

"I'm going with you to Adamant, Corr," he said at last. "After all, I'm a Stormrider now."

4

THE NEWS BROUGHT BY the Red Duke of Tintamarre—that Nightbane were massing north of the Bourne—had spread quickly through Fable and the surrounding towns and villages. Riders of the Errantry hurried through the countryside, sounding the alarm and urging all inhabitants to leave their homes. By the evening of that day the high road was filled with a steady stream of wagons, carts and people on foot.

Many sought refuge in Fable, which was already crowded with fleeing Storyfolk from other lands. All too soon Lord Caliburn, the Marshal, was forced to close the gates to all newcomers. There were angry words, and some folk who had been shut outside came to blows with the sentries. A few who had been turned away set up camp on the hillside and in the woods around the city, while most headed back on the road for the towns to the south.

At the same time, more armed companies had begun to arrive. The larger forces were preceded by heralds, who sought permission in the name of their commanders to join the defence. Other, smaller bands of armed men came, as well, many of them makeshift companies of those who had joined in common cause after the Nightbane had overrun their homelands.

The Course began to fill with more and more tents and pavilions, and the people of Fable, who were used to solitary travellers from strange lands, saw the greatest gathering of Storyfolk that anyone had ever witnessed. And each arriving band or troop or handful of armed men had a strange tale to tell of what had brought them here.

Not all who came to Fable were soldiers or warriors. Some were farmers and villagers who were tired of running and hiding and wanted to make a stand. Others were folk whom the people of Fable would never have thought of as allies. There were unwelcome, even alarming faces among the new arrivals: hulking troll-men from the distant Bone-lands, midnight hags, masked nomads of the Sand Sea, and the strange, unsettling people with sea-green skin and eyes like those of cats who were known only as the Otherfolk. All had come at great risk, for when they met scouting parties of the Errantry, they had been challenged and even attacked. But they all lay down their weapons and offered no resistance. They explained that this was as much their realm as anyone's and they had come to help defend it.

Late that evening, Lord Caliburn and the Mayor of Fable, Dame Oreande, left the city to join a council of the leaders of the still-assembling forces. The gathering was held in the great ivory-and-gold pavilion of the Red Duke, which had been chosen as the command post for the new and growing army. The captains and commanders assembled in the lantern light under the gently stirring silks of the pavilion, and many glances of surprise and suspicion went back and forth as the new allies got their first close look at one another. Some recognized those who had once been enemies, while others saw strange, outlandish faces and stared rudely or looked away in disdain. The mood in the pavilion was tense and threatening to worsen, when the Duke stepped into the middle of the crowd and raised his hand for quiet.

The Red Duke of Tintamarre was an elderly but still powerful-looking man, with a mane of snow-white hair and a trim white beard. His cloak was a huge bearskin clasped at the neck with a silver chain, the thick reddish-brown fur flecked with grey. A scabbard of polished wood inlaid with a pattern of green and white stones hung from his belt, but the scabbard held no sword.

The Duke began by welcoming everyone warmly. His voice was deep and commanded attention, but it did not threaten or attempt to master. It was a calm, reasonable voice, acknowledging everyone present without distinction of rank or race. The commanders heard the quiet authority in the Duke's voice and the good sense and submitted to it. The muttering died and the sharp glances ceased.

The Duke, as host, thanked everyone for coming and then he invited the Mayor of Fable to speak for her city. Dame Oreande was a tall woman with iron-grey hair cut severely short. Her gown was dark green and plain, her only adornment a shoulder brooch in the shape of a swan. She stepped forward and expressed the thanks of the people of Fable to all those who had travelled from near and far to help defend the city and the Bourne.

"There is much to discuss and plan, and time is against us," the Mayor went on, "but we needn't cast aside courtesy as a result. We should learn one another's names and hear the story of what brought us here. That must happen first if we're to rely on one another in the days ahead."

She introduced herself and the Marshal, and then invited the Red Duke, as the first of the allies to arrive, to come forward again and speak. The Duke bowed to the Mayor and then briefly told of his search for the city he had seen in his dream. He described how on their march his army had passed through the devastation caused by the gathering Nightbane hordes. He also said that he knew of other commanders and their troops who were now cut off from reaching Fable because the enemy was in their path. Some of these allies had managed to get messengers through to him to say that they were seeking other roads into the Bourne, but it meant that they would likely not arrive in time to join the defence.

When the Duke was finished, he invited the other commanders to tell their stories. Two people seated near him, side by side, rose at the same time. One was a sharp-faced, red-bearded man in sleek furs, the other a tall, proud-looking woman in a coat of shining mail. They eyed each other uneasily and then gave their names and titles, which none of the Bournefolk present had heard before.

"A year ago today," the bearded man began, "our two armies met for what was to be the final battle that would bring our long war to an end. All that day by the sea the fighting raged. Many brave men and women on both sides fell. Blazing pitch flew from catapults. Great volleys of arrows darkened the sun. The earth ran red with blood.

"When evening fell, there was still no clear victor. Our armies gathered and rallied under their banners one last time for the final clash that would decide all. We marched toward one another, hammering our swords and spears against our shields and taunting with hoarse voices. Only death lay ahead and we all knew it."

"Then the ranks slowed and came to a halt," the woman said, picking up the story. "Each of us fell silent and stared in wonder at what had appeared on the narrow strip of bloody ground that lay between our armies. A small child walked there. A child in spotless white, fair of face and without any mark of war or wound. He walked through the filth and blood as if strolling through a summer meadow. And all of us knew that the fighting was over for that day. The banners of war were lowered and flags of truce were raised. And then the two of us"—she glanced at the bearded man— "stepped forward and met for the first time between our two armies. We went to the child and spoke to him. We asked him which side he had come from and who his parents were, since we assumed he was the child of some man or woman on the battlefield that day. The child did not speak. We understood then that his wits were gone. And looking into his empty eyes, we saw our own madness at last. We saw the doom we were bringing to both our peoples. So we lay down our weapons and took each other's hands and vowed there would be peace between us."

"But peace made in a moment can easily fall apart in a day," the man went on. "Many on both sides opposed the armistice. Blood had been spilled for so long that vengeance had become our daily bread. We knew the truce was too fragile to last and so we did the only thing we could. If our people wished to fight, we would seek out another war, so that instead of being turned on one another, our swords would be united against a common enemy. Then perhaps we would learn to trust one another again."

The bearded man and the woman grasped hands and sat down in their places.

One by one the other commanders rose to tell their tales. Some had come from other distant wars that they had believed would be the last they would ever have to fight. A few of the younger commanders had never led their people in battle before but had seen no other choice. Many had made the journey to Fable because an omen or a prophecy had called them here, while some admitted they had come only because they had heard of a chance to kill Nightbane.

The last to speak was the dwarf Mimling Hammersong, who had arrived with his six brothers and thirty of his kinfolk from the hills west of the Bourne. Mimling limped into the middle of the ring of commanders, abashed by all the stern martial faces around him. He cleared his throat and began.

"I'm not here because of a dream or a legend, like most of you, or even because I like smashing Nightbane skulls," the dwarf rumbled. "Though I used to enjoy that a lot. No, I'm here for my lady Rowen of Blue Hill. Most of you have never heard of her and don't know who she is, nor do you care, but I promised Will Lightfoot that I would return to Fable for Rowen's sake and here I am. My brothers and cousins are not warriors. They never took up the questing life as I did, but they've brought their hammers and shovels and axes for whatever work needs doing, whether it be strengthening defences or, should the defences fail, smashing Nightbane skulls."

When they had all given their names and told their stories, Lord Caliburn rose. The Marshal of the Errantry was grey headed and stern looking and had no gracious words of welcome for the assembly. Of all those gathered there only Dame Oreande knew that he had not always been so sombre and cold, that there had been a time, before the death of his son, that the Marshal had been known for his hearty laugh and his warm, open way with others. But little of that man remained now, and the news he had was grave. In his usual clipped, unadorned way, Caliburn gave the latest report of the movements of the enemy and how close their growing force had already come to Annen Bawn, the Errantry citadel that defended the Bourne's northern border. Before the stir his words caused had fully died down, he went on to relate what he had learned from Balor Gruff about the even more terrible threat of the armoured fetches.

"As far as I can understand it," the Marshal said, "they're something like mechanical men, puppets that can move on their own. But these armoured spectres aren't puppets made to amuse. There are thousands of them, each one bound to the will of our enemy, and they will not tire or halt or heed pleas for mercy."

"How far away is this host, my lord?" the Red Duke asked.

"Gruff tells me they neither rest nor sleep, which means they can cover a hundred miles in a single day and night. They could be here in as few as seven days, by his reckoning. I've learned to trust his reckoning."

At that voices were raised in alarm and dismay. The Duke raised a hand for quiet, and when it had been restored, the Marshal went on.

"I have sent Gruff to Annen Bawn to give the garrison there warning and such knowledge as he has about the threat," he said. "A company of reinforcements has also been outfitted and will start within the hour for the citadel. What *we* must decide is whether our alliance should make its stand here or join the defence at Annen Bawn. For my part, I believe it is too late to march our still-gathering force to the Bawn before the Nightbane assault it. The walls at the Bawn are thick and strong, and the valley narrow. Three hundred can hold the citadel as easily as three thousand. Once the fetch host reaches there, however, it is hard to say what will happen. From what Balor Gruff has told me, these creatures are not likely to be turned back by walls or difficult terrain. If they find their way blocked at the citadel, they may simply

climb into the hills on either side of it and so come to Fable
by other paths. One thing is certain: whatever strange call
or prophecy or dream has brought all of you to Fable has
brought our enemies, as well. This city is their goal and they
will not stop until they reach it. And so I say this must be
where we make our stand. All that we can ask of the brave
souls at Annen Bawn is that they purchase us some time,
which we should spend preparing to meet this threat."

At that a debate began. Many voices were raised in support of the Marshal's view, while others urged they all march
at once for the citadel. Still others put forward more elabo-
rate plans that involved various movements of troops to divide or surround the enemy forces. In the end, however,
most of those present, including Lord Caliburn, turned to
the Red Duke and waited for him to speak. One thing alone
seemed to have been agreed upon without the words having
to be spoken: that the Duke would lead this alliance and his
would be the final say.

When silence had fallen again and all eyes were on him,
the Duke rose and stood beside Lord Caliburn.

"The Marshal's plan seems most sound to me," he said.
"If it's true our enemy has no purpose other than the taking
of this city, we should not divide our forces at this late hour.
But I will not have it said that a few stood alone shielding the
rest of us while we waited here, so I will also send some of
my men to Annen Bawn."

His words brought swift and general agreement among
the commanders, and many also pledged troops to the reinforcements the Marshal was dispatching to the citadel. Then
the Duke spoke again, saying there was still much to plan
and prepare, but for now those who had just arrived should
have time to rest from their journey. At that the gathering
broke up, though there was still much loud talk and debate

among the commanders as they filed out of the pavilion, only now it was talk among allies rather than strangers.

Lord Caliburn and the Mayor remained behind with the Duke after the others had left, at his request. The Duke wished to know everything they could tell him about the city itself, the strengths and weaknesses of its walls and other defences. Yet he also made it clear he would not set foot in Fable himself, nor would he permit any of his men to do so, and he would encourage the other commanders to follow his example.

"We're here to prevent an invasion, not become one," he said with a smile.

The Marshal had brought a map of Fable with him and now he unrolled it on the Duke's chart table and went over the plan of the city point by point, with the Duke asking questions and making observations. The Mayor added her own thoughts from time to time, but for the most part she simply listened, studying the Duke. There was something in his voice and manner, she thought, something calm and direct and unconcerned for his own dignity, that would inspire trust and loyalty in anyone. The strange notion struck her that in some other time and place, perhaps in another realm altogether, this white-headed Duke with his bearskin cloak had worn a grander robe, and in that empty scabbard there had been a sword as renowned as its bearer. The longer she observed and listened, the more certain she became that she was right. And that thought gave her hope.

5

THE SAME NIGHT THAT the commanders met in the Duke's pavilion, the mage Ammon Brax returned to the toyshop at Pluvius Lane.

He was not alone. With him came Captain Thorne and six hand-picked Errantry troopers. It had taken some doing, but Brax had persuaded Thorne to free the Marrowbone brothers from custody and bring them along, as well.

As they approached the dark, silent shop, Brax glanced back and eyed the huge, pig-faced brothers with distaste. Hodge and Flitch Marrowbone were trolls of a kind known as hogmen, and it was not difficult to see where the name had come from. Flitch, the older of the two hogmen and the one who always took the lead, strode along with a gloating sneer on his face, clearly delighted to be free at last. The other hogman, Hodge, was larger and more powerfully built, but he looked frightened and miserable and kept glancing around nervously.

The brothers had been locked up at Appleyard for their crimes, which included, if the rumours were to be believed, eating people. They were vicious and stupid, and could be intimidating to anyone who didn't know what cowards they really were. That made them useful.

Between the brothers, looking small and frail next to their grotesque bulk, stood the young Skalding woman Freya Ragnarsdaughter. Her jaw was set defiantly, but in her eyes Brax saw the fear she was trying to hide. He'd brought her along because he suspected she might also be useful to him in the dangerous game he was about to play here. She would have to be watched, though, and that was another reason for bringing the hogmen. Freya and her people had captured the Marrowbone brothers and turned them in to the Errantry, and the hogmen had been waiting for their revenge. They were not about to let her out of their sight.

Captain Thorne reached the door first. He was a large man with a craggy face and thick black brows. An imposing figure, Brax thought, if you didn't notice his darting eyes and the nervous pursing of his lips. Thorne was one of those men with dreams much greater than his abilities. There were always a few like that on the council at Kyning Rore. If you knew what men like that wanted, you had them.

Brax drew a deep breath and gripped his ivory staff tighter. If this attempt to take back the toyshop failed, it was all over for him in Fable. He needed the Loremaster's power. He needed to control that mysterious, secret force that some called werefire. Without it, he would have no choice but to flee back to Kyning Rore and wait with the other mages as their powers slipped away and the destruction that was about to fall on Fable came to their doors, too.

The fading had begun quietly, with rumours of far-off lands falling into shadow and silence. The council of mages had watched and waited, unwilling to intervene in matters that seemed remote and of little consequence to them. Too late the mages understood that the fading had already reached them: their own power had begun to wane. They still knew all the spells and incantations, but there was little force in them anymore. Water, earth, fire and stone: the elements no longer obeyed their will. And as they felt their magecraft dwindle, their trust in Brax waned, as well. At times he had been reduced to conjuring tricks, mere sleight of hand, to maintain his hold over the council.

What power still remained to him was contained in the staff, and even that was not his own: he had wrested it from the dead hand of a sorceress he'd been forced to kill after he stumbled upon her secret lair. No one at Kyning Rore had suspected the staff was a weapon of dark spellcraft, for he himself had banned such things from the island. He had kept it as a last resort should his enemies on the council attempt to depose him. He knew the staff held enough power to unleash one last deadly strike, and so he'd held it in reserve and waited while he watched his own powers trickle steadily away.

And then word had reached him of the rebel mages at Skald and how they had unleashed a plague of werefire. The name of his old teacher, Nicholas Pendrake, was mentioned by those who brought the news. Pendrake, they said, had tamed the dreaded fire single-handedly and driven it back to wherever it came from. It was then that Brax knew what he had to do. The risk had been tremendous, leaving the council leaderless to make the long journey in search of the old man. But that danger paled against the threat of Malabron and the possibility of learning Pendrake's secret, of seizing control of the secret fire. Only the fire could save him from the power of the Shadow Realm.

The captain lifted a hand to knock on the door, then he paused and turned to the mage.

"Master Brax, you said the boy had the wolf with him," Thorne began. "He's said to be very strong."

Hodge whimpered and Flitch muttered a spittle-flecked curse at him.

"Listen to me, you two," the captain growled at the brothers. "You'll be going right back to your cell once this is over, make no mistake about that. You conduct yourselves well here, though, and you might just earn your freedom one day."

"We understand," Flitch said sullenly. "We will not disappoint you, Captain."

Thorne turned back to the mage. "Master Brax, tell my men what you told me at Appleyard. About what we might be facing here."

Brax faced the six uneasy-looking troopers.

"You've all heard of this boy, whom some call the Pathfinder, and his protector, the wolf," the mage said. "They are friends of the Loremaster's granddaughter and they will fight for her if she tells them to. They must be prevented from interfering by whatever means necessary. If force is required, do not hesitate. You may not get another chance."

"What about the old toymaker?" asked one of the troopers, a burly man with a shaved head. "They say he's got *powers*."

The old toymaker, Brax thought. He recalled how strange Pendrake had seemed when he'd returned from wherever the thrawl had taken him. There was that strange yellow gleam in his eyes, and he had glanced at the girl nervously, as if taking his cues from her. It had struck him then, with absolute certainty, that this was not Nicholas Pendrake. The girl had found someone—or some*thing*—to impersonate her grandfather. She was far more resourceful than he'd suspected.

"Listen to me," he said now to the troopers, "the man who returned to the toyshop earlier today may look and act very much like Nicholas Pendrake, but he is an imposter. I know this for a fact. Whoever he is, he has none of the old man's powers or he would have tried them against me already. Still, he is cunning and desperate, and therefore dangerous. Do not heed anything he says. And do not listen to the girl. She is under the imposter's spell and will obey his wishes. As long as she stays in the toyshop, she is in grave danger. We must take her into custody, too, for her own good."

"He's lying," Freya shouted, starting forward. "He's just after Father Nicholas's secrets."

At a gesture from Thorne, Flitch grabbed hold of Freya's arm. She struggled, her eyes fixed on Brax.

"I'm here to save your friends, Freya of Skald," Brax said in his most calm and reasonable voice. "I know they do not trust me, any more than you do. That is why I brought you along. I'm hoping they will listen to you. Please, help me to help them."

In Freya's eyes he saw anger wrestling with doubt. She knew he might be telling the truth about this false loremaster. At last she stopped struggling against Flitch's grip.

The Skalding woman's outburst had unsettled the troopers, but Brax saw that his words had worked on the captain. Thorne's eyes narrowed and glinted like those of a hunter who has just caught the scent of his prey. The thought that he, Emric Thorne, might unmask a dangerous imposter and bring him to Appleyard was a powerful goad to the captain. Such a coup would only make it clearer to everyone that he was the best man to lead the Errantry.

Thorne stepped up to the door and knocked on it sharply. He waited, then tried the door handle.

"Locked," he said to Brax.

The mage stepped forward. He touched his fingers cautiously to the door handle and in a low voice uttered an unbinding charm. He felt the lock resist the charm, and as he had so often lately, he silently cursed the fading of his magecraft. Not long ago, opening a door like this would have cost him little effort. Now he was thankful the others could not see the strain on his face. After a long struggle the lock finally gave way and the door swung slowly inward without a sound.

Brax let out his breath and carefully turned. Thorne's troopers were hunched and ready, their hands on the hilts of their swords.

Brax raised his lantern and the light fell into the dark front hall of the toyshop.

There was no one to be seen.

Thorne took the lead again. He stepped past Brax and strode into the hall, his shadow rising menacingly in the lantern light. "Master Pendrake," he called. There was no answer. "Master Pendrake, it's Captain Thorne. I've come at the request of Master Brax. I wish to speak to you about matters of importance to Fable."

Silence.

Brax stepped through the doorway, followed by the Errantry troopers.

The hall was cold and unlit, and for an instant Brax wondered if the girl and her friends had abandoned the toyshop. But he stood still and waited, and his keen senses, honed over the years to detect anything threatening, told him that the silence was not that of an empty house. He and the others were being watched.

The mage glanced back and saw that the hogmen were still standing just outside the entrance with Freya Ragnarsdaughter between them, their gross, sweating faces more pallid than usual. It was the wolf they were afraid of, Brax grasped. In his need to learn what they knew about the werefire, he had been forced to sit and listen to Hodge's blubbering story about their long, weary travels with their older brother, Tuck, and how a garm-wolf had torn him to pieces and everything had gone wrong for them after that. The boy's companion, the creature Shade, half looked like a garm-wolf. Not for the first time Brax doubted the hogmen would stand their ground, but at the least they might keep the beast busy long enough for the mage to launch his own attack. Angrily Brax gestured for them to get inside, and after exchanging a nervous glance, they obeyed.

"Master Pendrake," Thorne called again. "If you're here, answer me. We've brought a friend of yours."

Brax took another few steps into the hall. A floorboard creaked under his boot and he heard one of the hogmen catch his breath at the unexpected sound.

"Nicholas," he said, "we have Freya Ragnarsdaughter with us. She has been very worried about you and Rowen, as you can imagine." He eyed Freya as he spoke, saw the distrust in her face, but she remained silent.

Brax turned and kept on up the passage. When he came to the kitchen doorway, he paused and looked in. The room was empty, but just as spotless and tidy as he remembered it. That thought gave him another idea.

"Madam Edweth is waiting anxiously at Appleyard, too," he called out. "She's afraid that some harm may have come to Rowen. We are all very concerned about her."

The silence remained unbroken. There was only the library left on this floor. Brax reached it and peered in. There was no one to be seen. He motioned to the hogmen. Reluctantly they joined him at the doorway into the library.

"This is where Master Pendrake was taken away by the servant of the Night King," Brax said. "It may have been a creature of werefire. Do you sense anything?"

He knew that the hogmen, having been in close quarters with werefire in the sewers of Skald for so long, could sense its presence. Especially Hodge. They were terrified of the fire, but their familiarity with it could be of great help to him now.

Hodge leaned warily into the room and sniffed. He turned to the mage with a shrug. "I don't know," he breathed. "I can tell something happened here, something magic. But it was days ago."

"I know that much already," Brax said tersely. "Go in. Check around."

"But the wolf . . ." Hodge murmured.

"He's not here," Flitch said, keeping a grip on Freya's arm. "Get in there, fool."

Hodge stepped cautiously into the room, for some reason on tiptoe. He looked absurd, Brax thought, like an enormous bloated child playing hide-and-seek. The hogman turned quickly in a circle, then gazed at Brax, his eyes wide with fear.

"There's nothing in the room, but . . . something's *here*."

"Brax," Thorne said in a warning tone.

The mage pivoted—and saw what the captain and his troopers were staring at.

On the staircase at the end of the hallway stood Nicholas Pendrake—or someone who looked very much like him. The old man was silent and unmoving, his eyes cast downward and his face shadowed by the overhanging arch of the stairwell.

"Father Nicholas," Freya cried. "Don't listen to him. He's a liar. He only wants—"

"Silence," Brax growled.

"Why have you come to my house with weapons?" Pendrake asked in a calm, quiet voice. "There's no need for any of this. Let Freya go and return to your business, all of you. There are far more important matters for the Errantry to deal with than bothering an old man in his home."

Thorne regarded the toymaker and swallowed hard. For a moment Brax feared he would give in, but then the captain drew himself up and stepped forward.

"I'm sorry, Master Pendrake, but a grave accusation has been made and it must be answered. You will accompany us back to Appleyard or I shall have no choice but to take you there by force."

"I am needed here, Captain," Pendrake said firmly. "If you wish to question me, you may do so now, but I will not leave the toyshop."

As he spoke, the old man raised his head. His eyes came into view and Brax caught the strange yellow gleam in them. He gave a shout of triumph.

"This is *not* Pendrake, Captain," he said. "Look at him. Look at his eyes. He's some kind of changeling or shapeshifter."

Still he felt the hesitation in the men behind him. The Loremaster was deep in the counsels of Lord Caliburn and was respected, even a little feared, as a figure of wisdom and a wielder of mysterious power. Brax, an outsider to them as yet, had crossed an invisible line. Even Thorne had frozen where he stood and seemed at a loss now.

"Go home to Kyning Rore, Ammon," Pendrake said in a voice of gentle chiding. "Your fellow mages need their leader. Men of the Errantry, return to your duties. You are not at fault here and you will not be held accountable for the folly of others."

"Don't listen to him," Brax yelled. "Arrest him before it's too late. This imposter puts us all in danger."

"There is great danger to Fable," the old man said, "but not from me."

"Where are Rowen and the boy?" Brax shouted. "What have you done with them?"

"I have done nothing with them and you will do nothing to me," the old man said, his voice deeper now and carrying a trace of threat. Some of the Errantry troopers shifted uneasily and a whimper of fear came from Hodge.

Brax took a step back to where Freya stood with the hogmen. He reached for her arm and held the obsidian blade of his staff to her throat.

"Reveal yourself," he said, "or the Skalding woman dies."

"What are you doing? I did not agree to *this*," Thorne hissed.

"I'm doing what's necessary and so must you if you care about the safety of this city. Arrest him, Captain. *Now*. Do you want the blame if he escapes?"

But still Thorne did not move or give any command to his men.

The Loremaster took one slow, cautious step down the staircase and raised his hand. "Do not harm the girl," he said.

Brax saw the yellow glow in his eyes flicker and brighten, as if whoever or whatever had assumed the form of the Loremaster was tensed and ready to leap out.

But it was the Skalding woman who surprised him. Freya drove her elbow hard into the mage's ribs. He let go of her with a gasp, and before anyone could move, she darted up the stairs and threw her arms around the old man.

"Father Nicholas," she cried. "Don't listen to the mage. You mustn't let them—"

She broke off, stepped back. She had seen what Brax had seen in the old man's eyes.

The mage moved swiftly. He caught Freya by the arm once more and brought the blade to her neck.

"Reveal yourself!" he roared at the old man.

In the next instant Nicholas Pendrake was gone and a huge tiger, its tawny coat rippling like fire in the dark hall, crouched on the stairs. Thorne let out a growl of fear and surprise, and the Errantry troopers raised their weapons. The tiger stared only at Brax and did not move. But now the mage had seen something else in the depths of those strange yellow eyes, and he knew that he had won. He thrust Freya away from him.

"You came from wherever the Loremaster's power does," he said under his breath. "The old man *made* you."

He raised his staff with both hands.

"We mustn't let it escape," he shouted to the troopers. "We have to keep it here."

Without warning the tiger gave a roar that seemed to shake the walls and then it sprang at the mage. At the same moment Brax swept his ivory staff upward. The tiger was caught in mid-leap and hung in the air on the point of the obsidian blade, but it had not been pierced by the knife-sharp stone. It was only held there, thrashing and writhing as though caught in an invisible net, its bright shape dimming like a guttering candle flame. Then, as if the flame had been snuffed out, the tiger vanished.

Brax lowered the staff with shaking hands. It was empty of its dark spellcraft now but that no longer mattered. It had been enough. Just enough.

Thorne and his men also lowered their weapons. Hodge and Flitch were still cowering on the floor. Freya had backed away when the tiger leaped and now she bolted for the door, but Flitch moved in time to bar her way. His huge hand closed around her ankle and twisted her sideways. She fell with a sharp cry.

Brax turned in a slow circle. He drew a deep breath, willing his hammering heart to slow. He was closer than ever to what he sought. The tiger, the shapeshifter, had come from the same source as the werefire, he was sure of it. Whether he had killed the creature or only wounded it, he didn't know, and so he would have to move quickly. Somewhere in the house, he knew for certain now, the source of the shapeshifter's power lay hidden. This time, with the help of the hogmen, he would find it.

Freya lay on the stone tiles of the front hall, clutching her ankle and grimacing in pain. Flitch stood over her, scowling. "You shouldn't have run," he muttered.

"Are you hurt?" Captain Thorne asked Freya, but she ignored him and stared with blazing eyes at the mage. The captain turned to Brax, as well. "You were right, Master Brax," he said. "Whatever that thing was, it was not Nicholas Pendrake. Fortunately it didn't harm anyone before you destroyed it."

If Thorne had been impressed with the mage before, his expression was now one of awe. He had seen him tear apart a powerful being of flame and dark magic, and now he would do almost anything Brax told him to without question. He had no idea he'd witnessed the very last trick up Brax's sleeve. There would be no more such displays if the mage did not find what he sought, and soon.

Thorne ordered his men to search the house for Rowen and the others. They hurried up the stairs and Brax watched them, trying not to let his impatience show. He wanted the captain and his men out of here. Time was against him. In a few days this city would be under siege, and not long after that, he was sure, it would be a smoking ruin. By then he had to have that power or he was finished forever.

"What was that thing?" Flitch said.

"It was the fire, brother," Hodge mumbled. "Not the werefire. The good kind."

"What do you mean, the *good* kind?" Flitch snapped. "It might have torn our throats out, like that damned wolf."

"The wolf isn't here anymore," Hodge said.

Brax turned to the hogman. "You're certain of this?" he asked.

"The wolf is with the girl and she's gone, too."

"How can you possibly know that, you gibbering dolt," Flitch growled.

"I just know."

"The two of you are coming back to Appleyard with me as soon as we're finished here," Thorne said. "In the meantime, keep your mouths shut."

"Actually, Captain, I would like to keep these two with me," Brax said. "Here at the toyshop. Whether the girl is found or not, this is a loremaster's house, and if I'm going to help defend Fable, I must continue my investigation into what happened to Nicholas Pendrake. These two hogmen can be of service to me in that. Let me care for the Skalding woman, as well. If she's broken any bones, I will tend to them."

Thorne frowned. "You want to keep the hogmen here? You know I must inform the Marshal about what's happened, Master Brax. He won't be pleased to learn these two aren't locked up at Appleyard."

"Then perhaps it's best you don't inform him of the fact— at least not right away. I will have to work quickly and unhindered to get to the bottom of all this, and I need you to stand with me, Captain. The threat to Fable is beyond anything Lord Caliburn has ever dealt with, and we can't wait while he deliberates and follows the old, safe ways of doing things. You understand that better than anyone. This city needs our boldness and our willingness to do what must be done, however unpleasant."

Thorne took a deep breath and then nodded. "The Marshal has other concerns," he said. "You may keep the hogmen with you, but they must not be allowed out of the toyshop."

Brax lifted his staff. He could feel the deep crack running through its heart. It held no more power now than any broken stick, but it could still be of use. He tapped the staff once, softly, on the floor, and the Marrowbone brothers quailed before it.

"Captain Thorne, I can promise you," he said with a thin smile, "they will stay put and behave themselves."

6

WILL HAD NO IDEA how long they'd been travelling through
the Weaving. It could have been moments or hours. Time was
different here. His awareness of its passing seemed to come
and go. He remembered walking into the raincabinet and
ducking his head against the falling water, and the next thing
he knew, he and Shade were following Rowen through vague,
shadowy streets between tall, lightless grey buildings. Then
the houses and streets had fallen away and they were hurrying through thick, gloomy woods.

They were moving much faster than should have been
possible through this trackless forest, Will had thought, until
he realized that everything around them was moving, too.
Moving and changing. Walls of foliage parted like curtains
to reveal a way forward. Tangles of thorny branches un-
coiled themselves or melted into nothing but shadows.

A huge tree rose up directly in their path, but as they drew closer, the tree divided into many smaller trees whose slender trunks they could pass between.

Eventually Will realized that Rowen was making a path for them to follow. She was bending and shaping this strange world around her, *telling* it the way she had told the rain-cabinet into concealing itself.

The woods melted away into a wide, open plain of grass, and then the plain buckled and heaved itself into rocky hills, and still they hurried on at an impossible pace. From time to time dim shapes of people would loom up out of the shifting shadows and swiftly melt away again. Some of them seemed to notice Will's presence: they raised their hands as if to hail him, speak to him, but he avoided meeting their gazes and kept moving, not daring to lose sight of Rowen. And like everything else in the Weaving the figures quickly melted and changed, becoming a stone or a tree or simply a trick of light and shadow.

Then it happened. A house swam up out of the shifting murk. A house tucked in among sleepy-looking trees, with a wooden front porch that needed painting, a peaked green-tiled roof and warm lights in the windows.

It was the house Will had grown up in.

He stopped in surprise. He took his eyes off Rowen and Shade only for a moment, but it was enough. When he turned to them again, they were gone.

Now he was standing in front of his old house, on the street of his childhood. He had grown up here. He had lived here until the day his mother died and then his childhood had ended.

It was all so real. The world was no longer changing around him. The familiar trees, fences, telephone poles—everything was where it belonged and just as he remembered it. The front walk was solid under his feet. It seemed he really had left the Weaving. He had come home.

Yet it was the middle of the day and the street was deserted. That was strange. Old Mrs. Morrison wasn't sitting on the rocker on her front porch. No one was mowing the lawn or washing the car. There were no kids riding their bikes or skateboarding, and there should have been because it was summer. Unless it wasn't summer here. Time passed differently in the Perilous Realm. He knew that. Maybe he had come home on a day when everyone was at work or at school. Or had he come home at all?

Will gazed around at the silent street and tried to think. If he had really left the Weaving, he had to get back. He had to find Rowen and Shade again. He couldn't leave them. But if he was still in the Weaving, what then? Rowen had told him the Weaving was like the world of one's dreams. If he was in a dream now, could he wake himself up?

Not knowing what else to do, he climbed the creaking steps of the porch. The front door was open. He went in.

The house was dark inside and cool.

"Dad?" he called. "Jess?"

There was no answer. No one was in the front room.

He walked down the hallway to the kitchen at the back and was reaching for the light switch when he saw a shadow move on the wall beside him. He whirled with a cry.

Someone was standing in the dark hall. Someone in a bulky hooded coat. In the dim light Will couldn't make out a face in the shadows under the hood.

"Don't move," said a man's voice that was out of breath and strained. Something about the voice was familiar, too, though Will could not place it. All he knew for certain was that this man had been running, hiding from something or someone.

"I live here," Will said.

"Take a step backward," the man said. "Just one."

Will hesitated, then did as he was told. He took a step and his face came out from the shadows into the light from the kitchen window.

The man gave a grunt as if surprised by what he saw. "It really is you," he said. "The threads are all tangled. It's happened before, the stories getting mixed up like this. But I've never seen you. You're still at the beginning and me . . ."

He was talking to himself, Will realized.

The man shook his head slowly. "No telling how long it will last," he murmured. And then Will felt rather than saw the man's eyes fix on him. "No time," he said. "You have to listen. You have to listen to me. Don't make the same mistake I made."

"I don't know what you're talking about," Will said in as calm a voice as he could manage. The stranger sounded desperate, almost crazed. His unexpected, menacing presence here in Will's own childhood home already felt like an act of violence, and he braced himself for whatever might follow.

The man seemed about to say more, then he lifted his head as though listening for something. Will's eyes had begun to adjust to the dim light and he could make out more of the stranger's face. He saw a sharp cheekbone, a thin fringe of beard and two sunken, haunted eyes. It was the face of a young man, but one who had lived through great terror or hardship. The eyes were familiar, too, like the voice. Will was sure he had met this young man somewhere or had seen him before, though he could not think when or where.

Then he heard whatever it was the stranger had heard: a distant roar and rumble, punctuated by metallic groans. Like the noise of great machinery at work somewhere not far off.

"They're getting closer," the young man said. "It won't be long now. Listen to me. Where you're going, you must stay with her. No matter what. Do you hear me?"

Will said nothing. This stranger, whoever he was, seemed to know him, and knew about Rowen. But Will wasn't going to give anything away. This could be a shape-changing creature, like one of those fetches, sent here to trick him.

"Do you hear me?" the young man repeated, his voice rising to a shout. "Don't play stupid. You understand who I'm talking about. Stay with her. Don't leave her, no matter what."

"Who are you?" Will demanded, with a terrifying awareness that he already had the answer.

"I'm not anyone. Not anymore," the young man said. "There are no names left. Almost everything's been swallowed up. First the Perilous Realm and then our world, too. No matter where I ran it was the same. I didn't expect to find this place still here. But wait . . . we're not really *here*, are we? No. I remember now. You followed her into the rain-cabinet and then you got lost and came here. Yes, now I see. That's where we are. This is the Weaving. The end can meet the beginning here. I can warn you. The story doesn't have to end the same way. It can be changed. *You* can change it."

The distant rumbling was louder now. The metallic groans rose to a piercing shriek before falling away again.

"They're so close," the young man said. "Listen to me. She still has the thread, right? The ball of golden thread her grandmother gave her."

Will hesitated. "I don't know what you're talking about."

"You do. And she has it. You of all people can't lie to me. She must use the thread on the wolf. Do you understand?"

"What do you mean?"

"She has to bind the wolf with the thread. That's what it's for. The wolf will agree to be bound, but she won't want to go through with it. She'll give in to her love for him. You must convince her. The wolf must be bound, or all is lost."

Will shook his head. "You're talking about Shade," he said angrily. "No. I couldn't do that to him. I won't."

"He's already started to change, hasn't he? Of course he has. I remember now. It happened at Corr Madoc's fortress. They gave him the fever iron. If she waits too long, he won't submit to either of you. He'll turn against you. She's seen it, and you know it's true."

Will said nothing.

"We had no choice," the young man went on, his voice choked with rage and despair. "I didn't want to harm my friend, but he would have killed us. We had to do it. We had to bind him."

From the street came a bang, followed immediately by a high-pitched crackling whine. The young man turned and ran to the front door but did not open it. Will followed. Beside the door was a small window draped with a thin lace curtain. The young man stood at the window and drew the curtain aside slightly. Will could make out little from where he stood, but the world outside had gone utterly dark save for a cold, white light that seemed to be falling out of the sky. The ghostly shadows of the lace curtain slid across the young man's face.

A flare, Will realized. A search light.

"She's found me," the young man said, and his voice had gone hollow and utterly hopeless. "She's coming."

"Who's coming?" Will asked desperately.

The young man didn't answer. The flare must have landed somewhere nearby. Its stark white light had stopped moving. And now Will noticed that the walls and the floor of the house were shaking. The glass hummed in the window frames and dust drifted down from the ceiling.

"It's over," the young man said. He turned, and in the cold light Will saw his haggard face clearly for the first time.

"You must get back to where you came from," the young man said. "Find her. Get back to her—stay with her. Don't leave her . . . like I did. I failed her, and because of me, she failed. It's too late now for me to change it, but not for you."

Will hesitated.

"Go," the young man shouted at him. "Run!"

Will stumbled back. The walls of the house were cracking and splitting, the floorboards buckling under him. He turned and ran down the hall to the kitchen, burst through the back door and down the crumbling steps. This was the way he had gone the first time he returned to the Perilous Realm. Maybe it was the right way to go now. He couldn't tell, but the street, the other houses, had vanished. He was surrounded once more by a rushing blur of vague, rippling shapes and shadows. There was a roaring in his ears, as if he had plunged under the surface of a swift, churning river. He didn't know if it was the sound of the Weaving or the unseen machines behind him.

Then he heard a voice calling his name.

Rowen.

He shouted back, and out of the rush of shadows she appeared. Solid and real. She took his hand, gripped it.

"I found you," she said through her tears. "I found you."

The next thing he knew he was blinking up into bright sunlight.

Rowen's hand was still gripping his. Shade stood nearby. No one spoke. It was as if they had been woken suddenly from a dream and were still too dazed to speak.

They were standing on a grassy slope that ran down to an expanse of water rimmed with dark forested hills. The water's surface gleamed like gold in the sunlight. Above the hills the immense dome of the sky was a brilliant azure, across which a few wispy white clouds drifted. Will could hear the wind sighing in the grass and waves lapping softly on the shore.

"Are you all right, Will Lightfoot?"

It was Shade speaking to him. Will nodded, still struggling to clear his head.

"And you?"

"I am better," the wolf said, "now that we have left that place. It was . . . strange. I saw things that made no sense to me."

"Have we really left the Weaving?"

"We have," Rowen said. "We're back in the Realm."

"I am sorry I lost sight of you, Will Lightfoot," Shade said. "Where did you go?"

Will didn't answer right away. He saw with anguish that the wolf's condition appeared worse than before they had gone into the Weaving. Shade was outwardly calm, as always, but Will could see in the wolf's eyes that he was suffering, and struggling to conceal it.

The young man's feverish warning that Shade must be bound came back to Will and he felt sick inside. He couldn't deny who that young man had been. Or would become. The thought terrified him, even as he struggled to understand how the two of them could possibly have met.

"I was back home," he said. "In the Untold."

He couldn't share with Rowen or Shade what he'd seen and heard. Not yet. It had happened in the Weaving, after all. Rowen had said you could get trapped there by things that weren't real. Maybe what he'd seen was something like a bad dream. Not the future, not the truth of what was going to happen. Only a dream. And maybe that's what the Dreamwalker's vision of Rowen had been, too. Only a dream. Something that *could* happen, not something that *would* happen. He hadn't told Rowen about that yet, either.

"I saw a house," Will said at last. "The house I grew up in. I wasn't sure if it was real or not. I looked away just for a moment, and when I looked back, you were gone. Both of you. It's exactly what you told me not to do, Rowen. I'm sorry."

She shook her head, and he was troubled to see how pale and exhausted she appeared.

"It wasn't your fault," she said. "It's the Weaving. That's what makes it so dangerous. I was the one who should've been more careful. But we're safe here—for now."

"Where is *here*?"

"I think this is the place where Grandfather and I left the Shee, the Fair Folk, on our way home to Fable. It was south of the Forest of Eldark. There was a lake there, like this one. With hills like those on the far side. When we—"

To Will's alarm Rowen dropped the Loremaster's staff and staggered as if about to fall. He caught her and eased her to the ground, where she sat with her head sagging forward. Shade joined Will at her side.

"What's the matter?" Will said.

"I'm just tired," Rowen said, looking up at them with a weak attempt at a smile. "I'll be fine. I didn't think going into the Weaving again would be so hard. I thought I could find the thread of the Fair Folk easily, but there were so many stories, so many threads. I couldn't shut them out. It's as if every time I go into the Weaving there's more of it—or less of me. I tried, but I couldn't keep the three of us together and search for the Fair Folk at the same time."

Will brought out his water flask, uncorked it and handed it to her. She took a drink and wiped her mouth.

"I had it, just for a moment," she said. "I could see the path, the way we had to go." Her voice was trembling. "But then I saw . . ."

The expression in her eyes now was one of awe and terror.
"Who did you see?" he asked.

"The Fair Folk," Rowen said. "The Tain Shee. But they
had changed, Will. They didn't look the way they did when
we first met them, after Moth died."

With a pang Will remembered the Shee archer. He had
saved Will and Rowen from Lotan, the terrible Angel of
Malabron, and died destroying him.

"I knew it was them, though," Rowen went on. "I think I
was seeing them as they really are. They were on horseback
and they were wearing bright armour and carrying long
swords. And their faces, Will. They looked the way Moth did
when he fought the Angel. Their faces were pale, but their
eyes were like fire."

"Where did you see them?" Will asked. "Are they near
here?"

"No, it was somewhere else. Not the Shadow Realm,
but . . ." She shook her head wearily. "I don't know where it
was. They were riding over a place of broken stones. There
were buildings, but they were strange to me, and there were
things I didn't recognize. Creatures I've never seen before.
The Shee were riding into this darkness that the creatures
were coming out of, a darkness that was . . . *screaming.* Then
I couldn't see them anymore. They were gone."

"Gone where?"

"I don't know. I don't know. I was frightened and I looked
away. Then there were too many threads between us and I
couldn't find them again."

Rowen made as if to climb to her feet, and Will helped
her up. She brushed the hair from her eyes and gazed out
over the lake.

"The Weaving is all torn and tangled now. So much of it is
already dark. So much has been swallowed up. I tried to find

the Shee again, but I went too far. Too far, too fast, and I left you and Shade behind. It wasn't you who lost me—it was me who nearly got us all lost. After I found you and Shade again I took us out of the Weaving while I still could. I brought us here, to the last place I spoke to the Lady of the Shee. And now we're here and the Fair Folk are not."

She was distraught, shaking.

"You did what was right," Will said firmly. "It's better to be here than lost in *there*." He gestured vaguely behind him and then realized he had no idea where the Weaving was. There was no doorway, as there had been in the toyshop. "You just need to rest for a while," he went on. "Once you're feeling stronger we can go back into the Weaving and search again."

Rowen looked at him with tears in her eyes.

"You don't understand," she said desperately. "We can't get back into the Weaving from here. I don't know how. The only way in I know about is the raincabinet in the toyshop. Maybe there isn't another doorway. And Fable is miles from here, on the other side of the forest. If we can't go through the Weaving, it'll take us days to walk there. Don't you see? I've failed. I'll never find Grandfather now, and Fable has no loremaster to protect it. I've failed everyone." She buried her face in her hands.

Will put a hand on her shoulder. Her despair had shaken his own resolve and he didn't know how to comfort her.

After some time Rowen stirred. She slipped a hand into her cloak pocket, pulled out a tiny golden ball and held it in her palm. It was the golden thread that Rowen's grandmother had spun for her in the Weaving and given to her before they parted.

Will glanced furtively at the wolf, then back at Rowen. She was gazing at the ball of thread.

"Grandmother said it was the strongest thread there is," she murmured. "She said I could weave with it, and what I wove could never be unwoven. But she didn't say what or how."

Will leaned closer, his own eyes caught and held by the tiny ball's golden shimmer. The thread was so fine that one could easily mistake its tight coil for a solid sphere of gold. How could something this frail and insubstantial, almost not there at all, bind a powerful creature like Shade?

Will asked quietly, "Are you going to use it now?"

"I wonder . . ." Rowen said hesitantly. "Maybe I was supposed to use it if we got lost. There's an old story about that. Grandfather told it to me once. A story about someone using a golden thread to find the way out of a labyrinth."

"I've heard that story, too," Will said.

"Maybe if I just let the thread out, it will unwind and lead us back to where Grandmother is. Or back to Fable."

"Do you think that'll work?" Will said.

Rowen didn't answer right away. Finally she looked up at Will and shook her head. "No," she said. "No, I don't think that's what it's meant for—as a way to go back. Grandmother didn't want me to search for Grandfather. She wanted me to stay in Fable and defend it. I think that's what the thread is for—to help Fable in some way. I need to save it for that. But we have to find Grandfather first, before we go back home. If we can find the way back."

Rowen gazed at the golden ball a moment longer, then slipped it back into her cloak and wrapped her arms around herself as if cold, even though it was warm under the bright sun.

"I'm lost, Will," she said in a hollow voice. "I don't know what to do."

Will turned in a circle, searching the hills although he had no idea what he was looking for. Watching Rowen with the thread, he had made up his mind. They would go on and he would say nothing about what he'd seen and heard in the Weaving. For all he knew his encounter there had been only an illusion. He would wait until he had more proof that binding Shade was the right thing to do. Or until he had no other choice.

One thing was certain: he wasn't ready to give up yet. He had been warned not to leave Rowen, no matter what. That much he was determined on.

"It'll be all right," he said at last, though he hardly believed it himself. "Do you remember what you told me? You said you needed me to come with you, to find a way into the Shadow Realm. You said it had to be. So you did that much right. And I'm still here."

Rowen faced him. "You're right," she said, trying to smile. "I saw you in the story. I saw you coming with me."

"So maybe it's up to me now," he said. He had been half joking before, in the hope of cheering her up, but he was serious now. "Maybe that's why you saw me in the story. Because I have to find the way from now on. Who knows, there could be a knot-path around here, one that the Fair Folk took to wherever it is they went. Did the Lady of the Shee say anything to you about that before they left?"

"All she told me was that they were going to meet their enemy and either defeat him or perish. She didn't say where they were going."

"Well, what about this place, then? I mean, why did they bring you here instead of somewhere else? Maybe they had a reason."

"I don't know. The Lady of the Shee talked about the hill where they met the Stewards at midsummer, under the great Tree of Story. The Lady said few such places like that were left in the Realm, places where time stops, but *this* was one of them. That's all I remember."

Will turned slowly in a circle. At the top of the grassy slope they were standing on rose a thicket of small flowering trees. The other way, the slope fell gently to the lakeshore and the shimmering water.

"I'm going to have a look around," he said. "Maybe I can find something that will help us. Shade, stay with Rowen, please."

"We should all stay together, Will Lightfoot," the wolf said.

Will glanced at Rowen, who still appeared as though she might drop again from exhaustion at any moment.

"I won't go far," he said. "Just wait here."

He set off down the grassy slope to the lake. At the bottom he passed the moss-cloaked remains of a low wall. Beyond a gap in the wall was a flight of worn stone steps, half sunk in the earth, that led him down to the shore, where a narrow stone pier jutted out a short distance into the water. The Shee must have been coming here for a very long time, he thought. The stonework seemed very old, but at the same time he had the strange feeling that none of this—the mossy wall or the sunken stones or even the lake itself—had existed more than a few moments before he set foot here. He remembered Moth and his sister, Morrigan, how they both looked so young and so ancient at the same time.

Will paused, listening to the water lapping softly against the stone, then stepped onto the pier and walked slowly to the end. The pier was low in the water, or had sunk over the years like the wall and the steps. If the waves rose just a little, he thought, they would wash over the top of the stone. Will stopped at the edge and stood looking out across the lake, shielding his eyes against the brilliant dazzle of sunlight on the water. He closed his eyes and listened to the rush of the wind. The lonely sound reminded him how far they were from where they were supposed to be, but he listened to it as if this wind had travelled a vast distance with a message meant only for him. He listened, but if the wind had anything to tell him, he could not understand it.

Then he realized something was missing. There was no sound of water.

7

HE OPENED HIS EYES.

The surface of the lake had gone completely still. No waves lapped against the pier. The perfectly calm, still water reflected the distant hills and the blue sky like a mirror.

With a start Will thought of the shard of silver glass that the Lady of the Shee had given him to help him find the way home. He took the shard out of his pocket and held it up, peered into it. The piece he carried was only half of the shard. Rowen had the other half, because Will had broken the shard in two before he left her to search for Shade. The Lady had told him the shard would protect him from harm, and he had wanted to keep Rowen safe, too.

Will searched for his reflection in the shard, but no matter which way he tilted or turned it, the silvered glass showed him nothing except blue sky and wisps of cloud. This had

happened the first time he had peered into the shard. Not
seeing his own reflection had startled him into an understanding of how his pathfinding gift worked: he had to stop
trying to make it work. He had to get out of his own way and
the path would be clear. But what did it mean that his reflection was missing now? He neither saw nor sensed any path
before him. Only the water, and he could not walk on that.
Like the sound of the wind, the empty sky in the shard was
a message he could not read. The glass in his hand and the
water at his feet were the same.

They were the same.

He turned and shouted to Rowen and Shade. They came
hurrying down the slope and joined him at the end of the
pier. He gestured to the lake's surface without speaking.
Rowen leaned over the edge and looked down.

"What's happened to the lake?" she asked. "The water's
not moving."

"That's because it's not water anymore. Or maybe it
never was."

"What do you mean?"

"There *was* a reason the Fair Folk brought you here," Will
said eagerly. "I think the Lady of the Shee wanted you to learn
about this place, so that if you were looking for her people
you would come back here. She must have foreseen that we
would be searching for a way into the Shadow Realm."

"I don't understand. Why *here*? How can this place help
us find them?"

"This lake—it's the mirror."

"The *mirror*?"

"The Mirror of Truth, the one that was shattered in the
first war with the Night King. Remember what the Lady told
us? Over the ages her people have been gathering the pieces
of the mirror together again. This is where they kept them.

I'm sure of it. When Moth destroyed the Angel, they finally recovered the last few shards they had been searching for, and they gave me one. Maybe the very last one. It came from here. It belongs here."

Rowen still looked incredulous. Will decided he would have to show her, and prove to himself, too, he was right. And there was only one way to do that.

Rowen gasped as he turned away and stepped off the end of the pier. As he had guessed, he didn't plunge into icy cold water but found himself standing on the smooth, still surface. The lake, or the mirror, was solid under his feet. He lifted one foot and stamped, saw the surface bow slightly under the sudden pressure, then go smooth and still again.

"Will?" Rowen said.

He realized he was holding his breath, and let it out. He turned back to Rowen and Shade. "Come on," he said. "I think we're meant to cross it."

Shade took the first careful step off the pier, and came slowly to Will's side, staring down at the glassy surface underneath him, his back arched and his paws splayed wide as if he expected at any moment to fall through. When he realized that the mirror would hold him up, he relaxed and took a few more exploratory steps from the pier.

"It looks like ice, but it's not cold or slippery," the wolf said. "How can that be?"

"I don't know what it's made of. I don't think it's glass, either."

Rowen joined them a few seconds later. Slowly they stepped farther away from the pier, glancing back often, still unwilling to leave the safety of the shore too far behind. But soon it became clear to them all that Will had guessed right. What they were walking on wasn't water, or if it was, it had changed somehow into whatever strange substance the

mirror was made from. They were able to walk across confi-
dently, without any sense that they might lose their footing.
Even so, they couldn't help looking down often as they
walked, not yet fully believing that they were really doing
this impossible thing.

Their own reflections looked back up at them in wide-
eyed amazement.

Before long they had walked far enough that the pier had
almost vanished in the glare. They could still see the grassy
slope and the darkly treed hills all around, but everything
appeared more distant than they would have expected after
such a short time. The shore had receded to a dark line on
the horizon, as if the lake, or the mirror, was growing larger
as they crossed it.

After they had walked on a little farther still, the shore
was nothing more than a dim green line on the horizon. To
find themselves surrounded both above and below by an immense blue dome dotted with a few small clouds was dizzy-
ing. They seemed to be suspended in an infinite sky.

"What do you think's on the other side?" Rowen said.

"I'm not sure we're supposed to reach the other side," Will
said. Rowen was going to ask him what he meant, but his
gaze was fixed on the mirror's surface a short distance ahead
of them. He was clearly looking for something. Just when she
was about to ask him what it was, he gave an excited cry.

"There!" he shouted, and broke into a run.

Shade and Rowen hurried after him. Rowen searched the
mirror for whatever it was Will had seen, and then she saw it:
a tiny spot of blackness in the shining blue of the reflected sky.

Will reached the black spot and went down on one knee.
Rowen and Shade joined him a moment later.

"This is it," he said. "This is where our piece of the mirror
fits in."

Rowen crouched beside him and saw more clearly what he had found. It was a roughly triangular patch of absolute darkness, as if a hole had been punched through the fabric of the world into a lightless void beyond. She shivered.

"This *is* where they came from," she breathed. "The broken pieces. You were right."

"The lake . . ." Will murmured. "It's the way the Fair Folk do things. The way they've stayed hidden all these years. By hiding in plain sight." He held out his hand. "Give me your half."

Rowen slipped the chain from around her neck, undid the tiny clasp and slid the chain out of the hole in the shard. Will took the shard from her, then held her half next to his in his palm. As she watched in wonder, the hole that had held the shard on the chain shrank and vanished and the two halves came together seamlessly.

"It's one piece again," Rowen said.

She waited for Will to put the shard in its place in the mirror. She wanted him to. She wanted that hole into darkness covered up, but Will didn't move. He was staring at the shard in his hand.

"Will?" Rowen said quietly. "What's wrong?"

"Nothing," he said, shaking his head. "It's just that the Lady gave this to me to protect me. It was one thing to break it in half. I only did that because I wanted you to be safe, too. I didn't think twice about it. But to just give it up like this, when we need it more than ever . . . I don't know if I should."

Rowen dared another glance into the dark place in the mirror. She thought of the clever wooden puzzles her grandfather made at the toyshop. How hard it was to fit the pieces together in the right places, and how pleased she felt when she got to the last piece and there was only one place it could fit.

"No, this is right," she said. "You were right. This is where the shard belongs."

Will frowned. "I don't know," he said. "But we have to do something."

Slowly and carefully he placed the two halves of the shard in the triangular black space. They fit exactly, and as soon as they were in place, the hair-thin line between them and along the edges of the hole began to melt away. Moments later the mirror was whole and there was no longer any trace of their shards, so that she could not even say for sure just where Will had placed them. All Rowen knew was that she was glad to see that terrible window into nothing sealed up.

At first it seemed that nothing else had changed. And then as they continued to gaze at the mirror, they saw its bright surface dim and darken. Their own reflections began to fade and waver.

"What's happening?" Rowen whispered.

"The mirror is becoming water again," Shade said, dabbing at it with a paw.

It was true. With each movement of their feet, the surface shivered and ripples spread outward. But the three of them didn't plunge through, and after a moment, Rowen saw why. The water was nothing more than a thin film over a stony surface. As if the lake had suddenly begun to drain away.

They looked up then from their dimming reflections to see that the wooded hills were gone. They were standing in the middle of a paved road lined with spindly shrubs and thin trees. The pavement was cracked and uneven, and sunken in places, so that parts of it were covered in water. They were standing in one of these shallow pools. The sky above them was no longer bright but sealed over with swiftly moving grey cloud.

"Where are we now?" Will asked, gazing around.

"We've gone where the Fair Folk went," Rowen said.

"Where is that?"

Rowen didn't answer.

Will glanced up at the sky. The low, dark clouds were churning, shredding apart and fusing again, as if a storm was brewing within them. Here on the ground the air was still and quiet.

He turned to Rowen. "Do you recognize this place?"

"No, but I think we're on one of the paths the Fair Folk take when they conceal themselves. One of their hidden ways."

"How can you be sure?"

"I can't," she said, and then peered down at the thin film of water at their feet. "But I don't think we can go back."

"This place we have come to," Shade said. "It is no longer my world."

"What do you mean, Shade?" Will asked. "This isn't the Realm?"

"It is . . . hard for me to find the words," the wolf said. "Where I come from, everything has a voice. The sunlight, the rain, the wind in the leaves. They are all part of a great speaking, and so am I. Here, that voice is very hard to hear. We are in the Realm, but we are not."

Will looked up and down the road. In both directions it ran straight until it vanished in the haze. Then he glimpsed a small green structure by the roadside and half hidden in the trees. "Let's find out what that is," he said. He set off, and Rowen and Shade followed.

The little building, whatever it was, turned out to have a roof and three walls, but was open on the side facing the road. The green paint was chipped and flaking. There was a bench inside the structure, also green, and a few scraps of paper and other things littering the dirt floor.

Shade sniffed at the bench and the walls. "Someone has been here. Not long ago," he said.

"What happened to the other wall?" Rowen said, glancing around inside. "Who would build a house like this and why?"

"It's not a house," Will said. "It's a bus shelter."

"A what?"

Will didn't answer. He toed the trash on the floor of the shelter, recognized a cigarette butt, a bottle cap, broken bits of amber glass that had probably come from a beer bottle. Rowen bent and picked up something from under the bench. It looked like a crumpled ball of paper, but it crinkled noisily as she unfolded it. The paper was transparent.

Rowen's brow furrowed. "See-through paper," she murmured wonderingly. "But there's nothing written on it. Have you ever seen anything like this?"

Will nodded. Rowen was holding an ordinary piece of plastic wrapping.

"This isn't some hidden path," he said. "The mirror didn't bring us to the Fair Folk—it took us back to my world. This is the Untold."

Rowen gaped at him. "Are you sure?"

Will gestured to the scrap of plastic Rowen was still holding.

"There's a lot of that kind of thing in my world. I don't recognize this place, but that doesn't mean anything. We could be somewhere far from where I live."

"But if we've crossed over into the Untold, why would the mirror . . . why would the Fair Folk bring us here?"

Will had no answer.

They left the shelter and kept on along the road, which rose slightly and then began to bend around a curve. The haze in the air had thinned somewhat and now they could see tall, bluish rectangular shapes rising in the distance beyond the road and the trees.

"Are those towers?" Rowen asked. "They're so tall."

Will nodded. "That's what a city looks like in my world," he said.

"Should we stay on the road, then, Will Lightfoot?" Shade asked. "You told me once there were few wolves where you come from, and most people had never seen one. If this road takes us to a city of your world, is that a place we want to be?"

"I don't know," Will said. "There's something strange about all this. We should've seen more people by now. More buildings. Cars. Road signs. I think we should just keep going until we know more about where we are."

Not long afterward the road plunged into a cutting between two high stone walls overarched by a wooden bridge. The cutting was filled with deep shadow and at its edge they halted instinctively. If some threat came at them in that narrow space, they would be trapped.

Without having to discuss it, Shade took the lead. Rowen and Will followed him warily. The paving stones underfoot were even more cracked and uneven than the rest of the road they had walked, but they hurried along faster than ever, eager to reach the light at the far end.

When they were halfway through the cutting, Shade pulled to a halt and lifted his head.

"Something is coming along the road," he said, "from the direction we came. I hear wheels, and hoofs."

8

AS ANOTHER DAY DAWNED pale and cold over the Valley of Fire, Corr Madoc's five remaining skyships set out for the city of Adamant.

Finn stood with Corr and Doctor Alazar on the bridge at the stern of the flagship. On the long main deck below them, sixty armoured Stormriders stood hunched against the relentless wind. At least twice that number were crowded into the hold below. The other ships were filled with men, too, and with Nonn's folk. This was the long-awaited day for the Ironwise, as well.

Corr scowled into the blast of the wind. His scarred face was a ghastly, mottled colour, but he showed no signs of fatigue or pain. Thanks to the *gaal*, Finn thought, which was also coursing in his own blood. He could not use his right arm—it was still a dead weight in its sling—but he had been taught to wield a sword with either hand. He could still be helpful. As long as there was fever iron to sustain him.

Finn glanced at Ord, the golem, who stood to one side of the bridge, the same impassive look on his grey features as always. If the ship fell to pieces and they all plummeted to their deaths, the expression on the clay man's face would not change, Finn thought.

I've become like him.

The ships were sailing above the low cloud cover to conceal their approach from any watchers below. As the sun rose, it flared like a newly kindled fire at the edge of the earth. Looking west, Finn saw snow-capped peaks marching off into shadowed lands where night was not yet over. To the north, gleaming white snowfields rolled away, seemingly forever.

"It reminds me of the deserts in my homeland," Alazar said to Finn, shielding his eyes against the blinding white glare of the snow. "You could travel for weeks without seeing anything but sand."

Since they'd set out, Finn had avoided speaking with the doctor. He didn't want to see the concern and pity in the older man's eyes.

"Balor told me that in the Sunlands you were the king's physician," Finn said.

The doctor nodded. "I entered Prince's service when he was a still a boy. The old king, his father, was terrified his son would contract the same disease that afflicted him: leprosy. And so the prince was never allowed out of the palace, and he yearned to know about the world outside its walls. For that he had to rely on what stories I could tell him of my own few travels. He spoke often of the great journeys he and I would make together when he was older and stronger, and I encouraged him, thinking that these were no more than a boy's dreams.

"Then came the day his father went hunting and was

unhorsed and killed by a lion. Suddenly the boy was king.
I saw very little of him after that. It was as though he'd been
walled in by counsellors and petitioners. And then one day I
was summoned to the young king's chamber. He showed me
a pale lesion he had found on his neck, and I knew that his
father's fear had come true. I told him that I would do all I
could to cure him, that I would seek out the finest physicians
in the Realm. But he shook his head. He said he was releasing
me from my duties as royal physician. 'I will never make
those journeys we used to speak of,' he said, 'and so I ask you
to make them for both of us. My only command is that one
day you return and bring me back tales of all the wonders
you've seen.' And then he put on a golden mask shaped like
the sun—the same mask his father had worn to hide his own
disfigurement. And that was the last time I saw his face."

The doctor sighed and glanced away.

"I think he wished to spare me pain," he went on. "The
pain of watching the disease take him a little at a time. I did
not want to leave, but it was his command. So I left his
service and went in search of the Realm's wonders."

He gazed out over the rolling white fields.

"Like snow," he said.

Finn was startled to feel tears sting his eyes. He had
thought the fever iron had killed any feeling in him other
than cold rage, but the sight of the snowfields had stirred
something. He had believed the Valley of Fire lay at the utter-
most edge of the world, but now he knew the Realm went on
past this hellish place, on and on into lands he would never
see or know. It might be that the Realm went on without end,
and if it did, then maybe no one, not even the Night King,
could ever conquer all of it.

"So one day you'll be leaving the Errantry and returning
home?" he asked the doctor, keeping his face turned away.

"That was my king's command," Alazar said. "And I think now, after all of *this*, I can return with enough to tell."

A Stormrider who had been leaning over the prow of the ship looked to the bridge and shouted something Finn did not catch over the wind's roar. Corr, still intent on the chart, straightened and barked orders. Men clambered into the rigging and the mordog at the helm eased off the huge treadle at his feet. There was a rumble and hiss from below, steam shot up in plumes from gratings in the deck, and all at once they were descending. The roiling cloudscape seemed to be rushing up to meet them.

Corr turned to Finn and Alazar.

"This is it," he said, gripping his brother's shoulder. "You and the doctor had best keep a hand on the rail. The ride down will be bumpy."

He had just finished speaking when the ships plunged back into the roaring wet and gloom of the clouds, into the reek of ash and sulphur.

The flagship shuddered and bucked as it descended. The timbers rattled and groaned under Finn's feet, and he wondered whether the ship would hold together long enough for them to reach Adamant.

All at once the planks seemed to drop away beneath him. His stomach lurched and he feared they were falling out of the sky. But in the next instant his knees buckled under him as the ship rose again, reassuringly solid, if shaky, under his feet.

"Heated air from vents in the ground below," Corr shouted in his ear. "Shakes the hulls something fierce, but not to worry. It means the ride is nearly over, brother. We're close to the city now."

Through a sudden gap in the clouds Finn caught a glimpse of the grey, barren valley still far below, and what looked like a path or road snaking through a field of boulders, but there was no sign of Adamant. Then a shadow crossed a thick bank of cloud beneath them and Finn looked up to see the hull of one of the other skyships appearing out of the mists.

Like the flagship, this ship and all the others had the same odd iron latticework that projected from the hull at a point midway between the rail and the keel. These were the lightning collectors that the dwarf-smiths had fashioned. The latticework ran along the hull, tapering to a single dark band when it reached the prow with its figurehead of an eagle. Finn did not understand how Nonn's folk had contrived such a thing, but the skyships harnessed the lightning, or the invisible, nameless power that sparked it, and held it in reserve until needed. When let loose by the gunner in the prow, a white-hot bolt of lightning would lance from the eagle's eye sockets.

The hull of a third ship appeared out of the mist just then and Finn knew the other two could not be far away. They were falling into formation now behind the flagship.

The mist suddenly lifted away. The roar of the wind fell off at the same instant and the ship's terrible shuddering ceased. They had dropped through the floor of the clouds, and the long trough of the Valley of Fire lay revealed beneath them.

Corr turned and beamed at Finn.

"There it is, brother."

Adamant had been built in the crater left by a great rock that fell from the sky ages ago, and that is what Finn saw at first: just another of the smoking holes in the earth that dotted the valley. But as they drew closer, he could make out more detail. All along the rim of the crater an earthen ring-wall had been raised, thirty feet high or more and topped with a stone battlement that bristled with huge spikes. A tall iron door was the only sign of a way through the great wall. The city itself lay within this fortified circle, but they were still too far off to see over the rim of the wall.

"The gate is shut and the wall seems intact," Corr said. "No sentries that I can see."

As the other ships emerged from the clouds and came level with the flagship, the Stormrider in the crow's nest high up on the mast gave a cry. They followed his outstretched arm and saw a pair of large winged shapes circling above the city. Finn found it difficult to tell how big these creatures were, but something in the slow, stately wheel of their flight told him they were very large. Corr shouted to the lightning gunner at the prow of the ship to stand ready, but almost before the words had left his lips, the winged creatures broke from their circling with slow, unhurried flaps of their wings. They beat their way northward through the smoky air, away from the city and the approaching ships, and swiftly vanished into the clouds. A cheer went up from the Stormriders.

"Dragons?" Finn asked.

"It looked that way," Corr said, "but no, they were scavenger birds."

"They must have been huge," Alazar said in wonder.

"Yes. They'll eat nearly anything, but most often they show up after a battle to feast on the dead. Anything else that might have been looking for a meal gets out of their way fast."

"They've arrived for dinner a little early, then," the doctor said grimly.

Corr laughed. "I would call their presence a good omen, Doctor. For us. Nightbane eat those creatures when they can bring them down. The birds won't usually fly anywhere near Adamant or our fortress for that reason. It's a sign the city has probably been deserted. That's why the men cheered."

The ships dropped ever lower, and as sails were furled, the forward movement of the ships began to slow, as well. Just as the flagship passed over the ring-wall, Stormriders threw grappling hooks on long ropes that caught on the iron spikes. The ropes went taut, and with a lurch and a shudder through its frame the flagship came to rest. One after the other all the skyships followed suit and were soon anchored above the wall, venting steam and groaning deep in their timbers.

Finn gazed over the side, awestruck in spite of himself. Just within the enclosing wall a broad walkway ran around the entire rim of the city. Within its circle a great crater yawned wide and deep, descending in ring after concentric ring of ledges, balconies, staircases and battlements far into the earth, until its lower circles were lost in smoke and darkness. There was no movement or sign of life in the depths that Finn could see, though he could make out small dark shapes that might have been bodies lying on some of the walkways. Directly beneath the flagship, an anvil-shaped projection of black stone jutted out into the central well, tapering to a pier. On the far side, a second pier reached out across the city's crater, but the two did not meet. A broad gap lay between them, though their jagged tips suggested that they were two halves of what had once been a slender bridge spanning the deep. The black stone, Finn guessed, must be the fabled adamant, the rare ore from which the city took its name.

"That's where we'll set down," Corr said, pointing to the nearer of the two anvil-shaped piers. "It's closest to the main gates. If anything unforeseen happens, we'll have the best chance of withdrawing from there with men and ships intact."

Below the upper parapet the depths of the city were lost in shadow and smoke. Flakes of ash whirled in the air, and the same acrid stench of sulphur and burning tar filled Finn's nostrils and stung his eyes, though a fainter but even more unwholesome reek accompanied it now: the smell of dead and rotting things.

"Where I come from we have a legend about a city like this," Alazar said to Finn. "It's where the spirits of the wicked go after death, to be tormented for all eternity."

Corr overheard him and turned with a cold gleam of amusement in his eye. "The spirits of the dead are down there indeed, Doctor," he said. "Don't you see them?"

Finn looked again and realized that some of what he had taken for drifting shreds of smoke and ash were in fact fetches: pale, wavering shapes of men, slowly moving about the parapets and platforms of the city.

"Will they attack us?" the doctor asked.

Corr didn't answer. He shouted another order to the helm and the ship began slowly to descend. When it dropped below the rim of the ring-wall, the sun's pale light was suddenly cut off.

In a few moments all five ships hovered little more than a man's height from the upper parapet and then came to rest on their flat keels. The sails sagged and the flagship's timbers knocked and groaned as they settled upon themselves.

Gangplanks were quickly lowered down the sides and the Stormriders hurried onto the pier. Corr ordered Finn and the doctor to wait on the ship's deck until he gave the word, and then he went over the side, followed by the golem and then the Stormriders. The other ships disgorged their crews, as well, and soon there were hundreds of Stormriders milling about the dull black surface of the pier. Finally Corr signalled to Finn and he climbed down with the doctor, who brought his heavy satchel with him.

"Welcome to Adamant," Corr said.

The flat, broad pier jutted out like a road, from the massive front gates of the city. The gates themselves were set deeply in the outer wall between two towering bastions that had carved stone heads of dragons set atop them. Finn thought it odd that these monstrous heads, their mouths gaping, should have been placed inside the city, facing inward, rather than glaring out at the valley to dismay enemies. But he was too busy surveying the rest of the city to think about it for long.

On either side of the pier the parapet curved away, and now Finn could see there were other structures built upon it: round sentry towers overlooking the central well, and vaults, like hoods carved of stone, over entryways to descending ramps and staircases that Finn guessed would lead to the city's lower levels.

The fetches Finn had glimpsed earlier from above had all vanished, as if they had been frightened away. He remembered Master Pendrake explaining that these spectres had no will of their own and drifted aimlessly unless bound by spellcraft. But they were drawn by the *gaal*, Nonn had said. That was how his people had trapped and sealed so many of them in armour alloyed with the fever iron.

Some of the Stormriders ran back along the pier to the gates and up staircases to the battlements, where they stood at watch while the rest of Corr's forces left the ships, carrying gear and supplies. Other Stormriders began to fan out and explore the platform and the adjacent tunnels and walkways. Corr's beastmaster, an enormous brute with a whip, came down from one of the other ships with seven of the wolves following him. They were agitated and wary, no doubt smelling the scent of blood and death in the air. And there were a few Nightbane corpses to be seen, lying on the stone or the stairs to the upper battlements. Some had had their limbs or heads hacked off.

Once the ships were securely at rest, Finn and the doctor walked with Corr to the tapering end of the pier, followed by the golem and two Stormriders. As Finn had seen from the ship, the walkway ended at a broken and jagged edge, as did the end of the pier on the far side. It seemed as if a central span that had once connected the two walkways had been smashed through by something falling from above. Or perhaps exploding from below. Chunks of black rubble littered the other pier, and Finn wondered what kind of weapon or force had been powerful enough to shatter something that was supposed to be unbreakable.

Together they gazed down into the chasm that was the city of Adamant, speechless for a while at the vastness that lay beneath them. Much of the building the Ironwise had done over the ages was damaged or had collapsed, but what remained to be seen—columned arcades, great arched doorways, sweeping staircases, slender bridges—struck Finn with amazement. This city had been beautiful once.

"The fetches will be drawn to the *gaal* in the ships sooner or later," Corr said. "We'll have to be vigilant. They may not be under the Night King's power, but their touch can still freeze the blood."

As if to fulfill Corr's words, Doctor Alazar gave a cry of warning. A pale figure had risen from the depths in front of them and hovered now just beyond the edge of the walkway. It was a fetch in the vague, wavering shape of a bearded man in long, flowing robes. Finn and the doctor stepped back in alarm, but Corr stood his ground.

The fetch hung in the air only steps from the broken end of the walkway, his sunken eyes fixed on Corr but without any expression in them that Finn could read: not fear or malice or even curiosity.

"Who were you in life, I wonder," Corr said. "A leader

of men, I think. Yes. A great lord or a king. That's why you came forward first, before the others. You were always first, weren't you?"

The fetch slowly raised a hand toward Corr and drifted closer to him, growing more solid and distinct the nearer it got.

Finn murmured, "Be careful, Corr."

"He won't harm me," Corr said over his shoulder, then he turned to the fetch again.

"It's *you*, isn't it?" he said. "The first Sky Lord. The one they named me for."

The fetch gave no sign of recognition.

"Hear me," Corr said. "I rule here now and the *gaal* is mine. There is nothing left for you or the others. Fade and depart as you should have done long ago."

The fetch gazed at Corr as if it had not heard, then at last it began to move away, dimming and growing thinner, its arm still outstretched, until finally it could not be told apart from the ash and smoke whirling up on the drafts from below.

"Will they all obey you like this?" asked Alazar.

"They bend to a stronger will, Doctor. Any stronger will. We've seen it before. One must face them down, and then there is nothing to fear."

The dwarfs' ship was the last to set down. When it had been secured like the others, Nonn appeared with his fellow elders, descended the gangplank and crossed the pier to where Corr and the others stood. To Finn's surprise the dwarf chieftain was no longer wearing the drab ring-mail and leathers he'd had on earlier. Instead he was dressed in a robe of sleek white fur embroidered with silver, and his lined brow was ringed with a thin circlet of bright gold. He walked with a staff now, too, a rod of roughly finished iron but topped with a spike of red stone.

The dwarf came toward them slowly and solemnly, like a monarch to his throne. He did not look at Corr or anyone else but strode past them all and halted at the very tip of the pier. He stood there for a time in silence, his head bowed, then he raised a hand.

"City of our fathers," he said in a deep, booming voice. "Great Qarqanaq. Adamant the imperishable. Your children have returned home. I join my life's blood with that of my fathers, and I vow I will not leave here again while yet a drop of that blood remains in me."

With that he drew the red spike of his staff across the palm of his hand and closed the hand in a fist. As the dark blood oozed from between his fingers, he held his arm out and let the drops fall into the depths.

Finally he turned away and strode back to where Finn stood with Corr and the doctor.

"This was our great public gathering place," the old dwarf said, gazing around the pier with its strewn bodies. "We gathered here on feast days and to welcome the sun at the end of winter. Oh, yes, we dwarfs loved the sun in those days. It wasn't always hidden behind veils of smoke and we weren't forced to hide in our tunnels then. We called our city Ban nor qalu, the circle of light and song. And now . . . now it is a charnel pit." He cursed in his own language. "The slaves of the Night King have defiled this ground, as they defile everything they touch."

"You and I will make this a living city once again, Nonn," Corr said. "And for that we will need the mines, if they can be reached."

"I have walked the path to those mines in my thoughts every day, Sky Lord," the dwarf said. "There is a main road that winds down through the city to the mine entrance, though it was damaged in the upheavals of the earth that

killed many of my people. The Nightbane may have re-
paired the road, but they are not Ironwise and it is very
likely that way is still difficult to pass. It would be best if a
company of my finest delvers go first, before anyone else."

"Until we're certain the Nightbane have left, nobody is
going anywhere without an armed escort," Corr said.

Finn thought the old dwarf would bristle at Corr's words,
but instead he smiled coldly.

"I agree," he said. "That's why I've brought one."

Nonn gestured toward his own ship. From its far side
now emerged a troop of thirty or more dwarfs in thickly
plated armour, carrying great square-headed hammers and
broad-bladed axes. Corr's eyes narrowed at the sight of
them, and Finn guessed that his brother had known nothing about this.

Corr studied the armed dwarfs in silence. Then he nodded.
"Very well," he said. "Have your delvers send messengers
back as soon as they've secured the mines. For now, though,
I would ask that you yourself stay with me. We're going to
establish our base camp here, as you suggested, and I will
need to consult you about many things."

"Of course. But one more thing, Lord. There may be
blockages and cave-ins that will be hard to clear, and that
creature of clay is stronger than thirty men. The work of
reaching the mines safely will go much faster for my delvers
with his help."

Corr turned and studied the silent, unmoving man of clay.

"The golem stays here for the time being," he said at last.
"If and when your delvers need him, I will reconsider."

Nonn's eyes burned. It looked as if he would protest, but
he nodded slowly and marched off without another word.
Finn watched him go. His suspicions about the old dwarf's
loyalty had been rekindled by the sight of the armed dwarfs

and Nonn's request for the golem. But before he could voice them, Corr spoke.

"Adamant has two masters now, it would seem," he said. "Nonn is no happier about that than the fetches."

"Can we trust him?" Finn asked.

"His little army isn't enough to protect him if the Nightbane return," Corr said. "He knows that. Nonn needs us as much as we need him."

Grath, who had captained one of the other ships, now hurried to Corr's side.

"My Lord, one of my men spotted two or three Nightbane as we came in. They were several levels down, on the far side of the city. They weren't fetches, the man was certain of that. And we've found cooking pots with food still in them, as well as weapons and other gear lying about. They left in haste, by all the signs, but a few are still skulking around. Maybe more than a few."

"We're being monitored, Grath—you can be sure of that," Corr said. "Strict watch is to be maintained at all times. Let the men know that anyone who fails to keep alert will have his ration of *gaal* suspended."

Grath nodded and strode away, roaring orders to the Stormriders who were unloading the ships.

To his surprise Finn saw that Doctor Alazar had knelt beside the nearest of the Nightbane bodies.

"You can't help that one, Doctor," Corr said.

Alazar stood and adjusted his spectacles. "This creature died of battle wounds," he said. "Who were they fighting?"

"One another, no doubt," Corr said. "There were Nightbane of many races here, Doctor. They hate one another almost as much as they hate us. If the order to march on the fortress was given before they were fully prepared, there was probably much disagreement over it."

Alazar hoisted his black bag over his shoulder. "I'm going to see if there are any others still living," he said. "If I may, I'll take one of your Stormriders as escort."

"Doctor, if my Stormriders see you patching up their enemies, they may just decide to stick a sword in you, too. Stay here, if you please, and let my men take care of any Nightbane we find alive."

"Take care of them?" Alazar laughed. "They'll kill them."

"They'll bring them to me first. We need to find out all we can about what's happened here. But whether they talk or not, we can't let them go, and I won't have you mending their wounds."

The doctor shook his head slowly. "You don't command me, Corr Madoc. If you won't give me an escort, I'll go myself."

"You'll stay right here."

Alazar didn't reply.

He turned to walk away, but Corr grasped his arm roughly. "You will stay here," he growled. "Or be put in chains."

Finn stepped forward. "My brother is right, Doctor," he said.

Alazar stared at him with surprise. "Finn, how can you—"

"My brother is right, but I will go with you. If we find any living Nightbane, do what you can for them, then I'll bring them to Corr."

Now Alazar stared at Finn as if he no longer recognized him. There was a long, tense silence, then at last Corr released the doctor from his grip.

"Very well," he said. "It's on your head, Doctor. Just don't stray too far. Night is coming, and we don't know what else still calls this city home."

9

AMMON BRAX STOOD OVER the smoothly polished table in the Loremaster's library. Several books were open before him and many others were stacked or scattered across the table. He was reading one of the open books, restlessly running a finger up and down the columns of print and then turning quickly to the next page. The scowl on his face deepened with each page he turned.

"Stories," he growled. "Nothing but stories."

He had already scoured Pendrake's workshop on the top floor. A tapestry on the wall there had caught his eye and held him: it depicted a blossoming green tree on a hill. A tree that glittered with silver points of light, as if stars had been caught among its branches.

He'd stared at the tapestry a long time, thinking and sifting through scraps of old legend he could only vaguely recall. Then he noticed with a start that words had been woven into the leafy pattern along the edges of the tapestry.

He'd traced the words slowly with a finger.

> *In the hand that grasps, it burns.*
> *In the hand that opens, it flows like water.*
> *Where you don't expect to find it,*
> *there it will be,*
> *the hidden fire.*

It was a clue—he was certain of it. The hidden fire was the source of the Loremaster's power. But where was the place you didn't expect to find it? He tore the tapestry down. Nothing but a solid wall stood behind it.

From there he'd scoured every other room in the house. In what he took to be the girl's bedroom he'd found another tapestry hanging on the wall that looked to have been woven by the same hand. It was a portrait of a man and woman whom he guessed must be Rowen's mother and father. The man was dressed in strange garments of a kind Brax had never seen before, and this troubled him for some reason he couldn't quite fathom. But perhaps that was just it. There was something about the girl herself he didn't yet understand. Something she knew, or something she *was,* still eluded him, just as she had herself.

Like water. Where you don't expect to find it.

Studying the graceful, delicate weave of threads that made up the tapestry, Brax guessed the work had been done by Pendrake's wife. All he had been able to discover about her in Fable was that she had gone away and no one knew where. That was a piece of the puzzle, as well, he was convinced. But he didn't have enough of the pieces yet to see how they all fit together.

He had thought he might find the answer in one of the old man's books, but so far they had proven nearly useless. There were scattered references to the Night King and the Broken Years and the dangers of werefire, but nothing that might offer a clue to how the fire could be summoned. And in every book Brax had found only more of what he didn't want: stories.

A loud, bleating laugh came from the kitchen down the hall. The hogmen. Brax had got them searching the toyshop top to bottom, too, like pigs sniffing out truffles. But even Hodge's supposed sensitivity to the werefire had failed to turn up anything. And now they were back to stuffing themselves and doing nothing useful.

Brax went back to the table and opened the only book he hadn't examined yet, which turned about to be another journal written in the Loremaster's own hand. And like all the others it was full of stories. More worthless old tales that Pendrake had gathered on his travels through the Realm.

There once was a poor woodcutter . . .
Long ago, in a faraway kingdom . . .
In the days when birds and beasts could speak with men . . .

More laughing and snorting erupted from the kitchen.

Brax snarled and swept the book off the table. He took up his staff and stalked down the hall.

The Marrowbone brothers were sprawled in upholstered armchairs they had dragged in from somewhere else in the house. Their feet were up on the table and they were chuckling about something. Both of them had dressed themselves in frock coats that they must have found among the Loremaster's things. The coats were too small for their bloated bodies and made them look even more grotesque and ridiculous than they usually did.

Hodge was gnawing on a bone, and other bones lay scattered over the table and on the floor, along with dirty plates
and other crockery in rickety heaps. Over everything hung a
rank stench of rotting food. Then Brax saw that the stove
woodbox was open and filled with half-burned books that
had been shredded to light fires.

Hodge lifted his feet off the table quickly when Brax appeared. Flitch, Brax noted, did not.

"Where did you get those books?" the mage demanded,
wrinkling his nose at the stench.

"We found them on the floor in the other room," Flitch
said casually. "We assumed you'd finished with them—"

"You don't assume anything," the mage snapped. "You
leave everything as it is unless I tell you otherwise."

"They're just paper," Hodge said in a wounded tone.
"What use is that?"

"How long have you two been sitting here stuffing your
faces?" Brax said, advancing on them. Hodge shrank into his
chair. "Get up and get back to searching the house."

Flitch set aside the sliver of bone he had been using as a
toothpick.

"We've searched, my lord," he said icily. "We've looked
everywhere. *Everywhere*. And you haven't even told us what
it is we're supposed to be looking for. If you ask me—"

"I am not asking you—I'm *telling* you. One would think
that following my orders has got to be preferable to the hospitality of the Errantry."

The hogman's lips quivered. Brax noted with some concern that it was more from rage than fear. He would have to
watch Flitch and not let down his guard for a moment.

"We're only taking some well-earned refreshment, Master
Brax," Hodge said quickly. "We've been working very hard—
honestly we have. As my brother said, we've looked everywhere.

In every room, every corner. Under everything. Lots of places more than once, just to be sure. We're very grateful for all you've done for us—truly we are. Aren't we, Flitch? And we're going to get right back to work."

"We are," Flitch echoed grudgingly, "but we do have one small request first."

"What is it?"

"The Skalding woman has been useless to you, from anything we can see. We'd like to put her to work for us. Pay her back for handing us over to the Errantry, you see. She can cook for us and clean and . . ."

His gaze strayed to a wooden knife block sitting on the sideboard. Then he met Brax's eyes again and grinned.

So it was true, Brax thought. The stories from Skald that the hogmen had eaten people were more than just rumours. In spite of himself, he shuddered.

Then he looked again at the filth in the kitchen, the blood-stains on the tabletop. This would be just the place to bring her, it occurred to him. The sight of the hogmen in their element might just loosen her tongue. Keeping her locked up was pointless. Flitch was right about that. And eventually word was sure to get out that she was being held prisoner.

Brax faced Hodge. "Bring her here," he ordered.

Hodge sprang to his feet. "I'll fetch her, Master Brax. Back in no time." He lumbered from the room, his jowls jiggling in his haste.

Brax went over to the block of knives, slid out a long carving knife and turned it to examine the blade. Then with all his strength he jabbed the knife into the wooden top of the sideboard. It wobbled there a moment and went still. Brax stepped back to survey the effect.

Flitch watched all this with mingled fear and eagerness in his eyes.

"We'll get her to put this place back in order, my lord," he said. "Back the way the housekeeper had it. Nice and tidy, the way you people like it. And if she won't do as we ask— well, I suppose that'll mean you won't mind us disposing of her for you."

"We shall see," Brax said. "For the time being she's my prisoner, and neither of you will lay a finger on her. Is that clear?"

Flitch glowered silently at the table, then raised his head.

"As you wish, my lord. But, in that case, my brother and I were also wondering if you'd let us out of the toyshop from time to time. To look for others who might . . . make dinner for us. And such. What with things in the city all astir, I would think no one would notice us or care too much if they did. I mean, we blend in, you could say, with all the outlandish folk taking refuge here these days."

The mage rounded suddenly on Flitch, whose beady black eyes went wide with surprise and fear. The sight pleased Brax even as it infuriated him. These creatures were more trouble than they were worth.

"Listen to me, hogman," he said, his voice low and cold with threat. "I have Thorne's sentries at the door as much to keep you from getting out as to prevent anyone getting in. I would prefer not to have your foul stench anywhere near me, but the last thing I need is the Errantry coming here looking for people who've gone missing and have ended up in your cookpot. And so you and your feeble-minded brother will do exactly what I tell you and nothing else, do you understand?"

"Very clearly, my lord," Flitch muttered.

"With a word I can have the two of you back to rotting in that cell at Appleyard. Or worse. Far worse." He raised his ivory staff and Flitch quailed. "You will do as you're told and there will be no more talk of guests for dinner."

Flitch pushed away his food. His thick hands were trembling.

"As you wish, my lord. My brother and I will keep searching. But—pardon me, I have to ask—isn't there anything else you can tell us about what we're looking for? It's some secret of the old toymaker's, we figured that out, but we've turned over all the toys in the place, shook them, took them apart. We've looked in every nook and cranny, under the beds, under the rugs, behind picture frames. I don't think it's really fair to get angry at us for failing to find this thing if"—he paused and glanced sideways at the mage—"if even *you* don't know what it is."

At that moment Hodge stumbled back into the room, breathing heavily.

"She's gone," he panted. "The room . . . it's empty."

Moments later the mage and the hogmen were standing in front of the broom closet. Two large metal-trimmed wooden chests stood stacked near the door, which was slightly ajar. Brax stepped into the broom closet and looked it over, top to bottom. He picked up a frayed length of rope.

"Her hands were bound tight as anything," Hodge wheezed. "No way she could have got out of that."

Brax stepped back out of the broom closet and studied the chests. "You say the door was shut when you came up just now and these were in front of it?"

Hodge nodded convulsively. "Yes. Yes. I swear it. We used those chests full of books you said you didn't need anymore because you'd looked through them. They were so heavy the two of us together could barely lift them. There's no way she could have . . ." He turned to his brother. "It was Flitch's idea to stack the chests in front of the door. I told you it wasn't enough. I told you—"

Flitch snarled, "You lying sack of tripe," and advanced on his brother.

Brax raised a hand. "Enough!" he bellowed.

Flitch backed away from Hodge.

Brax crouched and examined the floor. Then he rose and set his hands to the two stacked chests. He gave a shove, grunted with the effort. "No, she could not have moved these away from the door," he said. "And there are no scuff marks on the floor. She had help. Probably from the shapeshifter."

"So that cat thing is still . . ." Hodge began, but his voice died to a whimper when he saw the look in Brax's eyes.

Flitch had to see the broom closet for himself. He stepped inside, sniffed and looked around. Then he faced his brother. "You didn't tie the ropes tight enough, gristlewit. Can't you do one simple thing without botching it?"

"You're the one who tied them," Hodge blubbered.

Flitch raised a fist and Hodge cowered beneath it.

"Enough!" Brax roared again.

Flitch lowered his fist, then cursed and gave his brother a shove. Hodge slammed into the back wall of the closet with a howl, then rubbed his shoulder.

Brax ignored them. He was gazing off down the corridor that led to Pendrake's library. "She may still be here some-where, hiding and waiting for a chance to escape," he said. "We'll have to check all the rooms again, one by one. Search everywhere. If she gets away, things will go very hard for the two of you."

The hogmen hurried out of the closet, first Flitch and then Hodge, still rubbing his shoulder. Brax shot them a look of dis-gust. He turned away and hesitated a moment, as if deciding which direction to begin the search. Then he turned back, more slowly this time, and peered into the closet a second time.

"We've searched there, my lord," Hodge muttered feebly.

Brax raised a hand. "Silence," he hissed. "Do you hear that?"
The hogmen shook their heads.

"Water," Brax whispered. "There's water here."

Brax crouched at the back of the closet. He could hear water trickling. He pressed a hand against the wall, slid his fingers slowly up and down.

"What is it, my lord?" Flitch asked.

"Must be like the sewers in Skald," Hodge whispered to his brother. "Pipes full of leaks."

Brax stood and took a step back from the wall. He raised his staff, useless to him now for anything other than brute force, and began to prod and scrape the wall with the obsidian blade. He managed to leave pale scratch marks on the stone, but the wall remained as solid and impervious as ever.

The words from the tapestry came back to him.

Like water. Where you don't expect to find it.

"This isn't really here," he murmured. "The wall . . . it's an illusion."

"What did you say, Master Brax?" Flitch asked.

Brax ignored him. He struck and hacked with more force now, and the ivory staff, already cracked when he struggled with the tiger, now split into halves. He picked the half with the blade off the wet floor and went on hacking and slashing at the wall.

"This isn't really here!" he shouted.

The obsidian blade broke and the pieces clattered at Brax's feet. He stepped away from the wall, his breath coming in gasps, his arms hanging at his sides. He had been so certain. So absolutely certain that this was it.

He turned to the Marrowbone brothers. "Don't just stand there," he growled at their terrified faces. "Find her."

Then he noticed that the hogmen's looks of fear were directed not at him but at the room behind him. And now he became aware of the roar that he had thought was his own blood rushing in his ears. He whirled.

The walls of the broom closet were gone.

A shimmering curtain of rain had taken their place. Brax stood open-mouthed, then he reached out his hand and thrust it into the falling water. After a moment he pulled his hand out and studied the glistening droplets in his palm. He watched them shrink into tiny grains of light and flow back into the rain.

"The hidden fire," he breathed. His hand began to tremble, and he closed it into a fist.

Without another word to the hogmen he took a deep breath and plunged into the rain, disappearing from sight.

Hodge and Flitch gaped at the spot where the mage had been. After a moment, they turned to each other with eyes wide.

"Where did he go?" Hodge whispered. "Is he . . . gone?"

Flitch shook his head slowly, then his eyes flicked to the chests by the door. "Quick, let's put those back," he said.

"What?"

"If we put the chests back against the door, we can shut him in there."

"Oh. Oh, yes. But, but what if he—"

"Just do it, fool. Quick!"

The brothers had just moved toward the chests when the mage reappeared out of the rain. His hair and cloak were steaming and luminous tendrils of pale green vapour were twining and curling about his outstretched hands. His face was whiter than when he had gone in, and to the alarm of the hogmen his eyes were glowing with the same unearthly green light. The Marrowbone brothers warily backed away. They had seen this light before, when they'd been in hiding under the keep in Skald. It was the light of the werefire.

"Master Brax?" Hodge whimpered. "What did you find in there?"

"We—we're sorry she got away, the Skalding woman," Flitch stammered. "But—but now I think you don't need her anymore, isn't that right, my lord? Isn't this what you've been looking for? And we helped you find it, if you think about it. We brought you here to the broom closet and if it wasn't for us, you wouldn't have . . ."

Brax seemed not to hear the hogman's frightened babbling. He moved slowly, his eyes unfocused, as if he were walking in his sleep. He glanced at the cowering Hodge, then at the chests full of books, and his eyes glittered feverishly.

"Stories," he said.

The mage lifted his hand, studying it as if it were something he had never seen before, and then he gestured almost casually at the chests. With a crack and a groan the iron corner braces and side straps sprang off and the wooden sides fell away. Books tumbled onto the floor like the spilled guts of a slaughtered animal. As they fell, they fluttered open, and then it was as if their leaves were being torn out by invisible hands and tossed away. Page after page flew up and went whirling about the corridor. And as they whirled and scattered, the pages burst into green flames and were swiftly consumed, leaving nothing behind, not even a puff of smoke or a trace of ash.

"Master Brax?" Hodge whispered. "Don't forget we helped you find it. I mean, if we hadn't put her in there, you might never have come up here to see and then you wouldn't have—"

The mage turned to the hogmen with a smile that was more terrifying than any look of threat or anger they had seen from him yet.

"You did help me," he said. "And for that I will let you live.

At least, as long as you obey without question. If you fail me, rest assured I will do to both of you what I did to those books."

"We understand, my lord," Flitch said, bowing solemnly and elbowing his terrified brother to do likewise. "We are yours to command."

"Yes," the mage agreed, as if there could be no other possible answer. "Yes, you are."

10

"DO WE RUN?" WILL began, but in the next moment he and Rowen saw and heard what Shade's keen eyes and ears had detected. A barrel-shaped green caravan appeared at the top of the cutting, drawn by a large piebald horse. Two people sat on the front seat of the caravan, but with the light behind them it was difficult to make out their features. Even though the caravan was not moving quickly, Will knew there wouldn't be enough time to outrun it to the other end of the cutting.

"Stay behind me," Shade said, stepping in front of Rowen and Will.

The caravan was descending the road now, and they could more clearly make out the figures seated on it. It was large but shabby looking, its once-bright green and gold trim faded and chipped. It had the bowed roof and tall spoked wheels of old-fashioned gypsy caravans Will had seen pictures of in his own world. The sides of the box were hung with all sorts of old and well-used things: a wooden wash tub, a shovel and rake, rolled-up lengths of cloth.

The two people seated on the box of the caravan could not have been less alike, yet something in the very oddness of their appearance made them look suited for each other. The driver was a stocky, muscular young man whose bald head was filigreed with tattoos. He wore a dark leather vest without a shirt underneath and his chest was darkly furred with hair. Beside him sat a small, sharp-featured older woman in a shawl over a faded green velvet dress. Her greying hair was matted and tangled. Both she and the driver had seen the three strangers and were staring at them with wary surprise. Then the driver flicked the reins and shouted at the horse, which broke into a quicker trot.

Whether he meant to overtake them before they could escape the cutting, or pass them more quickly, Will had no idea, but his hand had already gone to his sword hilt. As the caravan approached, the driver turned his head to the side and shouted something that Will could not hear over the clatter of the horse's hoofs. Will thought he was speaking to the woman, but a moment later a third figure appeared, pulling open the yellow curtain that separated the front seat from the caravan's interior. It was another young man, very tall and even more muscled than the driver, his head covered with a mop of unruly red hair. His one hand gripped the side rail of the shaking caravan and the other clutched a thick wooden cudgel.

"I will hold them off while you run," Shade said.

"No, wait," Rowen said. "We must stay together. I don't think these people mean any harm."

"We can't take that chance," Will said. He looked again at the caravan and saw the woman speaking quickly to the driver, her mouth close to his ear. The driver was shaking his head and muttering something back to her, then with a scowl he pulled up on the reins and slowed the horse. The man with the cudgel did not seem threatening: his eyes were wide and his mouth slack, as if he was merely curious about these strangers. Will understood then that the driver had increased the horse's pace out of fear. Rowen had been right. The people in the caravan were just as alarmed by this unexpected meeting as they were.

The caravan had already rattled past the three of them by the time the horse drew fully to a halt, whinnying nervously and tossing its head. Obviously the animal was very aware of Shade's presence and disturbed by it.

The driver's tattooed head appeared over the side of the caravan.

"We'd have a word with you young folks," he said sullenly, as if it was the last thing he wanted to do. "Just the two of you. Keep the beast away."

Will exchanged a glance with Rowen.

"We should speak with them at least," Rowen said. "We need to find out where we are."

"They are afraid of us, Will Lightfoot," Shade said. "They do not mean us harm, but they may strike out of fear."

"I'm pretty sure it's you they're afraid of. And Shade . . ."

"I know, Will Lightfoot. I will not speak. There will be fewer questions that way."

Will and Rowen left Shade by the wall and walked along the side of the caravan to the front. Will made sure he stopped in a spot where he and the wolf could still see each other. The man hunched in the caravan doorway still clutched the cudgel as if ready to use it.

"So where might you three be headed?" the driver said.

As an attempt to sound friendly it was not convincing. Will

studied the man. The dark blue tattoos on his bald head appeared to be ornate letters, but Will could not read them. The vest he wore, embroidered all over with a bright floral pattern in yellow and silver, was at odds with his stiff, guarded manner. A dull, dinted sword was slung through his belt, along with two smaller, unsheathed knives. The other man, who was much larger but clearly the younger of the two, gaped slack jawed at Rowen and Will. The woman's sunken, staring eyes, Will noticed with unease, were fixed on Rowen.

"We're looking for friends of ours," Rowen said. "We think they may have come this way."

"Odd place to be looking for friends," the driver said. He was younger than Will had thought at first, probably not much older than Finn Madoc, but he had a thin, rasping voice that did not carry well.

"Why is that?" Rowen asked. "We're not from here."

"No one is," the driver said with an edge of bitterness in his voice. "Tell us about your friends. Maybe we've seen them."

"They're travellers like us. They live in tents and pavilions. They have horses. Have you seen anyone like that?"

The driver exchanged a look with the woman. Her bony fingers plucked at his sleeve, setting the bracelets on her wrist jingling, but he shrugged her off. Clearly she wanted something from Will and Rowen, but he was not of the same mind.

"We're going to a place where folk live mostly in tents," the driver said at last. "A big camp on the outskirts of the city. There are horses there, too. A few, anyhow, most of them like this one—not much good anymore. Nothing worth stealing, either. But it's a big place, with folk from all over coming and going. Maybe your friends are there."

"Is the camp far from here?" Rowen asked.

"Not far," the woman said to her eagerly. "We've been out gathering things we need and we're going back now."

From the look of all the worn and beat-up objects hanging off the sides of the caravan, Will guessed that they had been scavenging for whatever they could find. Will glanced at the younger man's bare, muscular arms and understood that he served as the protection for the other two, just as Shade did for Rowen and him.

There was something else about these people, something that struck him as strangely familiar. The driver's gaudy vest, his tattoos and phony-looking sword, the woman's once-elegant but now-faded dress and her bracelets, so out of place on her bony wrists. Costumes, he suddenly realized. The hulking younger man with the cudgel could be a strongman. The woman would easily pass as a fortune teller. The driver might have been a sword swallower or knife thrower. They were dressed like performers from some shabby circus of long ago. They were sideshow people.

"It's not far," the woman repeated. "Lots of people. Good people. It's safe there."

"The thing is," Rowen said, "we've come a long way and we're not sure just where we are. What city is that over there?"

"If it has a name, we don't know it," the driver said. "We don't go there. No one from the camp does. It's . . . not a good place to be."

"Why is that?" Will asked.

"People who go there don't come back," the driver said.

Will wanted to ask if they had heard the name of his town, or any place that he knew of in his own world, but before he could speak, Rowen said, "Will you show us the way to the camp? All we want is to look for our friends."

"My sons and I will show you the way," the woman said.

The driver glared at her but nodded. "You can come with us," he said grudgingly, "but I'll tell you right now your friend there won't be welcome." He nodded at Shade, who hadn't moved from where he stood.

"He won't harm people unless they try to harm us first," Rowen said sharply. "If the people at this camp are peaceful, they'll have no trouble from him or us."

The driver did not appear convinced, but he had clearly given in to the woman's wishes.

"Just make sure the beast keeps his distance."

"There's food where we're going," the woman said. As if to sweeten her words, she managed a strained smile, showing many gaps between nubs of yellowed teeth. "There's no need to be afraid. It's safe at the camp."

She held out a hand for Rowen to take, to climb up on the seat.

"There's room, girl—you don't have to walk. Vardo will stay in the back. He won't hurt you. He wouldn't hurt anyone 'less we told him to." She gestured to the red-haired young man, whose dull gaze passed from the woman to Rowen and back again.

Rowen shook her head. "No, thank you," she said. "We can keep up."

The woman shrugged, but Will could see she was stung by the rebuff.

"Suit yourself," she said offhandedly, then turned to the red-haired young man, who was still hunched in the caravan doorway. "Vardo, it's all right. These children won't hurt us."

The red-haired young man set down his cudgel obediently but remained in the doorway.

"Very well, then, let's get moving," the driver said with a nervous glance at the close walls of the cutting. He gave the reins a flick and shouted a loud *yah* and the horse lurched into motion again. The caravan started off with a clatter. Will and Rowen began to walk after it and Shade joined them.

"These people are strange," Rowen said in an undertone to Will as they hurried along beside the caravan. "That woman won't stop looking at me. I think there's something wrong with her."

Will quickly told her of his guess that they were circus folk. She had not heard the expression before, but when he described what he meant, she nodded eagerly.

"Travelling carnivals like that sometimes come to Fable," she said. "With clowns and tumblers. But these people don't seem very"—she searched for the right word—"merry."

"We don't have to follow them if you don't want to," Will said.

After a long pause, Rowen said, "No, let's keep going. Shade's right, I'm sure. They don't mean any harm. I think it's safe to trust them."

The horse walked very slowly now as it climbed the rising road on the far side of the cutting. Rowen and Will were able to keep up alongside. The driver ignored them, his gaze fixed on the road ahead, but the woman, who was sitting closest to the side of the caravan they were walking on, continued to glance at Rowen with eyes that were full of concern but also a strange intensity that Will found unsettling.

They went on in a tense silence for a while. A brief rain fell out of the churning, restless sky and then quickly drew off, leaving a humid mist behind. The towers of the city loomed closer. Finally the woman seemed unable to contain herself, and she spoke to Rowen.

"What's your name, child?" she asked.

Rowen glanced at Will, who gave a barely perceptible shrug.

"I'm Rowen. I'm from a place called the Bourne. Have you heard of it?"

"Rowen's a pretty name," the woman said. "How did you end up out here? Does your family know where you are?"

"The friends we're looking for are sometimes called the Fair Folk," Rowen said. "Or the Tain Shee. Have you ever heard of them?"

The woman gave the driver an odd glance, as if happily surprised, then she turned back to Rowen.

"Fair Folk, yes," she said with a strange smile.

"You know them?" Rowen exclaimed.

"Yes, yes," the woman said with matching eagerness. "We've heard of them."

"We think they came this way, but we're not sure," Rowen went on. "We're not really sure where we are at all. Nothing looks familiar to us. What do you call this country?"

"We don't call it anything," the woman said. "We're not from here, either. But if you're looking for Fair Folk, you're in luck. That's us."

Rowen frowned. "You are not," she said angrily. "You can't be. We . . . we would know it. You would know *us*."

"We're the Fair Folk," the woman said firmly. "That's what we're called. Ain't we, Vardo?"

The red-haired giant, who had yet to say anything at all, nodded solemnly.

"This caravan has seen better days, it's true, but it was once part of the Great Travelling Circus of the Plains, and so were we," the woman said importantly, confirming Will's guess. "But nobody ever called us that other name you said. *Tain* . . ."

"Tain Shee," Rowen said. "They're not circus folk."

The woman shrugged. "There are people from all over at the camp. Some are travelling performers like we was. Some ain't. Some of them might be your Tain Shee, I suppose. But everyone calls our camp the Fair," she went on, "because you can trade anything for anything there. And there's music and magicians and rope walkers." She shrugged. "So that makes us the Fair Folk, don't it? Anyhow, you'll see when we get there. You'll see what it's like, and maybe . . . maybe you'll want to stay. That is, if she allows it."

"*She*?" Rowen asked.

"The Witch," the woman said, lowering her voice. "We didn't tell you that before. Maybe we should have. But you needn't be afraid. The Witch won't do you no harm if you're good and don't do nobody no harm yourself. She watches over everyone in the camp and makes sure nothing bad gets in. She looks after us Fair Folk. She's our protector."

"Or our keeper," the driver muttered.

"None of that now, Arn," the woman snapped with a sideways scowl at the driver. "We'd be dead or scattered by now if it wasn't for the Witch. That's why you should come with us to the camp. It's the only safe place to be around these parts. There's bad folk wandering these roads. Robbers. Murderers. And worse things. The Witch will protect you, too, if she decides you can stay."

"We won't be staying," Rowen said.

"Child," the woman said, shaking her head. "You just don't know yet. You don't know how it is. There ain't nowhere else to go."

"What do you mean?"

"Everyone you meet on these roads is lost. All of us was going someplace else and ended up *here*, instead. Sometimes a few try to find the way home again, but they always return to the camp. It's like the roads never go nowhere except around in circles."

Rowen and Will shared a troubled glance.

"Your families must be worried about the both of you," the woman said. "Did you run away from home?"

"We didn't run away," Rowen said. "We meant to come here, to find our friends. Tell us more about this Witch."

"She sees and knows more than anyone. Maybe she can tell you where your friends might be. If she'll speak with you, that is. She don't speak to almost no one. Least that I know of it."

"And that's a good thing," the driver said.

"You shouldn't be talking like that, Arn," the woman said with an edge of fear in her voice. "You don't know she can't hear you."

"All the way out here?"

"Even if she can't, she can tell what's in someone's heart. You know that."

"I do. I've seen it. She protects the camp, it's true, but—"

"But nothing," the woman snapped. "There ain't no more to say about it."

The man shook his head angrily but made no reply.

The news that these people called themselves the Fair Folk gave Will and Rowen much to think about. Did it mean they had lost the Tain Shee entirely and were following a false trail that would lead them nowhere? It seemed there was only one thing to do: keep going and hope to get some answers.

The road crossed a rusting metal bridge over a dried-up stream bed. On the far side the pavement gave way to an uneven track of sand and gravel. The caravan jolted and rocked as it trundled along, the wheels grinding on the rough surface. The noise kept the woman from speaking to Rowen and Will for the time being, though clearly she still wished to. Instead she began to croon a wordless melody that rose and fell along with the rhythmic creaking of the caravan's wheels. The strongman grinned open-mouthed as she sang.

They crossed a train yard, where the caravan juddered and bounced over rusty rail lines. Brown and dull green train cars decorated with colourful but unreadable graffiti sat here and there on some of the tracks. The air was smoky, metallic tasting. Not far off rose the skeletal silhouettes of what Will guessed were electrical transmission towers marching off into the distance. Faint but recognizable sounds came to him now, as well: the surf-like roar of traffic, the whoop and wail of sirens, other distant rumbles and hisses of machinery, all of it merging into the background noise of a city, a kind of mechanical breathing so familiar that once you were used to it you didn't even hear it anymore. Familiar to him, anyhow. He glanced at Rowen and saw concern on her face, and realized that these distant noises were strange and alarming to her.

"Don't worry," he said. "Where I come from that's what a city sounds like."

Yet there were no vehicles on the road and no other people anywhere in sight. Will didn't know what to make of that. If not for the distant noise of its life, he would have said the city was abandoned.

On the far side of the train yard they came to a chain-link fence. One section had been dismantled or had fallen down, leaving a gap wide enough for the caravan to pass through.

Beyond the fence lay a straight asphalt road lined with squat, windowless buildings. Warehouses or storage sheds of some kind, Will thought, though they looked more like mausoleums in a graveyard.

"Where are all the people?" he wondered aloud to Rowen. "There should be people. Lots of them."

It was like a derelict neighbourhood in the cities of his own world, Will thought, except for the tall grass growing along the sides of the road. There were even a few stunted trees growing up right out of the pavement in places, as if the city and the natural world had somehow clashed here and neither had given way completely.

By the side of the road ahead, half hidden in the tall grass, were what looked to Will at first like three large reddish-brown boulders lined up in a row. As he and the caravan got closer, he realized they were cars—or the remains of cars. They were badly rusted, the glass was gone from all the windows and most of their tires were gone. Will saw Rowen's baffled look and as they passed, he quickly explained what they were.

"They're sort of like carriages," he told her. "Like this caravan, except they don't need a horse to pull them. They have an engine inside that moves them."

"Engine," Rowen echoed. "I've heard that word before but not for something like this. An engine is something used in war to break down gates or walls . . ."

Her voice trailed off and a frightened look came into her eyes. Will guessed her thoughts had gone to the same place his had: what was happening in Fable? It was hard to say how much time had gone by while they'd been in the Weaving. For all they knew the armoured fetches were already at the gates of Rowen's city. Yet here he and Rowen were, following these strange folk through this deserted, nameless land, seemingly no closer to finding the Fair Folk and the way to the Shadow Realm.

The road ended at a high wooden fence plastered with faded posters for music concerts and theatre performances. Beyond the fence rose the abandoned shell of a building. Its windows were devoid of glass, and bits of yellow insulation and tangles of wiring hung from many of them. The road did not really end here, Will saw, but branched now to their left and right. Neither direction appeared any more inviting than the other.

The driver took the caravan to the left and at last they reached a gap in the high fence.

"Here it is," the woman said. "The Fair."

Beyond the fence lay an open space, a large square field across which were scattered a motley collection of patched and faded tents, lean-tos and shelters, most made of unmatched scraps of wood and topped with canvas or plastic tarpaulins. There were many people milling about the camp, though, engaged in all sorts of activity: some were tending cooking fires, some hanging washing on lines, others putting up or repairing some of the shelters. A gang of small shrieking children were kicking a ball around on a flat patch of dusty bare earth. There was a garden patch to one side, and geese and chickens in pens, and they could hear the bleating of sheep and the barking of dogs. Around the entire camp ran a fence like the one they had just been following.

Despite the strangeness of the surroundings, Will recognized almost at once what he was seeing. The news at home in his world often showed such places. The Fair was a refugee camp.

But as they passed through the opening in the fence, Will noticed other things that made this unlike any refugee camp he had seen: banners; colourful decorations hung from posts and tent poles; and the way that many of the people were dressed, in bright clothes and hats, as if they were getting ready for some kind of celebration.

At the far end of the camp stood a long platform of painted wood, really the bed of a wagon, Will saw after a moment's examination, with its wheels removed and replaced by wooden piles. The platform was topped with a curtained wooden frame and at the back hung a dark blue cloth painted with stars. A stage, Will realized.

Beyond the stage and the fence rose a tall building that Will immediately thought would have been an old-fashioned grand hotel in his world, with its stone facade, peaked green roof and gabled windows. The appearance of such a building here was so unexpected that Will could only think the hotel had been uprooted from some elegant street in another place and time and dropped here by accident.

When the caravan passed through the entrance, a young boy standing nearby shouted what might have been a warning or a greeting, in a language Will didn't know, and ran off. Other people came out of the tents to see what was going on. At the sight of Will, Rowen and Shade, the people gawked, especially at Shade.

The boy returned with a tall grey-bearded man wearing a sheepskin coat and leading a large black mastiff on a leash. The boy halted some way off from the caravan, but the man strode right up. A knot of smaller children gathered around the boy and curiously eyed the newcomers.

"Who have you brought with you, Arn?" the tall man demanded. The mastiff strained against the leash and growled when it saw Shade.

"It's all right, Holt," the driver said. "They're just looking for friends of theirs."

"What about the . . ." the man began. He was apparently about to say *dog*, then he had a closer look at Shade, his eyes narrowing, and he shook his head. "That animal isn't coming in here."

"He won't hurt no one, Holt," the woman said, rising from the seat. "And you know *she'll* have them out of here if there's any trouble. No need to worry yourself. Go back to your workbench."

The man named Holt studied Will, Rowen and Shade for a long moment, then shrugged.

"Very well," he said, "but Arn, you're responsible for them. Don't forget that."

He tugged the mastiff's leash sharply and marched off without another word. The crowd began to clear away and go back to their own business as Arn brought the caravan to a halt not far from the gate. He and the others climbed down, while Will, Rowen and Shade waited nearby. Some of the children had gone off with the man called Holt, but a few were still milling around, interested more in Shade than anything else. Arn had begun to unhitch the horse, then he paused and shouted at the children to clear off and they finally wandered away.

"These are friends, Hulda," the woman said to a frightened, ancient-looking face peeping through the flap of the nearest tent.

"Thank you for letting us come with you," Rowen said. "We'll leave you be now and go search for our friends."

The woman turned to Rowen with a beseeching look.

"We'll be having our dinner soon," she said. "You should stay. Have something to eat, I mean." She gestured to a nearby firepit surrounded by crude benches made of split logs. "You can sit there."

Rowen shook her head. "We really have to go now. It's a big camp and—"

"Bigger than it appears from here," the woman agreed quickly. "And you're both tired from the road. Sit and rest and I'll get Vardo to fetch the Scholar." She said the word importantly, like a title. "That's who you need to see. The Scholar keeps a record of everyone who comes to the camp. He'll know if your friends are here. Better than wandering around asking everyone questions. Go ahead now. Sit."

With a droop of her shoulders Rowen gave in and sat down on one of the benches. Will was relieved. He was worn out from the long walk and he knew Rowen was about to drop from weariness, though she was trying not to show it. She met his eyes and he nodded his agreement and sat down beside her. Shade hunkered down close to them.

The woman smiled and spoke to Vardo, who lumbered off down the main thoroughfare of the camp. Then, with another intense look at Rowen, she climbed into the caravan. The driver brought a bundle of thin sticks to the firepit and soon had a crackling fire going. He set a small iron kettle on the grate over the firepit. Shade, as they had agreed when they first met the caravan, sat silently nearby like an obedient dog, ignoring the man's many nervous glances.

Will had noticed that ever since they'd entered the camp, Rowen had become quiet and withdrawn. Now he saw that she was shaking her head slowly as if to drive away some troubling thought.

"What is it?" he whispered.

"They *were* here," Rowen said. "The Fair Folk."

"You've seen that?"

"I'm seeing it right now," Rowen said desperately. "They were here. But it was somewhere else. Or this place was different. I don't understand."

"What do you see?"

Before Rowen could answer, the woman reappeared, carrying a big cast-iron pot, which she set beside the kettle on the grate.

"It's only leftover stew from yesterday," she said apologetically, "but it'll fill you up."

"So you don't know what this country is called?" Rowen asked her.

"Like I said, if it has a name, we don't know it. But I don't think it does, because the Scholar says it's between places. Or it's bits and pieces of many different places, all sort of jumbled together somehow. Like a lot of voices all speaking at the same time so you can't understand what anyone's saying. It's a kind of . . . what does the Scholar call it, Arn?"

"Limbo," Arn said.

"Yes, limbo," the woman echoed. "And if there's a way out, no one's found it yet."

"You said you were on your way somewhere else when you ended up here. Where were you going?"

"Away," the woman said, and now a look of immense sadness fell over her lined features. She seemed suddenly bowed by a great weight.

"Away?" Rowen echoed quietly.

The woman slowly stirred the pot with a wooden spoon. It seemed she wasn't going to answer Rowen's question, then finally she spoke.

"Folk never trusted us where we're from. Never. Oh, they came to our shows, all right, and bought our potions and remedies, but they never trusted us or let us stay for long in their towns. They called us thieves and sorcerers. Then the weather changed. Lots of storms. Too much rain. The crops rotted in the fields and folk went hungry. Some started blaming us, the travelling folk, for what was happening, and that idea caught on quick. One night they came with torches to burn the caravans. Only a few of us got away. Only a few."

She looked searchingly at Rowen.

"My Hana," she said. "She had long hair. Not like yours, no. It was dark, dark hair. In curls. Beautiful curls, like mine used to be. But she was about your age, maybe a bit younger. And she was a sharp one. She spoke her mind like you. Didn't she, Arn?"

The driver, busy brushing down the horse, gave a short, mirthless laugh.

"What happened to her?" Rowen asked.

The woman stared into the fire.

"The ones that came to burn our caravans—they took young girls. They took my Hana."

"We don't know that, Mother," Arn said, and in his voice

they heard a very old argument. "She might've got away. She could have escaped."

"She could have escaped," the woman echoed without conviction. "But she didn't leave with us and now we can't find the way back. We can't look for her. She might be out there looking for us, too. And we're here."

"I'm sorry," Rowen said.

The woman went back to stirring the pot of stew and said nothing more. No one spoke until Vardo returned, hurrying up the path followed by an old man dressed in what appeared like a dingy suit of armour. As they approached, Will saw that the armour was made of cut sheets of cardboard painted a dull silver and held together with twine. The man had a wispy white goatee and his face was deeply lined, but it was a disguise: he was wearing stage paint and the beard was pasted on. He was actually quite a young man, Will realized.

"This is our Scholar," the woman said with sudden, feverish enthusiasm. "He'll be able to tell you about your friends if anyone can."

"Forgive the attire," the young man said with a gesture at his costume and an embarrassed smile. His cardboard armour was much creased, Will noticed, and frayed at the edges, as if it had been worn many times. "We've been rehearsing for tonight's performance. I hope you'll be able to attend. It will be our first ever staging of the famous tale *The Knight of the Sorrowful Countenance*."

"We're trying to find the Fair Folk," Rowen asked. "They're sometimes called the Tain Shee. We think they came this way. We were told you know everyone in the camp."

"I am the record keeper, yes, as well as master of the revels," the Scholar said. His polite, formal way of speaking was at odds with the shabby surroundings, and when he talked, his thin little stage beard twitched up and down.

"I gather the histories and tales of everyone who joins us here, many of which we enact on our stage in the evenings. But no, I have never heard of anyone called the Tain Shee. As for the Fair Folk . . ."

He gestured to the woman and her son.

"No," Rowen said. "These are not the folk we're looking for."

"Well, then . . ."

"Is this the Perilous Realm?" Will asked.

The question seemed to baffle the Scholar, as if Will had asked him whether they were on the moon.

"The Perilous Realm? Well, we performed a story about the Perilous Realm once, quite a while ago. About a boy who ran away to that mysterious land and the adventures he had there. But that was just one of the stories we tell here. You see the Fair is a place to trade for what one needs and seek shelter from the dangers of the road, but the truth is it's the stories everyone really wants, and it is our task to provide them. That's what they've lost, those who find their way here. Their stories. That's the one thing that gives us common ground. What we've lost. Have you heard of *The Tale of One-Armed Lodovic the Fiddler*? Or *Brave Meena and the Hen of Wisdom*?"

Both Will and Rowen shook their heads.

"Of course you haven't," the Scholar said. "That's to be expected. They're almost forgotten, those stories. They came from places that have been left behind or lost, and all trace of them is likely to vanish forever if we don't keep them alive."

"We're trying to do the same thing," Rowen said. "It's why we need to find our friends."

The Scholar raised his hands in a gesture of helplessness.

"They're not here, not unless they have concealed their true identity, though that's doubtful. We have many performers and stage folk here who play many roles, and the

Witch allows our playing—in fact, I believe there are times when she watches our performances in secret. But sometimes folk come to the Fair, you see, to hide from their crimes or with some wicked intent. They give false names and spin a hard-luck tale to gain admittance, but their goal is theft or worse. And the Witch, well . . ."

"*She* finds them out every time," the woman said. "The Witch sends them packing in a hurry."

"Our friends aren't wicked," Rowen said. "They only hide who they are because of their enemies."

The Scholar glanced up at the hotel that rose beyond the far end of the camp. "Be that as it may, only the Witch would know for certain if they're here or if they've ever passed this way," he said.

"Is that where she lives?" Will asked, noticing the Scholar's glance. "In the hotel?"

"Hotel?" the Scholar said with a frown. "We call it the castle. But yes, that's where she lives."

"The Witch wasn't always here," the woman said. "Before she came, this place was as bad as anywhere else. She made the camp a safe place."

"It's true," the Scholar said. "We were always under threat from whatever ruffians and cutthroats happened to pass this way. One gang of armed men would show up regularly and make off with whatever they wanted. They killed a man who resisted them the first time and after that no one gave them any trouble. Then one night we saw lights in the castle for the first time and a figure at the windows. The Witch, though we didn't know that at the time. We didn't know who or what had set up residence in the castle. Not until the gang came around again a few nights later. They took a young woman, Holt the carpenter's daughter, started dragging her out of the camp screaming. They had guns, you see. Have you heard of guns? Terrible weapons that shoot bits of metal into people and tear their flesh. Anyhow, there was nothing anyone could do. Then *she* appeared. The torches all dimmed, and we could barely see what it was, just a pale blur, like fog. We heard a voice, a woman's voice, and it said, 'These people are under my protection. Anyone who harms them will suffer.' The gang leader must have thought this was one of our stage tricks, because he just laughed and kept dragging the girl away. Then the fog . . . well, it seemed to rush at him, and it passed over him and when it was gone . . ."

He hesitated and the woman broke in.

"He just stood there staring," she said with a fierce, dark joy. "Couldn't say a word, like my poor Vardo. Then he reached for his knife and he cut his own throat. Did himself in, just like that."

"He did," the Scholar confirmed with a haunted look. "The rest of the gang took to their heels and they haven't been back since. When they were gone, the Witch's voice came out of the dark again. She told us that those who lived in peace with others and did no evil would be safe in the camp from now on, but that she would reappear and punish anyone who did harm. And she's been up there in the castle ever since. We see a shape now and then in the windows at the very top, though she never ventures down here any-more—at least, not that I'm aware of."

"She don't need to," the woman said. "Everyone knows she's there. When people show up here with the idea of caus-ing trouble, they leave right quick."

Arn, who had been listening while he brushed down the horse, spoke up now. "Sometimes she drives out people who've been in the camp a long while," he said sullenly.

"Yes," the Scholar agreed, "she's done that to those who steal from others or drink or spread evil rumours."

"How does she drive them out if she doesn't leave the castle?" Will asked.

"She has a way," Arn said uneasily.

"Usually the person she doesn't want here anymore will start behaving oddly," the Scholar explained. "Nervous. Fearful. Sometimes he'll come right out and confess to all of us what he's done wrong. As if he knows somehow that she's found out his secret. Then he'll pack his things and slip away."

"Sometimes people just disappear," the woman said, "and everybody says the Witch took them."

No one spoke after that, and Will couldn't help glancing up again at the structure beyond the fence. A few cold drops of rain had begun to fall, some with a hiss as they fell on the cooking grate.

More of the camp folk were emerging from their tents now and heading for the stage. Some were dressed in costumes like the Scholar. Will saw a man in brown robes, a girl dressed as a milkmaid, a soldier in tall black boots. Some of the people carried shabby umbrellas, while others held cloaks or straw baskets over their heads.

"It promises to be a most memorable evening, despite the lack of cooperation from the weather," the Scholar said brightly, as though hoping to lighten the dark turn the conversation had taken. "You are very welcome to attend. And who knows, if you stay, perhaps you would be interested in joining our company of players." He eyed Shade. "Your friend there would certainly add a touch of verisimilitude to an old story we'll be performing at the next full moon."

"Thank you, but we aren't staying," Rowen said. "We're going to see the Witch."

Will turned to her in shock but held back his protest. Now was not the time to argue, not in front of these people.

The Scholar's eyebrows rose. "*See* her?" he said, plucking nervously at his false beard. "No one sees her. The castle is forbidden to everyone, even those of us she protects. If the Witch wants to speak to you, you will know it."

"Well, we're not waiting here to find out," Rowen said, and she climbed to her feet. Reluctantly Will joined her. Shade came to his side.

The woman gazed at Rowen with a desperate longing.

"Don't go yet, my dear," she said. "You can stay the night with us and go in the morning. That's a better time. Not at night. Not in the rain."

"We can't wait that long," Rowen said. "What's the quickest way to the castle?"

The Scholar rubbed his forehead and then pointed down the path to the stage. "I think this is a mistake," he said, "but so be it. Go around to the far side of the stage to the fence at the back of the camp and you will find some loose boards there. You can climb through and then it's just a short walk. I went that way once with a delegation from the camp to officially thank her for all she's done for us. We didn't get far beyond the fence before we knew we weren't welcome. So we turned back and no one from the camp has gone to the castle since."

"How did you know she didn't want you there?"

"We knew."

"The stew is ready," the woman said. "Stay and eat first. You can go later."

"Thank you for all you've done," Rowen said to her. "I hope . . . I hope you find your daughter."

"My dear, don't go—"

"Mother," Arn said sharply. "That's enough now. Let them go if they want to. It's none of our business."

The woman bit her trembling lip. Her eyes filled with tears and she turned away.

Rowen and Will thanked the Scholar and set off with Shade. People watched them as they passed, but no one spoke to them and Will had the strange feeling the entire camp already knew what they were doing here. He had been waiting until the three of them were out of hearing of anyone else, and now he took hold of Rowen's arm and forced her to halt.

"What are you thinking?" he said. "They told us nobody goes to see this Witch, and it sounds to me like that's how she wants it. What if she does to us what she did to the leader of that gang?"

"What choice do we have?" Rowen said in a desperate undertone, tugging her arm out of Will's grasp. "I know that the Fair Folk were here, the *real* Fair Folk, and maybe this Witch knows what happened to them. They're the only chance I've got of finding Grandfather."

"Maybe the witch knows what happened to them because she's on *his* side," Will said. "She could be one of his servants. Did you think of that? Maybe *she's* the reason the Fair Folk aren't here anymore."

"Will, whoever she is, you heard what the Scholar said. She looks after these people and only punishes those who harm others. That doesn't sound like a servant of the Night King to me. Maybe she can't help us, but that doesn't mean she's going to hurt us. I have to find out what she knows."

Will shook his head but said nothing more.

They passed the stage, where several people were busily lighting lamps and setting up a large canvas backdrop painted to look like a sunny countryside dotted with windmills. The people on the stage glanced at them curiously as they passed but like everyone else said nothing to them.

From the other side of the stage it was only a short walk to the fence. There was no difficulty finding the loose boards, which hung crookedly among the others. To Will it seemed

strange that no one, not even the carpenter, Holt, had bothered to repair the fence, given all the trouble they'd had from
outsiders. Then Will looked up at the hotel, looming darkly
over this end of the camp, and he thought he understood
why the fence had been left as it was. Closing up the loose
boards would make it seem they were hoping to keep the
Witch out. As much as these people had benefited from her
presence, clearly they were still afraid of her and wished to
avoid doing anything that might offend her.

Will, Rowen and Shade slipped through the gap. On the
far side they found themselves on a cracked and stained concrete platform with fading painted lines that Will took to be
the remains of a parking lot. At the far end rose a retaining
wall with a crumbling staircase. They crossed the lot and
climbed the staircase with care. It led them up into the deserted street where the hotel stood, facing what looked to be
a public park with aisles of gaunt, leafless trees. A row of
electric lamps ran along the street, and several of them had
come on in the failing light, the nearest one flickering and
buzzing and the others casting a weak yellow glow. There
was still electrical power, Will thought with a strange min-
gling of relief and unease, even though the city seemed to
have been deserted.

As they walked up the street, the park's rusted gate
creaked in the wind. The rain was falling in earnest now, a
fine cold drizzle wetting them and raising a humid odour of
wet dust and ashes.

The hotel was of a type that Will had rarely seen with his
own eyes. The exterior was made of thick stone blocks and
had ornate mouldings and high turrets. But despite the elegant facade, the hotel was in poor repair. Windows up and
down the frontage were broken or missing altogether. The
walls were pockmarked with what looked like bullet holes

and the front doors were gone, leaving the deep stone entry-way resembling the entrance to a cave strewn with pebbles of glass. They halted here, both finding themselves suddenly unwilling to approach any closer.

"You called this place a hotel," Shade said. "I have never heard that word before, but this does not seem like a place we should go."

"In my world a hotel's a place where travellers stay for the night. Like the Golden Goose in Fable."

"This looks nothing like the Golden Goose," Rowen said.

"I know. And it's not like any hotel I've ever stayed in. This would have been a hotel only for rich people. But I don't think it's been used that way for a long time."

"Well, I'm going in there," Rowen said. "You and Shade can wait out here if you want."

Will and the wolf exchanged a glance.

"We're not splitting up now," Will said. "Let's go."

Slowly and hesitantly they stepped through the doorway and into the lobby. As they did so, Rowen tapped on the glass of the waylight and Sputter, the wisp, awoke, casting a pale blue light a short distance into the gloom. They could hear his faint flutter through the lantern's glass panes.

The lobby had marble columns and a high ceiling and was carpeted in a rich maroon with an ornate floral pattern. But the columns were cracked and chipped, and the carpet stained and rucked up in many places. There was a fountain in the centre of the lobby, but it was dry and filled only with dust and debris. To the right of the front desk, with its brass lamps and shelf with cubbyholes for keys, rose a wide carpeted stair-case, and on the far side of it, in an alcove, was a bank of three elevators, their doors open. On the other side of the lobby was an entryway into another room, where they could see dark leather chairs and side tables. A lounge, Will thought.

Over everything hung a thick, pervading smell of dust and damp.

"Hello?" Rowen called. Her voice echoed.

Will walked over to the front desk. He looked behind it, found nothing but scraps of paper and a mound of ash, as if someone had built a fire there once.

"Hello," Rowen called again, louder this time. "We've come from the camp. We only want to ask you some questions and then we'll go."

After a long silence Will wandered into the lounge and Rowen and Shade followed. A large stone fireplace stood on one wall, and above it hung a large painting in a gilt frame. The painting showed a group of slender people in red coats, men and women, galloping sleek horses across an autumn countryside. The artists had painted the scene as if the people and horses had no weight, Will thought. As if they were gliding on air.

Nearby, a large globe rested in a three-legged stand. Even from a distance Will recognized the familiar shapes of the land masses he knew. Rowen went over to it, placed her hand on the globe and turned it slowly.

"It's a map, isn't it?" she asked Will. "I've never seen one like this. Why is it round?"

"That's the shape of the world," Will said, surprised.

Rowen looked at him quizzically, then went back to examining the globe. Perhaps she didn't believe him or understand what he meant, but clearly she had chosen not to ask any more questions about it.

"I don't know the names of any of these places," she said at last, shaking her head.

Will was about to join her, and find the name of his town or at least point to its location, when Shade raised his head sharply and turned to the doorway.

"Will Lightfoot!" the wolf called out in warning, and gave a menacing growl.

Will and Rowen whirled to see a figure coming slowly toward them down the dark stairs.

Will stood frozen with horror. He hadn't known who or what they might encounter in this eerie, abandoned hotel, but the last thing he expected to see was a tall figure shrouded completely in a flowing white cloak.

The Angel.

The flowing white form moved across the long maroon carpet like a drifting bank of fog.

"It can't be," Rowen whispered, backing away. "He was destroyed. Moth killed him."

The sight filled Will with such terror that he was rendered immobile, unable even to cry out.

Shade snarled and bounded toward the Angel, but in the next moment he was brought up short, his paws scrabbling on the tiled floor, by a voice. A woman's voice that seemed to echo through the entire lobby.

"Children, why are you here? You should not be here."

The voice sounded angry, but there was something else in it, a deep sadness. It was a voice that Will remembered hearing before but couldn't put a name to, though Shade apparently had no doubts. He padded up to the white figure as if by command. A slender hand emerged from the sleeve of the shrowde cloak and touched the wolf's forehead.

Then Will knew. He gripped Rowen's shoulder to keep her from fleeing.

The white figure drew back the concealing hood and they saw a face that they remembered well, the face of a young woman with dusky skin and jet black hair. It was Morrigan of the Tain Shee.

"My friends," she said. "You should never have come here."

11

FREYA STOOD IN THE wind and the snow and wondered where in the Realm she had come to.

She had been locked in a lightless room in the toyshop for hours. The Marrowbone brothers had bound her hands and closed the door, and then she had heard them moving something heavy in front of it. When their footsteps had died away, she had tried pushing the door with her shoulder. No matter how hard she tried it wouldn't budge, and she couldn't climb to her feet because of her ankle. Flitch had broken it; that was almost certain. The pain wasn't going away, and she felt cold all over and couldn't stop shaking. So she had sat on the stone floor, hopeless and in agony, dreading what would happen the next time the door opened.

She was sure of one thing only: that Brax had not yet discovered whatever he was looking for. She was still alive only because he suspected she knew more than she had admitted about Father Nicholas's secrets. If he did find the cabinet, she would be of no further use to him. And then the hogmen would have their revenge on her, as they'd promised when they were shutting her up in here.

She couldn't tell how long she had waited in the dark, but after a long time she became aware of a light. A warm yellow flickering, like candle flame. It was coming not from the crack between the door and the floor but from behind her, from the back of the closet, as if the back wall had opened onto a vast darkness. With effort she turned and the light swiftly grew and then she saw that it was the tiger, padding out of the dark toward her.

There was nowhere to run or hide, even if she'd been able to. And so she had pushed herself up against the door and waited.

The tiger had stopped a few paces from her, and then she could see that it was not as solid and catlike as it had been when it had sprung at the mage. It was more a thing of separate flames woven together, with patches of nothingness in between. The flames themselves appeared frayed and wavering, as if they might go out at any moment. Even so, their light was strong enough in this dark place to hurt her eyes. This thing had been pretending to be Master Nicholas, and she hadn't understood how or why. Then she felt the rope around her wrists loosen and fall away, and as she gazed into the tiger's glowing yellow eyes, she finally grasped what Rowen had done.

"You're Riddle, aren't you," she had said, rubbing her chafed wrists. "You were guarding the toyshop for Rowen while she went to search for Father Nicholas."

The tiger did not speak, but its eyes were fixed on her and she was certain that it wanted something from her, though

she had no idea what. Some of its flames fluttered as if about
to go out.

"He hurt you, too, didn't he?" she finally said. "The mage.
Can you still talk to me?"

Again the tiger said nothing, then it turned and took a
few paces away from her, back into the darkness where there
should have been a wall. It halted and looked back at Freya.

"You want me to follow," she said. "I understand. But I
can't walk."

The tiger came close to her. She couldn't help pulling
back in fear, but it had no intention of harming her. Instead it
ducked its fiery head under Freya's arm and lifted it. She
understood immediately: Riddle was offering to carry her.

So she had climbed on the back of the tiger, and to her surprise the creature of fire was solid enough to hold her and
the flames did not burn. He had plunged with her into the
dark and then they were in a place she could not understand,
where everything around her was shifting and rippling and
changing. She had no idea how long they travelled through
this impossible world, when without warning the whirl
and rush stopped. They were in a place of dim light and
softly falling snow. The sudden quiet and stillness made her
head spin.

The next thing she knew Riddle was coming apart: the
many small, fluttering flames that composed him drifted
farther and farther from each other. Freya found herself sinking slowly into the soft, thick snow. Then all the flames went
out, one after another, and Riddle was gone without a word.

Now she was here, and Riddle had left her with no explanation why he had brought her to this place. Was she miles
away from Fable? She could not even be sure of the time of
day. At least she did not feel cold, which was very strange
when she thought about it. She should have been freezing

to death out here, but all she felt was a briskness to the air
that seemed to revive all her senses and ease the pain of
her ankle.

And then she thought, *Snow.*

Snow was the reason she had made the long journey to
Fable in the first place. The dragon, Whitewing Stonegrinder,
had come to Skald one night in the form of fog, snow and hail.
He had given her a message for Father Nicholas and for
Rowen. His message was that when Rowen saw snow in a
high place, she would know he had come to help her. Snow
had fallen on Fable one night in the middle of summer and
they knew that Whitewing Stonegrinder had come as he'd
said he would. Rowen had gone willingly to Appleyard that
night, no doubt hoping to meet with the dragon at the top
of the hill, which was the highest place in the city. But then
Freya had been taken away by order of the mage, and she
had no idea what had happened to Rowen after that.

Freya held out her hand now and the flakes of snow fell
onto her palm, but they did not melt. They lay there, glittering in the dim light.

"Old One?" she whispered, her heart pounding. She remembered that this was the right way to address an ancient
power of the earth like a dragon.

She had seen him in his dragon form once before. He had
been terrifying to behold, a great winged being with scales
that held the blue light of ancient ice. But crouched here in
the snow, she thought back to the first time she had met the
dragon, when she was just a child.

Her father had taken her into the mountains to search for
a rare kind of yellow-grey stone he used to sharpen the
blades he forged in the smithy. Finding these stones was one
of the many things she needed to learn as his apprentice in
the craft.

People from Skald didn't go into the mountains very often. They were afraid of the mountains, though she didn't know why. On that trip her father had brought her all the way up the valley of the Whitewing River to the foot of the great river of ice. There they stopped and her father built a small fire to warm them with wood he'd gathered on the way. He'd already found the stones he was looking for, and now Freya understood they had come here for something more. Snow began to fall, large soft wet flakes drifting down all around them, enough snow to put the little fire out. Her father had whispered then that the dragon was here. She had looked around, frightened but not entirely believing him, then asked her father where the dragon was.

"He is dreaming," he had said. "Listen, you can hear him stirring in his sleep."

She listened, and she heard faint sounds of creaking and rumbling from deep from the ice, as if something huge and very powerful was indeed stirring within it.

"One day," her father had said, "the dragon will awake."

"Old One," she said now, a little louder this time. "Are you here?"

There was no answer. The pain in her ankle had subsided to a dull throb. She thought she might be able to stand. Slowly and carefully she climbed to her feet, keeping her weight off her injured leg. She balanced there, straining to see through the veils of falling snow.

The snowflakes in her hand were glittering even more brightly now. Then she looked past her hand and saw that the snow all around her was glittering, too, in softly pulsing lines like veins under the skin.

"It *is* you, Old One," she said, scarcely daring to breathe. "You're here."

Then she heard a voice that seemed to come both from

inside her and the cold air around her. A voice she had heard once before, when hail fell on the roofs of Skald at midsummer.

His voice was not as strong as she remembered—it was little more than a whisper—but it carried a rolling undercurrent within it as of great storm clouds in the distance. And beneath the voice a faint creaking and rumbling that she remembered from that day at the foot of the ice with her father. The dragon stirring.

Freya Ragnarsdaughter, said the voice. *Welcome.*

"Riddle brought me here, Old One. The shapechanger. I don't know what's happened to him."

I sent him to find you and bring you to me. He was injured and now he has returned to the weave of things, to heal.

"You sent him for me? Why, Old One?"

We have a task to perform, child of Skald. One that we can only accomplish together.

"My friends," Freya said, and now all that she had been through and seen welled up in her and she could not stop the tears that slid down her face. "Father Nicholas and Rowen and Will—they're in danger. Can you help them?"

They are far away, Freya Ragnarsdaughter. We cannot reach them now. It is too late for that. And I have need of you here.

"Me, Old One? What can I do? My ankle is broken."

Listen now, mortal child. What you see around you is all of me that remains. You call me Old One and that is right, for I am old. Old—and the sun is strong. Stronger now than I have ever known in the long ages of my life. What strength I have left I must spend to keep the clouds above us, to keep the sun from finishing me. I have sent my roots into the earth to seek out the lightless underground rivers that are always cold. But they are deep here and difficult to reach. I am weary. I need a living heart and will to keep me from surrendering to the sun. I need your heart and your will, daughter of Skald.

Freya felt her fear rise up. She struggled to keep the weight off her injured leg. "What must I do, Old One?"

I will share with you what I know and what I am. You will be changed, as will I. We will become something that is both mortal and dragon, yet neither. Together we will gather our strength, and when the time comes, we will return to the Loremaster's city together.

"Then I give you my heart and will, Old One," Freya said, and she closed her eyes and waited.

It was then that she truly felt the cold. The true, deep, deathly cold of the dragon that he had been shielding her from until now. It burned her hands first and her feet, and then it moved inward. There was a terrible icy fire in her veins and she had to struggle not to cry out. Tears ran down her cheeks and dropped into the snow. She felt the cold flowing over her and stabbing deep into her. She felt it move into the broken bone of her ankle and the pain vanished. The cold itself was knitting the bone back together, healing and binding it. Soon she would be able to walk once more.

Then the dragon spoke again and his voice pulsed through her as if it was the voice of her own heartbeat.

Mortal child, tell me what you feel.

"I feel ice in my veins, Old One," Freya said. "I'm afraid."

Do not fear. You will not die of this cold. It will preserve you and strengthen you for what lies ahead. It will become you and you will give it thought and purpose.

What the dragon said was true. She felt now that she was nothing but the cold and that time itself seemed to have frozen to a halt along with her. Yet when she looked up, she saw, through a gap in the clouds, the stars wheeling through the sky, as if the night that had fallen while she stood here was rushing past. When she drew a breath, the air moved in and out of her as slowly as the sea's tide rising and falling. She was aware of her body standing on the hilltop, but she was more than just that small frail form lost in the snow. *That was still a part of her, it was true.* That was the Freya she had been. She knew that she cared for that Freya and wished her not to suffer. But now she had been taken up within this greater self, whose eyes and thoughts travelled out into the falling snow and farther still.

Tell me now, daughter of Skald, the dragon said. *What do you see?*

There was something at the foot of the hill, a little cottage. She knew without knowing how she knew that it had been Rowen's home when she was a child and that it was a day's walk from Fable. No distance at all for the dragon when it came time for him to rise again. Then her gaze seemed to sharpen, as if her eyes had turned to crystal, and she saw farther and farther.

"I see high mountains, Old One," she said. "I see the place where you were born, a wall of ice towering into the sky. I see that you were once mightier than anything in the Realm. Your body was the rivers, the streams. The rain. Your wings were the clouds. You were everywhere."

Our life is long. It flows forward and backward through the river of time. We are seeing what once was and may be again. If we do not fail.

Freya wandered then through visions and memories that were both the dragon's and her own. She saw her city as the dragon saw it, from a great height; saw her fellow Skaldings preparing for siege and war. And then her vision swooped down and she saw her father, hammering sword blades on his anvil. She saw her little brother and her mother at the doorway of the house, looking out into the dark and cold. Wondering where Freya was and what was happening to her.

She reached out a hand. They were so close, right in front of her. She could almost touch them. Her vision clouded with tears and then the voice of ice returned, thundering through her.

Turn our sight to where we are now, the voice commanded. *Look and tell me what is happening on the borders of this country.*

Freya's vision tore itself away from Skald and rushed back over the miles to the edge of the Bourne. It seemed that what she saw was happening at this moment, but it had also happened not long ago and yet was about to happen. She looked and then she tried to find words for what she saw.

She saw the day come, the sun lifting over the dark hills to the east. She saw the thin silver ribbons of the streams, and the deserted fields and farmhouses, and the folk upon the roads, riding and walking, driving goats and cattle, most of them hurrying southward, bringing with them the few possessions they could carry. To the north she saw a great gathering of Nightbane like a dark stain on the earth, moving along the road toward the rocky, steep-sided pass that was the way into the Bourne.

The citadel of Annen Bawn was there, an arch of stone over the place where the pass was narrowest. She saw the swarm of Nightbane flood into the gorge until it was stopped at the citadel walls like a raging torrent breaking upon a dam. She saw the defenders mustering on their battlements and walls. She saw a hail of arrows, and men and monsters screaming, falling, dying. She saw the great iron battering ram hammering at the gates, and with each blow she felt the stones of the walls shudder. The gates had been reinforced and they held. For now they held. Then her gaze swept north again, to a dark line on the horizon. Something still distant but moving swiftly, raising a great cloud of dust.

"Something else is coming to Fable," Freya cried. "Another army, but not like any army I've ever seen or heard of. They are covered in metal and they have no faces."

This army was perhaps less than two days away from

Annen Bawn, marching tirelessly day and night. The warriors were not Nightbane. She did not know what they were, but she knew that they were on their way to destroy. She was about to tell the dragon, but it came to her then that her vision was his now. It was as he had said: they would see and know as one, and that meant she had no need to speak her thoughts. Yet deep down she felt her own frail heart still beating, a tiny pulse of warmth in the depths of the icy immensity that was Whitewing Stonegrinder. She was still Freya of Skald, daughter of Ragnar, the blacksmith.

"Old One, we have to help the defenders at Annen Bawn," she said, gasping for breath in the icy air. "The gates won't hold. You can strengthen them. You can make a wall of ice across the gorge and seal the enemy out."

These things you have seen are happening now, the dragon said. *The walls of Annen Bawn are about to fall. We cannot prevent it. The defenders who remain will retreat to Fable and the Nightbane will follow.*

"But we can't just wait here, Old One. We have to do something."

Our powers are not yet ready. If we go to defend Annen Bawn now, we will fail and the enemy will carry on to Fable. We must wait, daughter of Skald, and draw the cold from deep in the earth. Another threat is coming that will require all our strength. A threat from the sky.

Freya joined her gaze to the dragon's once more and saw what he had spoken of: even stranger creatures than the faceless warriors, following them from the north on vast wings. Creatures that carried fire within them, like flying forges.

Where were they from? Freya looked northward past the fire-bearers, straining to the limits of the vision the dragon had granted her. She saw a fortress on the edge of a lifeless valley of smoke and fire, and beyond it a city in the earth, and in the city she saw Finn Madoc. His face was pale, his arm in a sling. His eyes feverish.

Finn was dying.

"There is nothing we can do for him," a voice said. "Many will die before this is over. We cannot save everyone."

Who had spoken? She didn't know if these were her own words or the dragon's. There was no longer any way to tell. She felt the last of her tears slide to a halt on her face and turn to ice.

12

"THEY ARE GONE," MORRIGAN said. "My people. They have passed into the Shadow Realm."

Will and Rowen stared at her, too shocked and dismayed to speak.

They had followed Morrigan up the wide staircase, flight after flight, and then down a long corridor to the room she inhabited in the hotel. It was a large room, half of a spacious double suite that took up one end of the top floor, but it was almost bare, containing only an armchair, a standing lamp and a dark leather sofa. On the far side of the room from the door was a large floor-length window that looked down onto the camp, where many lanterns and torches now glowed in the deepening twilight.

Morrigan stood at the window, tall and regal in a dark green gown. She had taken off the shrowde cloak when they first entered the room, and it had slid away across the thickly carpeted floor like a snaking tendril of white fog, curling up at last in the farthest, darkest corner.

"How can that be?" Rowen said, the colour draining from her face. "How can they be *gone*? Your people are powerful and wise and . . ."

Morrigan turned from the window. She was as beautiful as Will remembered, but her dark eyes burned with a terrible half-mad light. Will had seen that look before, in the eyes of her brother, Moth, when he faced Lotan the Angel. It was the look of someone who had abandoned all hope and lived only to die for the sake of what she held dear.

"Tell me what you see," Morrigan said now to Rowen, her voice low and urgent. "You have the gift of the loremasters to see into the weave of things. Use it now."

"What I see? You mean of your people?"

"Yes. Tell me what happened to them in this place."

"I saw them when we were in the Weaving, but now . . ." Rowen shook her head. She was sitting upright on the leather sofa with her hands braced on either side of her, like someone who'd just been through an earthquake and was waiting to see if any more tremors would come.

"You are like me when I first found this place," Morrigan said. "You do not wish to admit what your heart already knows. Tell me what you see."

Rowen drew a deep breath, then she nodded.

"I do see them," she said in a hollow voice. "The Fair Folk. I didn't want it to be true. But it is true, isn't it? Your people revealed themselves here to the Night King. It was like the sun emerging from behind clouds. The way we see them most of the time—the way we see you right now, Morrigan, wearing a disguise to keep yourself hidden. Your people took off their disguise."

She closed her eyes.

"It happened down there, where the camp is now. I can see their bright armour. Their horses with snow-white manes. I can hear their spurs jingling and their banners snapping in the wind. And they're singing. I don't know the words, but I can tell what the song means. They're singing a farewell to the Realm. To everything."

She kept her eyes closed and did not speak for a while. Her brow furrowed and her hands clenched into white-knuckled fists. She swayed a little as she stood and Will was startled to see beads of sweat on her forehead.

"What else?" Morrigan said. "Tell me."

"Wait," Will said. "Just let her rest, Morrigan. That's enough for now."

Rowen opened her eyes. "No, Will," she said. "I need to do this. I'll tell you what I see, Morrigan. There's a shadow rising in front of them, a huge dark shadow as tall as the sky. It's *alive*. It's a cloud of tiny flying things, so many of them they're filling the sky. The cloud is growing larger. It's blotting out the sun. I can hear it, too—a roaring sound, getting louder."

"I have seen and heard this cloud, as well," Shade said. "Long ago, when we battled the Storyeater."

Rowen stared at the wolf as if she hadn't understood what he'd said. Then she looked past him and seemed to be searching for something beyond the walls of the room.

From below came faint sounds of voices raised in shouts and laughter. The Scholar's play had begun.

"But the Fair Folk are still there," Rowen said at last. "I can see the light in their eyes, their faces. So bright. They're raising their swords and their spears and charging forward. And they're still singing. They're riding into the cloud, and now it's being torn open. It's like a black curtain tearing and falling to pieces. The earth is shaking, and the light . . ."

Rowen put a hand in front of her eyes. "It's just the way Grandfather used to tell of the war long ago, when the Shee first battled Malabron. But this time the Fair Folk are alone. There are no Stewards. Your people are alone, Morrigan, against all the hate there is."

Tears slid down Rowen's face.

"Then the cloud returns," she said in a whisper. "It returns stronger than before." She shook her head slowly.

"What is it?" Morrigan. "Go on."

"It swallowed them up. Their light went out. It took them. The Shadow Realm took them. All of them."

Her voice broke with a sob. Will put a hand on her shoulder. He looked up angrily at Morrigan and saw that her eyes had gone cold and hard.

"Yes, this is where it happened," she said, and her voice was like her gaze: there was no trace of the feeling with which she'd spoken when she first met them in the hotel lobby. "Or this place came to be because of the battle."

"What do you mean?" Will asked. "The battle created the Fair?"

"My people know of many hidden paths between the realms, Will. Paths that people from the Untold have stumbled upon from time to time, as you did. I think that my people took one of these hidden paths in the hope of approaching Malabron's realm undetected. They arrived at his borders and revealed themselves there or were discovered. Then the battle tore through the walls that keep the worlds apart, so that they have become entangled here. Like three broken threads knotting together, into something that was never meant to be. Now Malabron's nightmare is bleeding into our realm, Rowen, and yours, Will, and poisoning them both."

"My world, too?" Will asked, and a cold dread slid through him. "But how could that happen? The Untold isn't part of the Realm. It has nothing to do with any of this."

"You're certain of that?" Morrigan said.

For a moment Will caught a glimpse of Morrigan as he had first known her, the sleek coal-black raven who perched on Moth's shoulder and fixed everyone and everything with a sharp eye. She had been enchanted by Lotan, a prince of the Shee who'd been corrupted by Malabron and turned against his own people. For years she'd been trapped in that shape, and so it didn't surprise him to see that the raven was still there within this sad and beautiful young woman.

"We call your world the Untold because it is so little known and its stories are so strange to us," Morrigan went on. "But I have seen it, Will. I have travelled in the Untold."

"You've been to my world?"

"My brother and I journeyed there once long ago. Our people often have, though few in the Untold know of it. We used the hidden paths between realms as a means of concealment from Malabron's hunters. Sometimes we strayed too far on those paths and we would cross over into the Untold and walk among its people in disguise. This castle, the tools and weapons that some here carry with them—these are things of your world, Will. Surely you recognized them."

Will let out a long breath. "I did. I thought I was back home, but so many things are strange, too. This *seems* like a city in my world, but where are all the people? Why can we hear cars and sirens and all that but not see anyone?"

"If I am right about what has happened, this place is not in any one of the three realms alone—it is in all of them at the same time," Morrigan said. "You've seen the trees growing from the pavement outside. You've smelled the rot and ashes of the Shadow Realm. This is your world, Will, and yet it is not. It's as if three different stories have been at war here, each struggling to be told."

"That's why those people in the camp can't find their way home," Will said. "Now I see what the woman meant. Everything's mixed up."

"Yes. The roads, the places, the landmarks they know are tangled with paths that lead elsewhere. Or nowhere. I fear there are many such lost places in the weave now. Places where the Shadow Realm has drawn close."

"Malabron's story is winning the struggle?" Rowen said.

"It is," Morrigan said. "What is happening here will happen to the Bourne and every other part of the Realm if he is not defeated. And not just in the Perilous Realm but in your world, too, Will. That is why the people in the camp act out their tales and legends every night, why they hold on so desperately to them. The rise of the Night King is bringing forgetfulness with it. The past is being unwoven, along with what is and what will be. Soon we will all accept Malabron's nightmare as the only story we've ever known."

Will sat down heavily in the armchair. His heart was thudding in his chest. Until now he had thought that his home, his family, his world were safely out of reach of the dangers that threatened Rowen's. He remembered what had happened last night outside the cottage at Blue Hill, the strange feeling he'd had that his home was very close, that he only needed to walk a short distance through the woods at the edge of the farm and he would be there, back in his own world. That thought had comforted him then. Now it terrified him.

"I still have to find Grandfather," Rowen said. "Nothing changes that."

"What has happened to Nicholas Pendrake?" Morrigan asked.

Rowen told her own story then in a frantic, jumbled rush. She told of her grandfather's abduction by the thrawl and her search through the Weaving, where she'd met her grandmother, who'd revealed that war was coming to Fable. Then she told how she and Will had set out in search of the Fair Folk and had come to the mirror-lake, and what had happened after.

"And now we're already in the Shadow Realm," Rowen said when she'd finished, "or at least on the edge of it. Isn't that right, Morrigan? So from here we should be able to get there easily."

Morrigan had listened to Rowen's tale in silence. Now she nodded to herself as though she had just made up her mind about something.

"Come with me," she said.

She moved away from the window and crossed the room. Will, Rowen and Shade followed her through an open doorway and into the other half of the double suite. This room held more chairs and two large beds and had a bathroom and a small kitchen alcove, as well. Here the floor-length window looked out on the towers of glass and concrete they had seen from a distance.

They saw the city at last.

Grey ruins of buildings, many with shattered windows and stained, crumbling walls, marched off into an ashen haze. It was so unlike the view from the other window, with its rolling green countryside and warm glow of the camp lanterns, that Will wondered for a moment if they had come through one of the knot-paths that took you to another part of the Realm. Even the light was different here: a dim, sickly pall had replaced the soft blue twilight falling over the camp.

"It used to be that the black river, the one that you saw in the Weaving, Rowen, was the only way into the Shadow Realm," Morrigan said. "To cross it almost certainly meant that you would be without mind and will once you reached the far shore. But paths have opened now that never existed before. That city out there is another way into Malabron's nightmare, a way that he may not even be aware of yet. The shrowde has been to the city and knows what lies beyond."

"The shrowde," Rowen said. She and Will both turned to the doorway at the same time, as the living white cloak drifted like a ghost into the room. "I thought she was the Angel's servant."

"She was bound to Lotan, yes," Morrigan said with a nod, "though she no longer serves anyone, not even me."

"The cloak is a *she*?"

"That is only one of the things I discovered when I took her from the Angel. The shrowde had been forced to do his bidding. After my brother destroyed him, the shrowde was finally free, as I was, but she was terrified and helpless. I took her with me when I rejoined my people and in time she came to trust me. She has no voice as we do, but when she submits to cloak someone of her own free will, the wearer can see and understand the shrowde's thoughts and reply in kind. That is how we learned to understand each other. The truth is, after so many years wandering in the shadows I felt closer to her than to my own people. I have grown to care for the shrowde very much and she for me. We will not be parted again in this life."

The shrowde stirred and flowed soundlessly over the carpet. Morrigan extended her arms and the shrowde rose swiftly from the floor, covering the Shee woman's green gown, flowing over her shoulders and down her back, mantling her once again from her feet to her neck, leaving only Morrigan's head bare. When the shrowde had settled and gone still, it once again resembled nothing more than a long white cloak.

Will thought how strange it was that Moth had given his life to save his sister from Lotan's curse and here she was, clothed in the guise of the one who had killed her brother. He doubted that Moth would have wanted this.

"She's afraid of us, I think," Rowen said.

"It's me," Will said, recalling his last encounter with the

shrowde. "I cut her with my knife when the Angel was fighting Moth."

"She remembers you both," Morrigan said. "I have told her that you were only trying to help your friends, Will, but it is hard for her. She has known only fear and hatred for so long. It will take some time for her to trust you."

"The camp folk told us about the night you saved the girl," Rowen said hesitantly. "About the man who stabbed himself."

Morrigan's face gave no sign that Rowen's words troubled her.

"He was one of those who believe he can harm others without consequence to himself. The shrowde showed him what was hidden in his heart, all the fear and suffering he had caused others. It was there inside him, too, and it overwhelmed him. We did not intend he should die, but neither would we allow anyone else to be harmed."

"Why did you come here, Morrigan?" Will asked. "Did you get lost, too, like the others?"

"We were seeking a hidden way into the Shadow Realm, like you," Morrigan said. "Then we found the camp, and the shrowde feared for the people here; she would not have us leave until we were sure they were safe. Keeping our true identities hidden seemed the best way to spread fear among any who would harm these folk. Now we know we cannot protect them any longer, not by staying here. The camp is only a tiny rock against the tide, and soon it will be overwhelmed. We have to finish what we came to do."

"That's what I was hoping when we found you," Rowen said eagerly. "We can travel together, Morrigan, and the shrowde can show us the way. Once we find Grandfather and your people, we can return to Fable."

"We did not come to find my people, Rowen," Morrigan said, her voice hollow and cold. "There is only one way to end this nightmare: a blade must be driven into the heart of the Shadow Realm. The shrowde and I will be that blade."

Will and Rowen stared at the Shee woman.

"Morrigan," Rowen breathed, "you mean to find *him*."

"I would not have the three of you set foot in that terrible place. Nevertheless I will not hinder you. It is not my place to do so. We will travel with you, the shrowde and I. We will help you search for the Loremaster. And when we have found him, you will return home to Fable and the shrowde and I will finish what we came to do."

Tears rose in Rowen's eyes. "Thank you," she said.

"This is crazy," Will blurted, unable to stop himself. "I never thought we had much of a chance, going to the one place we should be trying to stay away from. And now you want to march in there and challenge . . ." He shook his head. "Morrigan, if all your people together couldn't defeat him, how can you hope to do it on your own?"

"One, or two as one, may succeed where many have failed, Will. My people's sacrifice has torn this hole between worlds, giving us this chance to slip into the Shadow Realm unnoticed, or so I hope. Besides, Rowen is determined to find her grandfather, and she would still go were I to stay here. Even with such a protector as Shade the three of you would not get far on your own. Malabron's domain is in-habited by far more dangerous beings than fetches. And it is a place with no clear paths and many false ones. But the shrowde knows the Shadow Realm. She went there many times with Lotan, the Angel. She has told me of a place beyond the dead city where the Angel always took his prey. A plain of silence and dust. Nothing lives in that place. It is the heart of Malabron's nightmare. The journey will be long and difficult, but the shrowde knows the way and can take us there."

"Then we should leave now," Rowen said. "There's no reason to stay here any longer."

"I understand your wanting to set out right away," Morrigan said. "But you—all of you—are tired and hungry and there will be little rest once we are in the Shadow Realm. We will wait until morning."

Rowen was about to protest, but Will cut her off. "Morrigan is right," he said. "We haven't eaten anything in hours and you can barely stand up. We're not going anywhere right now."

"I'm fine," Rowen said angrily.

"No, you're not. For once just listen to me."

Rowen glared at Will. She looked from him to Morrigan and back again. At last she lowered her head and her shoulders sagged.

"In the morning, then," she said.

"You may sleep in this room without fear," the Shee woman said. "No one has dared set foot here since we came except you. The shrowde and I will keep watch."

"But then you won't get any rest," Will protested.

"We do not sleep."

Rowen looked at the beds, one on each side of the window, with its view of the dead city.

"I can't sleep here," she said, shaking her head. "Not while Grandfather is out *there* somewhere alone."

"There's the sofa in the other room," Will suggested.

After a long silence Rowen nodded. Mutely she followed Will to the other half of the suite. She sat down on the sofa as she had before, with her arms braced on either side of her, as if she might spring up at any moment. Shade lay down heavily in the doorway.

"I will stay here, Will Lightfoot," he said.

Rowen stared at the far wall without moving, then stirred and glanced up at Will as though she'd just remembered he was there. For the first time in a long while she looked at him with concern.

"What about you, Will?" she asked. "Where will you sleep?"

"This'll do fine," Will said, sitting down in the armchair.

"No, you can't sleep in that thing," Rowen said. "You won't get any rest. There's room here."

"Are you sure?"

"Yes. Please, Will."

He got up and came over to the sofa. Rowen lay down then and awkwardly, shyly, Will lay beside her. After a moment Rowen reached over and drew his arm around her.

"She doesn't intend to come back," Rowen said.

"Morrigan?"

"You can see it in her eyes. Like Moth's when he was facing the Angel. She's ready to give her life for this."

"The shrowde is a powerful being, probably more than we know, and so is Morrigan. Maybe they can defeat him."

"Do you really believe that?"

Will didn't reply. To admit what he felt about Morrigan's chances would be the same as revealing that he saw no hope for themselves. He closed his eyes. From the camp noises of laughter and clapping drifted up. The merrymaking sounded hollow in his ears. The people down there were trying to convince themselves that everything was fine, even as darkness threatened to close over them.

Just like us, he thought.

Rowen sat up with a cry. She had been asleep, though she had no idea how long. Groggily she looked around the room. Will was not lying beside her—he wasn't in the room at all. And Shade was gone, too. There was no sound or movement below in the camp and most of its lights were out, but she could see a pale rose glimmer on the horizon that told her dawn was not far off.

She found Will and Shade in the other room with Morrigan. Morning may have been coming to the camp, but the sickly half-light over the city had not changed. Morrigan stood at the window in the shrowde cloak, a pale figure that seemed to belong to that dim, deathly world below.

"We wanted to let you sleep," Will said.

He and Rowen ate what little food they had left in their packs. There was barely enough to fill their stomachs now, let alone sustain them on what might be a long journey.

"I have seen cabinets in other rooms, with food and drink in them," Morrigan said when she noticed they had no more provisions. "At least, something *like* food and drink. None of it is to my taste, but I have tried it and it is safe."

Will stood. "I'll go have a look," he said. "Come on, Shade."

The wolf joined Will at the door.

"We'll check the other rooms on this floor," Will said before leaving. "We won't stay away long."

When they had gone, Morrigan turned to Rowen.

"Where was Shade poisoned with *gaal*?" she asked, her voice even colder than it had been last night.

Now that they were ready to set out, she seemed to have smothered all trace of warmth and concern. They hadn't spoken of Shade's condition yet, but clearly Morrigan had guessed what had happened to the wolf.

"At the fortress of Finn's brother, Corr Madoc," Rowen said heavily. "Just a few days ago. They used the fever iron on him. They wanted to turn him into one of their killer wolves. He hasn't been getting any better. In fact, he's . . . I didn't want him to come with us. I saw what would happen to him in the Shadow Realm. But he wouldn't leave Will. He says he can withstand the poison, fight what's happening to him.

Is there anything you can do for Shade, Morrigan? I'm so afraid for him."

"I might be able to help if we were somewhere wholesome, with sunlight and grass and clean water. But here there is little I can do, Rowen. With each passing moment this place falls further under the shadow. And if Shade comes with us deeper into Malabron's domain, his sickness will worsen and it will be much harder for him to resist. You and Will must be on your guard at all times."

"On our guard? You mean you think Shade would . . ."

"It is very likely he will turn against you. I have seen the power of Malabron overthrow other brave hearts and minds. It is what happened to Lotan, after all."

"Shade wouldn't . . . he could never . . ." But Rowen faltered. She could not deny what her sight had shown her.

"You spoke last night of the thread your grandmother gave you," Morrigan said. "May I see it?"

Rowen nodded. She took out the tiny ball of shimmering golden thread and handed it to the Shee woman. Morrigan examined it in silence for a long time.

"This is finer than any thread I've ever worked with," she said with admiration.

"You're a weaver, too?" Rowen asked.

"I was before my people left their home by the sea and became wanderers. The very last thing I wove was a tapestry telling of the battles the Shee fought against the Night King. I was so certain of our victory. And proud of my skill in weaving. As if the work I was doing at my loom was somehow as important as the fighting and dying that others were doing in my name."

"What happened to your tapestry? Did it survive?"

"I left it when my brother and I fled with the others. I suppose it burned along with everything else."

"I've never woven anything," Rowen said. "I never learned how. Maybe you should have this instead of me. You might be able to understand how to use it."

Morrigan gazed at the gleaming ball of thread as if considering Rowen's offer. Then she shook her head and handed the thread back to Rowen.

"I have never seen anything like this. The power in it is deep, beyond my understanding. But I see a way that you could use it to protect us all from Shade when the time comes."

"How? You mean . . . ? Oh, no, Morrigan, I couldn't."

"Once bound, he would likely be unable to break such a thread."

"That's what Grandmother said: that once I wove with it, the thread could never be broken. I don't know why. But it can't be for this. Not to harm Shade. I'm supposed to help Fable with it somehow. I'm sure that's what Grandmother wanted."

"To help your people you must first find the Loremaster and then return home. You will not accomplish any of this if Shade turns against you. We must be ready to act, Rowen, when the time comes."

They did not speak again until Will and Shade returned. In his arms Will was carrying a bulging pillowcase, which he emptied on the bed nearest the door. Out fell a jumble of bottles and other objects, pouches or bags made of shiny, crinkly paper.

"I found a few things," he said. "Things we can eat. And bottled water. I don't know if it's enough, but it will help."

"There's food inside these?" Rowen asked skeptically, eyeing the strange pouches.

"Potato chips," Will answered, holding up a crinkly yellow bag. He tore it open and handed it to Rowen. A strong waft of oil and vinegar rose from the bag and her mouth began to water.

Will held up one of a pile of smaller packages with colourful lettering on them.

"These are candy bars," he said. "We should save them for the journey. They'll help keep us going when we get tired."

Last night Rowen had noticed a strange metal object sitting on a shelf by the door. It had a glass jug fitted into it, and several mugs and a basket of small paper packets beside it. Will went over to this device now and touched something on its side. A red light appeared.

"This still works," he said with a satisfied nod. He picked up the glass jug.

"What is it?" Rowen asked. "Does it make tea?"

"Something like that."

Rowen sat in one of the chairs and watched while Will set to work. He filled the jug with water from a tap in the other room, poured it into the device and put the jug back in its place. He opened one of the paper packets and put a small bag into a slot in the device, as well. A few moments later the device was hissing and burbling and a thin stream of amber liquid began to dribble into the jug. When the liquid stopped flowing, Will filled three mugs and added some sugar from another packet. He carefully handed one mug to Rowen and another to Morrigan.

"It's called coffee," he said in response to Rowen's doubtful look. "My dad drinks it all the time. I don't, usually, but it's better than nothing."

Rowen sniffed at the mug, took a tentative sip. The drink was bitter even with the sugar in it, but she felt it warm her and tilted the mug again for another sip.

"It's good," she said. "Not like tea, but good."

A shriek outside brought Rowen up out of her chair. She and Will moved closer together and joined Morrigan at the window. The public park lay below them.

"Malabron's creatures," Morrigan said. "They lurk in the trees down there. I have already shown them the folly of coming near the hotel or the camp. But they are many and they will not stay away forever."

"Can we hide from them?" Will asked dubiously.

"There is a way to hide in plain sight," Morrigan said. "We *will* march in, Will, just as you feared. With the shrowde to conceal me the creatures of the Shadow Realm will believe I am the Angel, returning to the Shadow Realm at last. They may wonder at Lotan's long absence, but few will openly challenge the Night King's messenger or dare to lay a hand on his prey."

"I see," Rowen said eagerly. "We'll be your captives."

"So it will appear to any who cross our path."

When they had finished the coffee and food, they made ready to leave. Morrigan went to the window that looked out over the camp, and Will and Rowen joined her.

"Will you say goodbye to them?" Rowen asked.

"If I did that, I would not be able to leave," Morrigan said. "They would plead with me to stay and I could not refuse. I have cast what charms of warding I know around the camp, but what matters more is that word has got around that this is a safe, protected place. The people of the camp will have some time before it becomes known that I am no longer here. Let us hope it is enough time."

They went downstairs to the lobby. Before they reached the doorway, Morrigan stopped and turned to Rowen.

"I will take the staff," she said. "And your sword, Will. Your packs, as well. The shrowde will keep them concealed for now. No prisoner would ever be permitted to enter the

Shadow Realm armed or carrying anything. If you are seen
with such things, it would only create suspicion."

Before she handed over the staff, Rowen opened the little
door of the lantern fixed to the top. Sputter, the wisp, pulsed
within, but more dimly than Rowen had ever seen him, as if
he had somehow understood where they were going.

"Maybe you should stay here, Sputter," she murmured,
regretting now that she had brought the wisp from one danger to an even worse one.

"It's best if he remains with us," Morrigan said. "We may
have need of him if we get separated."

After a moment Rowen reluctantly agreed. Leaving Sputter here alone would be like abandoning him and she could
not do that.

She held out the staff and her pack, and Will his pack and
sword, and the shrowde stretched out two tentacle-like arms
and took everything within itself. Rowen could not help but
shiver, remembering how she herself had been swallowed
up by the shrowde when the Angel found her and took her
captive. Inside the living white cloak she'd had the unsettling feeling that there was a vast nothingness all around her,
much deeper than the shrowde could possibly contain.

"Now, walk ahead of me, the two of you," Morrigan said.
"We will make it seem as if I am driving you on."

"Wouldn't the Angel bind our hands or something?" Will
asked. "It might look strange if we're allowed to walk freely."

"The Angel had no need of such bonds," Morrigan said.
"No one ever slipped out of his grasp—other than you,
Rowen."

Morrigan turned to Shade and seemed to be considering
something.

"I know what you see when you look at me," the wolf
said. "You see one who belongs where we are going."

"Walk by my side, Shade, as if you are my servant," she said. "This will give anyone who thinks to challenge us another reason to keep a distance."

With Rowen and Will in the lead, they stepped out through the shattered doorway and into the street. The rain had drawn off. Just as when they had first arrived, there was no one to be seen. They already knew which way they had to go and so they did not hesitate now but started off across the wet, silent street and through the gates of the park, where the leafless trees bent and swayed in the wind.

After they had gone a short distance, Rowen glanced back at the hotel. She could no longer see it through the dark tangle of the branches, which seemed to have knotted together like some hideous spider web.

They were in the Shadow Realm.

13

AS HE KNEW HE would be, Ammon Brax was summoned
at last by the Marshal.

The mage climbed the rising path of the grounds toward
the Gathering House, the citadel of the Errantry on Appleyard Hill. It was high summer and the apples were green
and growing on the trees, Brax noted with a kind of de-
tached surprise, as if it was strange that ordinary life was
still going on when so much had changed. At least for him.
He had little doubt about the reason he had been summoned by Lord Caliburn. Word had finally reached the
Marshal about the activities at the toyshop. So be it. The
word had come too late.

When he reached the doors, the sentries let him pass, and
he walked swiftly through the great hall, with its tapestries
of past knights-errant, trying not to show his haste.

Captain Thorne was standing in the shadow of a pillar, just outside the door to the Marshal's chamber. The sullen scowl on his face spoke plainly: Caliburn had found out what had been going on and Thorne had just been called to account for it.

"He knows," the captain said. "He's waiting for you."

In the man's tone Brax heard the hint of a challenge, though his eyes betrayed his fear. Thorne wanted to learn what his new master was going to do about the old one.

"Stay here," Brax said. "Make sure no one disturbs us." Brax knocked at the slightly open door. Just before he went in, he took a deep breath and composed his face into a look of grave concern.

The Marshal was studying a map that lay unrolled on his desk. He glanced up when Brax entered, and in the older man's eyes the mage saw what he had expected to: his welcome in Fable was at an end.

"Master Brax," the Marshal said coldly. "Thank you for coming."

"Your servant, my lord," Brax said.

"Yes. Well. We have much to discuss and I have little time. As you must know by now, the Nightbane massing beyond our borders are not the only enemy we're facing."

"I've heard the report of these armoured fetches, my lord, yes. Grave news."

"The latest reckoning from our scouts says that these . . . *things* will reach the Bourne within five days."

Five days, thought Brax with a surge of fear and excitement. So little time left to gain mastery of the secret he had uncovered. Yet if he succeeded, that army could be his. He was certain now the girl had entered the raincabinet with the boy and the wolf, but where they had gone he didn't yet know. So far he had only dared short forays into that shifting, disquieting nowhere, sensing he might become lost if he strayed too far or stayed too long. Yet from those brief visits he had already gained more power than he had ever wielded in all his life as a mage. It was just *there*, to be taken. It flowed into you. Just like water, as the verse had said. Why had Pendrake never wielded it?

"I am here to help, my lord," he said. "Rest assured I will do whatever I can to counter this threat."

"If there was ever a time we needed Nicholas Pendrake," Caliburn murmured, looking away. Then he turned a cold eye on the mage again. "But this is not why I called for you. A short time ago I spoke with the Loremaster's housekeeper, Edweth Little. She has caused quite a stir since she was brought to Appleyard, demanding to speak to me, but I had no time to see her until this morning."

Brax nodded. He took a step closer to the Marshal's desk.

"Of course," he said. "The poor woman was not happy about being evicted from her home. I understand her feelings, but we both know it was for her own safety."

"That may be, but Madam Little has made some troubling accusations about you, Master Brax."

Brax raised an eyebrow. "Has she indeed. Goodness, it appears I've made an enemy."

"She accused you of removing her and the Loremaster's granddaughter only so that you could gain access to Nicholas Pendrake's secrets."

Brax gave a casual shrug. "Madam Edweth is angry with me. I don't hold it against her. I'm only surprised she would resort to such wild stories."

"Are they wild stories?"

"Of course, my lord," Brax said with a smile carefully crafted to reveal both amusement and mild offence. He took a step closer to the desk. "Surely you can't think that—"

"I wasn't sure what to think, Master Brax, but just now I've been informed of some of your other activities. It appears you've been giving orders to the city guard."

"That is so. When I discovered that the girl had left Apple-yard, I told the sentries to be on the lookout for anyone of her description coming to or going from the city. She is in great danger and I was concerned about her. She's a headstrong child, and with her grandfather missing I had no idea what she might do.

"Then she returned, and brought Will Lightfoot and the wolf with her to the toyshop, but you didn't feel it necessary to inform me of the fact."

"I regret that, my lord. It was a . . . difficult situation. The girl brought someone who appeared to be Nicholas Pen-drake, but I suspected—"

"I've already heard the story from Captain Thorne," the Marshal said tersely. "Though he, like you, didn't think it worth bothering me about at the time. It was one of his own troopers who finally let me know what's been happening at the Loremaster's house. Who or what was this creature that took the form of Pendrake?"

"I am not certain, but rest assured I have rendered it harmless. It may even be dead."

"What about Pendrake's granddaughter and her friends? I'm told they're no longer in the toyshop."

"No, my lord, and I am not certain where they are, though I suspect the girl fled when she realized that the imposter was not really her grandfather. She may have gone looking for Master Pendrake again. I only hope no harm has come to her."

"I hope so, too, Master Brax. Though I have to wonder why the girl didn't turn to you for your help in all this. At any rate, I spoke with Thorne just now and he admitted to releasing the hogmen from custody and bringing them to the

toyshop in the dead of night, along with six Errantry troopers and a young woman from Skald whom you used as a
hostage—a *hostage*—to subdue this imposter. None of which
you felt necessary to inform me about yourself."

"My lord, if word were to get out about a shapeshifter at
large in Fable, it would spread fear at a time when we must
reassure people and keep order. Captain Thorne was only
doing what we thought best for the city."

"Or what you thought best for Ammon Brax. The fact remains that you have been giving orders and taking command of my men, and now I understand you're kept the
hogmen with you at the toyshop."

"The Marrowbone brothers are vile brutes, my lord, but
they have keen senses that I saw I could make use of in my
search," Brax said. "And for all we know, their presence near
Fable might have had something to do with the Loremaster's disappearance. It made sense to keep them near me
until I got to the bottom of all this."

"I'm told you promised the hogmen they would be set
free if they helped you. Is this true?"

"I told them what I thought would ensure their cooperation. Surely one doesn't have to honour a bargain with creatures like that."

"At Appleyard we stand by our word," the Marshal said
heatedly. "We don't make promises we have no intention of
keeping. The point is, Master Brax, you've apparently decided
your authority as head mage of Kyning Rore extends to the
Errantry. Let me assure you it does not. Where is the Skalding woman now?"

"I gave her leave to rejoin her people waiting outside the
walls, my lord, and I believe that is what she did."

"We shall see. I've sent a man to confirm that she's with
her friends. In the meantime, you do not 'give leave' in Fable,

sir. You do not remove prisoners from their cells and you do not conscript Errantry troopers for your own purposes."

"Lord Caliburn, rest assured I would never attempt to undermine your authority."

"You *have* undermined it, Master Brax. Quite successfully. It appears that Captain Thorne sees you as Fable's best hope in the coming conflict, and he's willing to keep secrets from me as a result. I don't know how you swayed the captain from his duty so easily, Brax, but the damage has been done. I've had to relieve Thorne of his command." The Marshal's face darkened. When he spoke again, his voice shook with barely suppressed rage. "I cannot lose good men at such a time and I will not tolerate anyone, not even the archmage of Kyning Rore, breeding mistrust and confusion among our ranks."

Brax bent his head as if the rebuke had struck home. He took another step closer to the desk, keenly aware that he had little time in which to act.

"Forgive me, my lord," he said. "It was wrong of me and it will not happen again."

"No, it will not. You will be allowed to return to the toy-shop under Errantry escort to gather your belongings, and then you will leave Fable and you will not return. Do you understand me, sir?"

Brax steeled himself. The time had come. Everything depended on what happened in the next few moments.

"I understand, my lord," he said in the most chastened voice he could muster. "And I deeply regret having lost your trust. But before I go, there is something you have not heard from the captain, a matter of the gravest concern, and I must speak of it."

Caliburn glared at the mage.

"Haven't you been listening, Master Brax? You are to leave this city. *Now*. Take whatever road will get you home to

Kyning Rore safely, but be gone by the evening bell. If you are not, I will have you marched out of here."

Brax quelled his fury. He had to remain calm and yet be ready to act without hesitation. He was not yet certain of his control over the fire and if he failed now, all he had gained might be put in jeopardy. But first he had to strike a blow with words that would throw the Marshal off his guard.

"So be it, my lord," he said, "but this is something you *must* hear. The safety of Fable depends on it."

It seemed the Marshal was about to erupt in further angry words, but he pursed his lips and nodded.

"Speak, then."

First Brax moved to the door and slowly, softly closed it. When he turned back, Caliburn was staring at him in disbelief. It was obviously no one's place but the Marshal's to decide when that door should be shut. Caliburn, however, chose to ignore the mage's latest breach.

"Well? I have no time."

"I hesitate to speak of this, my lord, knowing how deeply he is in your counsel—"

"Who do you mean? Enough games, man. Out with it."

The mage leaned across the desk. He pressed a hand to the front of his cloak. "While I was looking through the Loremaster's things, searching for any clue to where he might have been taken, I found something disturbing. Something that casts doubt on everything we think we know about Nicholas Pendrake."

The Marshal's eyes blazed. "Choose your next words with care, Master Brax."

Brax drew a breath that was heavy with the pain of what he had to reveal. "From what I have seen, there can be no doubt that the Loremaster, Nicholas Pendrake, is in league with the enemy. He staged his own abduction and he was behind the return of the imposter."

Caliburn shook his head slowly. The muscles in his jaw pulsed. "That cannot be. I have known Nicholas Pendrake since—"

"My lord, I have the *proof* of it here with me."

"What proof?" the Marshal growled. "What have you found?"

The moment had come. Caliburn was outraged now, his deepest trust shaken. He would not be thinking clearly. Brax slipped a hand into his cloak and withdrew a rolled-up tube of yellowed parchment.

"What is this?" Caliburn asked, scowling. He leaned forward across the desktop and thrust out his hand. His anger and doubt were strong enough now that all other thoughts had fled.

Just as Brax was placing the scroll in the Marshal's palm, with a lightning-fast movement he dropped the paper and clutched Caliburn's wrist. The Marshal tried to wrench his hand away, but Brax held fast. The tips of his fingers, digging into the older man's flesh, glowed from within like ampoules of green glass.

"What are you doing?" Caliburn demanded furiously, and then his eyes went unfocused. He swayed forward, and set his other hand on the desktop to keep from falling. "How dare . . . you . . ." he said thickly, labouring to get the words out. He looked to the door and opened his mouth as if to shout for help, but no sound came out.

"Do not struggle, my lord," Brax said. "It might kill you and neither of us wants that."

Caliburn's hand went to his throat. He was gasping now for air.

"Madam Little was correct," Brax said, watching the Marshal's eyes. "I *was* searching for the Loremaster's secrets, and I found one of them. The only one that matters, as it turns out. It's the power to remake the way things are. To mould the world and men's minds. Now please sit, for we have much to discuss and very little time."

Brax let go of the Marshal's wrist. The skin was bone white where the mage's hand had gripped it. Caliburn gazed dully at his own hand, then stepped backward and sat down heavily in his chair. He stared up at the mage, stunned, uncomprehending.

Brax picked the scroll up off the desk where it had fallen and unrolled it. The parchment was blank.

"Sleight of hand," he murmured. "It still has its uses."

He set the scroll on the desk, then leaned close to the seated Marshal and lowered his voice to an urgent whisper.

"Are you listening, my lord?" Brax said. "It's very important that you listen to me now. For the sake of Fable and the Errantry."

The Marshal blinked and struggled to focus on the mage's face. "What's happened?" he muttered. "Brax, I can't seem to remember . . ."

"You have been poisoned, my lord. I am here to help."

The Marshal shook his head slowly. His eyes searched the room wildly and then focused again on Brax.

"You," he growled. "No, it was you."

"It was the *enemy*," Brax said sharply. "You have to listen, or Fable is doomed. The enemy *out there* has done this to you. The enemy who will destroy everything and everyone you love unless we act now. You must listen. Something was slipped into your food or drink. Do you remember?"

"Remember? No. Who would have . . .?"

"You don't have long, my lord. Neither does Fable. You must listen to me or all is lost. Soon the poison will make you weak and feverish. You will be unable to carry out your duties. The Errantry will be leaderless, which *cannot* happen now with the enemy already here in Fable. If the Loremaster has turned against us, then no one is safe, no one is to be trusted. But we can still save this city, you and I. First you must invoke martial law. Shut the gates, keep everyone at home. No public gatherings. Then assign me my own company of troopers. I must have the freedom and authority I need to root out any other traitors."

"Give you . . ." the Marshal muttered, struggling to rise. "No, wait. I must call the duty sergeant."

"You're confused, my lord. It's the poison working in you, clouding your thoughts. You've forgotten you summoned me when the enemy first struck. Think. *Remember.* You called for me. That's why I'm here. You knew that only I can stave off disaster. I am here to help, but you must concentrate and do as I tell you—or all is lost."

The mage spread his hand across the map on the Marshal's desk. Dark blotches began to appear at the edges of the parchment, as if fire was eating at it from underneath, though no flames appeared. The dark blotches grew in size and began to move inward, toward the city drawn in careful ink lines at the centre of the map.

"Our enemies are closing in on us," Brax said. "They've already wormed their way into the city. They've corrupted those we've held in trust. They've even reached you, my lord. We must act now, for the sake of the Errantry. For Fable."

"For Fable." The Marshal nodded, gazing in horror at the map. "We must keep the people safe. The enemy is—" He broke off and held up his arm. The band of white flesh around his wrist was fading now but still visible. "*No*," he rasped. "No. It was *you*."

The Marshal locked eyes with the mage and Brax recoiled at the fury he saw there. The man was resisting the power of the werefire with everything he had. His white-knuckled fists shook and the sweat stood out on his brow. It was a terrible thing to see, and as Brax watched the struggle, he felt an unexpected admiration for the man. Caliburn was stronger than he would ever have imagined. How he fought to hold on to the truth, to all that was slipping away from him.

During his time in Fable, Brax had taken care to learn all he could about the senior commanders of the Errantry. Now he saw he would have to put some of what he'd discovered about the Marshal's past to use. He leaned close to Caliburn and put a hand gently on his shoulder.

"Don't forget what happened, my lord," Brax said softly, "to your son."

Lord Caliburn's gaze turned inward. His face crumpled with pain. The words, Brax saw with satisfaction, had dealt the final blow. The Marshal's son, he'd learned, had died trying to prevent an outlaw named Corr Madoc from stealing Errantry horses.

"You weren't vigilant enough then," Brax said, his voice low and almost soothing. "You didn't see the true danger until it was too late. That must not happen again. The Errantry needs you to be strong, now more than ever. We must make sure that no more young men die needlessly."

The Marshal passed a hand over his eyes. He looked up again at the mage, but now his gaze was beseeching. "Help me, Brax," he said. "They're all depending on me. What . . . what should I do?"

"First, my lord, before anything else you must sign an order invoking martial law in Fable and throughout the Bourne."

"The Errantry . . . has never . . . ruled by force of arms."

"The threat to the Bourne demands it. There is no other way. And Thorne must be restored to his command and appointed acting Marshal before the poison incapacitates you any further. Thorne is one of the few we can still trust."

"Yes. Emric. He must take command when I . . . when I am no longer able."

"Sign the orders, my lord, and Thorne and I will see to what must be done. As you know, I am the only one who can detect any imposters that remain among us. I must have the power to apprehend and detain them. The men Captain Thorne hand-picked to guard the toyshop have already proven their loyalty, but I suspect I will need more. Perhaps many more."

"Yes, that is best," the Marshal said quickly. "You'll have the men you require. We must unmask the traitors and root them out. Find them, Master Brax."

"Sign the orders, my lord, and I will get to work at once. Oh, and there is one other matter. Something has to be done about those who've been sowing fear and making false accusations about me. It's regrettable, but Pendrake's housekeeper must be locked up and kept under guard to stop her from spreading any more lies. For all we know she may be in league with the false loremaster."

None of what Brax had just said, which moments ago would have goaded Caliburn to outrage, had roused him to the slightest protest. The mage permitted himself a smile. The Errantry would be his. He would have the time he desperately needed and no one could hinder him. After that the rest of Fable would follow swiftly. Let the Nightbane come. Let the opposing armies batter each other to dust on the field. By then he would be the master of the secret fire. He would remake this city into a stronghold, a fastness, a fortress to withstand anything. The warriors of a thousand banners would bend to his will. In time he would reach out to command armies, nations. Even perhaps to force a truce with the power of the Shadow Realm.

He came out of his thoughts to find the Marshal waiting, like an obedient underling, for him to speak again.

Brax slid the blank scroll across the desk. "Sign the orders, my lord."

The Marshal nodded. He dipped a quill pen in its inkwell and began to write on the parchment in a slow, laboured hand. "This will . . . give you the powers you need, Master Brax."

When he had finished he pressed the silver ring on his finger into the parchment, then rolled it up and handed it back to the mage. Then the Marshal dully, unsteadily climbed to his feet. His face was ashen and he looked haggard and ancient, a very different man from the one who had confronted the mage only moments ago.

"You were right, Master Brax. The poison is doing its work. I ask you, tell no one about this. It would only spread fear. No, we will say I have taken ill, that is all. Thorne will assume command for the time being. You will be his second, with emergency powers to arrest and detain as you judge necessary. I am counting on you to rid Fable of its enemies and keep the people safe."

"My lord, I am yours to command."

"Yes. Good. Now . . ."

Once more the Marshal seemed to be searching for words. He looked again at the mage, his gaze suddenly sharp and penetrating, and for a dreadful moment Brax thought that Caliburn was about to remember what had really happened here. There would no choice this time but to strike a killing blow and deal with the consequences. With this paper in his hand he already had what he needed. Brax readied himself, but then the older man's eyes clouded over again. He raised a trembling hand and placed it on the mage's shoulder.

"Thank you, Master Brax. You're a true friend to Fable."

The mage smiled warmly and gripped the Marshal's shoulder in turn. "I am your friend, as well, my lord. Never doubt it. And I beg you, call me Ammon."

14

ALL THE NIGHTBANE THAT Finn and the doctor came across were already dead, but Alazar would not give up the search.

From the upper parapet, where the skyships had landed, they found their way to the level beneath by way of a wide stone ramp probably meant for the passage of wheeled vehicles as well as foot traffic. The ramp led into a long vaulted hall with passageways branching out in every direction. Deep slits in the roof, lined with some kind of reflective metal, let in shafts of sunlight, but most of the passageways beyond the hall were dark. Finn borrowed a lantern from one of the Stormriders and he and the doctor set out to explore.

With growing awe Finn began to grasp the true size and extent of Adamant. Each circle, as the Ironwise called the descending levels, was fronted by a broad curving platform that formed an outer walkway. Set in from this projecting walkway

were the inner chambers, halls, vaults and connecting passageways of that circle. Each level thus extended deep into the rock,
so that the city was actually much larger and far wider in circumference than it appeared from the central well.

Adamant had a system of pipes, sluices and troughs to
deliver water up and down the levels. Some of the troughs
fed into basins that lined the outer walkways. Cold, fresh
water still trickled into a few of these basins. The water was
in great demand by both Ironwise and Stormriders, as the
city was stifling hot and everyone's throat soon parched in
the dry, smoky air.

Realizing how easy it would be to get lost in such a place,
Finn and the doctor did not venture far from the hall in the
first circle. Each chamber they explored they marked with a
piece of chalk to help them keep their bearings and find their
way back.

The farther they went, the fewer bodies they found. Finn
was startled to discover that not all the dead were mordog or
other races of Nightbane. There were a few men among
them. "This army isn't all that different from your brother's,"
the doctor observed as he examined one of these dead men.
Finn had been thinking much the same thing.

They moved on and in the adjoining chamber they found
a party of Nonn's delvers clearing rubble from a partially
collapsed passageway. The dwarfs warned them away, telling them that Nonn had forbidden anyone to venture farther
into the city until they had made sure it was safe.

They returned to the pier and enlisted four Stormriders
to come back with them to the rooms they had already visited
and load the dead bodies on a wheeled wooden cart they
had found in one of the passages. Alazar's plan was to burn
the corpses, but Kern appeared as they were dragging the cart
into an open court for that purpose. He quickly took in the

situation and ordered the Stormriders to throw the bodies into the central well.

"We're not holding any funerals, healer," Kern said calmly when Alazar protested. "This will send a message to the rest of the Nightbane still hiding in the city."

The doctor objected angrily, but Corr's lieutenant could not be swayed. The Nightbane bodies were lugged to the edge of the parapet and tossed over like so much trash. Kern watched without expression, then made a note in the little book he carried with him and strode away.

Finn and the doctor returned to the pier exhausted, grimy and sombre in mood. They found that Corr's men had been busy setting up tents near the ships and stringing lanterns between the masts. By now it was late afternoon and the light was failing. As the last of the sunlight climbed slowly up the walls, the circles of the city seemed to recede farther into the depths.

Finn and the doctor sat with a party of Stormriders near a cooking fire that had been set up in a large brazier. Neither had any desire to return to the flagship where Corr had set up his command post. None of the men they sat with had *gaal* pouches on their belts, and Finn remembered that the rank and file in the Sky Lord's army were not given their own supply. But some kind of warm brew was being ladled out into cups and from the steam Finn caught a scent he knew very well by now. There was fever iron in the drink. He felt his craving clutch at him again, but he refused a cup when it was offered to him because he feared his hand would shake from eagerness. He wondered how many of these men knew what means had been used to save his arm.

The Stormrider who sat next to Finn, a squat, broad-shouldered man with a squashed nose whom Finn remembered seeing at the defence of the breach, gave him the last piece of the loaf that was being handed around. Finn told him to keep it for himself, but the man insisted and Finn at last yielded.

"How's your wound, young master?" the man asked him in a kindly voice.

"Better, thank you," Finn said, unpleasantly surprised to be called *master*. As Corr's brother he received respect and honour that he hadn't earned and didn't want. Then he had a sudden thought. "At the breach there was a Stormrider younger than me, with dark hair. He died just before the battle ended."

"I think you mean Ferret, my lord. That's what we called him, anyhow. Never heard if he had another name or where he was from. He wasn't with us long."

"I wonder how old he was," Finn murmured. He saw again the dead, blank, dust-caked face. It could have been anyone's face. His own.

"I couldn't tell you, young master." The man shrugged and then grinned toothlessly. "Not really sure what age I am myself."

Someone shouted a warning and the Stormriders jumped quickly to their feet. Several fetches, faint and almost shapeless, hovered at the edge of the pier, nearly invisible under the glare of the lanterns. Their eyes were like dark holes in smoke. One of the Stormriders stepped forward and threw an empty stoneware tankard at them. It passed right through one of the fetches, who seemed utterly unaware of it.

"Damned rotting ghosts," the man growled. "What do they want?"

"They hang about like the fumes from your backside, Borlak," someone said to the man who had thrown the tankard. "That's probably what they are."

The other Stormriders laughed uproariously. The man named Borlak growled and drew his knife. He approached the dim shapes, brandishing his blade and shouting crude curses. The fetches drifted away and then faded from sight in the darkness.

The men returned to the warmth and light of the brazier and sat back down, laughing and joking at the easy victory, although Finn could tell they were rattled and on edge. Despite what he had told the old Stormrider, his wound had begun to burn and throb again some time ago. When the pain had become nearly intolerable, he excused himself on the pretext of getting water from one of the basins.

Once away from the light and voices he took a small pinch of the *gaal*. The bitter grains melted quickly on his tongue and in a matter of moments the pain lessened and his head seemed to clear. Finn drew a deep breath and closed his eyes, then opened them again.

It was not enough. Nowhere near enough.

As if observing someone else's actions, he watched his hand reach into the pouch, lift out a larger pinch of the coarse black grains and place them on his tongue. In no time at all the quickening fire was hurrying through his veins.

He was not dead yet. That dust-caked face was someone else's, not his.

"Finn?"

It was Doctor Alazar. He was looking on with his brow furrowed in concern.

"Are you all right?"

"I am what my brother has made me, Doctor," Finn said with a cold smile. The icy fire was rushing through him now, and as the pain vanished, so did his heavy thoughts. Everything stood out sharp and brilliant and clear, as though carved of diamond. He could sense the fetches hovering just beyond the reach of the torchlight. He could hear their faint, hollow voices and feel their hunger for the *gaal*. If he wished

it, they would bow to his will as they had Corr's. So would
the men sitting around the brazier joking with one another,
pretending their thoughts weren't on the fever iron and how
to get more of it. He was the Sky Lord's brother, after all. He
could have as much of the *gaal* as he wished. He could command it. And then he could command them.

"Only a few grains, Finn," Alazar said. "Any more than
that . . ."

Finn gritted his teeth. He was tired of the older man's
warnings. Tired of him always nearby, watching, offering his
useless advice.

He thrust the pouch toward Alazar. "Here, Doctor. If
you're going to tell me how to take my medicine, you should
try it for yourself, don't you think? Go ahead. Just a few
grains should be enough."

"If someone drinks poison, Finn, you can't help him by
drinking it yourself."

"That's a fine saying. You should set it down in your journal if you haven't already."

Finn returned to the circle around the brazier and so did
Alazar, though they sat apart and did not speak. After some
time the group of Stormriders broke up: some went on sentry duty and others to their tents to sleep. A messenger sent
by Corr found Finn and informed him there was a cabin on
the flagship set aside for the doctor and him, but they both
chose to stay where they were. Alazar sat down against a
broken piece of stone, and with his cloak for a blanket he
soon fell sleep. Finn knew he should do likewise, but with
the *gaal* racing through him he was no longer tired. All he
could do was sit and watch the dying coals in the brazier and
wait for morning.

He sat like this as the night crawled past, alert and ready
to spring to his feet every time he heard the echoing clatter

of a stone falling somewhere in the city. There were other sounds, too: the night wind moaning as it slipped through some narrow passageway, and faint skitterings and rustlings of rats or other unseen creatures. The effects of the *gaal* began to wear off, the pain was increasing, and his hand went to the pocket that held the pouch.

Just then a Stormrider came with a torch to say that both Finn and the doctor were wanted urgently on the flagship. Quickly, without speaking, he and Alazar washed their faces in a basin and hurried up the gangplank.

Corr was in his low-ceilinged cabin at the aft of the ship. One of Kern's patrols had caught one of a party of Nightbane they had encountered on a lower circle. Corr's chart table and its chair had been pushed to one side of the cabin and the prisoner was half sitting, half sprawled against the port bulkhead as if he had been thrown there, his hands bound before him with thick rope. Corr, Kern and several other Stormriders stood over him.

The captured Nightbane was wearing the tattered and bloody remains of a suit of dark red leather armour, but his head was bare and Finn saw with surprise that he was very young. His face was long and sharp boned, his slate-coloured skin burnished with sweat. One of his eyes was swollen almost shut and an ugly purple bruise discoloured his jaw.

"I sent for Nonn, as well," Corr said when he saw Finn and the doctor. "Where is he?"

"I don't know, my lord," Kern said. "My men haven't seen him for hours."

"We found a live one at last," Corr said to Finn, gesturing to the prisoner. "He wasn't as fast on his feet as his friends."

The Nightbane's unswollen eye went to Corr and stayed fixed on him.

"Did your men do this to him?" Alazar demanded.

"Why do you ask, Doctor?" Corr inquired. "Perhaps you'd like to carry out the interrogation in a gentler fashion."

"Why did you send for me?"

"He's lost a lot of blood. For a young one he put up quite a struggle before my men were able to subdue him. It's a shame we don't have any of his kind fighting for us."

"Let me look at him, please."

At a nod from Corr, Grath and the other Stormriders stepped aside. Alazar moved forward and knelt beside the Nightbane, who stared at him out of his good eye without expression.

"I am a doctor," Alazar said, then turned to Corr. "Does he speak our language?"

"He understands enough," Corr said.

The doctor turned back to the prisoner and cautiously lifted aside the torn edge of his bloodied leather breastplate. The Nightbane let out a hiss and stiffened.

"I will need some clean water and bandages," Alazar said over his shoulder.

"I don't want him back on his feet and dancing a jig, Doctor," Corr said. "Just stop the leak if you can. That's all I ask."

"I'll do my best, but his life may get saved by accident," Alazar shot back. "I hope that won't inconvenience you."

Corr glowered at the doctor's back, then nodded to one of the Stormriders who hurried out and returned a short time later with some torn strips of cloth and a small metal basin. Doctor Alazar wet one of the strips of cloth and dabbed at the Nightbane's wound, eliciting more hisses and grunts of pain. He dug in his bag, extracted a small glass jar of some strong-smelling unguent and applied it to the wound, then covered it with one of the torn cloths. The Nightbane did not watch what the doctor was doing but continued to stare at Corr.

When Alazar was finished, he faced Corr. "I've done what I can, but"—he glanced at the Nightbane, whose good eye was still fixed on Corr—"he doesn't have long."

"Then I'll ask you to step out of the way, Doctor, and let us finish."

"Wait," Alazar said, holding up a hand. He stood, came close to Corr and spoke in a low voice so that the Nightbane would not hear. "Let me try. Let me speak to him before you start in again. I know what race he belongs to. It may help, since a beating clearly won't."

Kern, who had stepped forward, glanced doubtfully at his commander. Corr frowned, then nodded.

"Very well, Doctor. Be sure to ask him how many Nightbane are left in the city."

Alazar turned back to the prisoner and crouched beside him. "You can understand me?" he asked. The Nightbane shifted his head to look at the doctor.

"Some," the Nightbane said in a weak, rasping voice. "I know you say—I die soon."

"Yes," Alazar said. "I am sorry."

The Nightbane shook his head. "Not sorry. If not dying . . . I kill you."

"You're Valkai, aren't you?"

"Of the Bloodlands. Yes. My people . . . never conquered." A tear slid from his eye.

"Your country is very far away," the doctor said. "How did you come to be here?"

"Doctor," Corr said in a warning tone, but both Alazar and the Nightbane ignored him.

"Lord of fetches called us in dreams," the Valkai said, and now there was more energy in his voice. "Visions. Called us here. To fight."

"You're talking about Malabron."

"The Deliverer. He who made all things. He was cast out, but he will rule all again. Our vision-seekers warned us of one who will rise against him. A demon child who will destroy everything. Destroy Valkai. Unless we fight."

"A demon child?"

"A girl. Hair like fire. She is young but powerful. Your kind are protecting her. Fools. If she is not stopped, she destroy you, too. She . . . tear the world apart."

"Rowen," Finn breathed as understanding struck him. "He's talking about Rowen."

"Who is this child?" Alazar asked the prisoner. "What is her name?"

"Doctor!" Corr said.

The Valkai warrior did not answer. He was shaking now, gulping and gasping for breath.

Corr stepped closer. "What about Adamant?" he barked at the Valkai. "Why was the fetch army sent out now? How many Nightbane are left in the city?"

The Valkai turned toward Corr, his mouth twisting into what looked like a smile of bitter amusement. Then he hunched forward, coughing. Dark blood spattered the planks.

"Where have the armoured fetches gone?" the doctor asked.

The Valkai lifted his head. "The iron warriors, they go to crush the destroyer's city. They find her and kill her. Nothing can stop them."

"How many of you are left in Adamant!" Corr roared.

The Valkai didn't seem to hear him. His good eye searched out the doctor's face and then slowly closed. His head slumped forward.

"Dead," Kern said matter-of-factly. "We've learned nothing."

Alazar touched two fingers to the Valkai's neck. "He's still alive. For now," he said, his eyes smouldering. "Let me fetch one of Nonn's healers. They have more knowledge of the Nightbane races than I do. Perhaps they can—"

Corr raised a hand to silence the doctor. "There's no time for that." He faced one of the Stormriders. "Give him the *gaal*. That should wake him up. And then, Doctor, we'll let my men finish the questioning, if you don't mind."

The Stormrider brought out a small iron box and began shaking the black grains from it into a cup that stood on Corr's chart table.

"In his state the *gaal* will kill him all the faster," Alazar said. "Finn, tell him. This is wrong."

"Giving him the *gaal* won't make any difference, Corr," Finn said. He found himself unable to take his eyes off the iron box in the Stormrider's hand. There was so much more of the powder in it than in his pouch, and he had already used more than half of what he'd been given. "Fable is where the real war is being fought. This battle doesn't matter anymore."

Corr stared hard at Finn, then he turned to Alazar.

"Your pointless questions may have cost us all dearly," Corr said. "I'm beginning to wonder whose side you're really on. Now, move out of the way."

The Stormrider with the *gaal* had poured water from a jug into the cup and was stirring it with the blade of his knife. Alazar watched him, then slowly he packed up his bag and began to clean his hands in the basin.

The Stormrider with the cup crouched in front of the prisoner. Another Stormrider forced open the Valkai's mouth while the one with the cup poured in its contents. The Valkai choked and sputtered, then began to thrash and struggle as the Stormriders held him down. When the cup was empty, the Valkai's good eye opened again and he lay panting and looking around at his captors in terror.

Corr crouched in front of the Valkai. "Listen to me," he said in a low, quiet voice. "You are going to die one way or another. The doctor says your lifeblood is slipping away. If you prefer to die as a warrior, on your feet in combat with one of my men, I will grant you that. But first you will answer my questions."

The Valkai stared back at Corr, his lips trembling.

"What do you say?" Corr asked.

But now the Valkai's eyes were on the planks at his feet. Then Finn felt it: a shaking underneath him as if the ship was shuddering into motion. Corr stood up quickly. The panes in the window were shivering and then there came a deep echoing *boom* from outside, followed by another and another . . . as if immense blocks of stone were falling somewhere in the city and bringing others down with them. The booming sounds finally merged into one long rumble they could feel as a tremor in the ship's timbers, and then there was silence and all was still again. Sawdust sifted down from the planks overhead.

"What in all the hells was that?" one of the Stormriders muttered.

Corr touched one of the beams above him, then looked out the cabin window. He turned to his lieutenant. "Go and see what's happened."

Kern nodded and strode out of the cabin.

"Nonn's people must have triggered one of their own traps by accident," Alazar said. "Or one of the tunnels they were excavating may have collapsed. I should go and—"

"Wait here, Doctor," Corr said, raising a hand. "We'll know soon enough."

"Corr," Finn said, "the Valkai was talking about Rowen, Master Pendrake's granddaughter. I'm sure of it."

"A girl with hair the colour of fire," Corr said, shaking his head. "You really believe this child is the *destroyer* he was babbling about?"

"It has to be her," Finn said. So much that he had only dimly understood was now falling into place. "Their vision-seeker said the girl was young and didn't know her own power yet. That's why Malabron was searching for Rowen when Will first came to the Realm. Because she is a descendant of the Stewards. She has their power to see into things, into the way things are, and shape them, Corr. Change them. I don't understand it, but I've witnessed it. The Loremaster returned to Fable to prepare Rowen for what only *she* could do: to stand against the Night King. The fetch host was sent out before everything was ready because of Rowen. Something she's done—or is going to do—has forced Malabron to act."

"Listen to what you're saying, brother," Corr said. "This *child* has the power to challenge the master of the fetches? No, it's nonsense. And anyhow, I put no faith in the prophecies of some mad Nightbane bone-caster. It doesn't matter why they abandoned this city. The fact is that they did. And this place, with its *gaal*, this is real. This is what I have faith in."

"You . . . should . . . not," the Valkai gasped out, and they saw he was grinning, his bloody teeth bared.

"You finally have something to say?" Corr growled, crouching in front of the prisoner.

"Your friends, the mole people . . . they are not your friends."

"You mean the dwarfs? What do you know about them?"

"This is their city. They want it back for themselves. Not for you."

"I know that much already, my friend—"

He broke off as Kern reappeared, with Grath following quickly after, ducking his head to enter the cabin. The mordog's hair and clothing were grey with dust, but his eyes blazed furiously.

"Nonn and his people," Grath snarled. "They're gone."

"They sealed off the lower circles, my lord," Kern said. "They've fled down to the mines, all of them, with their tools and supplies."

"That treacherous old snake," Grath roared. "He wants all the iron for himself. Always has. I knew he couldn't be trusted."

"All the passageways are sealed off?" Corr asked.

"All the ones we know of," Kern said. "Somehow they brought down stone slabs that have blocked every doorway and stair to the lower levels."

"Some of my men were trapped on the other side when the slabs came down," Grath said. "We heard them shouting to us at first and then nothing. We tried moving the slabs, but . . ."

He trailed off, then slammed his huge fist against the bulkhead.

"They were planning this all along," the mordog seethed. "My lord, we can take one of the ships down into the lower circles. We can find them and blast them with the lightning. Bury them under the rubble of their own city."

"And bury the mines, too?" Corr said. "No, we'll keep the ships here for now. There may be another way. Where is the golem?"

"He's with my company," Kern said. "One of my men was pinned under falling rock and the golem lifted it off him."

"Is your man badly hurt?" Alazar asked.

"His leg is broken."

Corr turned to the Stormrider who had given the Valkai the *gaal*. "Keep at him. Send word immediately if he talks. Kern, Grath, with me. Finn and Alazar, you, too."

With that Corr strode out of the cabin, followed by Finn, the doctor and the two lieutenants. They hurried down the gangplank and set off across the pier. A choking pall of dust hung in the air, and soon they were coughing and covering their mouths with their hands.

Corr had nearly reached the wide end of the pier when he stopped and raised his head as if he had caught a sound. A moment later they all heard it: a faint, slow metallic clanking from somewhere far below. Everyone went still and listened. The clanking grew louder, then was abruptly drowned out by a great, echoing roar. It sounded as if fire-breathing dragons were at war with each other somewhere in the deepest chambers of the city.

"What in all the hells is that now?" Grath breathed.

"They've relit the forges," Corr said. "They'll be smelting the ore soon."

"Bastards," Grath said. "May they burn themselves up like the black-hearted devils they are."

The roaring subsided but did not entirely fade away. It went on, a deep throbbing pulse that sounded to Finn like the beating of an enormous heart.

"What can they do with the *gaal* even if they mine it?" Alazar asked. "They've trapped themselves down there."

Corr shook his head. "You can be sure Nonn knows of other ways out of this city. He does nothing recklessly. And he's made an alliance with the Nightbane if that Valkai is to be believed. This was all carefully planned."

"We must take a ship down there, my lord," Grath said. "Let's strike back, before they strengthen their defences."

Corr glanced at Kern. The lieutenant, impassive as always, shook his head.

"The ships would be difficult to manoeuvre in the lower circles, and they would be vulnerable to attack," he said. "Nonn will have thought of all this."

"You're right," Corr said. "Nonn will be expecting us to strike back with the ships. He'll have something ready and waiting for them. No, we won't fall into another trap. First I want to see what the golem can do about these slabs."

Grath led the way down the nearest of the ramps. The passage at the bottom was blocked with a huge slab of gleaming black stone. The golem stood in front of it, as impassive as ever. A pile of broken stone from a partially collapsed pillar lay in a heap nearby, and the injured Stormrider sat near it, propped against the wall and watched over by two of his comrades.

Alazar hurried over to the wounded man and began to tend to him.

Corr stepped up to the golem. "The disc," he said. He gazed at the golem's feet. The black disc of fever iron that had compelled the golem to obey Corr's commands lay in pieces in the dust.

"Nonn . . . he broke it," Grath said. "It must have been him. Why would he do it? He could've taken the golem with him."

"Ord wouldn't obey him," Corr said, "so Nonn had to break the stone to keep the golem from raising the slabs."

"Then this thing is useless now," the mordog lieutenant snarled. He cuffed the towering clay man with the back of his massive hand. Ord did not move in the slightest, but Grath grimaced and clenched his hand in pain.

"If there are any Nightbane still about," he muttered, "and they find out the golem doesn't work anymore . . ."

"Enough," Corr said. He touched the polished surface of the stone slab, then stepped back. For a moment there was a blank look on his face. Then he turned to Finn.

"Brother, the green stone from my ring. Do you still have it?"

Finn nodded. Corr had given him the ring the day he left the Bourne. Years later, when Finn and his friends encountered the golem by chance in the Bog of Mool, Finn had set the ring's green stone in the clay man's forehead and it had sent him marching across the Realm in search of Corr. Master Pendrake had guessed that the stone had infused the golem with Finn's own greatest desire: to find his brother.

Reluctantly Finn slipped his hand into the inner pocket of his Errantry tunic and brought out the stone.

"Put it in his forehead, Finn," Corr said eagerly. "It worked before. It brought him here to me."

Finn looked down at the gleaming green stone in his palm. He thought of his friends in Fable and the armoured fetches drawing closer to them with every passing hour.

"What are you waiting for?" Corr said. "Do it."

Finn reached up and set the stone into the shallow round cavity in the golem's forehead. Immediately the clay man shuddered from head to toe. Finn stepped back, as did Grath and Corr. Ord's head turned slowly and his eyes, two grey featureless orbs, fixed on Finn.

"Ord," Corr said, stepping forward again. "Lift the slab."

The golem did not move at the sound of Corr's voice.

"Ord, do you hear me? You serve the Sky Lord. Obey my command."

The golem did not stir. Its seemingly sightless eyes remained on Finn.

"What's wrong with him?" Grath muttered. "What did that damned dwarf do to him?"

"This isn't Nonn's doing," Finn said. "Ord won't listen to you, Corr, because you gave *me* the ring. The ring is mine. The golem was obeying my wishes when it went in search of you. And now it will obey my wishes again."

He turned to the golem. "Ord," he said, "lift one of those stones."

With a low, grinding sound the golem bent at the waist, grasped one of the broken chunks of the pillar on the chamber floor and lifted it easily.

"Now crush it," Finn said. "Crush the stone."

There was no visible sign of effort as the golem's thick fingers closed around the stone. A moment later it shattered with a loud crack and a plume of dust. The bits and pieces clattered to the floor.

"I didn't know he could do *that*," Grath murmured in awe.

"It looks like you're right, brother," Corr said. "But this can work, too. If he'll do only what you tell him, Finn, then tell him to obey *me* in all things. As long as the order comes from you, he'll have to listen."

Finn gazed at the towering clay figure before him. He saw himself returning to Fable with the golem, saw Ord plowing through the ranks of the Nightbane. The Errantry's enemies would break like water on a stone. If he could only get there in time.

"Finn," Corr said urgently. "Command him."

Finn drew a deep breath. He felt distant from what was going on around him, as if seeing it all from a great height. His blood was on fire, but his heart was like ice in his chest. He knew what he had to do.

"The golem is no longer yours, Corr," he said. "I'm returning to Fable and taking Ord with me."

15

AFTER EDWETH HAD SPOKEN with Lord Caliburn about the mage, she had expected to be shown back to the toyshop. The Marshal had taken her accusations seriously. And so she hadn't complained when she was escorted once again to the room they were keeping her in at Appleyard. She was prepared to wait there patiently until word was brought to her that Brax had been evicted from the toyshop and she would be allowed to return.

She was all the more surprised, then, when the guards who came to fetch her led her down into the lower levels of the Gathering House to a smaller room with a locked door. The furnishings were even sparser than in the room she had just left. There was a low, narrow cot and one wooden chair, and to her horror nothing but a bucket to relieve herself in. The tiny, high window was barred. She had been so certain the Marshal would help her that it took her longer than it should have to understand that this was a cell and she was now a prisoner.

She had called the guards who locked her in every name she could think of and demanded to see the Marshal, but no one answered her. The door was locked and she was alone.

Hours went by. A guard arrived with a meal for her, but he made no response to her angry questions, as if he couldn't even hear her.

So she was left with her questions, which went around and around in her mind without answers. Why had the Marshal done this to her? What was going on at the toyshop? And where in the world was Rowen?

Night fell and then dawn came, and she was still alone in the cell. Edweth had slept a little, but not deeply. She was sitting on the edge of the cot when she heard a key in the door.

As the wildman stooped and entered, Edweth stood, her hands clenched, ready to defend herself. She had never spoken with Balor Gruff and had only seen him from a distance on rare occasions. With his outlandish features and hulking size he had always looked ridiculously out of place to her, as if someone had mistakenly draped an Errantry cloak over a cave bear.

They stood looking at each other uneasily, and then Balor made a stiff bow. She noticed he had a dark cloak under one arm.

"Madam Edweth," he said in a booming voice as the door was shutting behind him. "I am here on the acting Marshal's orders, to ask you some further questions about the events in the toyshop."

"*Acting* Marshal?" Edweth said with a start. "What's happened to Lord Caliburn?"

"He's been taken ill, ma'am," Balor said, moving closer and lowering his voice. "Captain Thorne is in charge of the Errantry for the time being."

"Thorne?" Edweth exclaimed. "That man is a far cry from—" Then she bit her lip and glared at the wildman. He stepped closer still, almost bending over her, and she drew back in fright. Balor lowered his voice to a near whisper and said, "Rowen sent me."

Edweth stared fearfully into Balor's eyes.

"Rowen?" she whispered back. "When did you see her? Is she . . ."

"When I left Rowen and Will, they were all right. They had Shade with them and . . . well, it's quite a story, ma'am, and I promise to tell you everything in full when there's time for it, but you must listen to me now. I believe you are in danger here and I am going to take you somewhere safe."

"Danger *here*?" Edweth said incredulously. "They may have locked me up to keep me quiet, Mister Gruff, but this is still Fable. There's been some misunderstanding, that's all—"

"Much has changed in a short time," Balor broke in urgently. "Lord Caliburn sent me to Annen Bawn with pressing news and I've only just returned. Otherwise I would have come to you sooner, as Rowen asked me to. But while I was gone, that scheming mage Ammon Brax seized power somehow. He's got his own personal company of Errantry troopers doing his bidding, and it seems even Thorne is answering to him now. The city is under martial law, and you're not the only one who's been arrested for defying the mage. I'm telling you on my oath as a knight-errant that even Appleyard is no longer safe. I have to get you out of here before worse happens."

Edweth studied the wildman's face for a long moment

and then she nodded. With her quick but rarely mistaken judgment she had decided to trust him.

"How will you convince them to let me out?" she asked, glancing at the door. "And even if you do, they'll suspect you, too, and lock you up."

"Leave that to me, ma'am. Now, I need you to put on this cloak and cover your face."

When she was ready, Balor turned and hammered on the door. It opened almost immediately and the sentry stood aside to let them pass without a word.

"I'm shutting the cell door now," Balor said to the sentry.

"Right, Balor," said the sentry. "And when I look in on the prisoner later, I will discover to my utter surprise that she's not there."

"You will," Balor said. "Hard to believe she managed to vanish from inside a locked cell without any help."

"No help at all," the sentry said with a wink at Edweth. "I didn't see you or anyone else down here. Must be more of that dark sorcery going on in Fable these days. Who knows what could happen next."

"We have to keep sharp," Balor said, and he nodded to the sentry and escorted Edweth up the stairs and out of Appleyard.

"I hope we're going straight to the toyshop, Mister Gruff," Edweth said when they had left Appleyard and Balor had steered her into a narrow alley. "I have some choice words for Master Brax."

Balor made a rumbling noise. "Er, that would not be wise."

"Why not? I'm not afraid of that phony, that charlatan—"

Balor fixed her with a sombre look that made her stop in her tracks.

"As I said, things have changed, ma'am."

She glanced around them then, and noticed for the first time that she hadn't seen any people on the streets. No carriages rattling past, no hawkers and sellers crying out their wares.

"Curfew," Balor said. "And no gatherings of three or more persons permitted at any time of day. There's been some panic, you see, about the coming battle, and the odd things that have been happening in Fable, thanks to the mage. There's been some rioting and looting, and Brax has the Errantry busy quelling what he says is a treasonous uprising. It's no such thing. It's just folk scared and angry, that's all."

"Brax did this? All the more reason, then, to hurry to the toyshop and put a stop—"

"We're not going there, ma'am, and I'll tell you why. When I got back from Annen Bawn, no one would tell me where you were," he said, "so I went to the toyshop. I wanted to make sure Rowen and her friends weren't Brax's prisoners. And I'd found out that Rowen's friend, Freya of Skald, had been taken there, as well. Ma'am, you wouldn't recognize the place anymore."

"What do you mean, Mister Gruff? Oh, I knew that horrible man would make a mess of things."

"It's much worse than that, I'm sorry to tell you. The shop, even the street it's on, has changed. I don't visit Pluvius Lane very often, but I know for certain it never looked the way it does now, all narrow and dark as a tunnel and cold, too. And all the other shops are gone."

"Gone? What do you mean?"

"Walled up. Nothing but blank stone from one end of the lane to the other."

"How can that be? I was there only two days ago, and Old Gimlet, the tailor, and Kyndle, the bookbinder . . . everyone was open for business."

"Well, they're gone now. Folk who live nearby say they

heard screams for help coming from *inside* the walls. Screams growing fainter, and then nothing."

Edweth put a hand over her mouth.

"It's the mage's doing," Balor went on with a grim scowl. "That's the only explanation. When I got to the end of the lane, I thought I must be in the wrong place because I didn't recognize the toyshop. Somehow Brax has turned the master's house into a fortress. The walls are covered in some kind of dark green stone, the windows are all gone, the door is barred with iron and half a dozen armed Errantry troopers are standing guard in front of it. And I don't know how to describe it, but there's something about the place now that . . . well, it just felt *wrong* to me, wrong in my bones. I've been to a lot of haunted and sorcerous places in my travels, ma'am, and I've learned to trust my bones when they shiver like that."

"Oh, no, no," Edweth said under her breath. "He must have found . . ."

She gave Balor an alarmed glance, as if she had said too much. The wildman shook his head.

"Ma'am, I know that Rowen had to get into the toyshop in order to go someplace else," he said, "and that's all I know. The rest is none of my business. But I'm pretty sure Rowen made it to wherever she was going and Brax does not have her. When I got to the door the sentries stopped me, so I made up some story about delivering a message from Captain Thorne that was for the mage's ears only. Then the door opened a crack and one of those filthy hogmen poked his head out. The scum was wearing the dress uniform of a knight-errant, with a lot of ridiculous gold trim and braid added on. I got pretty steamed when I saw that, but I kept the lid on and told him I'd come on Errantry business to fetch the Skalding woman back to Appleyard. I thought I'd start with Freya, you see, in the hope he'd let something slip. And he did. For an instant he had this panicked look, then he sneered and said that the mage released prisoners to no one, and I knew then that Freya had been in their clutches and escaped somehow and it was the hogmen's fault. Then he seemed to think of something, and he asked me if I was the scout who'd arrived two mornings ago with the news of the fetch host. Brax must've learned I was with Rowen when she got back to Fable, and he was wanting to question me about her. That means he doesn't know where she is, and he's worried she'll suddenly show up and ruin his plans. So now I think that Rowen succeeded at whatever she went back to the toyshop to do, and she's safely out of his reach. At least, it's what I hope."

"I'm sure you're right, Mister Gruff," Edweth said. "But please go on."

"Well, before I could say another word, the hogman's face got all crafty-looking and he told me to come inside while he fetched Master Brax. I hope you won't consider me a coward, ma'am, but I peeked through that doorway into what had once been the master's toyshop and I didn't see a front hall. I saw . . . well, I saw the throat of a beast. And I knew that if I set foot in there, I wouldn't be coming back out—I couldn't hope to stop the mage in his own lair, not by myself. I also knew that Rowen and Freya were safe, and that's what I'd come to find out, so I called the hogman some fitting names and hurried back to Appleyard. And then I found out where they were holding you. I had to keep my promise to Rowen, you see."

"You were right not to challenge Brax, Mister Gruff, and I consider you very brave indeed, but that wicked man must be removed from the toyshop, somehow. If he's been stealing the master's secrets, there's no telling what terrible things he might do."

"Or has already done. The way the Marshal took ill so suddenly . . ."

"Oh, do you think the mage *poisoned* him?"

"That or did something to his mind. The last orders he gave to Thorne, well, they were not like the Marshal at all. Anyhow, I'm not finished with Brax or those hogmen yet. And there are still plenty of us in the Errantry who haven't signed on with the new management, let me tell you. We're working on some plans of our own."

"I'm glad to hear it, Mister Gruff. And when the time comes, you can count me among you."

"I've no doubt of that, ma'am. But in the meantime I've thought of a place where we can keep you safely out of sight. Have you ever been to the Golden Goose?"

A short time later, Edweth and the wildman were at the bridge across the canal that ran through Fable. On the bridge itself was the Inn of the Golden Goose.

"You're bringing me here?" Edweth said doubtfully. "I'm grateful for your pains, Mister Gruff, but this must be the busiest spot in all of Fable. There are travellers and foreigners and other riff-raff coming and going at all hours."

"Yes, and that's why this is the last place anyone would think to search for you, ma'am, if you see what I mean. Besides, I've got a good friend at the Goose. He may look after an inn where people talk each other's heads off, but *he* knows how to keep quiet when need be."

A troubled look crossed Edweth's face.

"If you mean the innkeeper, Miles Plunkett, I can tell you right now he is not going to want me under his roof."

Balor looked startled.

"Why not, ma'am?"

"We had a falling-out some years ago, and I don't think he would care to see my face again. You see, one evening Rowen slipped out of the toyshop—she was only eight, the headstrong thing—and I finally found her here at the inn, perched on a chair by the fire with her legs dangling, telling stories to a roomful of strangers and vagabonds of the road. And Mister Plunkett hadn't done a thing about it. He hadn't sent word that she was at the inn, or had her escorted home. In fact, I found him sitting there with all the other idlers and ne'er-do-wells, just listening to the child spin some far-fetched tale. And, Mister Gruff, I told him in no uncertain terms what I thought of him, and we have never spoken since."

"I'm sure Miles has forgotten all about it, ma'am," Balor said. "I can tell you on my honour he's never had anything but words of praise for you."

Edweth gave the wildman a sharp glance, but she took a deep breath and followed him up into the inn.

The rickety stairs rose steeply to a small door set into an arch in the brickwork of the wall. Balor knocked softly and after a few moments they heard a bolt being drawn back and the door opened soundlessly, as if it had just been oiled before they arrived.

The innkeeper, Miles Plunkett, stood before them, a checked dishcloth over his shoulder and a lit candle lantern in his hand. He was a broad-shouldered, thickset man with a balding head and calloused red hands.

"Balor," he said in a low, urgent voice. "Good to see you. And you, too, ma'am," he added, nodding stiffly in Edweth's direction, though he wouldn't look directly at her.

"Mister Plunkett," Edweth said curtly, eyeing the many stains on the innkeeper's apron.

Plunkett beckoned them inside and they found themselves in an unlit corridor cluttered with chairs, crates, casks, and other odds and ends stacked along its sides.

"Come this way—quickly," Plunkett said, raising the lantern, "and watch your step, please."

They followed him along the dark corridor and up another flight of stairs to a small door that he unlocked with one of the many keys on the ring on his belt. The door creaked open into a long, low-ceilinged storeroom filled with more crates and squat barrels. He led them down the one narrow passage that was left, Balor having to bend nearly double to avoid bumping his head on the roof beams. At the far end of the room Plunkett reached up and pulled on some sort of hidden catch, which brought a concealed flight of steps swivelling noiselessly down on metal brackets.

"If you would, ma'am," the innkeeper said.

And Edweth, followed by Balor and Plunkett, climbed the steps. They led to a room that must have been right under the roof of the inn. It had a steeply sloping ceiling with a small round window set in the roof. In the room were a small, bare table and an armchair made of braided willow wands, a cot in one corner and even more crates stacked against the far wall. Old books stood leaning against each other in a row on a shelf. Cobwebs hung in every corner and there was the dusty, close smell of a room that had not been used or aired for a long time.

Edweth looked around and sniffed.

"I realize it's not the most pleasant accommodation, ma'am," Plunkett said, passing his dishcloth quickly over the layer of dust on the table, "but no one will be likely to look for you here. In fact, I'm the only person at the inn who knows about this place."

"Why do you keep a room like this, Mister Plunkett?" Edweth asked, unable to keep a note of suspicion out of her voice.

"It was for my Nell," the innkeeper said, resting a hand on the back of the armchair. "She was a lighthouse keeper's daughter, Nell was, you see, and she used to talk about how lovely it would be to have a place where she could climb up out of the noise and bustle and have a wider view of the world. So I built this for her. She could be alone here, knit, read her books, and no one would bother her. She was a great one for the books, my Nell. Smart as a whip, not like me at all. Can't have been easy for her, being an innkeeper's wife when she could have been, I don't know, a scholar or a doctor . . ."

He trailed off with a worried glance at Edweth as if he might have said too much.

"Forgive me, Mister Plunkett, my question was rude," Edweth said, her face flushed. "I did not know your wife well, but I was sorry to hear of her passing."

The innkeeper at last summoned the courage to look Edweth in the eye.

"Thank you, ma'am," he said huskily, and cleared his throat. "Balor's told me what's been happening, Master Pendrake going missing and the mage taking over the toyshop and all of that. It got my blood up, I can tell you. And now the girl off on her own somewhere." He shook his head slowly. "Those were always the best evenings around here, when the toymaker dropped by with Rowen and they'd tell their stories. The best evenings. I hope they'll both get back to you safe and sound, ma'am."

For once, Edweth seemed unable to speak. Her eyes welled with tears.

"There isn't much that someone like me can do to help make things right," the innkeeper went on quickly, "but as I told Balor, you're welcome to stay as long as need be, ma'am, and not a soul will hear of it from Miles Plunkett. I know the room's in poor shape and I haven't kept it as I should have, what with things always so busy."

"The room will be just fine, Mister Plunkett," Edweth

said firmly. She stepped under the sloped ceiling, glanced out the little window, then faced the innkeeper again. "Thank you for your kindness. And I wanted to tell you . . . about that time I found Rowen here in your common room and . . . well, I said some things to you."

The innkeeper flushed to the very crown of his balding head. He wrung the dishcloth in his hands.

"I don't remember a word of it, ma'am," he replied. "That is to say, I'm sure I deserved every word of it, even though I've forgotten what you . . . what I mean is . . ." He frowned, clearly desperate for a way out of the tangle he'd gotten himself into. Then he cleared his throat again and squared his shoulders. "What I mean to say is that Nicholas Pendrake is a good friend, and no harm would ever come to Rowen here, not while the name of Plunkett is on that sign above the door."

"I know that, Mister Plunkett," Edweth said warmly. "Let us both put all of it behind us for good, shall we? And please, call me Edweth."

"I will, if you'll call me Miles."

They smiled at each other and shook hands. Balor stared slack-jawed from one to the other as if witness to the most unlikely thing he'd ever seen in his life. And now both Edweth and the innkeeper seemed unable to find words, so the wildman came to their rescue.

"You're a good man, Miles, to do this," Balor said.

"It's what anyone would do," the innkeeper mumbled. "Just watch out for yourself, my friend, and stay alive." He turned to Edweth. "I have to be leaving now, ma'am, before everything goes to rack and ruin downstairs. But I'll come see you, I promise, when I have any news."

"Thank you, Miles."

With that he made an awkward bow and ducked out the low doorway.

"He's so kind," Edweth said to Balor when the innkeeper had gone, and her face glowed with more than its usual colour. "I'm sorry to say I had Miles Plunkett all wrong."

"He's one of the best, ma'am," the wildman said. "But I must leave now, too, before I'm missed. Will you be all right here?"

"Of course, Balor," she said, and to the wildman's surprise she rose up on tiptoe and kissed his cheek. "But what are you going to do? What if they find out you were the one who got me out of Appleyard?"

Balor grinned.

"You let me worry about that, ma'am. I've got some other friends to see. Brax may think he's running things now, but he doesn't have everyone in his pocket, not yet."

16

THEY HAD LEFT THE last of the working streetlights long behind.

Rowen, Will, Morrigan and Shade walked in an unending grey half-light through the silent city. Heaps of broken wood and masonry, bent and twisted scraps of metal and shards of glass were scattered everywhere. It was impossible to take more than a few steps without having to climb over or go around some obstacle. Fallen electrical wires lay across their path like dead snakes. They passed mounds of refuse and many abandoned vehicles, including a car that stood in the middle of a pool of oily water, on fire. Black smoke billowed from its burning interior. Apart from that, nothing moved. The air was cold down at the bottom of the city's canyons, and still and dry as dead bone.

This place had been well named, Rowen thought. It really was like being inside a shadow.

She remembered a trip she had taken with her grandfather a few summers before to visit the old cottage at Blue Hill. They'd reached the farm just as the sun was setting. One moment they had been walking through a warm, buzzing, honey-coloured world, and then the sun had dropped below the brow of the hill and they were inside its shadow. The air was suddenly chilled and damp, as if they had plunged under water, and it was then she'd understood that a shadow wasn't just a flat patch of darkness stretched over the ground. A shadow was a place itself. It had height and depth. When you passed into the shadow of something, you really were inside it. Except that here, in the Night King's realm, there was no hill casting the shadow. It was simply everywhere, a part of this dead world that never changed. And it was not a cool, welcome twilight like the one they'd entered that evening at Blue Hill, but an unrelenting ashen greyness, neither day nor night, which seemed to have seeped inside things themselves.

It was seeping into her, as well. She could feel it in the heaviness of her steps and the bleak thoughts she couldn't help thinking. When they had stopped to rest in the concealment of an underpass, Will had handed her one of the bottles of water he'd brought from the hotel. He'd given her a smile, too, to cheer her, but a voice in her head said, *How much longer will he stay with you before he gives up and runs away? He's just a weak, scared boy. He can't help you anyway.*

She'd looked away, ashamed of herself. Where had these hateful thoughts come from? It was the shadow. What was happening to Shade was happening to all of them, she was sure, if more slowly.

Since leaving the hotel they had seen no one, and now

even the distant roar of traffic had faded away, leaving only
the sound of their own footsteps as they slowly picked their
way through the rubble-choked streets. From time to time they
did hear faint rustlings and skitterings that might have been
rats or other small creatures scuttling through the debris. And
yet Rowen was sure that these were not the only inhabitants
of this city. The farther they walked, the more certain she
was they were being watched by hidden eyes.

"Do you feel it?" she whispered to Will when her eyes
caught his.

He nodded without speaking and she knew he understood what she meant.

If Morrigan sensed the watchers, she, too, gave no sign.
Rowen and Will were walking ahead of her, as they had
been since leaving the hotel, and it often happened that they
were forced to stop when they came to a crossroads and were
uncertain which way to proceed. Then Morrigan would
quickly indicate with a nod which path to take and they
would go on. She kept her face hidden under her hood at all
times, so that Rowen could not help but wonder if their
friend really was still concealed within the silent white
shrowde that covered her.

For his part Shade stayed close to Morrigan, but sometimes, at a word from her, he would trot on ahead to scout
beyond some obstacle or around a corner and then report
back to her whether the way was clear. He kept his distance
from Rowen and Will, not even glancing at them when he
passed them on the way back to Morrigan from his scouting
forays. Since he was playing the part of the Angel's servant, it
made sense for him to ignore them like this, but Rowen had
the troubling feeling that Shade's avoidance was more than an
act. Ever since they set foot in the Shadow Realm, the wolf
had grown increasingly agitated and withdrawn. His hackles

were up all the time now. Rowen's heart went out to the wolf as he struggled. She wanted to speak to Shade, find some comforting words if she could, but she dared not drop her own role as a prisoner even for a moment.

Both Rowen and Will had lost any sense for how long they had been walking. The dead sky showed no familiar signs, no lengthening shadows or changing light to mark the passing hours. The fact that they did not speak to each other only added to the feeling that they were wandering in a timeless dream. If anything changed at all, it was the buildings themselves, which looked more shattered and desolate the farther they walked, until they could hardly be distinguished from the heaps of rubble that filled the streets. The pavement under their feet also grew increasingly broken and heaved up, so that eventually they were doing as much scrambling up and down as walking. This slowed them considerably when they had to take a meandering path around some crevasse in the roadway or carefully pick their way over ridges of loose, fallen stone or brick. Morrigan and the shrowde moved easily over the rougher terrain, but Rowen and Will were soon breathing hard and stumbling from weariness. Even Shade seemed to be having difficulty.

At last, when Rowen felt she could barely take another step, Morrigan called a halt. She told them that back in the world they knew it was now night. They had been walking for many hours and it was time to rest.

Shade nosed around and found a shelter that would offer some concealment. It was a small dome-roofed structure that jutted out from the front of a blackened, burned-out building.

"What sort of place was this before?" Rowen wondered.

"It looks like a ticket booth for a theatre," Will said.

She wasn't sure what that meant, but there was enough room inside the booth for both Will and her to lie down on the paper-strewn floor with their heads on their packs. Rowen and Will shared some of the food and water they had brought from the hotel, while Shade hunkered down outside the door and Morrigan stood at the building's entrance. Neither she nor the wolf appeared to need sleep, but Rowen was exhausted and she soon found herself nodding off.

She was jolted awake several times out of frightening dreams to find Will asleep beside her, breathing softly, and Shade in the doorway, his eyes open and observant. Each time, she wondered whether she was really awake or still dreaming. Maybe in this place, she thought, they were the same thing.

She awoke once to find Shade watching her.

"You cannot sleep, Rowen of Blue Hill?"

"Not very well, Shade. I'm sorry if I'm disturbing you."

"You are not. It is this place, as you warned me."

To her shock she saw that he was shivering, as if cold or feverish. It was the sickness in him. It was worse than she had thought.

"Shade, you don't have to stay here," Rowen said, her heart breaking as she understood how much the wolf was suffering. "You could go back. To someplace with sunlight and trees. We have Morrigan and the shrowde with us now. You don't have to protect us any longer. I'm sure Will would say the same."

"It is too late for that. I have come too far already."

"What do you mean?"

"I told you how the Stewards found me dying in the forest and gave me life and speech. They made of me something that no wild creature had ever been. I think now that they should not have done this."

"You can't believe that, Shade. What would have happened to Will if he hadn't met you? He would never have made it home. Probably none of us would have."

"I am glad that Will Lightfoot found his home again. And I have lived much longer and travelled farther than any of my kind. That is good. But those years are all here. They've gathered in my bones and I feel them now. The wolf in me is dying, Rowen of Blue Hill. When he is gone, what remains will be only what belongs here, in this place."

"If you went back to Fable," Rowen said, struggling to hold back her tears, "maybe you could sleep again, like you did before Will found you. Then you could restore yourself."

The wolf lowered his great head.

"What I wish," he said, "is to be only *wolf* again. To run and hunt with the pack. To live the swift seasons of my kind and then die as a wolf dies, returning my flesh to the earth. But the First Ones are gone. They cannot take back the gift they gave me."

For the first time since she had known Shade, Rowen heard pain and even despair in the wolf's voice.

"We'll find my grandfather soon, I'm sure of it," she said desperately. "Then we can get back home and he can help you. He'll know how to heal you. He must know. Then maybe someday you can go back to where you came from and—"

"I will not be going back. You know this. You warned me of it. And now I know it, too."

"I saw what would happen if you stayed with us, Shade. That doesn't mean it *will* happen. It doesn't have to. You can get away from here. You can change what I saw. No path has to be the only one."

"Look at me, Rowen of Blue Hill. Speak the truth. Will the one you know as Shade ever leave here?"

Rowen gazed into the wolf's eyes and he into hers. Tears slid down her cheeks.

"No, Shade," she whispered. "You won't."

"I see what you see," the wolf said. "The other wolf, the one that belongs here, is running toward me faster than I can flee him. Even if I turned back now, he would be here before I could reach the border of this realm. Soon I will give in and he will walk in this flesh. To kill him you must kill me. And I would let you."

"Shade, no," Rowen gasped, "we could never—"

"I understand that I cannot force such a choice on you or Will Lightfoot. So I will leave. Soon, before that other one arrives. But I will not try to return to where I came from. Instead I will find some way to die here. Then I can be sure you will be safe from me. I only ask you, Rowen of Blue Hill, not to speak of this to Will Lightfoot."

"I won't—I promise. But, Shade, there is another way. The thread my grandmother gave me. It's stronger than anything. Morrigan has seen it and she agrees. I can use it to bind you and even you couldn't break it. If you're bound, then you— then *he*—won't be able to hurt anyone. Only . . ."

She hesitated.

"Only, I will be helpless," Shade said.

"Yes. The things that live here, they'll find you and . . ."

She couldn't finish.

"If it comes to that, it will not be me they find," Shade said. "Yes, you are right, Rowen of Blue Hill. This is a better way and I will submit to it. Rest now. I am still here, the Shade you know, for the time being. We will speak again of the thread."

Later Morrigan roused them. It was time to move on. Rowen watched Will go over to Shade and place his hand on the wolf's matted fur. She knew he could see what she had seen earlier, how much Shade was suffering, but she was certain he hadn't overheard their conversation.

Will looked up at her then and gave her a smile. *He wouldn't have dared come this far if it wasn't for the wolf*, she thought, and then she was shocked at herself once more. She turned away.

Morrigan stood beside her, her face cloaked in the hood of the shrowde as always.

"If you cannot do as he asks when the time is at hand," the Shee woman said, "the shrowde and I will kill him, as he wishes. If we can."

They walked on and once more time didn't seem to pass in this lifeless city. As he had the previous day, Shade scouted ahead often and returned to report what he had found. On one of his forays the wolf was gone for a long time, and Rowen began to think the worst. But at last Shade reappeared from around a corner, moving quickly, at a near run. Rowen froze in fear as the great beast bounded toward her. But Shade swept past her and Will and drew to a halt beside Morrigan.

In a voice just loud enough for Rowen and Will to hear, Shade said, "There are creatures ahead. Of a kind I have never met before. I found a place where we can watch them without being seen."

"Take us there," Morrigan said, and without another word the wolf loped back the way he had come.

They followed. Around the corner the street ran out from between the looming towers into an open space bordered by long, low buildings and paved with flagstones. A kind of city square, Rowen thought, much like those in Fable.

Shade did not stop but set out across the square and they hurried after him. Keeping up with the wolf was easier now because the pavement here was clear of the broken stonework, cables and glass that had made their passage difficult. Yet the square was littered with other things: scraps of paper,

a worn leather shoe, a cane, a book splayed open, a child's
cloth doll with the stuffing falling out. Rowen had the unsettling feeling that a great crowd of people had filled this
square only moments earlier, just before she and the others
arrived here.

Then it struck her: she could not see or hear them. The
people who had left these belongings or were forced to abandon them should have been causing a clamour in her story-
sight. But there was no more story in these objects. Or almost
none. She pressed her hands to her temples, struggling to find
a thread of who they were and what had become of them.

Will noticed her distress.

"What is it?" he whispered. They were in an open space,
far from any buildings or places of concealment, so it seemed
safe to talk.

"I can't hear them," she whispered back.

"Who?"

"There were people here, Will. I should be able to hear and
see them. See the paths that brought them here, and where
they went. But there's nothing."

"What happened here, Morrigan?" Will said. "What is
this place?"

"These streets were once part of a city in the Perilous
Realm," Morrigan said. "Not long ago, by the look of it. Then
its people fell under the shadow, either willingly or by force.
That is how Malabron's empire of fear grows. My people
have seen it happen too often already. Those who once called
this place home have become fetches by now. They will have
scattered aimlessly through the Shadow Realm, forgetting
who they were."

They were nearing the far end of the square, where the
enclosing buildings drew closer again. The street rose steeply
beyond the square, climbing to a bridge or overpass supported

by massive concrete pillars that arched over another paved roadway running beneath it. Or the bridge would have done so, but when they reached the middle of the great span, they discovered that the other half of the arch had collapsed into the road below. Iron reinforcing rods jutted out into the gap like exposed roots.

The bridge had a low parapet on either side and Shade led them to the one on the right. Part of it had crumbled away, and through one V-shaped gap they were able to look out over the expanse of the city, which stretched away into a dim grey haze. Beyond the bridge they could see what Rowen first thought to be great heaps and ridges and drifts of rubble, some rising like hills almost to the tops of the highest buildings. Then she caught the sour stench of damp and decay and she looked more closely. With a shock she realized that these heaps and ridges were not rubble but great mounds of cast-off objects like the belongings in the square.

What lay before them was a sprawling wilderness of trash.

And it was silent. No threads of story came or went from any of it.

Several times as a girl she had gone to Fable's trash midden with her friends. It was not a place they were supposed to go and so it was irresistible to them. But the first time she'd seen the pit where people threw out what they didn't want anymore she had been speechless. She'd hated the stink of it, too, and the feeling that her own things—toys and books and everything else—would end up here sooner or later, discarded and forgotten. Now it came to her that the Shadow Realm was a trash heap itself, only a thousand times larger and more hopeless.

"It must go on for miles," Will said under his breath.

"Untold miles," Morrigan confirmed. "When a part of the Realm falls to the shadow, all that lives *becomes* the shadow.

Becomes part of Malabron's nightmare. Everything else is left to rot."

"All the people," Rowen breathed. "The stories. Just . . . *gone*. No threads. Nothing."

She saw Fable in her thoughts then. Just like this. The streets she knew. The Golden Goose. The toyshop. Nothing but rubble and trash. Lifeless. It would happen soon, and there was nothing she could do to stop it.

Shade growled and hunkered down below the rim of the parapet.

"There they are," he said.

They all looked out to see a dark, distant figure on one of the hills of trash. The figure was hunched over and moving slowly across the slope, stopping now and then to scrabble in the refuse as if searching for something. A moment later Rowen caught sight of a second hunched figure not far from the first and then a third, climbing another of the trash heaps. All three of these beings, whatever they were, seemed to be dressed in the same grey rags, but it was hard to make out any other features or to be sure of their size.

Just then one of the three figures stood upright and gave a rasping shriek. For one terrifying instant Rowen thought they had been discovered, but the figure bent again and began digging furiously in the hillside. The other two straightened and began to make their way over the mounds toward the first.

"What are they?" Will whispered.

"Harrowers," Morrigan said. "The scavengers of the Shadow Realm. They search for anything or anyone that might still have a little life, a little of the fathomless fire, and they feed on it."

Rowen stared at the digging harrower and then she looked away, not wanting to see what it had found.

"It's horrible," she said, shaking her head. "They're horrible."

"We have no choice but to go that way, into their midst," Morrigan said. "The shrowde says it is the swiftest path to the heart of the Shadow Realm."

"What if the harrowers see us?" Will asked.

"They fear the Angel, as most of Malabron's slaves do," Morrigan said. "He was once their overseer and treated them cruelly. The sight of the shrowde should be enough to keep them at a distance."

They turned from the parapet and descended the bridge, following Shade. Once at the bottom again they set out across a broad pavement toward the trash mounds. The stench was far worse here than it had been above. It assaulted them so powerfully that both Rowen and Will had to stop several times to retch before they could go on.

There was a path of sorts through the mounds. It was a narrow, trampled trail, slick with some kind of foul-smelling oily leakage. They climbed in single file, going slowly to avoid slipping. The heaped garbage rose steeply on either side of them like the walls of a canyon.

The path made the walking easier, but Rowen guessed that the trail had been made by the harrowers themselves in their comings and goings, and that meant it was all the more likely they would meet one of these creatures.

Sure enough, they had not gone far when Shade stiffened and his ears flicked forward.

"What is it?" Will whispered.

Shade sniffed the air. "Something very close, coming this way," he said. "Two creatures. Maybe more."

They turned to Morrigan.

"We keep going," she said.

Around a corner the path fell away steeply. Below them

lay a pool of dark, stagnant water with a long, warped wooden board thrown across it. At the top of the slope Morrigan halted and Rowen looked up to see two figures working their way down another mound of trash on the far side of the pool. They could not be seen clearly at this distance and in the gloom, but to Rowen they appeared to be much larger than even Morrigan in the shrowde cloak. Both were hunched over, like the three they had watched on the bridge.

The nearest of the harrowers began scrabbling at the trash with its bony arms, and with a shiver of horror Will realized it was digging through the carcass of some large dead animal. As it dug, it was singing to itself in a cracked, tuneless voice.

> *Run mouse run,*
> *your tale is done.*
> *Tale is done, and all is one.*
> *We his eyes, we his teeth.*
> *We his claws for catching meat.*
> *Catch you, claw you.*
> *Nibble you, gnaw you.*
> *Tale is done and all is one.*
> *All is one, and one is—*

The creature abruptly raised its head and sniffed the air. Will dimly made out glittering black eyes in a bone-white face. The creature hissed at its companion, who also raised its head and then hunkered down, making a low moaning sound.

"They've seen us," Rowen whispered, her voice tight with fear.

"Do not speak, whatever happens," Morrigan ordered. "You must act as if you have no will or hope left."

She led the way down the slope. At the bottom she stepped onto the board that lay over the pool and stood there, silently watching the approach of the two harrowers. Will moved close to Rowen. She saw him put his hand to where his sword would have hung. Morrigan had taken it, she remembered. They were supposed to be defenceless prisoners.

The creatures descended the trash mound toward them, and now Rowen could see the harrowers more clearly. They were terrifying. The nearest, the one who had been singing, had the head of an old woman, with hanging hanks of clotted, filthy hair, but her body was grotesquely elongated, her arms bony and bent weirdly at the wrists, like those of a praying mantis, so that when she wasn't using them to dig in the trash her huge clawed hands lay tucked inward. She wore a tattered grey robe; a pair of gnarled, clawed feet poked out from the draggling hem. Even hunched over she was well above six feet tall, her hideous head straining forward on a stalk-like neck, her small eyes squinting, searching.

The other harrower was naked except for a filthy rag that served as a loincloth. A thickly braided rope was knotted around its neck. This harrower climbed down toward them more slowly, moving its head from side to side as it came, and then Rowen saw the reason for its caution. It had no eyes. On its broad, flat face there were only two tiny slits for nostrils and a round, many-fanged hole for a mouth, like a lamprey eel's, that opened and closed with a wet sucking sound. The rope around its neck, Rowen realized, was a noose.

The harrowers drew closer, and Rowen felt their malice and hunger like a blow. She knew that if not for Morrigan in the shrowde cloak, these creatures would rend her and Will in an instant. Absolute, blind terror seized hold of her then and shook her so that she could barely stand. She was about to run—she couldn't help herself.

Then she felt Will's hand slip into hers and grip it, and she knew he felt the same. There was the smallest comfort in that. Just enough.

The thing with an old woman's face bowed low, her bony hands scraping across the trash. A stench came off her of excrement and rot.

"Prince of Hunger," the harrower croaked, lowering her head slightly but keeping her sunken eyes fixed on Morrigan.

The harrower was frightened herself, Rowen now saw, but there was also a cold, measuring appraisal in her look, as if she were watching the one she believed to be Lotan for any sign of weakness.

"Mighty Angel. What joy for us unworthy ones. We did not know if we would see you again."

Her darting eyes fell on Rowen, Will and then Shade. Morrigan did not reply to the harrower's greeting, and Rowen could not help but glance up at her, suddenly afraid that she would reveal herself.

When Morrigan did not speak right away, the harrower moved closer and raised her head slightly higher.

"Lord?" she said. "How may we serve you?"

At last a voice came from the shrowde, and it was not Morrigan's.

"Dirge. The Angel remembers you. Return to your task."

Or it was still Morrigan's voice, Rowen thought, but it had changed almost beyond recognition, and sounded like a hiss of steam escaping from deep under the ground.

"We are humbled and thankful for your gracious notice, Mighty One," Dirge said, drawing closer but hunching over even more as she approached, so that she was nearly crawling by the time she reached the bottom of the trash heap. "And we rejoice, don't we, Gibbet, to see the Prince has returned at last."

The harrower with the eel's mouth let out a long bleat that sounded more like a cry of despair than one of joy. It raised its eyeless head and sniffed, its nostril-slits flaring.

"Why would you rejoice, Dirge?" Morrigan said. "You could not have doubted you would see me again."

"Mighty Angel, forgive the ignorance of the worthless," the creature called Dirge said, "but rumour reached us that you had been . . . *ended* in the Uneaten Lands. Now here you are, and we can scarce contain our happiness at finding that it is not true, that you are not ended, that it was only some hateful lie. Tell us how you escaped, for we always long to hear of your journeys, your victories. It is not our lot to venture into the Uneaten Lands, though we hear they are filled with spoils. With so many tasty things."

"The Angel cannot be ended, Dirge. You know that. Even to have such a thought is blasphemy."

"Oh, Great Prince," Dirge replied, cowering even lower. "Mighty One, we did not truly believe those wicked rumours. It is just that we . . . no, it was Gibbet who feared . . . if anything happened to you, not that it could, but—"

"Return to your work, harrowers. I have captives to be brought before the One."

Dirge bowed her head again, so low this time that her lank hair trailed in the pool.

"Pardon our babbling, Prince of Hunger," she said. "We did not know that these morsels were for the One. In our joy at seeing you again, we allowed ourselves the hope that you had brought these dainties for us, a gift for your most loyal friends. Just as we captured the shrowde and brought it to you, so long ago, as a gift."

"We have never been *friends*, Dirge," Morrigan said, and the shrowde cloak billowed like a storm cloud. "It was no more than your duty to bring me the shrowde."

Dirge ducked her head, but her eyes remained fixed on Rowen and Will. She inched closer, and Rowen could not stop from taking a step backward. It was clear the harrower could not stop herself, either, even with the threat of the Angel hanging over her.

"Just look at them, so rich with fear," Dirge moaned. "We can smell the swift, sweet blood running in them. Fresh little mice. They must be strong to be so lively yet."

Dirge reached a claw toward Rowen, but in the next instant a tendril of the shrowde cloak shot out and curled itself around her wrist. The harrower shrieked and tugged to get free, but the shrowde did not let go.

"You are filth to be wiped from one's shoe," Morrigan said. "Remember your place or I will grant you your own ending here and now."

For an instant the hag's face, half concealed behind her hair, contorted with rage. Then she whimpered submissively and the shrowde let her go. Her arm dropped and she backed away with her head down, her long bony fingers slithering in the dust.

Morrigan glided past, with Will, Rowen and Shade following quickly, but they had only taken a few steps when a woman's voice brought them to a sudden halt.

"What of me, my lord Prince? Are we friends?"

Rowen looked up in search of whoever had spoken and saw a figure at the top of the mound of trash. It appeared to be a dark-haired woman in an ash-grey gown with a ragged, spreading cape. Then Rowen saw the woman was hovering just above the trash mound, and what she had taken for a cape was a pair of huge mottled grey-and-black wings.

The harrower called Gibbet gave a moan of fear at the sight of the hovering woman and cowered in the trash. Dirge lowered her head even closer to the ground and dug her claws into the muck.

The third harrower's wings fanned out with a shiver and she descended slowly toward them, her bare feet gliding just above the trash. Her long hair was as dark as Morrigan's but pulled back severely from her face. She would have been beautiful, Rowen thought, if not for the shark-like blackness of her eyes, in which cold points of light glittered.

"You have been gone such a long time, Lotan," the woman said, raising her hands in greeting. Her fingers ended in long curved nails like a bird's talons. "You and I have much to speak about."

Her voice was soft and even musical after the harsh croaking of Dirge, but Rowen heard the threat under its sweetness and she tensed, expecting violence. The woman hovered just above Morrigan, her wings still outspread and beating slowly. Too slowly, Rowen thought, as if she had some other means to keep herself aloft.

Then it struck Rowen: the woman had called the Angel *Lotan*. She spoke to him as an equal, and that meant she was far more dangerous than the other harrowers.

The woman studied Shade, then Will, then finally Rowen.

"This must be the child we have heard of," she said. "I congratulate you on finding her, though it is difficult to believe that such a pitiful thing could have cost the mighty Angel so much time and trouble. But now that your task is accomplished, surely you can spare a few moments to talk with me."

For a long while Morrigan did not reply. Rowen guessed that the shrowde knew nothing about this third harrower and Morrigan was uncertain how to respond without giving anything away.

"My task is not finished," Morrigan said at last. "And I have come too far to be waylaid with trifles."

The woman's eyes narrowed. Her cold gaze travelled up and down the shrowde cloak.

"It is no trifle, the matter between us, as you well know," she said, all trace of pleasantness gone from her voice. "Our agreement was made long before you clothed yourself in that *creature*. Before you rose so high above the rest of us. You cannot walk away. Not from me."

"What is done is only what the One commands," Morrigan said. "I will hear you when I return."

She moved to go around the woman, but the huge wings spread even wider to bar the shrowde's way.

"You will *hear* me?" the woman echoed, and then she laughed, a deep, harsh, hateful laugh that sent a shudder through Rowen. "No, we will speak now, because your life was once in my hands and I returned it to you. I will not be denied."

"You have your place here and your tasks to perform," Morrigan said. "We all have our place. Nothing can change that."

"My place," the woman hissed scornfully. "My place was beside you. Or so you swore to me. So you promised when I saved your life. We were to be consorts, equals in power and honour. That is what you told me. You swore on your flesh and spirit that you would raise me above *this*."

She gestured at Dirge and Gibbet, neither of whom had yet dared to look up in the woman's presence.

"That is what you swore to me when we were in each other's arms, my lord," the woman went on. "You cannot have forgotten. We were to rule together in the name of the One when the last of the Uneaten Lands had been devoured. You would not *dare* to pretend you have forgotten your oath."

Her voice shook with anger and wounded pride, and Rowen understood that the woman had once loved Lotan and had been loved by him in return.

"You will stand aside, harrower," Morrigan said, her voice weighted with such threat that the woman actually drew back a pace. Her black eyes glittered feverishly.

"I will stand aside," she said, "in exchange for the wolf and the boy."

"These uneaten ones are not for you or me. Stand aside."

"It is the girl who matters. She was the one foreseen. These others are of no consequence. Give me the wolf for a servant and the boy to feed upon, as a token of your good faith."

"Do not presume to know what is of consequence to the One," Morrigan said in a voice so low and menacing that Rowen took an involuntary step away from her. "Now stand aside or I promise you will be cast down lower than these wretches at your feet and you will never rise again."

The woman's pale lips trembled. Her grey wings stirred and then went still once more.

"At least speak my name," she said. "Show me that courtesy, my lord, before you break your word."

Her voice was mocking and despairing at the same time, yet Rowen had the feeling that this was also a carefully crafted performance. She feared the woman had guessed it was not Lotan underneath the shrowde, and her suspicions were about to be confirmed. And if that happened, Rowen was braced for an attack.

Morrigan did not answer the woman's question. The shrowde had known the names of Dirge and Gibbet, Rowen guessed, because she'd met them before, but she had never encountered this other harrower.

"Speak it, my lord," the woman said. "Why do you hesitate?"

Just then Dirge, still cowering at their feet, reached out a bony hand to the fringe of the shrowde cloak.

"Great Angel, if you punish Dama, do not harm poor Dirge," she pleaded. "Destroy Gibbet, the worthless, if it

pleases you, but do not punish poor Dirge, the faithful, who
has grown old and feeble in the service of—"

"Silence!" the woman shrieked, and Dirge shrank from
her with a terrified moan.

"Whatever agreement there once was between us, Dama,"
Morrigan said, "it is as dead and finished as if it had never
been. All things begin and end in the One. Stand aside or be
cast into the void."

"Now you remember my name," the woman said, her
eyes wide in a mockery of surprise. "I find it strange that
you did not until Dirge spoke it. What happened to you in
the Uneaten Lands, Lotan? Why were you gone so very long
and what of the rumours that you had been ended? Why
have you come this way, on this road you have never taken
since you were given the keys of the realm?"

"Enough of this," Morrigan said, and the shrowde cloak
reached out lashing white tentacles. Dirge and Gibbet groaned
and blubbered in fear, burrowing themselves into the trash
mound, but Dama did not move. One of the shrowde's tentacles encircled her neck like the noose around Gibbet's,
but still she did not stir.

"Do as you will, my lord," she said, her voice fallen to a
strained whisper. "Cast me into the void, since I am already
nothing to you. But let me look upon your face as you do it."

Rowen held her breath. The shrowde drew its tentacle
ever tighter around Dama's neck. Then it loosened again and
withdrew.

"I will return when there is time and grant you the ending
you seek," Morrigan said. She swept past the winged woman,
and Will, Rowen and Shade hurried after her. Rowen dared
not glance back. She kept as close as she could to Will. Their
eyes met, but only for an instant. It was too soon to let down
their guard.

They had crossed the pool and gone a short distance up the rising path on the far side when from behind them there came a sound of rushing wings. Rowen threw herself down, but it was too late. She felt claws bite into her shoulders and she was plucked from the ground and lifted helplessly into the air.

She was in Dama's clutches, rising powerlessly above the trash mounds.

Rowen struggled and kicked her legs, but the woman's arms held her fast. She heard Will shout "Let her go!" and saw him charge forward before the shrowde billowed out and held him back.

"The boy dares to speak and to struggle?" Dama said, her breath cold on Rowen's neck. "His spirit is not broken. How could the Prince of Shadows allow this?"

"You will let the girl go, Dama," Morrigan said in a slow, threatening voice. "She belongs to the One."

"Show me your face, Lotan," Dama cried. "Do not hide from me behind that *thing* you befriended. Let me see your face or I will tear this mortal open and suck out her life, I swear it. And *I* do not break my promises."

The woman's grip tightened and Rowen let out a cry of pain. Morrigan did not move.

"Show me your face," Dama repeated.

Slowly Morrigan's hands went up toward the hood of the cloak. Rowen looked on in despair, knowing that in another moment the deception would be over and with it would go all hope of finding Grandfather.

Then a dark form sprang up the mound and leaped at Dama from the side.

It was Shade.

Dama turned to ward off the wolf, and Rowen was suddenly free of her grip and fell onto the trash mound, stunned.

The harrower was knocked out of the air by the force of Shade's attack. She and the wolf slammed into the mound near Rowen, who rolled out of the way. Dama snarled in rage and fear as the wolf snapped and clawed at her, snagging her robe and preventing her from rising. She beat her wings frantically and slashed at Shade, but the wolf evaded the blow and sank his fangs into her leg. Dama gave a shriek. Her talons swept down and this time they found their target. They raked across Shade's muzzle and clawed at his eyes, until at last the wolf let go his grip and Dama writhed away, her wings billowing.

She was rising now, escaping, but Shade made another leap and collided with her in the air, and then they were locked together, clawing and thrashing and struggling violently.

Shade's weight was pulling Dama down out of the sky, and now Morrigan was moving up the slope toward them, the shrowde cloak seeming to glide effortlessly over the jumbled trash. Dama saw her coming at almost the same moment Rowen did. The winged woman let out a hideous scream and struck Shade a torrent of vicious blows that finally succeeded in breaking his hold on her. Shade fell from the air and disappeared on the far side of the trash mound.

Dama beat her bloodied wings and flapped away, shrieking and sobbing, until she was lost from sight. Rowen saw both Will and Morrigan climbing the slope toward her. She tried to rise, but the world seemed to tilt and slide underneath her. She fell back again and the shadows seemed to close over her head.

17

CORR STARED IMPASSIVELY AT Finn.

"Brother," he said with icy calm, "you know that even if I allow you to leave with the golem, you will have no chance of crossing the Valley of Fire alive, let alone reaching the Bourne. When you run out of *gaal*, how long do you think you'll survive out there? Hours, at most."

"I know that, Corr. That's why we'll be taking one of your skyships."

Corr broke into a soft laugh.

"You're still feverish from your wound," he said. "You can't believe I would give you one of my ships for this fool's errand."

"You will, Corr. Because if you don't, I'll command Ord to push every ship you have left over the edge of the pier."

Corr's smile hardened into a grimace of rage.

"Think carefully about what you're saying, brother," he breathed.

"I'm going home in one of your skyships, Corr," Finn said, turning away. "And, Doctor Alazar, I hope you'll come with me."

"I will, Finn. There's nothing more I can do here."

"You don't turn your back on me, boy," Corr roared, and he gripped Finn's shoulder and spun him around. Finn offered no resistance. The golem, who had started forward at Finn's command, stopped and waited.

"I raised you," Corr growled. "I taught you to hunt and fight and track. I taught you everything you know and this is how you repay me? Those Errantry fools swayed you against me."

"It wasn't the Errantry, Corr," Finn said, his voice shaking. "You gave me the *gaal*, remember? You taught me about that, too. I'm only doing to you what you do to everyone and everything around you."

Corr's eyes blazed. He raised his fist as if about to strike Finn down. Finn did not move.

A shout came from farther up the tunnel. Everyone turned to see three Stormriders with staves striding down the ramp. Between them were two dwarfs.

"What is this?" Corr demanded.

"My lord, we found them hiding in one of the other tunnels. They wouldn't say anything other than to demand we take them to you."

The larger and younger of the dwarfs stared with frightened eyes at Corr and the others, his head shaking with a slight tremor that was not fear, Finn realized, but some sort of palsy. The other dwarf was very old. He was bald except for a few wisps of white hair about his ears, his seamed face crisscrossed with livid scars, his deep-set eyes two clouded and

unseeing orbs. He looked familiar, and then Finn remembered
seeing him at Corr's fortress, on the observation platform. He
was the ancient-looking smith whom Nonn had asked about
the repairs to the ships.

"What are your names?" Corr said, his voice calm and
commanding again. He appeared to have forgotten Finn's
threat for the moment. For his part Finn waited to hear what
the dwarfs had to say.

The younger dwarf stepped forward.

"I am Nar," he said in a flat, guarded voice. His shaking
head was hunched into his shoulders, as if he expected a sword
blade to lop it off at any moment. "This is Tholl, my father. We
weren't hiding, my lord. We were trying to find you."

"Why didn't you get away with the others?" Corr barked.

"We did not know of Nonn's plans, my lord, until he
was already leaving. We did not wish to betray the Sky Lord,
so we stayed behind."

"I don't believe you. You're trying to save your skin now
that you've been caught."

"They left us behind because we are worthless and slow,
my lord," said the old dwarf, his voice deep and ponder-
ous, like the sound of something heavy and hollow being
dragged across a stone floor. "I cannot see and so Nar must
be my eyes. We cannot move quickly with all the rubble and
filth choking the passageways. When Nonn saw his chance
to bring down the slabs and abandon you here, we were
busy helping your men figure out how to work the water
pumps. We could not get away in time, so Nonn left us to
your mercy."

Corr looked from father to son with a cold, calculating
expression.

"I think you were left behind on purpose," he said. "I think
Nonn ordered you to stay as spies or saboteurs, believing I

wouldn't suspect a blind old smith and his son. I should just throw the both of you over the parapet and be done with it."

"My lord, we are not spies," Nar said quickly, his voice hoarse with fear. "I swear to you we had no part in Nonn's plans."

"Nonn is my sister's son," the blind dwarf said, "but he has no love for us, his own kin. I lost my sight from years hunched over a workbench, crafting gears, ratchets, pins so fine that few could match them. My son, Nar, was my apprentice, but Nonn forced him to work in the tunnels below the fortress, scraping and scratching for just a little more of the *gaal*. There are poisonous fumes deep under the earth, and what they did to Nar you can see for yourself, Sky Lord. He can no longer carry on the work I trained him for, the craft that has been passed down in our family for generations. We have your precious *gaal* to thank for that."

"Father . . ." Nar said warningly.

"You may not know or care, Sky Lord," the old dwarf went on without heeding his son, "but mighty furnaces and bellows alone do not keep your ships in the sky. They would not obey the hand at the wheel so readily without hidden workings of great subtlety and precision. But the knowledge of these intricate devices will soon be lost, because Nonn tosses his tools away when they get old and worn out—tools like my son and me. He cares only about weapons. Crude, unskilful things good for nothing but killing."

"I knew nothing of your work, Tholl," Corr said, "but if my ships fly because of it, then you have my thanks."

The old dwarf bowed.

"I have served our people for longer than Nonn has been alive," he said. "He styles himself the heir of the Eldersmiths of old, but his greed has driven him mad. Rather than share Adamant with you, he made a pact with the enemy. He will destroy the Ironwise. I curse him, Sky Lord, and I turn my back on him and his followers, and so does my son."

Corr studied the two dwarfs again without speaking. Nar kept his shaking head bowed, but Tholl's seamed, scarred face was raised toward the Sky Lord.

"What were you doing in the tunnel where my men found you?" he asked at last.

"When Nonn brought down the slabs, your men ran and left us, my lord," Nar said hastily. "We were on our way to find you and warn you. There is grave danger for you and all your men. Now that Nonn has relit the forges, he has the means to destroy your ships."

"How can that be? If he's sealed off all the doors, he can't harm us any more than we can him."

Just then the sound of frantic shouting and running feet came from above. At first the shouts were all a confused babble of voices. Then one word was clearly heard above the din.

Fire!

Corr stood frozen, and to Finn it seemed that for the first time he saw fear in his brother's eyes. Then he turned to Kern.

"Finish questioning them," he said. "Grath, with me."

Corr wheeled around and strode up the tunnel with the mordog lieutenant. Finn and the doctor, for the moment, had been forgotten. They glanced at each other and then followed.

They walked out onto the parapet to a scene of frantic disorder. Some Stormriders were shouting orders, others rushing with buckets to the water troughs and back to the ships.

Small burning objects were rising out of the central well, hundreds of them, like a cloud of glowing fireflies. They were hard to make out in the smoke and darkness beyond the torches, but they appeared to be small metal braziers filled with bright, leaping fire and kept aloft by whirling wooden blades.

The braziers were rising on the updraft of hot air from the forges, Finn realized. And now that they had reached the colder air of the upper circles the blades were slowing down. The braziers were starting to fall, and the ships were directly below them.

With the others Finn hurried after Corr, who was roaring to his Stormriders to form into lines to pass the buckets hand over hand to the ships. And then Finn stumbled over something and looked down and saw a Stormrider lying dead on the black stone with an arrow in his chest. An arrow with black fletching.

He peered across the gap to the other pier and saw furtive figures there, crouched among the scattered stone rubble. Figures shooting up from concealment, drawing back bows, loosing arrows.

"Nightbane!" someone cried as another black-feathered shaft whistled past Finn's ear and clattered across the stone behind him.

But now a few of the braziers had fallen into the rigging and spars of one of the skyships. When they struck, they spilled their blazing contents, and sails and cables burst into hungry flame.

Corr's flagship was closest to the edge of the pier and its furled sails were already a mass of crackling flame. Blackened cloth was falling onto the deck, and Stormriders were scurrying about with water buckets and wet rags to put these new fires out, some frantically stamping at them with their boots.

Then the falling braziers reached two more of the skyships and their sails and decks began to burn. Other Stormriders on the pier had formed into lines as Corr had commanded and were handing along buckets from the water troughs. But black-fledged arrows were flying thick and fast now from the

Nightbane on the far pier, and every so often a Stormrider would cry out and drop with an arrow in him. The wounded had to be carried to the shelter of the stairways and sentry towers, which left fewer men to fight the fires.

Corr had already charged among his men, directing the work of saving the ships, seemingly oblivious to the arrows whistling around him. A few of the Stormriders had crept as close as they dared to the edge of the pier with their lightning staves, but the crackling white bolts they loosed fell short of the Nightbane. There were archers with longbows among the Stormriders, as well, and they clambered up the sentry towers along the parapet and launched their own volleys at the Nightbane.

The doctor was soon busy looking after those who had been struck by arrows or burned by the falling fire. Finn stayed close to Corr, and the golem strode along behind him. He had a plan to take a company around the parapet to come at the Nightbane archers from behind. He was about to share his thoughts with Corr when he saw another obstacle: massive pillars had fallen across the parapet on either side of the pier, likely deliberately brought down by Nonn's people. The far side of the upper circle of Adamant could only be reached by climbing over the fallen pillars, and their flanks were too tall and smooth for that to be a simple task. The golem might be able to lift or move one, Finn thought, but by that time it would be too late. All the Nightbane had to do was hinder the attempt to save the ships, and then the Stormriders would be out in the open and nearly helpless, for the pier was now cut off completely from the rest of the city.

Just then an arrow tore through Corr's cloak. He didn't seem to notice. His eyes were fixed on the flagship and he hastened toward it, shouting at the Stormriders who were scrambling down the gangplank, coughing and shielding their eyes from the smoke, commanding them to stand their ground and save the ship. One of them ran blindly past him.

"Corr, we have to stay back," Finn said, clutching his brother's arm. He looked around for Alazar, wondering where the doctor had gone, but he couldn't see him anywhere.

"The *gaal*," Corr breathed. "We must save it."

"There's only a little of it left, you told me. It's not worth your men dying for."

"No, you don't understand. In the hold of the flagship—there's a secret compartment filled with the ore. Enough to keep the ships aloft for days. I kept it hidden from Nonn in case he ever betrayed me. If the fire reaches the hold, the *gaal* will go up. The pier . . . the camp . . . everything will be destroyed."

Corr halted, his face stricken as he watched the flames consuming the flagship's sails and spreading along the masts and spars.

"We can raise the ships," Corr said, speaking more to himself than to Finn. "Take them up above the rim of the city. Yes, we must raise the ships."

"It's too late," Finn said. "They're only death traps now."

Corr turned to him with a look of rage and it seemed for a moment he didn't recognize his brother. Before he could speak, somewhere nearby a man cried, "The water!" and they both pivoted at the shout.

"The water's stopped flowing!" another Stormrider called to Corr.

Finn glanced down at the narrow trough underfoot. Where once there had been a steady stream, now there was nothing left but a thin trickle.

"What's happened to the water?" Corr roared at the nearest of his men. The Stormrider stared back at him blankly.

There was another shout, but this was a cry of amazement and relief, and Finn saw several men pointing at the two towering bastions on either side of the gates. From the gaping mouths of the dragons came frothing white plumes of water, falling like a miraculous rain on the ships. Finn's gaze swept over the entire circle of the city and he saw now that there were dragon-headed bastions all around the great curve of the parapet and that water was gushing from these spouts, too, and splashing and cascading over the walkways below. And now he understood why the dragon heads had been carved facing inward: they were there to protect the city, not to warn away enemies.

"Who's done this?" Corr said in wonder as the braziers that were still hovering among the ships were struck by the falling water, their flames going out with a hiss and gush of steam. The water fell upon the decks and spars of the burning ships, as well, and the fires were dimming and going out.

In a short time the jets from the dragon mouths drew off to a weak drizzle, but it had been enough. There were only a few small fires left burning on the decks of the ships and among the tents on the pier, and Corr's men had rallied and were rushing to put those out. Even the Nightbane across the circle seemed to have been dismayed by this unexpected turn of events, for the volley of feathered shafts fell off to a few scattered arrows and dark shapes could be seen scurrying away into the shadows.

"Who has done this?" Corr said again, gazing up at the mouths of the stone dragons. Then he turned to Grath. "Where is the old dwarf and his son? Find them and bring them to me."

The mordog marched off just as the Stormriders who had fled the flagship were returning to it, hurrying up the gangplank with buckets to douse the last of the fires.

Corr turned to Finn then, and the rage had gone from his face, replaced with his usual icy glare.

"You haven't left yet, brother," he said coldly. "My ships are damaged, but it's possible one of them may still serve to get you home."

"Corr, I—"

He didn't finish. The doctor had appeared on the deck of the flagship with the Valkai prisoner. The warrior's head was down and he was struggling to walk, his hands still bound. The doctor had one arm around the Valkai's waist and one of the Valkai's arms was over Alazar's shoulder. In a flash Finn understood that the doctor had deliberately climbed aboard the burning ship to save the Nightbane prisoner.

Finn left Corr and dashed up the gangplank.

"They left him to die," Alazar shouted. "Help me, Finn."

Finn reached for the wounded Valkai's other arm. The young warrior cried out as he was moved but was still able to hobble along.

"I've got him, Doctor," Finn said. He felt the doctor's hold slip away and he struggled down the gangplank with the wounded Valkai, fighting to keep him upright. When he reached the pier, the Valkai gave a groan and his legs buckled under him. Finn set him down as carefully as he could upon the stone, just as two of Corr's Stormriders rushed up to take the prisoner from him.

"Should've let this one burn," one of the Stormriders muttered.

Finn ignored them and looked back up the gangplank for the doctor, wondering why he hadn't come with them. He saw Alazar sitting beneath the main mast, his shoulders slumped. The doctor's spectacles had come off and he was groping about to find them, as if he had gone blind.

Finn climbed back up the gangplank. A burnt spar came loose and crashed to the deck a few feet from where he stood.

"Doctor, it's not safe here," Finn said, but the older man did not answer. His trembling hand was still feeling its way over the planks. Finn knelt beside him and finally saw the black-feathered shaft protruding from the small of his back.

"My spectacles, Finn," Alazar said. His face was ashen and he was breathing in shallow gasps. "Can't seem to find them."

Finn picked up the spectacles and put them in Alazar's hand. Shakily the doctor raised them to his face and slid them on. Then his hands dropped into his lap as if the effort had exhausted him.

"We'll get you out of here, Doctor," Finn said, and he shouted for help. "Corr's men will know what to do about the arrow."

He felt a presence near him and looked up to see that the golem had followed him onto the deck and was standing over him now, unmoved and unmoving as always.

"You're no use here," he muttered angrily at Ord. "Not now."

"Don't let them touch the arrow, Finn," Alazar said. "I'll just bleed out faster."

"Tell me what to do, Doctor. There must be something I can do."

He shouted again and the Stormriders on the deck turned at his voice.

"Bring Corr! The doctor needs help!"

One of the Stormriders ran for the gangplank. The doctor raised a hand and grasped Finn's arm. His grip tightened.

"Finn, my bag . . . where is it?"

Finn glanced around the deck and saw the battered black leather bag lying at the top of the stairs into the hold. He ran over, picked it up and carried it back.

"I've got it, Doctor," he said. "What do you need?"

"My journal," Alazar said hoarsely. "Find it, please."

Finn dug in the bag and brought out the journal.

"Is there something in it that will help?" he said. "A remedy or—"

"There's no remedy for this, Finn. Not for any of it. I want you to take the journal. It was nearly full, anyhow. Take it with you when you leave."

Finn understood at last and tears stung his eyes. "Doctor, the journal is yours. You'll be writing in it later about all this, I'm sure of it."

Alazar blinked up at him through his spectacles and smiled.

"You're a good man, Finn. I wish there had been time for us to become better friends."

"There will be time, Doctor."

"Finn, please. You're the only one I can trust. Keep the journal. Maybe one day you can visit the Sunlands. Give the journal to my king, if he still lives. Tell him I kept my word."

"You'll do that yourself, Doctor," Finn said, and then he glanced over at a sound. Corr was striding toward him across the deck with the two Stormriders that Finn had sent to find him.

"Corr," Finn said. "It's a Nightbane arrow. Can you help him?"

Corr did not reply. He crouched beside Finn and put a hand on his shoulder.

"Corr, the arrow . . ." Finn began again, then he looked down at the doctor and saw that he was dead.

The ships had been saved and the Nightbane attack had drawn off, but the Stormrider encampment was still frantic with activity. Men were clambering over the ships, salvaging whatever they could of the sails and ropes that had burned or replacing them with spares. Other Stormriders were busy setting up a system of winches and buckets on cables in case the ships were threatened again with fire. Still others had begun clearing the rubble that had cut the pier off from the rest of the upper parapet.

The doctor's body had been placed with the Stormrider dead on a pyre of charred wood from the damaged ships. With Alazar's journal tucked in a pocket of his cloak Finn summoned the golem to follow him back onto the pier. For a long time he stood with Ord like a silent tower beside him and watched the Stormriders going about their tasks. What had brought most of these men here he had no idea, but it seemed certain that many of them would never leave.

With all the urgent activity, no one took any notice of him. At last Finn gave the golem a final command and then went in search of Corr.

He found him with his lieutenants in his cabin on the flagship, planning a counterassault on the mines. The old dwarf and his son were there, too.

"Nonn's Nightbane allies will likely have reported by now that the ships weren't destroyed," Corr was saying as Finn appeared. "He'll be wondering how we got the dragon spouts working again. He may figure out it was you and your son, Tholl, who helped us."

"Even if he does, my lord," the old dwarf said, "there is much he doesn't know about Adamant. Many secrets were built into this city as it was delved through the ages. Secret ways of dealing with enemies from both without and within. I am the last who knows of some of them."

"There was a time, long ago, when the Ironwise nearly went to war with one another," Nar added. "There was much distrust then, and one of our chieftains had secret traps and defences built in case of need. My father helped build them."

"The secret defences were never used," Tholl said. "Eventually they were forgotten. Only I remember."

"Is there a way to get through those slabs?" Corr asked.

"There is no means to raise the slabs from this side, Sky Lord," Nar said. "They were a last defence against invaders and were made so that the mechanism that lowers them would break once they were used. Even if the clay giant could raise the slabs, which my father says isn't likely, Nonn will have set other traps and obstacles in your path. But—" He hesitated and glanced at his father apprehensively.

"In those long-ago days," Tholl said, picking up the story, "I helped construct secret waterworks to flood the forges and mines if the other faction gained control of them. Nonn knows nothing of this."

"You can flood the lower circles?" Corr asked.

With great care the old dwarf rolled back the sleeve of his tunic to expose a withered forearm that was covered with a web of old scars.

"As we built the secret traps and defences, I made a map of them, Sky Lord. A map that would survive the years and that no enemy would discover, not on a body that was already as scarred as mine. But I no longer need the map. I can see it all, every hidden passage and trap, with my eyes closed, and so can my son."

"My father and I will rechannel the water, my lord, so that it will douse the forges and drive Nonn's delvers out of the mines," Nar said. "And then I can lead you by hidden passageways so that you may take Nonn unawares."

"You would do this for me?" Corr asked doubtfully. "You would have someone who is not of your kind rule the city of the Eldersmiths?"

"Better an alliance with the Sky Lord than with Nightbane," the old dwarf said, and for the first time Finn saw the ghost of a smile crease his ancient face. "My son and I saved your ships, and we will help you seize the forges and the *gaal* for yourself. But in return I ask something of you."

"What is it?"

"Nonn has been ruthless, and most of those who follow him do so only out of fear. Spare my people, Sky Lord, and they will serve you well. They will restore this city to what it once was, to the glory of the Adamant of old. We cannot do this without you and you cannot do it without us. We need each other so that what is almost lost can be preserved."

Corr regarded the old dwarf impassively.

"Those who do not resist will be spared," he said at last.

"You are gracious, my lord. And so I dare one further request: Should Nonn be captured alive, bring him before me and my son in chains. Let his punishment be for us to decide."

"Very well. If he lives, Nonn will be yours to deal with as you please."

"Swear to what you have promised, Sky Lord, on your life's blood."

Corr hesitated a moment, then he slid the knife from the sheath at his belt and drew the blade across his palm, as Nonn had done on the pier. He made a fist and the blood dripped through his fingers and onto the stones below.

"On my life's blood," Corr said.

The old dwarf bowed his head.

"I will show you how the water may be diverted, and Nar will lead your men through the secret passages."

Corr gave orders to his lieutenants to prepare for a counter-assault. Then he glanced up and saw Finn at the door.

"You'll be leaving now, I gather," he said coldly.

"I will," Finn said.

"The ships won't be skyworthy for some time yet, but if

you're not willing to wait, you can use one of the undamaged skiffs. I can't spare anyone to go with you, but Kern will supply you with the ore you'll need and show you how to keep the thing aloft."

"I'm not using one of your ships, Corr. Your men need them. The golem is yours, too. I've already given him the command you asked for. He will obey you again."

Corr stared hard at his brother.

"Finn, what do you think you're going to do? *Walk* out of here?"

"That's right. I've come to say goodbye."

"You've come to . . ."

Corr shook his head in disbelief. Then he reached out and gripped Finn's shoulders.

"We *have* him, brother," he said. "An hour ago I thought we were finished and I would have agreed with you that leaving was our only choice. But now we have him and soon we'll have all the fever iron we need. Don't throw your life away, not when we're so close to victory."

Finn set the pouch of *gaal* powder down on the chart table. He looked up at his brother but found he was unable to speak.

"Even if you make it across the valley," Corr said, "which no one ever has, not on foot, it would take you weeks to reach the Bourne. By then whatever's going to happen will be over and done with."

"Corr, you and the Nightbane were killing each other over this poison, and now you're at war over it again, this time with your allies. If you defeat Nonn and the mines are yours, someone else will come hoping to take them from you. And even if you win that battle, one day the ore will run out and your Stormriders will be killing one another for the little that's left."

"You heard what the doctor said, didn't you? Without the *gaal* you'll be dead in a matter of days, Finn. If the beasts out there don't get you first, that is. At least take the suit of fetch armour. It'll give you a fighting chance."

"I'm not putting on that armour, Corr. When I woke up in the infirmary, I thought I had a choice between joining you or dying, but I see now it was no choice at all. The fever iron is death, and death is all you and your men will ever find in this place. It will find me, too, soon enough. But it won't find me here. Goodbye, brother. We won't see each other again."

Corr came around the table. He stood in front of Finn without speaking. Then he put his arms around him and embraced him.

"I love you, little brother," Corr said under his breath. "You know that, don't you?"

"I did—once."

Finn left the flagship and went among the Stormriders on the pier, saying goodbye to the few he'd fought alongside. Then he strode across the pier to the great doors. He was carrying water, what little food the quartermaster could spare and the doctor's journal, wrapped in a clean cloth. Before stowing it safely in his pack, he had turned the journal over in his hands, feeling the worn leather cover, the thin paper, soft at the edges with many thumbings. He knew the journal was not for him, but he could not keep himself from leafing through the pages and reading a few lines in the doctor's neat, precise hand. *I have stayed in Fable much longer than I ever intended to,* the doctor had written on a day several years earlier. *The knights of Appleyard wish me to remain and join their ranks. They tell me they have need of my skills, such as they are. I'm not certain yet whether I will accept, though it's true I have grown very fond of this peaceful city and its people.*

The sentries at the doors had already been informed Finn was leaving. They hurried to the winch and raised the small portcullis. As he was about to duck through the low, narrow doorway, Finn heard his name called. He turned to see Grath hurrying after him. He was wearing his battle mail and had a cloth pack slung over one shoulder.

"I hear you're deserting," the mordog said brusquely.

"If you want to put it that way."

"You're going to die out there, you know."

"I wish you well, Grath. I hope one day you'll find the freedom you've been searching for."

"Well, this seems as good a day as any to look for it. I'm coming with you."

"You're . . . Does Corr know about this?"

"I told him. His first thought was to have me clapped in irons. Then he changed his mind and decided I might be of use to you, since I am no longer of any use to him. Kern was happy, though. My leaving suits his ambitions." He shrugged almost imperceptibly. "Together we might manage to stay alive a little longer than we would by ourselves."

"Have you ever been out there?" Finn asked, gesturing to the doorway and the cold grey light beyond.

Grath grinned crookedly.

"Out there, Finn Madoc," he said, "is where I come from."

18

WILL HAD ALREADY STARTED up the trash mound when Shade first attacked Dama. As he struggled through the jumbled, sodden refuse to the place Rowen lay, he saw Shade's fall and Dama's escape. Then he lost his balance and banged his shin painfully against a sharp-edged piece of protruding metal. He bit back a cry and kept going, his vision clouded with tears of pain and grief.

He reached Rowen's side. She was picking herself up, apparently unhurt but with a shocked, glassy stare in her eyes. He took her hand and helped her to her feet.

"I'm all right," she said shakily. "We have to help Shade."

Will looked around wildly, but he could no longer see the wolf. At that moment Morrigan joined them. She had glided up the slope in the shrowde cloak without making a sound.

"We must not linger here. Dama will raise the alarm and

others are sure to come," she said. "I saw where Shade fell. Follow me."

They made their way slowly along and down the slope. Will was slowed by his bruised shin, which sent pain knifing through his leg whenever he put any weight on it. And Rowen was still unsteady on her feet. He stayed close to her, alarmed at how pale she was.

At last they came around to the far side of the slope and found another narrow gully below them, like the one where they had met the harrowers. At the bottom they saw the wolf on his side in a shallow pool of filthy water.

"Shade!" Will cried.

He plunged down the trash slope, heedless of his injured leg, crying out the wolf's name. As he reached the bottom, Shade stirred and climbed with great effort to his feet.

Will came to a halt a few steps away. He couldn't help himself. For a terrible moment he wasn't even sure this was his friend at all.

Shade had grown larger. Much larger. Will had always been able to stand face to face with him, but now he had to look up into the wolf's eyes. Shade's fur was darker, too, and matted into thick hackles spattered with blood, his own and likely Dama's. From his heaving chest came a deep, shuddering rasp, like a saw being drawn through knotted wood.

"Shade?" Will said. "Are you all right?"

The wolf's eyes, dull and bloodshot, regarded Will without seeming to recognize him. By now Rowen and Morrigan had reached the bottom of the slope.

"Keep a distance," Morrigan said, placing a hand on Will's shoulder.

The wolf looked at each of them in turn, his chest still heaving and his eyes showing no sign that he knew them. Then he took a step toward Rowen, who stiffened and backed away.

"Shade," Will said. "What's wrong? It's us."

The wolf took another slow step toward Rowen, then he stopped and lowered his great shaggy head. Will saw that his limbs were trembling, as if he was struggling to hold himself back, from either bounding away or leaping to attack. Slaver dripped from his jaws and a low, strained growl came from deep in his throat.

"He's trying to say something," Rowen said desperately. "What is it, Shade? Can't you speak? What did she do to you?"

The wolf gazed at Rowen with a beseeching look, then lowered his head again.

"You know what this means, Rowen," Morrigan said. "What he is asking of you."

"I know," Rowen said, shaking her head, "but I can't do it. I can't."

"You must. He cannot speak because the other wolf is winning the struggle. Shade is giving us this chance, before it is too late."

Rowen nodded. "Forgive me, Shade," she whispered.

Will watched in disbelief as she slipped the ball of golden thread from her pocket. This was the moment that the young man in the Weaving had warned him of. It had come already. He had thought there would be more time.

In his mind he saw the young man's feverish eyes, his look of a hunted thing.

That's not me, he thought. *Not yet.*

"No," he said with quiet force.

Rowen turned to him with a look of anguish. "I have to do this," she said. "Shade asked me to bind him before the shadow took him over. He wants this. It's the only way he can keep us safe when the other wolf comes. Isn't that right, Shade?"

Shade's great head nodded once. Rowen stepped forward and the wolf hunkered down and stretched out his front paws.

"No, there has to be another way," Will said. "Shade would never hurt us. I don't believe it."

"If Rowen does not act now, Shade will become like those others," Morrigan said. "Like the harrowers. He will turn on us. Either we bind him with the thread, or he must die here, now, at my hand."

"You're both giving up on him," Will said, clutching Rowen's arm. "How can you do that? He's never given up on us!"

Rowen shrugged off his grip.

"If you won't help me, then stay out of my way," she said, her voice breaking.

Will stepped back. He stared at Rowen, who turned away from him and knelt before Shade. Quickly she teased out the end of the thread and began to draw it out from the ball.

"Shade, don't submit to this," Will said. "*Run.*"

The wolf gave no sign he had heard. His red-rimmed eyes were fixed on Rowen. When she had a good length of the fine, gleaming thread, she began to wind it tightly around Shade's huge front paws. He lifted them from the ground to make it easier for her, but her hands were shaking so that she worked clumsily and slowly. Will watched, not understanding how something so thin and fragile could ever be expected to hold his powerful friend. And yet he knew that Rowen's grandmother had told her that once she had woven with it, the thread could never be broken.

When she had bound Shade's front paws, the wolf lay over on his side so she could reach his back paws. Soon those were also tightly wound with the thread, which now seemed to shine even more brightly than before. Will glanced at the golden ball in Rowen's palm and saw to his surprise that it seemed to be no smaller than when she'd started.

He was jolted from his thoughts by Shade, who stirred suddenly and gnashed his teeth together.

"He doesn't want this," Will cried. "You're telling us not to do this, isn't that right, Shade?"

"He wants you to bind his jaws as well," Morrigan said. "That's what he is asking."

Again Shade lowered his head to confirm she was right.

"But he'll be completely helpless then," Will said. "You saw those harrowers, Rowen. You know what they'll do to him!"

"His jaws must be bound," Morrigan said coldly. "Finish it."

Rowen started to bring the end of the thread to Shade's muzzle.

"No!" Will shouted. "I won't let you."

He crouched beside her and blocked her with his hand.

"I have to finish," Rowen said, tears sliding through the grime on her face. "I have to, or the thread won't hold him."

"How do you know that?"

"I just know. Or maybe it's the thread that knows."

"But it's not working. The thread isn't being used up. There's still as much left as when you started."

"I know, and I don't understand it either. Grandmother didn't have time to tell me everything. All she said was I would have to weave—"

"Listen to me," Will said as a memory suddenly came to him. "When I met the Dreamwalker, the old man of the Horse Folk, he said he'd seen you in the dream country. He saw *you*, Rowen, coming here, to the Shadow Realm. He knew it would happen even before your grandfather was taken by the thrawl."

"The Dreamwalker saw *me*?"

"He called you the weaver of worlds. He said you would find a great power in yourself. He called you a *weaver*. I think he must have been talking about the thread. You're supposed to do something with it, but not this. This can't be it. This whole journey is not just about finding your grandfather.

You're supposed to change everything, the Dreamwalker said. Everything in all the worlds. There's something else you have to do here, and if you bind Shade with the thread, you won't be able to do it."

Rowen's eyes were wide with shock and fear.

"Why didn't you tell me, Will?" she whispered.

"I didn't want to make things harder for you. I didn't . . ."

He was about to say more when he felt a sudden sharp pressure on his raised arm, and turned to see what had caused it.

His wrist was caught between the wolf's jaws.

"Shade?" he whispered.

The wolf's eyes burned into his, but Shade did not move or release him. Will held his breath and went still. He could feel the points of Shade's teeth on his skin. The wolf was holding his arm with just enough force to keep him from pulling away. A cold chill crawled over him. He knew that with the slightest clenching of those powerful jaws, Shade's fangs would bite through his flesh and bone as easily as snapping a twig. Will's heart thudded in his chest and every nerve was screaming at him to pull away, but he dared not move a muscle.

"He does not wish to harm you, Will," Morrigan said. "He is warning you. He wants you to stay out of the way so that Rowen can finish binding him."

Shade's eyes moved to Morrigan and the steady look in them confirmed what she had said.

Will swallowed hard. "Shade, listen to me," he said in as calm a voice as he could muster. "I am not going to let Rowen do this. If you want her to finish, you'll have to take my arm."

"No!" Rowen cried. "Will, don't say that."

"Will," Morrigan said warningly. "You cannot survive a wound like that. Not here in this place."

"You were there, Shade, when the Dreamwalker told me about Rowen," Will went on, ignoring them both. "About what she had to do. The thread isn't meant for this. Binding you won't help any of us. You'll just die for nothing." He was crying now, his words coming in gasps. "If you really wanted to, you'd have taken my arm off already. But you're still you, and you always will be, no matter what. You would never hurt me or Rowen. I know that because I love you, Shade. And I trust you. So trust yourself."

For a long moment the wolf's eyes stayed locked on Will's. Then they closed, and tears slid down his ravaged face.

Will felt the points of Shade's teeth lift ever so slightly from his skin. Slowly and carefully he pulled his arm back until it was free of the wolf's jaws. Shade's head sagged down. His muzzle nudged Will's hand.

"Unbind him," Will said.

"Will . . ."

"Do it."

Rowen hesitated, terror in her eyes, then she began to unwind the thread from Shade's paws. Will looked at his arm with a kind of numb shock, as if he couldn't quite believe it was still there. Shade's teeth had left a livid half-circle on his skin. The sick fear of what had almost happened was still churning through him and he struggled to climb to his feet.

In a few moments the wolf was free, and Rowen was weeping and stroking Shade's fur.

The wolf pulled away from her and climbed unsteadily from the ground, his fur dripping where it had lain in the filthy water. He gazed at each of them, Morrigan, Rowen and finally Will.

"Shade," Will said. "Go. Run. Find the way home."

The wolf's huge body burst into motion. He bounded away from them, a blur of black and grey, and was soon lost from sight. Will touched his arm. The marks of Shade's teeth were already fading, but the words of the young man in the Weaving came to him again: *The wolf must be bound, or all is lost.*

Will and Rowen didn't know how long the Shee woman led them along winding paths through the mountains of trash. Their thoughts were on Shade and they paid little attention to their surroundings. After a while, though, Will couldn't help noticing that the litter of devoured stories was changing around them. The broken glass and crockery, the books and clothing, the tools and toys—it was all blending together, the colours fading, the edges of things blurring, each thing becoming indistinguishable from everything else until it all seemed to be turning into one lifeless grey mass.

Like everything's becoming more of the shadow, he thought, and then he realized it was true. Everything around them was turning into more of the Night King's realm.

The words of Dirge's nonsensical song came back to him then. *Tale is done,* she had croaked as she rooted in the trash for something living she'd sniffed out. *Tale is done and all is one.*

Rowen stumbled beside him, but when he put a hand on her arm she moved away from him. He fell back without a word and watched her struggle on. *Everything is becoming more of the shadow,* he thought again. *Even us.*

Finally Morrigan said that they should stop and find a place to rest.

"The shrowde says that we are close now," the Shee woman said. "The place where the Angel brought his prisoners is not far."

She looked around. In the face of the steep wall of trash to one side of the path, she found a squarish hollow opening that looked like a cave entrance. As they crouched and climbed inside, Will saw two rows of bench-like seats and realized the cave was the interior of a large vehicle, probably a school bus. It had been buried in the wall of debris with only its rear door open to the air.

The bus was dark inside, the windows blocked completely by refuse. Rowen sat down heavily on one of the seats. Will sat beside her and handed her a water bottle, but she didn't drink from it. Once they were all inside, Morrigan drew back the hood of the shrowde cloak.

"We must not stay here long," she said. "Only until you are both able to go on again."

"Morrigan," Rowen said weakly, "may I see Sputter?"

The Shee woman brought out the waylight, still fixed to the end of the Loremaster's staff. Rowen took it from her and opened the little door. For a moment Will wondered if the wisp was even still inside, and then a faint blue glow appeared, pulsing feebly.

"This place is hurting him, too," Rowen said. "But it's too late to send him back. He'd never make it."

She shut the door of the waylight and handed it back to Morrigan.

"You're shivering," Will said to her.

"I'm all right. I just need to rest."

She leaned forward and wrapped her arms around herself.

"Will," she said after a long silence. "The Dreamwalker . . . did he tell you anything else about me? About what I'm supposed to do?"

"I don't remember everything he said. Only that there's something you would have to do here, for the sake of everyone in the Realm. He said it would be your task to make a new story."

"A new story." She shook her head slowly. "I don't know what that means. I can do a few things that Grandfather taught me. But they're just tricks. I'm not one of the Stewards.

They were the only ones who ever had the power to create stories. Isn't that right, Morrigan?"

"They, and Malabron," the Shee woman agreed. "But remember, you are their descendent. And your grandfather believed you would do greater things than any loremaster before you."

Rowen's head sagged. "He was wrong about me," she murmured. "He only said it because he loves me."

"Whatever the man of the Horse Folk saw, we should keep to our original purpose," Morrigan said. "For all we know, Rowen, searching for your grandfather is what you are meant to do. Surely no one has dared go as far into the Shadow Realm as we have. Our very presence here brings something new into this nightmare."

Rowen did not reply. She stayed hunched forward with her arms wrapped around herself for a long time. At last she sat up, but she didn't speak or look at anyone. She remained very still, her eyes fixed on the doorway.

At last she said, "You were right about Shade, Will. You were right to stop me from binding him. I'm sorry I lost faith in him. In both of you."

"Do you think he'll come back?" Will asked.

"I don't know," Rowen said. "I can *see* him, Will. I can see his thread, but it's very faint and far away. I don't know if he'll come back. But none of the others out there have dared to go near him. I can see them, too. The harrowers and the fetches." Her voice was quiet and distant, like the voice of someone talking in her sleep. "I didn't think they had any story left once they came here. But they do. Or it's all one story now. *His* story."

"Does *he* know we're here?" Will whispered.

"I can't see him," Rowen said. "There's just more shadow ahead, and all the threads of story lead into it. I can see the path, but not where it ends."

"What about the Loremaster?" Morrigan. asked. "Can you see him?"

Rowen closed her eyes tightly. Her lips trembled. At last she turned to them both with a lost, hopeless look.

"I can't," she whispered. "I can barely see you. Even right here it's like you're far away. Or I am. I think . . . I think what happened to Shade is happening to me. I can see whatever has become part of this place, but not Grandfather." She pressed her hands to her temples. "My story-sight didn't work here before, not because it couldn't but because I wouldn't let it. I was afraid to. Because it's telling me I'm going to be like *them*. Like Dirge and Gibbet." She buried her face in her hands.

"We're here with you, Rowen," Will said, trying to keep the fear out of his voice. "We're not far away. We won't leave you."

"You should leave me, Will," she said. "I should never have brought you here. Any of you. This nightmare turns everything into more of itself. That's how it grows. It only happened to Shade first because of the *gaal* inside him."

"Shade resisted," Will said, desperate for words that would give them both some hope or comfort. "He's still out there somewhere, our friend. This place hasn't defeated him yet. You have to be like Shade, Rowen. You have to fight against it."

"I'm trying," she said sharply, looking up at him with eyes blazing. "You don't know what it's like. You can't understand."

Again she had lashed out at him, and it hurt. But something of her former spirit had showed itself, like a curtain parting briefly to let sunlight into a dark room. That reassured him, just a little. In spite of what she had said, the Rowen he knew was still there.

Then her gaze softened. She took his hand and gripped it. "Will, I'm sorry," she said. "I didn't mean . . ."

He shook his head. "Don't think about it. Just rest now."

With an exhausted sigh she closed her eyes and lowered her head to his shoulder. Will could feel the feverish heat of her forehead through the sleeve of his shirt and it alarmed him. He turned to Morrigan with a pleading look, in the faint hope there was something she could say or do. But the Shee woman seemed to have withdrawn into herself as well. She gave Rowen an almost cold glance, in much the same way she had looked at Shade.

They let Rowen rest, and Will even thought she slept for a time. Then abruptly she stirred and sat up, staring around wildly as if she had no idea where she was. She was still deathly pale, and when he helped her up her hands felt cold to his touch.

"Rowen?" he whispered.

"We'll keep going, Will," she said. "Morrigan is right. I don't know what else to do, so I'm going to keep searching for Grandfather. All the threads I can see lead into the shadow. He must be there, too."

They were getting ready to leave the shelter of the bus when she halted suddenly and said, "Wait."

They turned to her. She stood without moving, staring straight ahead. Slowly she raised her hand and moved it back and forth, as if she were brushing invisible cobwebs out of her way. Will exchanged a glance with Morrigan, but neither of them spoke.

At last Rowen turned to them.

"They've found our trail," she said. "We're being hunted now. But the place the shrowde knows about is not far. I see the way there. I can take us by a path that'll make it hard for them to follow."

*   *   *

After a while it seemed to Will that each step took more effort. Soon he was breathing hard, as if he were trudging up the steep slope of a mountain into thinner air. But unlike a mountain climber, he had no sense that he was coming closer to a goal. Instead it seemed they were dropping farther and farther into a pit, a forgotten place without life or meaning or even names. He found he had to keep reminding himself, as if he was about to forget, *My name is Will Lightfoot. I am with Rowen and Morrigan of the Shee. We are trying to find Master Pendrake so we can return to Fable.*

Then, without warning, the trashlands ended.

They had climbed another slope and were forced to halt at the brink of a sheer wall that plunged at least a hundred feet straight down. There were no more hills and gullies of stinking grey rubble before them. From here they could look out over a vast flat expanse of barren earth, bleached almost white and scarred with a web of cracks and crevices, like the floor of a dried-up lake. The white plain stretched away, seemingly without end, into a haze of dust and shadow.

"This is where the shrowde says the Angel always brought his captives," Morrigan said. "The shrowde does not know what dangers it might hold, but she has heard there is a place at its heart called the Silence, from which nothing ever returns."

"Did she ever see what happened to the people Lotan brought here?" Will asked.

"She supposes that they became fetches, but the Angel never lingered in this place once he cast his prisoners from him. She thought that he feared it, too."

"There won't be anywhere to hide out there," Will said.

"I'll keep you both concealed in the shrowde," Morrigan said. "She will be less visible on the plain, and we can go faster that way."

They waited for Rowen to speak. She hadn't said a word since they'd halted at the top of the ridge, and now Will realized he and Morrigan had silently agreed that Rowen was the one making the decisions.

At last she stirred and turned to them.

"No, Morrigan," she said. "We can't hide in the shrowde because it's her trail they're following. They're looking for the one pretending to be the Angel. That's who they're after."

"You're saying we should leave the shrowde behind?" Will asked.

"Out there is the place all the threads lead to," Rowen said. "That's where we have to go, and it's not far. Will and I can make it, Morrigan, but only if you draw off the hunters."

"I cannot leave the two of you to cross the plain alone," Morrigan protested. "There is no defence. Nowhere to hide."

"Rowen, we can't even get down this cliff without Morrigan and the shrowde," Will said.

"We can," Rowen said firmly. "There's another way, Will. You'll see. Morrigan, please. You must do this. The hunters are so close. If we stay together, they'll catch us. I can see it. I see their threads and mine weaving together, but that doesn't happen if you leave now."

The Shee woman looked back the way they had come, then she turned to Rowen again, her face set with grim resolve. Without a word she brought out the Loremaster's staff and Will's Errantry sword, and handed them over.

"The shrowde and I will draw the pursuers away," Morrigan said. "As soon as it is safe we will find you again."

"Morrigan, if they catch you . . ." Will began, but he couldn't finish.

"Then we will do our best to thin out their numbers, Will. If they threaten to overwhelm us, the shrowde has agreed she will leave me and seek you out."

She reached out a hand and touched Rowen's cheek.

"Go safely," she said. Then she turned and they watched the flowing white form of the shrowde glide away over the ridge until it disappeared from sight.

19

THE MORNING AFTER ANNEN Bawn fell to the Nightbane, the sky over Fable was clear and the air mild and warm. The field before the city was dotted with tents of so many kinds that to anyone looking over the battlements it seemed as if the harvest festival had come early. But the mood in the city was far from festive. Errantry troopers patrolled the silent streets, and the shops and taverns were all shut.

In the eerie hush, the pounding of hooves could be heard by those on the Course, and a lone rider appeared on the north road, galloping hotly for Fable. He rode up into the city and silence fell again, but a rumour quickly spread that he was a herald from Annen Bawn, sent to report the fall of the citadel. It was not long before the rumour was verified, as the few survivors of Annen Bawn soon appeared in his wake, in ragged companies with bloodied armour and bowed heads. And everyone knew this meant that the enemy could be at the walls of Fable by the next evening.

Preparations for battle and siege went even faster now, and the stream of folk fleeing the northern part of the Bourne increased to a flood that clogged the roads and led to arguments and in a few cases blows. With the Marshal unable to perform his duties, it was up to Captain Thorne to meet with the Red Duke and the captains of the other allied forces. The Duke's great pavilion was even more crowded than it had been the first time.

"We've been informed," the Duke said to Thorne, "that your city is under martial law and there have been arrests."

"It is true," Thorne said, darting nervous glances at the assembled commanders. It was clear he felt out of his element and was struggling to maintain his poise. "The archmage, Ammon Brax of Kyning Rore, has discovered a plot to overthrow the Errantry. We had no choice but to take these measures, for the safety of the people."

"This is troubling news," said the Duke. "If you require additional troops to help—"

"We do not," Thorne said brusquely. "The mage will soon have the traitors unmasked."

The Duke nodded doubtfully, as if he wished to say more, but then he turned the business of the council to the coming threat. It was almost a certainty that the Nightbane would use the high road from the north, since that would be the quickest and easiest route from Annen Bawn. The enemy would know by now they could not hope to take the city by surprise, yet it was unclear whether they had any inkling of the size of the defending force. And so it seemed to the Duke and the other commanders that they themselves might have an element of surprise that they could put to their advantage, along with the fact that the enemy would be coming uphill to meet the defenders.

"We need not wait for a siege to begin," the Duke said. "And I believe we should not. The walls of Fable were not built to withstand the kind of onslaught that is on its way. They are neither high enough nor strong enough to last even a day against siege towers and battering rams. And to pen our combined forces up inside walls would be to hobble what strength we have. I say we take the fight to our enemy. We strike them hard and fast, and hope to break their lines and scatter them before they get anywhere near the city."

The various forces were divided so that if a company was made up of both archers and foot soldiers, the archers were separated from their fellows and assigned to one of two large companies of bowmen. They were to be situated on either side of the narrow, northern end of the valley, and their task would be to rain arrows down on the enemy from both sides. But this order would not be given until the main Nightbane force had come some distance into the valley. A shallow stream that often dried up in the hottest summers meandered across the northern end of the Course, and this was chosen as the point at which the enemy was to be stopped and driven back.

Teams of diggers went to work on the banks of this stream, which was nearly dry now in the late summer heat, hollowing out the banks and making them deeper and more sheer. Stakes were driven all along this new trench on the Fable side. The plan was to let the enemy begin crossing the stream, and while they were struggling up the near bank, when their lines would be in disarray, the main force of defenders would launch its assault. A company of horsemen concealed in the woods on either side of the Course would charge out at the same time, with the intent of cutting through the enemy and breaking it in half. Then the archers would let loose their volleys.

What remained was to decide how the Errantry itself, with its troopers and its small contingent of mounted knights, would be best deployed. The Duke had a plan for this, as well. The knights, he suggested, would form part of the concealed cavalry brigade on the west side of the Course, nearest to Fable, while the foot troopers would join a reserve force that would remain closer to the city gates. These troops could be brought up to reinforce the main army if the battle turned against them, or they could be sent back into the city to defend it should the attack be repelled and the battle become a siege.

"And what of the archmage?" the Duke asked Captain Thorne when the plans had been debated and approved. "I have had mages for counsellors myself in the past and have seen their power and the way they can stir hope and fighting spirit in men. Once the threat of treason in Fable has been dealt with, will Ammon Brax help us?"

"Master Brax has informed me that he will stand with us," Thorne said, though the nervous working of his jaw was at odds with his words. "I know he is making preparations for a great feat of spellcraft that he'll unleash on our enemies in the hour of need."

"That hour may be soon," the Duke said.

The next day dawned as bright and serene as the last, and some began to question what they had been told, doubting whether there really was any Nightbane host on the march or whether these strange foreign armies—which counted among their number goblins and trolls and other such creatures of darkness—had gathered here under false pretences in order to lay siege to the city themselves. This fear, combined with rumours of dark sorcery in Fable, brought people out into the streets to demand answers. The Errantry troopers had to quell several near riots as they attempted to disperse the crowds and send everyone home. When it was all over, there were some bloodied heads and broken bones, among not only the people but the Errantry as well.

Balor Gruff was kept busy all that day restoring order, although he sent two of the older Errantry apprentices he knew and trusted to keep watch on Pluvius Lane in case anyone entered or left the toyshop. Finally, late that evening, he turned his steps toward Appleyard, weary and disgusted with the force he'd had to use to keep peace in the streets. As was his duty, he went to report to the acting marshal, a task he had been avoiding ever since taking Edweth to the Golden Goose.

Thorne was pacing in Lord Caliburn's chamber, his hands knotted together. He didn't wait to listen to Balor's report but muttered broken phrases about traitors in their midst and punishment for those who broke their oath to protect Fable.

"Even Dame Oreande," he said, shaking his head in disbelief.

"The mayor, sir?"

"I've had her taken into custody. Brax uncovered proof that she was one of the plotters. And if she—" He broke off suddenly and looked at the wildman as if noticing him for the first time. "You're one of the few I can trust, Gruff. I cannot leave Appleyard now to meet with the commanders. No, the archmage requires my presence here to keep order in the city while he prepares his great stroke against the enemy. We must not—" He broke off once more, and wiped a shaking hand across his mouth.

"Sir?"

"We will commit no troops to the defence outside the walls. Master Brax has advised me on this and I agree with him. This Duke and the others . . . well, we must be on our guard. We don't know what their true motives are. Balor, listen. I'm making you special constable of the watch. I've already signed the order. Keep your troopers on patrol in the streets and allow no one to leave the city. The Errantry's duty is to the people of Fable."

"Sir, the enemy is almost here. There will be battle tomorrow, by all reckoning. Our allies need us to stand with them."

"No one leaves the city until I give the order," Thorne repeated. "Is that clear?"

"If I may speak freely, sir. The mage created all this fear and confusion in the first place. He's been using us—using the Errantry—for his own ends. His only concern is protecting himself. He's growing more powerful all the time and we can't let him—"

"You have your orders, Constable," Thorne growled furiously, his lips trembling. "If you will not carry them out, you will be stripped of your rank and confined to your quarters. You are dismissed."

After he'd left the Marshal's chamber, Balor paused on the steps of the Gathering House and looked back at the great doors. This had been his home for many years now, ever since childhood, when he was found by Errantry troopers and brought to live at Appleyard. How proud he had been to take the oath of a knight-errant.

Then he hurried to Pluvius Lane, where he'd left the two apprentices to keep watch. They were still there, concealed in the shadows.

"People are being marched in there, Balor," they told him. "Those who break curfew or protest what's happening are taken in there and they don't come back out."

"Time to spread the word, lads," Balor said. "We will have to act soon."

In the night's cool quiet, above the creak of frogs from the nearby ponds and the crickets chirring in the long grass, a faint noise could be heard, a rumbling like distant thunder. The sky was clear, but in the middle of the third watch a vast cloud rose and hid the stars. It was the cloud of dust raised by the approaching enemy.

In the first grey light before dawn a thick clot of darkness could be made out at the far end of the Course, where the northern road emerged from the hills beyond. As the light grew, the darkness resolved into a great mass of bodies. Shouts and calls and the clatter of weaponry drifted across the field.

The Duke and his fellow commanders watched from a knoll at the other end of the Course, but no one from the Errantry had yet joined them. Then Balor came riding from the city alone. He dismounted before the Duke and saluted.

"The acting marshal has sent me in his stead, my lord. He is . . . preoccupied with the threat of treason and cannot leave the city at present."

"It would seem the threat is worsening," the Duke said.

"It is, my lord. Captain Thorne has issued an order that while the Errantry is engaged in rooting out this insurrection, he will not commit troops to the defence outside the walls."

A shocked and angry murmur spread through the gathered commanders. The Duke raised a hand.

"The captain is aware, is he not, of the enemy force that has just arrived on his doorstep?"

"He is, my lord."

The Duke breathed deeply. He turned his gaze to the city for a moment, then back to his fellow commanders.

"Very well," he said. "We pledged to defend this city, and we will do so. Balor Gruff, I ask you to remain at my side for the time being. There may be news that you can take back to your acting marshal, should he be interested in hearing it."

Balor had a spyglass, an instrument unknown to many

of the other leaders. The Duke borrowed it from him and peered through it. After a moment he gave a grunt of surprise and handed the spyglass back.

"There are men in the Nightbane army," he said.

Balor looked where the Duke pointed. He saw a company of foot soldiers and another of horsemen, the metal of their pikes and spurs glittering with the morning dew. They looked like they could just as easily have joined the side of the defenders.

The sun climbed in the sky and burned the mist away from the hollows and thickets around the city, but still the enemy did not advance. No horn sounded; no signal was given. Instead the besieging force slowly fanned out on either side of the road—as if the plan was to encircle the defenders— then came to a halt.

"Why aren't they attacking?" asked Balor.

"They haven't brought any siege engines," one of the other commanders said. "There are no catapults, no battering rams."

"The fetch host will be their battering ram," the Duke said. "That's what they're waiting for."

Soon an unnerving sound could be heard, a squealing that pierced the silence and swiftly grew louder. At last the most distant of the enemy ranks parted and a great, towering carriage came into view, square and windowless and made of some dull grey metal. The wheels were metal, as well. The carriage was pulled by four huge, unknown beasts in plate armour that covered most of the enormous bodies.

The carriage stopped at the rear of the Nightbane army and again there was silence. Then a single rider on a black horse appeared. He sat stiffly upright, clutching his arms before him, like someone unused to riding, but still his mount came swift and sure up the Course to the far edge of the stream, where it halted. The rider's face was bowed, and he carried no weapon that anyone could see, nor made any gesture of greeting or parley.

"It must be a herald," the Duke said. "We will meet with him."

The Duke had his horse brought and he rode down with Balor and two other commanders.

When the four reached the stream, they saw why the rider sat so stiffly in his saddle. He was an older man with cropped white hair and a long sharp face, and he had been strapped to his mount because he was dead. His fine plate armour had been defaced with obscene taunts scrawled in blood, but the clasp of his torn cloak was the five-petaled flower of the Errantry.

"Who is this?" the Duke asked, his face darkening with anger.

"He was the garrison commander at Annen Bawn," Balor said, swallowing hard. "Captain Bayard Kells."

As if in answer to its name a voice issued from the dead man's mouth, though the mouth did not move. The commanders' mounts snorted and stamped in fear.

"Greetings to the Red Duke of Tintamarre and his allies," the voice said. It seemed to rise from a deep pit.

"Who are you?" the Duke demanded. "Who dares speak through the dead?"

"I speak for the Viceroy of Malabron, who commands these legions. I am his voice."

"I've never heard of this viceroy," the Duke said. "What is his name? What land is he from?"

"He has no name, for he is many. The many that is the hand of the One. The Viceroy bids me say to the leaders of your alliance: this is not your city. It belongs to the true lord of this world and he will have it. If you lay down your arms now, you will be allowed to depart in peace for your own lands."

"Tell your viceroy we will not lay down our arms," the Duke replied. "He is the one who must leave this field. He and all this rabble of invaders, before they are all destroyed."

They waited, but the voice did not speak again. The dead man's empty eyes gazed at nothing. A fly landed on his forehead and began to walk across it.

"We cannot leave your comrade to this indignity," the Duke said to Balor. "His body should be taken back to Appleyard."

Balor nodded. He dismounted and was clambering down the stream's newly steepened bank when the dead man's horse reared up and galloped down the field the way it had come. The commanders watched as horse and lifeless rider were swallowed up by the Nightbane horde and vanished from sight.

Balor climbed back up the bank and the four rode back to the knoll.

"We were all offered the chance to leave here unharmed before the battle begins," the Duke told the waiting assembly. "Even if our enemy honours his pledge, which is unlikely, it will only be a matter of time before this host appears at our own doorsteps. Even so, I present this viceroy's offer as it was given, and I leave the choice to each of you to go now or stay and fight."

There was much stirring through the ring of commanders, but no one spoke and no one moved forward, until at last one figure made his way through the crowd to stand before the others. It was the dwarf, Mimling Hammersong.

"I've been on quests and fought battles, likely nowhere near as many as the great lords among us, but I've learned one thing," he said. "Those who fight, fight together. Those who run, run alone. I for one am not going to scuttle home and wait for the axe to fall."

20

THEY HAD BECOME PREY.

Finn crouched with Grath in the shelter of a huge tilted slab of rust-coloured rock. They had been walking for hours, until the walls of Adamant dropped away below the ridges and slag hills. They had skirted gaping cracks in the earth out of which scalding hot steam rose in hissing clouds. They had waded through pools of lead-coloured water and scrambled over heaps of shattered stone. The sun was high in the sky, though little of its light or heat penetrated through the smoky haze.

And then something that lived in this lifeless waste had picked up their scent and was now following them, though they could not see it. Grath had become aware of it first. He'd halted, listened and sniffed the air, then turned in a circle and said, "We're being stalked. Keep your blade ready."

Finn had not caught whatever sound or scent the mordog had picked up, but from time to time he thought he heard the soft clink of a stone being disturbed.

Grath had not increased his pace, though, but kept on at the same steady gait, and Finn was grateful for that. It had been hours since his last taste of the *gaal*. The throbbing pain in his arm had returned, worse than ever. His eyes burned and his head swam. He noticed his legs had begun to tremble, too, and he wondered how much longer he would be able to keep going before his body simply gave out.

Finally Grath had seemed to notice that he was in difficulty and called a halt. They had come to the foot of a huge tilted slab of stone. Finn dropped heavily to the ground. His face and clothing were drenched in sweat, and dark spots had begun to appear before his eyes. The mordog handed him a waterskin but remained standing himself to keep watch. Finn noticed there was no longer a pouch at the mordog's belt.

"You're not taking the *gaal*?" he asked.

The mordog glanced down at him with a crooked grin.

"Kern asked me to surrender my share. Thought it would be a waste since I was certain to die out here," he said, then studied Finn more carefully. "You're feeling the lack."

"Aren't you?"

"I've felt it every day since I joined your brother's cause, but this is the worst." He bared his teeth in a sour grin. "If they have any fever iron left at the fortress, I may be forced to kill someone for it."

They had already agreed they would stay together until they reached Corr's fortress at the far end of the valley, where a small contingent of Stormriders remained. There they hoped to find some shelter and rest, and then decide what to do next. Finn's goal was to carry on south out of

the valley and come upon some place where he could bargain for a horse. If there was any chance he could make it
even that far. Grath had yet to say what he planned to do
beyond the fortress.

"How much farther?" Finn asked. He still had not been
able to glimpse the fortress on its height through all the
smoke and steam.

"Hours yet, by my reckoning. We won't get there before
nightfall at this rate."

Finn heard the annoyance in his voice. "You should carry
on, then," he said. "I'll only slow you down."

The mordog laughed coldly.

"What does it matter?" Grath said. "I've already broken
the most important rule for getting across the valley alive."

"What's that?"

Grath eyed Finn's sling.

"Never come out here with a one-armed man."

To his surprise Finn found himself laughing, too.

"I know what the doctor told you," Grath went on. "That
you're little better than a walking corpse without the *gaal*. If
I had any sense, I would go now and leave you here to be
eaten by whatever's been following us. I'm not going to do
that, though."

"Why not?"

"Because if you die, then there's just me out here, and
wherever I go I'll be hunted either by my own people or by
those who hate my people, and they are many. Even my fellow Stormriders at the fortress will likely stick my head on a
pike when they find out I've deserted. No, Finn Madoc, you
and I are proof that the cunning ones and the mordog don't
have to be at each other's throats until the world ends.
Maybe we're the only ones who believe that, but still, it's in
my best interest to keep you alive as long as I can."

Finn studied Grath's face and then held out his hand, and the mordog helped him to his feet.

"Let's go," Finn said.

They struggled on, taking only brief rests, while the distant sun crawled down the sky, until they neared the edge of the largest and broadest chasm they had seen yet, at least fifty paces across. Its sheer sides dropped away into blackness and stretched away out of sight on either hand.

"I've seen this hole in the ground from the skyships," Grath said. "I thought we were east enough to avoid it, but this place can fool even the best trackers."

"So what do we do?"

"We go around it."

Finn nodded, hoping the mordog wasn't also wrong about the direction he had chosen. He took another sip from the waterskin, which was growing alarmingly light in his hand, he noticed. Then he followed where Grath led.

They were mostly climbing now, over a tumbled terrain of porous black rock that gave off heat as if it had been molten not long ago. Finn was soon gasping for breath. Grath seemed less affected by the heat and before long he was far ahead.

Then the mordog stopped and gestured urgently to him. Finn pushed himself on and when he reached the place Grath stood, he saw that just a few paces ahead the chasm narrowed to a thin crevice and came to an end. They would be able to cross now, but an even greater obstacle still lay ahead.

The far side of the chasm was higher than where they stood, and at this end it had grown to a sheer escarpment that they would have to scale if they wanted to proceed.

Finn gazed up at the rock face rising above them and then looked into himself and felt the death there, worming its way toward his heart. He would not make it to the top of this wall. He would never see his friends in Fable again. He would not deliver the doctor's journal to King Shakya.

Yet he had no choice but to try.

He stepped forward, except Grath's arm shot out and barred his way.

"Listen," the mordog hissed.

Finn froze. All he could hear was the chill wind that had blown at their backs all day.

"What is it?" he whispered.

The mordog didn't reply. His head was raised and he was sniffing the air again. Finn gripped his sword hilt with his good hand and waited, and it was not long before Grath nudged him and said softly, "There," nodding toward the way they had come.

There were three of them. Long, sleek things with skin the same reddish-black of the stones over which they were slinking. Finn studied them with a strangely calm interest, as if, like the doctor, he was observing creatures he had never seen before. He knew this wasn't curiosity, though, only cold certainty about what would happen next.

The hunters were something like wolves, he thought, but with a catlike roll to their shoulder muscles and a supple grace in their every footfall. They had horns, too, that curved down from the spined ridge of their foreheads. Their eyes were black in their blood-red faces. Eyes that gave away nothing.

"*Slar*," Grath muttered. "I thought there might be more than one."

Finn had never heard the name before, but in Grath's voice he heard something worse than fear: resignation. The creatures had spaced themselves far apart and were moving slowly and cautiously, but it was clear all three were headed toward Finn and Grath. The creatures had chosen their moment well: the prey was trapped now, with a sheer wall at their backs.

Grath had his crude cleaver already in hand, but he took a moment to survey the terrain at their feet. Then he sprang onto a nearby boulder with a roughly flat surface and pulled Finn up after him. He tossed his sack at his feet and Finn did the same with his pack.

"Stay on my right," Grath said. "They'll have more trouble reaching us from that side."

Finn nodded and raised his sword. It occurred to him suddenly that he no longer felt any pain. His wounded arm had gone numb, and even his other hand, the one in which he held the sword, barely had the strength to grip the hilt. He had nothing left to fight with, but still he raised the sword and watched while the creatures climbed steadily and unhurriedly toward them. One of the three *slar,* the one that had come closest so far and seemed to be the leader, was larger than the other two. Finn guessed that this was a mother and her two offspring, but that thought did not bring him any comfort or hope. Obviously all three knew what they were doing and had hunted together like this many times before.

"What are you thinking, my lovelies?" Grath whispered, and Finn realized he was talking to the *slar.* Trying to guess what they would do next.

Without warning the largest of the three burst into motion. She lunged toward the boulder on Grath's side, a blur of rippling hide and muscle. The mordog crouched to meet her attack, but at the last instant the *slar* swerved, darting out of the reach of Grath's blade. A feint, Finn realized, and he turned just in time to see one of the other two *slar* where it hadn't been a moment before, impossibly close and coming at him, leaping, and he was too slow—

Grath's blade swept down. There was a shriek and the *slar* fell limp at Finn's feet. Grath gave the body a kick and it slithered down the side of the boulder, trailing a streak of bright blood.

The other two *slar* stood frozen a few paces away. They appeared to take no notice of the one that had fallen but kept their eyes fixed on their prey.

"You moved too soon, my beauties," Grath taunted. "We're not making it that easy for you." He nudged Finn. "They'll likely wait us out now. Night's approaching. They'll bide their time until we tire and drop our guard."

Finn's head was swimming, his breathing little more than a strained gasp. He felt his knees buckle and he clutched the mordog's sleeve.

"Stay on your feet or we're dead," Grath growled, but his words seemed to come from very far away. Finn felt his fingers losing their grip on the hilt of his sword. He could see the *slar* advancing slowly once more. He thought of Will and Rowen, and Freya, and he wished them well, wherever they were.

Before his eyes was rough, pitted black stone. He had fallen. He could not see his sword. He heard Grath cry out, and then there was a roaring in his ears and a glare of white light that filled his head.

There was nothing else for a long time. Nothing but the roaring and the light, and a feeling that his body had become weightless and was drifting like a leaf blown about by the wind.

Then he was aware that the roaring had fallen to a murmur of air, rising, falling away and rising again. There was still a light in his eyes, but it was dimmer and it wavered. It was above him, a warm yellow light. It was coming from a lantern that was swinging on a hook. He fixed his gaze on

the light for a while, and then he became aware that the soft
rising and falling of air was his own breathing.

He stirred. His body was solid again, heavy. Encased in
something hard that weighed him down.

"Can you hear me, Finn?" said a voice. A voice he knew.

Finn looked away from the lantern swinging on its hook.
A figure swam up into his vision.

It was Corr.

"Yes, you're still alive, brother."

Finn lifted his head. He was lying on the cot in Corr's cabin.
He was on the flagship. He felt the ship's timbers shuddering beneath him, and through the aft window he could see sky
and drifting clouds. A wave of dizziness swept over him and
he clutched at the side of the cot.

"Where . . . are we?"

"Over the fortress just now," Corr said. "We're landing to
take on provisions before we make the rest of the journey.
I left a few men from the Bourne here, too. Some might be
willing to join us."

"Journey . . . where?"

"Home," Corr said. "Fable."

Finn stared at his brother. "To Fable." He struggled to sit
up and fell back. Whatever had been placed on his body was
still weighing him down. "Why?"

Corr laughed. "Why? You begged me to do this and I'm
doing it. Now you want me to change my mind?"

"No. But Adamant, and the *gaal*—"

"It's all been left in good hands," Corr said lightly, but
there was bitterness and even rage in his voice. "Turns out
Kern has been working hard to persuade the Stormriders
he's the one who'll bring them all the fever iron they want.
They've got a new Sky Lord to lead them now."

"Your men rebelled?"

· "I'd decided to split up the forces, half to stay in Adamant and the other half to follow the fetch host. That's when Kern played his hand. He already had most of the mordog on his side. It looked like there'd be bloodshed, but they let me and the few men still loyal to me leave in the flagship, since it was the most damaged. He knew about the *gaal* hidden in the hold, too. He took most of it."

"Grath," Finn said, suddenly remembering the valley of fire and the *slar*.

"He's alive, and with us."

Finn looked down at his body. It was clad from neck to feet in black armour.

"The fetch armour," Corr said. "Heavy, isn't it? You'll get used to it soon enough."

"I won't, Corr. I'm taking it off."

"You can try, I suppose. But I had the plates riveted together to prevent that. The armour is the only thing keeping you alive, brother. And I want you alive. After all, you've got a task to finish. You swore to bring Corr Madoc to justice, and I'm going to make sure you keep your oath."

21

WHEN MORRIGAN HAD GONE, Will and Rowen turned back to the cliff wall.

"I still don't see a way down," Will said.

"I do," Rowen said, and before he could move to hold her back, she stepped off the edge.

Will cried her name in fear, but Rowen didn't fall. He looked down to see that bits and pieces of the trash that composed the wall—chunks of bricks, scraps of wood and metal, and other unidentifiable odds and ends—were slowly sliding out of the grey mass of the cliff, as if drawn by some force he couldn't see. They were coming out of the wall at what seemed to be regular intervals all down the cliff face in a slanting line. *Steps,* Will realized. Rowen was already standing on the uppermost of them, a slab of grey cinderblock, her head bowed as if she was deep in thought.

Rowen looked up at Will. Beads of sweat had broken out on her brow.

"His story is so strong," she murmured.

"You did this," he said, and realized that the effort had nearly exhausted her. "Like the raincabinet. You made these steps."

"They'll hold us for now, I hope," she said, descending to the next step. "But we have to hurry. Follow me."

Will steeled himself and set a foot on the first step. It was uneven and narrow but not slippery, and it held firm underneath him. He kept as close to the wall as he could. If he slipped, it would be a long fall and he doubted even Rowen's powers could save him then.

The stairs descended at a steep angle, and in a much shorter time than he expected they had reached the bottom. Here Rowen put a hand to the wall and closed her eyes. Will glanced up the way they had come and saw the steps were already vanishing, their various bits and pieces withdrawing again into the wall.

"There," Rowen said. "Now it'll be harder for anyone to follow us."

Will glanced around and shivered. It was even colder here than on the height above. The air was so utterly dry and lifeless that he instinctively pulled out one of the water bottles. He had a small sip and handed the bottle to Rowen. She paid no attention, her gaze fixed on the bleached expanse before them, as if she was waiting for something. She took a few steps forward and paused with a hand in the air as if feeling for something she couldn't see. Then she turned to Will.

"What is it?" he asked.

"Something's out there," she said. "Something that guards this place. It's not a harrower. I don't know what it is, but it's a threat. I can feel it. Stay close to me."

She started off, and Will followed.

The cliff wall soon dwindled behind them and vanished in the haze. The dust rose in sluggish clouds at their footfalls, as if they were the first beings to disturb it for centuries. The earth under their feet was as flat as a tabletop and covered all over with cracks and crevices like dried mud.

They walked for a long time without speaking to each other, and it felt to Will as if the emptiness itself was a presence, a thing walking along with them. In the silence his own thoughts seemed to him as loud as shouts. He felt a strange urge to stamp his feet and scream, as if it would prove he was really here, but more than anything he wanted another drink of water. The thought of the two bottles that remained weighed heavier with each step, but he resisted. There was no telling when they might return to a place with drinkable water.

He saw a movement then and halted, gripping Rowen's shoulder. Something pale and indistinct was walking near them, going in the same direction they were.

"Did you see—?" he whispered. His own voice startled him, as if it had been years since he'd heard himself speak.

Rowen nodded.

"Fetches," she whispered back. "Drawn here by *him*. They won't harm us."

They walked on, and now Will saw more of the pale forms, all trudging slowly or simply drifting like thickened clots of dust across the plain. *We'll be like them if we keep going this way,* he thought. *Unless we already are.*

He stopped again as Rowen's hand touched his shoulder.

"Wait," she said, her mouth close to his ear. "Do you hear that?"

He went still and listened. There *was* a faint sound. A thin whispering, little more than a stirring of air, that appeared to be coming from a great distance.

"It's wind," he said in surprise. "There's actually a wind here."

"It's what I sensed earlier," Rowen said. "It's the threat, Will."

"What is it?"

"I can't tell yet, but it's drawing closer."

Will looked back at the two lines of their footprints in the dust. "Well, there's nothing else we can do," he said, "except keep going."

They hurried on, listening for the sound they'd heard. It rose and fell, sometimes vanishing completely into the silence and then returning, and each time they heard it again it was stronger and more shrill. Still there was nothing to be seen anywhere around them but the same cracked, lifeless earth stretching away in all directions.

Suddenly Rowen halted again.

"Don't move," she whispered urgently. "Don't run, whatever happens. Hold your breath."

Will knew better than to question her. He did as she said, and a moment later the sound rushed up, louder than it had been yet. It whined and shrieked all around them, but still Will could see nothing. Then the sound died down and disappeared again.

Rowen let out her breath and Will did the same.

"What was that?" he said. "I couldn't see—"

To his surprise she put a hand to his mouth to keep him from speaking, then began to draw lines in the dust with the end of the Loremaster's staff.

She wasn't drawing, he realized. She was writing words.

Wind is threat. Hunts what moves or speaks.

He took the staff from her and scraped a reply.

What can we do?

Her answer: *Keep going. Stop when wind comes. Can't see us then.*

Go where?

Fetches go this way. So do we.

They set off again. He resisted the urge to glance around and kept his gaze fixed ahead of him, waiting to see anything that would tell him they had reached the place Rowen was looking for. But what lay ahead was the same as what lay behind: haze and shadow.

Then Rowen halted and gripped his arm tightly. He went still and listened, heard the wind returning, its hollow whine growing louder. This time it did not seem to come as close to them, and soon trailed away into silence.

They waited awhile longer, still holding their breath, then walked on. Nothing about the lifeless earth under their feet or the dull grey sky changed in the least, and after a while Will began to wonder if they were really moving at all or somehow plodding over the same patch of ground again and again.

And then he became aware of something ahead of them. At first it seemed only a faint darkening in the endless haze, but as they walked on, it began to take on more shape and definition.

Before them stood a vast pillar of dust, rising from the earth and into the depthless heights of the sky. A pillar of dust that, as they came closer, they saw was silently revolving, like a cyclone that had somehow slowed down until it was almost motionless. At its base the pillar looked as large in circumference as the walls of Fable.

"This must be the place Morrigan told us about," Rowen murmured. "This is the Silence."

All around them the fetches kept moving forward, until they reached the pillar of dust and vanished into it.

"Do we go in there, too?" Will said. "Remember what Morrigan said. Nothing ever returns from the Silence. What if that's where *he* is?"

"I don't know what else to do, Will," Rowen said. "Grand-father may be in there. I have to find out."

They started forward. Will's throat was parched and all he could think about was the water in his pack. They needed to drink something, he decided, before they entered that wall of dust. He was reaching to touch Rowen's hand, to get her to stop so they could take a drink, when he caught his foot in one of the cracks in the earth and stumbled forward.

He hit the ground hard, letting out an involuntarily grunt and raising a cloud of dust. Rowen turned at the sound and hurried to his side, then froze and lifted her head.

Will heard it, too: the wind was coming again, but this time with a roar more frenzied and insistent. The wind wasn't searching blindly now. It was coming straight for them.

Rowen glanced around wildly, but she seemed unable to move. Will scrambled to his feet, gripped her hand in his and whispered one word in her ear.

"Run."

Together they burst into headlong flight. At first Will could hear only the noise of their breathing and pounding feet, then the wind's shrieking rose above those sounds and grew louder. The dry, lifeless air seemed to pull the very breath out of Will's lungs, so that in no time he was gasping and panting.

They ran on. The shrieking filled Will's ears. They were almost there, almost in the pillar of dust, and something was clutching at his cloak. He heard the cloth tearing.

They reached the wall of dust and kept going straight into it without slowing. Will felt Rowen's hand slip from his, but he could no longer see her. The earth seemed to have vanished from underneath him and he was tumbling over and over through the thick, choking dust.

He ended up on his back with dust in his eyes, nose and mouth and the wind roaring somewhere close by like a wild animal in a rage. He couldn't see his hands in front of his face. He couldn't see Rowen. All he knew was that he had to keep perfectly still, even though his every nerve was screaming at him to flee.

At last the noise lessened and seemed to move away. The wind died to a whisper, then to silence.

Will wiped at his eyes. He sat up and blinked. The dust around him was falling now, thinning out.

"Rowen, where are you?" he said softly, not daring to speak any louder. His words seemed to vanish as soon as he spoke them.

"I'm here, Will."

As the dust settled, he saw her, picking herself up, a few feet from him. He hurried over to her and helped her to her feet.

"I think the wind is gone," he said.

"It can't come in here," she said, and then her eyes widened. "Will, your cloak."

He tugged the end of his travelling cloak around to see what she was looking at. One side of it was shredded to ribbons, as if by a beast's claws.

He let the cloak drop and looked up.

The dust had settled enough now that they could see they'd fallen into a large circular hollow, almost as deep as the cliff at the edge of the Silence had been high, but with more gently sloping sides. Like a crater on the moon, Will thought. Thick drifts of dust had settled at the bottom of the rim, where they stood now, but farther out the earth was as hard and bare and lifeless as it had been in on the plain. The pillar they were inside rose like a towering grey wall around them, closed over with a hanging cloud of dust at some height they could not guess. There were no fetches to be seen anywhere.

At the centre of the hollow stood a tree.

It was immense, leafless and looked long dead. The trunk and the many twisted, skeletal branches appeared to be made of the same dust that filled the hollow.

"What is this place?" Will asked.

"I don't know," Rowen said. "I can't see the threads anymore. Not Shade's. Not anyone's."

"What happened to the fetches?"

"I think they were drawn up into the pillar. Maybe it's from here that they get sent to do the Night King's bidding."

"At least we're safe from the wind now."

"Where's Grandfather's staff?" Rowen cried. She glanced around wildly and then saw it, half buried in the dust near the place they had fallen. She hurried to it and lifted it. The waylight was still attached, but its door hung crookedly and the glass in its panes was broken. Rowen peered into the lantern's interior.

"Sputter's not here," she said. "What happened to him?"

"There he is," Will shouted, pointing. The wisp was coming toward them, skimming low over the floor of the hollow. When it reached Rowen it flew up into her open palms, trembling and bobbing, its light pulsing brighter than they had seen it in a long time.

"He's excited about something," Rowen said.

The wisp leaped up from Rowen's hands and sped off again the way it had come. It didn't go far, though, before it halted in midair and waited for them to catch up.

"He's taking us to the tree," Will said.

They set out across the floor of the hollow, the dust sifting down from their hair and clothing as they hurried along. The closer Will got to the tree, the sharper and more defined it seemed to grow, as if it was becoming more real only because of their presence.

At last they reached the tree and drew to a halt beneath it. In size and height it was even more enormous than Will had first thought, its trunk squat but thick and broad, larger around the bole than any tree he had ever seen back home. It rose straight out of the dust without any roots visible, its barren branches towering into the ashen sky. Will thought of a dead spider lying on its back with its legs in the air. It was a sight of such utter hopelessness that he felt all his own hopes had finally ended here.

Only Sputter didn't seem to think so. The wisp danced around them frantically, then shot up to the tree's heights and back down again to settle on Rowen's outstretched hand.

"What have you found, Sputter?" Rowen asked, and then she looked up with her eyes wide and said, "Oh."

"What is it?" Will asked.

Rowen didn't answer. Slowly she reached up and touched the rough, knotted bark.

"It's *their* tree," she whispered. "Or it *was*. This was it, Will. The tree of the Stewards. The one that stood on the green hill where they met at midsummer with the Fair Folk and the Speaking Creatures."

"But it was destroyed a long time ago. Wasn't it? That's what Shade told us."

"This is how Malabron destroys," Rowen said. "Like everything we've seen here, it all becomes more of the shadow. The same thing happened to the tree. But this is it. Sputter knows. He recognizes it. This is the Tree of Story."

The wisp sprang from Rowen's palm and whirled into the air, dancing and crackling and buzzing like a firecracker that has spun out of control. Then, before they could do more than stare in surprise, the wisp shot toward the base of the tree and vanished into a furrow in the bark.

"Sputter!" Rowen cried. She pressed her hands to the

place the tiny creature's light had vanished. There was no sign or sound of the wisp.

Rowen stepped away from the tree.

"He's gone back to where he came from," she said sadly. "At least he'll be safe here for now."

"But we have to keep going," Will said. "Master Pendrake isn't here. This isn't where he was taken."

Rowen lowered her head and stared at the ground as if she was deep in thought. Then she looked up and gazed around the hollow with a startled expression, as if she was seeing it for the first time. She reached out a hand and touched the tree again at the place where the wisp had disappeared.

"No, Will," she said. "We don't go anywhere from here. I didn't understand before. Or I didn't want to. But Sputter showed me. *This* is the place all the threads lead. It all began here, at the tree, just like Sputter did. Everything that the Stewards wove and cared for began here."

"But there's nothing here."

"That's just it. Nothing. All the stories lead here, to the tree, and then they just . . . *end*." Her voice had gone faint and hollow. "It's just like Grandmother told me. *Nothing* is what will happen, forever, once *he* wins. Everything will end, in the same place it began."

The cold despair in her eyes terrified Will. The words of Dirge's song came to him again: *Tale is done, and all is one.*

"Then where is Master Pendrake?" he said desperately. "You said he'd be where all the threads ended up."

She didn't answer but stared past him, at the tree. Her eyes seemed to burn in the gloom.

Will turned to where she was gazing. In the furrow where Sputter had vanished, a slender, pale green shoot had grown out of the bark. Rowen crouched before it. She raised her hand but didn't touch the thin, fragile tendril, as if she wasn't sure it was really there. In the grey emptiness of the hollow this one tiny thread of life and colour held him spellbound, too, as if he had never seen such a thing before.

"It's *him*," she murmured. "Sputter did this."

She set her hand on the bark beside the shoot, then pressed her ear to the tree, like someone listening for a heartbeat. After a long silence she gave a cry and looked up at Will with a gleam of hope in her eyes, the first he'd seen in a long time.

"The tree isn't dead, Will," she said. "Not yet. Sputter knew. That's what he's trying to show us. That the fathomless fire is here. It's so faint. It's barely here at all. But Sputter felt it. The tree is still alive, Will."

"Can Sputter heal it?"

"I don't think he's strong enough, not by himself. Not in this place. Malabron's story is too powerful." She took a deep breath and brushed her hair out of her eyes. "Sputter's returned to where he came from. This is his home, but he's still weak. He needs my help. Maybe together we can make the tree grow again. If that happens . . ."

"Will it stop Malabron?"

"I don't know," she whispered. "I don't know, but I have to try."

She fell silent, closed her eyes and crouched, pressing herself up against the tree once more.

Will watched and waited, not daring to speak and disturb her. He glanced up often at the rim of the hollow, dreading to see figures there: Dama and whatever creatures she had gathered to hunt them. But the hollow remained silent and Rowen did not stir.

Then Will heard the faintest of sounds from the tree. He looked up in surprise to see another slender, pale green tendril rising from one of the crevices in the bark. It was so quick and fine that at first he thought it must be a tongue of werefire. Then he looked closer and realized the tendril was real and solid. It was another shoot, like the first, and it was uncurling as it came, growing longer and thicker. Tiny buds like green droplets of water appeared along its length.

Then he looked higher up the massive body of the tree and saw that other shoots were appearing there, as well, some growing out from the trunk and others from the branches. The sound he had heard was the buds on all of these new shoots opening to the air, the leaves inside them stickily unfolding. Not all of the tree was growing, though, he noticed. Most of the branches remained lifeless and bare. And yet it seemed to him that the grey dimness of the hollow had lightened just a little.

Rowen was still pressed to the tree, her eyes closed, her brow furrowed in concentration. She hadn't given any sign that she knew what was happening. Will was about to let her know what he was seeing, but he held back, not wanting to disturb her. He caught the warm, sweet scent of sap and green life and breathed it in deeply. It seemed to him a lifetime since he had smelled anything but dust and decay.

Then he glanced down at his feet.

Green shoots were slipping from the cracks in the earth, too. These were stalks of grass, he realized. They were growing all around the tree, more and more of them appearing each moment. Each slender stem seemed lit with its own inner fire, as if the light of a sun that Will could not see was shining on them.

He heard Rowen take a sharp breath and turned to her. Her eyes were open and she was marvelling, as he was, at the change that had come over the hollow. They shared a look of wonder but didn't speak. Rowen climbed to her feet.

The grass was growing with impossible speed. Instead of scattered blades poking up here and there through the

barren earth, a deep, living carpet of green was spreading
out on all sides, climbing the slopes to the rim and rising
there, growing taller, the stalks tangling and intertwining to
form a living wall. A moist, earthy smell filled the air. Will
even thought he heard the sound of water trickling somewhere not far away. *Water*. It was something else he had
wondered if he would ever see again.

"You've done it," Will said excitedly. "You and Sputter."

Rowen faced him. Beads of sweat glittered on her brow
and she was shivering as she had been when they were hiding in the bus.

"Now they know where we are," she said. "We can't hide
anymore."

As she turned away from the tree, she staggered. Will
caught her just as she was falling into the grass. He lowered
her down and crouched beside her.

"So tired," she murmured, closing her eyes. Her breathing was deep and laboured.

He waited for a while, not daring to disturb her. His own
body so craved rest that he was tempted to sink down beside
her and close his eyes, too. But her own last words kept returning to him, prodding him to stay awake.

At last he could wait no longer. He touched her shoulder.

"Rowen?"

She opened her eyes but didn't look at him.

"They haven't found us yet," he said. "We should keep
going. We don't want to stay here and wait to be caught."

She didn't seem to hear him. Will gripped her by the
shoulders.

"Rowen, listen to me. You have to get up. It isn't over yet.
If we find Morrigan we can—"

"They're bringing him," Rowen said.

"What?" Will said. "Bringing who?"

Rowen sat up suddenly. Her fingers clutched the grass.

"They're bringing Grandfather here," she breathed. "They're bringing him to me."

Will followed her eager gaze to the hollow's rim. Beyond the newly green slope there was nothing to be seen but the same slowly churning wall of dust.

"We have to get out of here *now*," Will said. "We can find Morrigan and—"

"There's nowhere else to go, Will," Rowen said. "And I'm not leaving. Grandfather is here."

"Where?" he said. "I don't see anything."

Rowen herself appeared uncertain. She turned in a slow circle, her brows knitted, then knelt and put a hand to the earth. She stayed like that, with her head bowed in concentration, as if listening for a heartbeat. Then suddenly she stood.

"They couldn't get through. I had to make a path."

Again Will looked where she was gazing, and this time he saw that the woven wall of green had collapsed in one narrow place, as if it had been mown or trodden down.

Dama stood there. Others were with her—Dirge and Gibbet, and creatures Will had never seen before. Among their hideous shapes stood a familiar figure in grey.

"Grandfather," Rowen whispered. The Loremaster did not raise his head.

Dama's wings spread. She rose into the air and then came gliding down into the hollow, leaving Pendrake and the others behind on the rim.

Will drew his sword and stepped in front of Rowen.

"No, Will," she said, clutching his arm. "That won't do any good. Let her approach."

Swiftly Dama crossed the space between them, but as she came Will saw doubt and even fear in her eyes. Not fear of them, he realized, but of this place. She had never set foot here before. She had no more idea of what she would find here than they'd had.

Dama descended to within a few paces of Will and Rowen, but her feet did not touch the grass. When her gaze fell on the tree a tremor crossed her face. A look, Will thought, of both fear and desire. At last she turned her eyes to Will and Rowen.

"The armies of the One are before the walls of your city," she said. "Soon all who dwell there will join you here. They will feed us. You have failed."

"What have you done to my grandfather?" Rowen asked.

"He is unharmed," Dama said.

"Let him go. It's me you wanted, and now I'm here."

"Whether he remains with us or goes free is of no consequence. But very well, we will bargain. If you want the old man set free, you must call off the wolf."

Will felt Rowen's grip on his arm tighten, and it was as if the thought passed between them without words: Shade was still alive. He was alive, and still fighting. Still resisting the power of the Shadow Realm. *He's hunting them*, Will thought with a terrible exultation. *He's hunting and killing the harrowers.* And more than that, he realized, the harrowers thought Shade was under Rowen's command.

"Let my grandfather go, and Will as well, and I will bring the wolf to heel."

"Rowen, no," Will said. "I'm not leaving you."

"We will let them depart unharmed," Dama said, ignoring Will's outburst. "The old man and the boy will have safe passage to what is left of the Uneaten Lands. But it is not enough. You, child of the Stewards, must remain. You must submit to the One and no longer use your power against us."

Rowen did not answer right away. Will felt her fingers dig into his arm, and then they let go and he knew what she was going to reply. He wanted to cry out, to stop her from answering, but his own voice was choked in his throat.

"I will stay and submit to you," she said. "But if you break your word the wolf will hunt you down and tear out your throat."

Dama snarled. She turned to the rim of the hollow, where the other harrowers waited, and raised a hand. Dirge and Gibbet, who had hold of Pendrake's arms, released him. The old man stirred. Slowly he raised his head and gazed around dully as if waking from sleep. Then he caught sight of Rowen and his eyes opened wide. He opened his mouth to speak, but his voice was too faint and the hollow's rim too far for them to hear what he was saying. Rowen raised her hand in a gesture of farewell. Pendrake seemed to understand now what was happening. He started forward, but Dirge reached out a bony arm and held him back.

"Take him," Dama called.

"Wait," Rowen said, and she held out the Loremaster's staff with its broken waylight. "Please give him this."

Dama took the staff from her. She gave it a quick sneering glance, as if she could not fathom the worth of such a pitiful thing. Then she raised her arm and threw the staff end over end across the hollow. It landed with a soft thump in the grass below the harrowers. Dirge scrambled down to retrieve it and handed it roughly to the Loremaster. Then she looked back at Dama as if awaiting further instructions. The winged woman nodded her head, and the harrowers turned and hurried away with Pendrake, as if they could not wait to escape from this place.

"They will take him to the edge of your realm," Dama said. "No harm will come to him."

"He's going," Rowen breathed, the tears sliding down her face. "He'll make it home."

Dama moved more swiftly than Will would have thought possible. She lunged and her talons sank into Rowen's neck, then she sprang away, rising on a powerful beat of her wings as Will slashed at her in vain with his sword.

"Leave or stay, boy," Dama cried as she soared toward the rim of the hollow. "It no longer matters."

Rowen staggered and Will caught her. He lowered her to the soft, cool grass. "What did she do to you?" he said, his voice breaking.

Rowen gripped his hand. "You must go, Will," she said. Her eyelids had begun to droop and her breath was coming in shallow gasps. "Find Grandfather and go with him."

"I'm not leaving."

"Sputter is . . . keeping the harrowers out. Making this place a refuge. But it won't last. They'll get through. You must go."

Will glanced back at the spot where the harrowers had appeared. The green wall had closed up again and there was no sign of Dama.

"I'm not leaving you," he said once more.

She grasped his hand and placed something in it.

"Take this," she said, and he saw that she had given him the ball of golden thread.

"Rowen . . ."

"I forgot it. When you get back to Fable, give the thread to Grandfather. He'll need it."

"But your grandmother gave this to *you*. There must be some way for you to use it, before—"

"Grandfather can save Fable with this, I'm sure of it. Take it to him, Will, and go now. Promise me you won't stay here after I'm . . ."

"Rowen, please don't."

"Promise me."

Her eyes implored him and he nodded. "I promise."

She closed her eyes. Her head fell back. Will spoke her name again, but she did not answer.

22

THE IRON CARRIAGE SAT at the end of the Course while more Nightbane poured into the valley and swarmed around it like a dark tide around a great black stone. There were no other heralds, and yet no assault began. Some of the commanders began to urge an attack of their own, to drive into the ranks of the enemy while they were still assembling. The Duke decided against such a move. The enemy numbered at least ten thousand and there might be many more concealed in the woods, waiting to surround them if they charged straight down the field.

And so nothing moved on the Course, and there was silence as the two forces waited and watched.

At midday a company of three hundred or more riders came up from the south, dark-skinned men in gleaming silver armour. Their leader, who wore a mask of gold, dismounted and sought council with the Duke in his pavilion. The allied troops waited, wondering who these new arrivals were and where they were from. It wasn't long before the news passed through the camp that King Shakya of the Sunlands had brought his finest warriors to join the defence. The young king wore a mask, it was said, to hide the disfiguring marks of leprosy on his face.

In the early afternoon, a dark cloud appeared in the sky to the north. It was thought at first to be drifting smoke, perhaps from the burning of Annen Bawn, but quickly it became clear that the black cloud was moving against the wind and directly toward Fable. Those with the keenest eyesight soon gave the warning that there were huge winged creatures within the smoke, and in a short time everyone could see that they were right. There were seven shapes within the cloud, and they flew with great flaps of their huge, translucent wings in a loose formation toward the city. The closer they came, the stranger they appeared. They were massive, swollen creatures, like immense black bags, with little in the way of limbs or tails. They had tiny eyes on the sides of their great heads and gaping mouths that belched black smoke and glowed red even in daylight.

Only Balor, watching with the Duke's retinue, knew what they were.

"Motherworms," he told those gathered around him.

"Not many of them whatever they are," the masked king observed. "The archers and musketeers should drive them off soon enough."

"They're more of a threat than you know," Balor said. He asked the Duke for permission to warn the city, and when it was given he rode back in great haste to the gates of Fable.

"You will need more hands to carry buckets," he told the sergeant in charge of the Errantry's fire brigade. "Our troopers won't be enough. The people have their own brigades."

"No one is allowed out of their houses, Balor," the sergeant protested. "The acting marshal's orders."

"There won't be any houses left standing if we don't act," Balor roared.

The sergeant hesitated, then sent three of his men to knock on doors and spread the word. Balor went with them.

When the dragons reached Fable, they did not descend but wheeled high over the city in wide, slow circles. Jodo Flyte's bowmen stationed, near the walls, were kept from shooting at the dragons for fear that their falling arrows would strike people within the city. The musketeers of Sarras fired a volley and the sounds of their guns cracked sharply through the air, but the cloud of shot they loosed appeared to have no effect on the circling dragons.

Then with a roar the motherworms opened their vast mouths and from them came what were seen to be small creatures of fire that moved with their own life and will. These lesser firedrakes fell on the wooded heights of Appleyard Hill, and on the roofs of houses in the town below, where they darted and leaped and burst into larger flame. Soon there were fires burning all over Fable, and still the motherworms circled and vomited their burning offspring onto the city. The Errantry's fire brigade had already been prepared, and thanks to their swift action most of the fires near the walls were swiftly doused. But the people who had been called out of their homes were only just beginning to organize their own brigades when the motherworms attacked. A few fires deeper in the city continued to burn, and spread.

Now the motherworms wheeled away from Fable and belched forth more of their offspring, and these fell, crackling and hissing, upon the army outside the walls. The blazing snakelike forms whipped and tore through the ranks, and men shrieked and dove out of their way. Some whose hair or garments caught on fire ran for the stream in the hope of putting out the flames, while others struck at the dragons with their swords and spears. When a spear point or blade struck one of the firedrakes, the creature burst apart with a spray of smaller flames that seemed still to move with life and purpose. Men who wore capes or tunics over their armour tore them off and used them to cover and then stamp out the flames.

The musketeers fired another volley, this one directed at the motherworm that had descended the farthest. The thick hail of shot succeeded this time: it tore through one of the dragon's wings. The monster let out an ear-splitting shriek and heeled, its torn wing crumpled into itself, then it plummeted through the air, keeping enough command of its fall to turn itself toward Fable at the last moment. It crashed onto the battlements not far from the gate, and a blazing cloud of its spawn exploded upward and fell upon the city.

Then another cry of warning went up. As the dragons brought disorder and fear to the allies, the Nightbane had seized this chance and charged up the field without the warning of chants or drums. A great mass of them strode up the Course toward the stream. Soon they would be across it.

The Duke's herald blew a rallying call on his horn and the allies hurried to re-form their tattered lines. Those who had run to the stream to douse the flames and who could still stand raced back to join their comrades, but some were injured too badly and could only crawl up the bank and cry out for help. The front lines of the allied force, made up mostly of the Duke's knights and King Shakya's mounted warriors, marched to the stream bank and formed a wall bristling with swords and spears. A few men ventured out in the face of the advancing enemy and carried the burned and wounded men out of the stream bed. The Duke himself rode out from the knoll with King Shakya to take command of the two cavalry units waiting on either side of the valley.

The vanguard of the Nightbane host was an armoured wedge of hulking creatures wearing hideous beast masks and carrying heavy iron clubs. They reached the stream, poured down the far bank like a black flood and began to cross. They were slowed down as a result, but their lines were not broken as the Duke had hoped. All too soon they were clambering up the near bank, their progress barely impeded by the stakes, and then the armies met.

A great clamour of metal ringing on metal filled the air. The wall of the allies held, sending the front ranks of the Nightbane sprawling into the stream bed. More quickly took their place, trampling their own fallen comrades and charging up the bank. The pointed wedge of the assault had shattered, but now a broad, ragged wave of the enemy flooded across the stream.

The Duke had reached his mounted knights concealed among the trees, and sat his horse at the head of the line. The enemy's column stretched across the Course like a great worm. The moment had come to shear into the ranks and break them apart. The Duke's herald brought him a long-handled silver mace, and he held it on high so that on the other side of the valley King Shakya could see its light winking from the shade of the trees like a star in the dusk. When that star swooped down, the charge would begin.

Then a chill wind rose and the sky darkened. A churning mass of cloud was rising over the Course.

The Duke did not bring the mace down.

A cold mist began to creep over the fields and through the trees around the city. The Nightbane army faltered and its armoured beasts bellowed in agitation.

The clash and roar of battle stilled.

Without warning a howling wind rushed up the valley, carrying a billowing cloud of snow and shards of ice with it. The blizzard tore through the lines of the enemy, blinding them and obscuring them from view. There were shrieks and the clatter of weapons, and some Nightbane were thrown into the air or struck down by the force of the blast.

The Nightbane charge was halted, and then the lines broke and the enemy stumbled and fled. The defenders would have charged after them, but the Duke appeared at the edge of the wood with his open hand held high, the sign to hold, and the officers in the front lines kept their men in check.

The blizzard gathered itself into a whirling mass, like a tornado, and streamed up into the sky. It plowed into the circling motherworms and tore their bloated bodies to shreds. Fire burst out from their death throes and would have fallen as a terrible rain on the city, but the whirling snow extinguished the firedrakes as they fell.

When the last of the motherworms had been destroyed, the white cloud began to descend, slowly now, like an ordinary snowfall, upon the burning roofs of the city. It became a mist and the remaining fires were dampened, and the people carrying buckets from the canal wiped their eyes, still streaming from the smoke, and cheered.

Some of the snow flurried down onto the Course, and as it settled, a young woman appeared in its midst. Her long hair and her cloak were white with frost, and her face was a bloodless white tinged faintly with blue.

Freya stared about her as if dazed, and then she turned to the long drift of snow behind her, already trickling away into the grass under the glare of the midday sun.

She knelt and placed her hand upon the snow.

"Rest now, Old One," she whispered.

Then she frowned. Her fingers had touched something that was not melting snow. Out of the dying dragon's body she lifted a sword with a snow-white hilt and a blade of translucent blue.

Whitewing Stonegrinder's last gift to her.

There was a shout, and she looked up to see her fellow Skaldings pushing through the ranks of the defenders. Eymund Spearbreaker led them, and with him came another man Freya had never seen before, wearing a faded and stained Errantry cloak. His face was lined and pale and his eyes sunken, as if he was or had been ill.

Eymund strode up to Freya and clasped her in his arms.

"How can this be?" he said when they'd drawn apart. "We thought you were in the city. We thought you were their prisoner."

"Eymund Spearbreaker," she said, with no trace of feeling in her voice.

"What happened to you, girl?" he asked her.

Freya gazed across the field to the retreating Nightbane.

"The dragon happened to me, Eymund. And he's still here."

The Nightbane were massed again at the end of the valley. They did not launch another assault that day, but once it became clear that the strange storm was over, they brought up their own archers, who loosed clouds of arrows that descended in long hissing arcs among the defenders. Men took cover behind their shields, but some were struck and wounded, and several killed.

The volleys kept coming all that long afternoon. The allied lines were forced back, inch by inch, from the stream, but still the Nightbane did not take advance, and it became clear that the rain of arrows was only meant to thin out the ranks of the defenders.

So began the siege of Fable. Neither army moved from its position, and both sides knew what they were waiting for: the fetch host.

The sun went down, and great bonfires sprang up in the dark, and soon the defenders could hear the bellowing of animals being slaughtered to feed their enemies.

Balor Gruff spent the day with the brigades, dousing fires and helping those whose houses had burned. In the evening the two young Errantry apprentices who had been watching Pluvius Lane found him washing his soot-blackened face at a fountain in one of the public squares.

"You need to see this, Balor," they told him. Their faces were white with fear.

Exhausted as he was, the wildman followed them. As they neared the lane where the toyshop stood, it seemed to Balor that the streets had grown narrower, darker and more twisted than the last time he'd come this way, only a day before. And instead of the shopfronts and windows he remembered, the walls on either hand had become solid grey stone, their surface gnarled and whorled as if molten rock had flowed over the buildings and hardened in place.

"It's spreading," Balor murmured. "He's turning Fable into a maze." He stopped and turned to the apprentices. "The people who lived here—did you see what happened to them?"

"We didn't see," one of the apprentices said. "We heard screams. When we got here it was like this."

They kept on and reached what should have been the entrance to Pluvius Lane. There was no lane to be seen. Like the rest of the street the entrance was sealed over with blank stone. The only indication that there might be a way through the wall was a shallow depression in the rough shape of a door.

"We'll get battering rams," Balor said. "We can break through this."

He touched a hand to the door-shaped depression, then immediately pulled it away. Something had *moved* within the stone.

"What is that?"

"We saw it, too," the young man said. "And we heard—"

He broke off with a gasp. The stone was moving again, bulging where Balor had touched it. For an instant they saw a face, its mouth wide in anguish. Then the face sank, as if into quicksand, and the wall was blank again. Balor took a step back. There were other shapes moving, as if just under the wall's surface.

"There are *people* in there, Balor," the apprentice breathed.

"We can't break this down with our own folk inside," the other apprentice said. "It's not even a wall. It's some kind of sorcery. There's nothing we can do to stop it. Or *him*."

Balor stood in silence, glowering at the wall, his arms folded across his chest. Then he looked up into the sky, where the faint red glow of the enemy's bonfires lit the evening clouds.

"Maybe we can't stop him," Balor said. "But we can still be of use before this is over. Go spread the word. Everyone who's with us is to gather at dawn in the square where you found me."

They heard a clatter behind them and turned. A small party of troopers, seven men in all, had surrounded them with pikes at the ready.

"Balor Gruff," said the leader, a young man with a sergeant's insignia on his uniform. His name the wildman could not bring to mind. "You have been accused of inciting rebellion against the Errantry. You and the others will accompany us to Appleyard to answer these charges."

Balor's hand twitched toward his sword hilt, then he glanced at the frightened faces of the two apprentices.

"Surrender your weapons," the sergeant said in a warning tone. "We have orders to use any force necessary."

The man's name was Kenning, Balor recalled. But there was something strange about him. A coldness in his voice, and his eyes. Brax had been at work here, too.

"You've been promoted, Hutch Kenning," Balor said. "Congratulations."

"Surrender your weapons. Now."

Balor gestured to the wall. "Do you see this, Sergeant? It wasn't here this morning. The man hiding behind this wall has taken over the Errantry for his own purposes. That's who you're working for now."

"I'm following the Marshal's orders, not the mage's," Kenning said. "Now surrender your weapons if you wish these fools with you to live."

Dawn on the second day of the siege came with a cold, cheerless rain.

The iron carriage still towered in the middle of the enemy host, but sometime during the night other wheeled conveyances had arrived or been brought into place. They were long wooden wagons, ten or more of them, and mounted on each was a long tube of iron.

"Cannons," the Duke said, for there were some among the defenders who had never seen such weapons before. "They've brought cannons."

Figures could be seen climbing up on the wagons and working with ropes and poles to set the great cannons in place, but there seemed to be no urgency in their movements. The rain fell, unrelenting and bleak, and the defenders waited, and then there was a puff of smoke from one of the cannons, followed by a boom that shook the ground. Some had never heard such a sound before and wondered what it meant.

Then something came screaming over their heads and thudded into the wet earth between the tents of the allies and the walls of Fable.

A shocked silence fell. They seemed to be holding their breath, every one of them.

"Is that all?" King Shakya scoffed.

"That was only a trial," the Duke said.

Soon after there came another puff of smoke, and a black ball hurtled out of the sky and struck the base of the wall several hundred paces from the gate. It was quickly followed by a shot from another of the cannons and then another. Each one hit the wall, and there was a crash and a shower of stone and dust.

In a short while the walls were cracked and rent with gaping holes, and if the attackers reached them, they were sure to be easily breached. This time the defenders waited in vain for an unexpected deliverance from this new threat. But no breath of icy wind or whirl of snow arrived—only the dreary rain and the spinning spheres of black metal falling from the sky.

"If Master Brax has indeed prepared something for our enemies," the Duke observed, "this would be a fine time to reveal it."

The Duke sent swift riders with new orders to the commanders of the bowmen and musketeers. They advanced over the ridge, and when they were close enough to the enemy camp, they let loose, aiming at the figures who manned the immense cannons. They managed to drive them away from the wagons and the cannonfire ceased, but a mass of Nightbane broke from the main host and charged up the hillside, and the archers and musketeers were forced back.

The cannonfire began once more.

* * *

The third day arrived with a chill wind that swept the rain clouds away, but the sun seemed pale and distant, shining through a veil of mist. The defenders could smell the new threat long before they could see it. When the wind shifted and blew from the north, they caught the scent of the dust that thousands of metal-shod feet had raised, and with it the smell of the ash and hot metal of the place where the armour had been forged and the fetches bound to it.

The sentries who still manned the half-ruined walls of Fable looked out across the Course, and in the growing light they could see the glint of what resembled a great armoured snake advancing up the road. The Nightbane army parted to let it pass.

The fetches had come.

23

WILL TOOK ROWEN IN his arms and lifted her. She was lighter than he would have imagined, as if there was almost nothing left to her.

There was a mossy place between two great roots of the tree. He carried her there and gently set her down, folding her arms over her chest. Her hands were cold and her face deathly white and still. He put his ear close to her mouth, but he could not hear or feel her breathing. He couldn't tell whether she was alive or dead. The three puncture marks on her neck from Dama's talons had become swollen and livid, like blisters. There had been some venom in the harrower's claws, he thought. Something that was killing her. Or had killed her already.

Struggling against his tears, he took the golden thread out of his pocket. There was nothing more he could do for her now, even if she was still alive. And if the Loremaster had the thread, as Rowen had wanted him to, maybe he could use it to save Fable, and the Realm itself. Then he and the Loremaster could return here for her.

He knew he could wait no longer if he was going to be of any help to anyone at all. He knelt beside Rowen one more time, and as his tears fell, he put his lips to her forehead.

It was warm.

Will pulled back and looked at Rowen's face. He could see the movement of her eyes behind her closed lids. He took her hand. It was warm, too.

She had not given in. Like Shade, she was still fighting. And that meant he had to stay with her. No matter what he had promised, his place was here. The Will he'd met in the mirror had told him not to leave her, no matter what. He had to keep her safe as long as he could.

He closed her hand within both of his own and leaned close to her ear.

"I don't know if you can hear me, Rowen," he said softly. "But I'm here, and I won't leave you. You're not alone. Keep fighting. I believe in you."

She did not stir.

Time passed. Will had no idea how much time. He spoke Rowen's name often, shook her shoulder gently. She did not wake.

He waited with his head bowed and after a while he felt cool air on the back of his neck. A flutter of breeze stirred his hair. It was the first wind he'd felt since they'd come to the Shadow Realm.

He looked up. Far above, the depthless grey roof of turning dust had been breached. A small opening, like a hole in a dome, showed him a patch of bright blue sky. The first time he had seen a colour other than grey in so long. It was like he was peering through a window into some other world.

Rowen and Sputter had done this, too, he was certain. They'd made a breach in the prison that was the Shadow Realm. The sight would have cheered him if he'd had any hope left. But now it was only more evidence that Malabron had defeated them. They had made this one little haven of green life within his dead grey nightmare, but it was not enough.

He thought of carrying Rowen out of the Silence. If he could find Master Pendrake, they might make it back to Fable, all three of them together. But it might be too late to catch up with the harrowers, and without their protection the knife wind would be on him in a moment. And he was so tired. The cold, hopeless weariness of their journey across the Shadow Realm was falling over him again.

One question still nagged at him. Why hadn't Dama killed them both when she'd had the chance? He'd seen fear in her eyes, and he'd thought then that it was fear of the hollow itself, as if she was trespassing where she'd never been permitted to go.

Now it became clear to him that Dama was afraid of Rowen. Terrified. She'd attacked and then fled. Not from Will's sword but from Rowen, from the power she'd revealed in herself by transforming the hollow.

He looked down at Rowen and cold fear shot through him. She was struggling against the poison from Dama's talons, he was sure of that. But what if it had not been meant to kill her? Only to weaken her. To break down her will, her resistance, so that when she woke—if she woke— it would be as one of them. It's what Rowen herself had feared, what she'd spoken of when they were hiding in the old school bus.

He thought of the young man he'd met in the Weaving. Was it really himself? The Will he would be someday, years from now? And if it was, then that is how he would end up: running and hiding from Rowen.

The Shadow Realm would have them both in the end.

The patch of blue sky remained for hours, then darkened to a deep indigo. Stars appeared. Somewhere far above him, Will thought, night was passing, but within the hollow the dim grey light did not change.

He spoke to Rowen again. He told her that he could see the stars, and that they were more beautiful than he remembered. But she did not stir. She slept on, her face a white mask. Will walked around the tree and crouched by the little stream that ran trickling through the grass. Where did it run to? He followed it from the small flower-fringed pool where it began and across the floor of the hollow, until it vanished back into the grass. Several times he climbed to the edge of the hollow and listened, but he heard nothing. The woven wall of green looked thicker than he had imagined. He pushed against it but could barely make it move.

When the hunger pangs in his stomach became too much to ignore, he finished what food was left in his pack.

He dozed once, for how long he had no idea, and shot awake with a cry to find Rowen beside him, still breathing faintly. There was a pale light in the little patch of sky far above and the stars were winking out.

On the second day, Will climbed the tree. Its lowest branches almost touched the earth and so it was easy for him to get his first foothold and then scramble up, branch after branch, as high as he dared go, still close enough that he could reach Rowen quickly if anything came for her while he was up here.

At last, as he clung to the highest branch he felt was safe to reach, he was just above the rim of the hollow. To his wonder he saw that encircling green wall, which he had thought was only a thin hedge, stretched away in all directions as far as he could see, to a greyish haze. The Shadow Realm was still out there as Rowen had said, but it was farther away than he'd feared, or at least it seemed to be.

Will climbed back down hastily and knelt at Rowen's side to make sure she was still breathing.

"I'm here," he said again. "I climbed the tree. There's green for miles, Rowen."

He placed his hand on her forehead and felt the heat of fever. She shivered and gave a faint cry.

"Rowen?" She went still again, but as he watched he saw beads of sweat stand out on her brow.

With his sword he hacked a strip off his cloak and wet it in the pool. With this he bathed Rowen's forehead, her face and her arms, hoping to cool the fever that was burning her from inside.

It seemed to help, or so he hoped. She had stopped shivering, at least. Most of that day she lay unmoving as if dead, but once in a while she would stir in her sleep as if caught in a terrible dream.

"It's not real," he told her. "You can wake up."

It occurred to him that if he concealed her, it might give them more time should anything come for her. He walked around the rim of the hollow, cutting away a few of the thicker, sturdier stalks from the hedge. When he thought that he had enough, he brought them back to the tree and arranged them around Rowen, working them carefully into the earth and twining them loosely together to make a kind of bower.

When he stepped back, he saw that this wouldn't help at all. The bower didn't look like a stand of thicker grass as he'd hoped, but only like what it was: an attempt to hide something. He let it remain, though. He didn't know why.

That night he heard them.

The nightmare creatures were still out there. He made out distant thrashing and crackling, as if huge machines from his own world were at work tearing through the thick wall of green. The sounds would stop for a while, then they would begin again. They didn't seem to be getting any louder or closer, but he stood over Rowen's bower through most of the night, listening, his body exhausted and aching for sleep.

When morning came, the distant sounds didn't die away. They continued through the day and into the evening. Now there were other sounds, as well. A low hum hovering just at the edge of silence. It was not the wind, he was sure of that, but he couldn't say what it was.

He awoke suddenly to find himself beside Rowen in the green shadows within the bower. He had tried so hard to stay awake, but he had fallen asleep again. Maybe not for long, but he cursed himself under his breath.

Rowen was breathing softly and looked much the same as she had the day before. Once he was sure she was no worse than she had been, he climbed out of the bower.

He froze.

Morrigan stood on the far side of the tree. The shrowde cloak shone coldly in the gloom. Will backed away, heart pounding, remembering what Dama had told them. And then Morrigan was gliding toward him, and he drew his sword.

"Will," she said. "Is Rowen with you?"

He didn't answer. She halted and looked at his sword.

"I am not one of them," she said. "Not yet."

Will heard the truth of it in her voice. It was a warm, living voice, the first he had heard in a long time. But his heart was still hammering and he wouldn't lower the sword. Morrigan glanced at the bower.

"Is Rowen in there?"

Will nodded. "What happened to you?"

"I led the hunters on a chase, then let them come to me. The shrowde took some of them, and the others fled. Then I was lost for a time, until I caught the scent of growing things and followed it. I knew right away that Rowen must have woven all this. It cost me much struggle to get through, but I was sure I would find you here."

Will at last lowered his sword. Morrigan walked with him to the bower and looked in at Rowen, and Will quickly told her everything that had happened since they'd parted. Morrigan knelt and put her hand to Rowen's forehead.

"Can you do anything for her?" Will asked.

The Shee woman shook her head.

"You were right. There is a poison in her beyond my power to draw out. Whether she will recover or not I cannot say. But if she does . . ."

She did not finish.

"Did you see Master Pendrake?" Will asked. "The harrowers promised to let him go."

"I did not see the Loremaster," Morrigan said. "I do not know whether the nightmare creatures kept their word. But they are tearing down this refuge and devouring it as they go. They will be here soon."

She had found some small golden-yellow berries growing within the encircling hedge as she made her way through it. She'd tried them and found they were safe to eat, and she shared them now with Will. He bit into one and his mouth filled with a sharp, sweet taste that made him think of sunlight.

"Is there anything we can do?" he asked. "I don't want to just sit here waiting for them to come."

"They have surrounded us," Morrigan said. "I barely escaped them myself. The moment we set foot outside this hollow they would be upon us. No, Will. All we can do is stay with Rowen, as long as she lives and breathes. When they come, you and I will make them pay dearly before this is finished."

They sat together that night, keeping watch over Rowen and waiting as the sounds from outside the hollow grew louder.

The third day came, and still Rowen did not wake. While Morrigan and the shrowde patrolled the rim of the hollow, Will stayed in the bower. He touched Rowen's forehead from time to time and was relieved to find her fever was lessening, but still she gave no sign of stirring.

He climbed from the bower to tell Morrigan about Rowen's fever breaking, but she was not in sight and he supposed she must be searching for more of the berries. Will went to the pool and crouched at its edge to drink. One of the large yellow-white flowers was near his lowered face, and he caught a flicker of movement from it.

He bent closer to look and jumped back with a cry as a greenish-brown, glossy-backed thing crawled out of the flower's cupped petals. It had many legs and a segmented back like a centipede, and it made a high-pitched chittering sound.

The creature dropped to the ground and went skittering on its many legs toward the bower. Will drew his sword and skewered it. The thing writhed for a second or two and then went still. Will drew out his sword, stared at the thing a moment and then crushed it under the heel of his boot.

He turned back to the flowers. There were more of the creatures crawling out of the blossoms now, and the flowers themselves were darkening, turning a sickly greyish-brown. Will stabbed another one that had crawled toward the bower and then another. More appeared, and he hacked at those, but others were getting past him . . .

Then Morrigan was there with the shrowde cloak spread, and when she passed it over the creatures, they shrivelled into themselves and went still.

"The nightmare is returning," she said. "Nothing is safe anymore. We must be watchful of everything, even the ground under our feet."

Will wiped his stained blade on the grass. The flowers by the pool were all dead now, their petals brittle and ashen.

They waited and watched as the hours went by. The sounds from outside the hollow had gone silent some time ago, Will realized with a start. He couldn't see anything along the hedge, but he knew for certain that something or someone was out there, watching.

"Stay here," Morrigan hissed. The shrowde billowed up around her, and its white form rushed across the hollow and into the hedge. Will waited breathlessly in the bower, and soon he heard a shriek that was abruptly broken off. All was silent again.

Morrigan reappeared at his side. "They are near," she said. "There are many."

He climbed to his feet with his sword drawn and stood beside her. Part of the shrowde fluttered like a sheet caught by the wind and hung behind him and over the bower.

The woven green wall began to shiver and rustle all around them. With a noise of splintering and tearing it began to buckle and then to topple in many places. Gaps appeared, holes through which plumes of dust began to roll down the slope.

Then they came. Slowly, cautiously, as if they were still afraid to tread here, the harrowers came.

"This is a place for the living," Morrigan cried. "If you set foot here you will be destroyed."

Laughter, some high-pitched and some a low rumbling, rippled through the throng. And still they came, some lumbering, others crawling and slithering. Will gripped his sword and willed himself to stand his ground, not to cry out and run. He saw Dirge among them, shaking her bedraggled locks out of her eyes to better see the prey before her. Behind her came Gibbet, his eel's mouth wide open, teeth bared. He saw other things he had no name for, their hungry eyes all fixed on him. He did not see Dama, and wondered if she hadn't dared return to the Silence.

Most of the harrowers had descended the slope by now and were coming across the hollow, moving more swiftly having encountered no resistance or threat.

"Little mice," Dirge called. "Little mice, your tale is done. It's them, Gibbet. Do you smell them? The little mice that got away didn't get away. There they are. They can't run any farther. Nowhere to go."

Gibbet raised his eyeless head and sniffed, then bellowed and shouldered his way past Dirge.

"Go on," Dirge said, pawing at the other harrower's shoulder. "Take them, tear them. We will be right behind you."

Gibbet came at a lurching run toward the tree. Will felt more than saw the shrowde cloak billow out on either side as Morrigan readied herself for the harrower's assault.

And then there was another sound, a great crashing that seemed to come from every direction at once. And with it the ground under Will's feet began to shudder. The harrowers froze and looked around wildly, snarling and gibbering. Whatever it was, it was clear they had heard this sound before and they were afraid.

Dirge came to a sudden halt, turning his head this way and that, his nostrils flaring, and then he roared and came on again, straight for Will.

He never reached him.

There was a burst of darkness, as if the pillar of dust had been torn open and night had come flooding in, and then Will saw that the darkness was a thing, a moving shape, vast and black, with jaws that opened and snapped shut, trapping the harrower between sharp fangs before he could take another step. A great dark head rose, shook Gibbet ferociously and then threw the harrower's limp, mangled body across the hollow.

It was Shade. Will knew it for certain, even though this monstrous thing with burning red eyes, the breath roaring from him like broiling air from a forge, looked nothing like the wolf he knew.

This was the Devourer.

Will cried Shade's name but his voice was lost amid the beast's thunderous growls and the shrieking and howling of the harrowers. Some were already fleeing out of the hollow, but many had turned to meet this threat. They were lunging and slashing at him now and he was turning, snapping at some and swatting others away with his great paws. Those harrowers that could leap or had wings had attached themselves to his heaving sides and were sinking their fangs into him and tearing at him with their claws.

Will watched in helpless horror as the savage battle raged before him. Even Morrigan seemed awestruck and unable to move. And then Will noticed that as Shade fought, as he clawed and bit and tore at his enemies, he was moving farther from the tree and from Will. He was doing it purposefully, Will understood with a surge of hope, trying to lead the harrowers away from their prey.

He was about to speak, to tell Morrigan that Shade was giving them a chance to get Rowen away from here, when a leathery arm slid around his neck and held him fast.

"Call off the beast, boy," a cold voice hissed in his ear. Dama's voice.

He struggled and felt a sharpness, like the tip of a knife, press against his throat. He knew without having to see it that it was the winged woman's talon. One of those that had poisoned Rowen.

There was a blur of white and Morrigan was in front of him, the shrowde rippling into agitated ribbons all around her.

"Let him go," Morrigan said in a low, threatening voice.

"Stay away, witch of the Shee," Dama snarled, "or the boy dies."

And then the talon was gone from his neck and Dama's arm had loosened its grip. Will didn't know the reason, but he took this chance to escape and struggled out of her grasp. He whirled to face her in case she attacked again, but she was not looking at him. She was staring in wide-eyed horror at the bower.

Rowen stood there.

She had awoken at last.

24

SHE DIDN'T SEEM TO know him at first, and then recognition came into her eyes.

"Will," she said.

"Rowen?" Of all the wonders and terrors he had seen in the last few days, Rowen standing before him again was the most wonderful and yet somehow also the most terrifying. Something had changed in her. Something he didn't understand.

Her face was still frighteningly pale and glistened with sweat, but her eyes were wide open and clear. She looked at Morrigan, and then her gaze shifted to Dama.

"You will no longer harm them," she said.

"You broke your word," the harrower growled as she backed away. "You promised to call off the Devourer and submit to the One."

"I'm not the wolf's master," Rowen said. "I never was. I made that bargain so you would let Grandfather go free."

"We killed the old man!" Dama shrieked. "We tore him to pieces!"

"No, you didn't," Rowen said calmly. "I see him. He's on his way home. He escaped you. The power I put into the staff helped him."

"You've still lost," Dama said. "If you see that far, you know your city is about to fall. He will return only to shadows and death."

Her wings rose and it seemed she would escape before anyone could reach her, but she did not ascend. Instead she stared down at her feet.

"What is this?" she gasped. "What are you doing to me?"

Will saw to his amazement that she was sinking slowly into the earth, or that the earth was somehow pulling her down. The grass was at her ankles now and rising. She reached down, her legs shaking, and desperately tore at the green blades, but still she sank.

Dama began to scream. She thrashed and threw out her arms, but the grass was above her knees now and all she could do was beat her wings helplessly.

Rowen stepped closer to the harrower. Dama grasped at her with a snarl but she stayed just out of reach.

"The One will come," Dama hissed. "The One will find you and torment you forever for this."

"Listen to me," Rowen said, sinking into a crouch beside her. "I'm sorry to cause you pain, but I can't let you harm anyone else. I'm going to tell you now what will happen to you. You'll return to the place you came from. The place everything comes from. It's called the Weaving. It's where we give back what we've been given."

Dama was up to her waist now and sinking faster. Her wings were caught next. They shivered but were held fast as terrified sobs wracked her body.

"No, no, no," she cried, clawing at the earth. "Let me live. I will serve you. I will worship you."

"You'll come back from the Weaving," Rowen went on. "Everyone does, in new bodies that have been woven for them. Nothing ever really ends. I know that now. You'll come back, but you won't have to be what you were. You won't have to serve this nightmare anymore. We all have a choice, every one of us. You can choose another way to be."

Dama had gone silent. The grass swallowed up her outstretched arms, and as it reached her neck and then her mouth, her eyes still burned into Rowen's, though with fear, hate or hope Will could not tell.

In another moment the green earth had closed over her head and she was gone.

Will stared in shock and wonder at the place where the harrower had been. Then from behind him he heard a sigh like a great rush of wind.

"Will," Morrigan said, and he turned and saw the giant form of the wolf lying at the edge of the hollow, his mighty sides heaving, his dark fur matted and glistening with blood. The torn and mangled bodies of harrowers lay all around him, but there were none still standing.

Will cried his friend's name. The wolf stirred and slowly raised his head.

"Shade?" Will said again, this time as a question. The wolf's eyes still burned with a red fire and his jaws hung open, with gobbets of blood and slaver hanging from them. Then he struggled to his feet, but instead of coming closer he began to limp away, the ground shuddering again with each of his great footfalls.

"Shade!" Will cried. "Don't go! You've saved us. Let us help you."

The wolf didn't seem to hear. Without looking back, he climbed the slope and vanished into the wreckage of the green wall.

"Let him go, Will," Rowen said, sitting up. "There is almost nothing left in him of the Shade we knew."

"But what will happen to him?"

Rowen didn't answer. She stood slowly, ignoring Will's attempt to help her.

"How long?" she asked. "How long was I asleep?"

"Three days," Morrigan said.

"Three days," Rowen echoed. She gazed around. "I'm so thirsty."

Will gave her the water bottle he had filled at the pool on the second day. She took a few sips. Morrigan was watching her, too, and Will saw that the Shee woman also wasn't sure what to think of what had just happened, or of the strange way Rowen was acting.

"What of the Night King, Rowen?" the Shee woman asked. "The harrowers may have been killed or driven away, but he will come for us, that is certain."

Rowen shot Morrigan a strange look, as if unsure whom she was speaking of. She was about to answer, it appeared, when she glanced away as though she'd heard a sound. Will and Morrigan went still, and then they heard it, too: a low hum, the same sound Will had heard on the second night of his vigil under the tree.

"What is that?" he asked.

"I heard it as well, when I was searching for you," Morrigan said. "Whatever it is, it is coming this way. We must leave here."

But Rowen showed no sign of concern. She stood calmly and waited, and so they stayed beside her.

The humming grew louder, rising to a heavy drone that reverberated in their ears. Then it was a roaring, almost a shrieking, that seemed to arrive from every direction at once.

The gaps in the green wall darkened even further, but with a trembling, crawling agitation, as if filled with count-less tiny flecks of ash churning over and over through the air. Then Will remembered Rowen's vision of the defeat of the Fair Folk, how they had been swallowed up in a cloud of tiny black creatures, and he knew that same cloud had come for them. A living darkness that churned and boiled in the hedge's gaps but came no farther into the Silence.

Will braced himself for what might happen next, but Rowen appeared unafraid. She stepped forward and raised a hand.

"You will come no farther," she said. "I rule here now. You know this to be true. You cannot harm me without harming yourselves."

Dread shot through Will at Rowen's words. What had happened to her while she slept? Fear clutched at him that she was not the Rowen he knew anymore, that she had be-come a creature of the Shadow Realm, and he recalled the terrified words of the other Will he'd met in the Weaving: *She's found me . . .*

The cloud of darkness shivered violently like a single creature, and many voices issued from it now, all speaking as one, with a sound that was both a whisper and a roar of rage.

You are nothing. You will be devoured and forgotten.

"That will not happen," Rowen said, and then she turned to Will.

"Do you still have Grandmother's thread?"

He nodded. He was about to take the ball from his pocket and hand it to her, but he hesitated. What if the golden thread was all she needed to become another Malabron? What if his older self had made the same mistake, and this is what led to him running and hiding for years until he was trapped at the ending of all the stories?

"Will?" Rowen said, and for the first time since she'd woken up, a look of concern crossed her face. "Give me the thread. It's all right."

He had to trust her. She had ended Dama and she could have destroyed him and Morrigan, too, if she'd wanted to. No, this was still Rowen.

He held out the ball of thread. She took it and set it in her palm, touching it softly with a finger, as if reassuring herself that it was really there. Then she held it up toward the seething darkness at the hollow's edge.

"I could destroy you with this," Rowen said in a loud voice. "So listen to me now. You creatures of the Shadow Realm, you've hidden the truth from yourselves for so long, but you've always known it, deep in your hearts. Lotan, the Angel, knew. He looked into the emptiness every time he came here, and he knew. He was afraid, and he served the lie and let it rule him, as you all did. For all the harm you've done in the name of this lie, I *should* destroy you."

You must not do this, the many voices roared. *Spare us and we will bow before you. We will serve you.*

"No one is going to bow to anyone anymore," Rowen said. "I'm opening a door for you. A door for everyone. I'm going to set you free. I'm going to set us all free."

"Rowen, what are you thinking?" Morrigan said in a low voice. "These are beings who have never known anything but hunting and killing the innocent. You cannot let them loose on the other realms. If you have the power to end them, do it."

"This story was their prison, Morrigan. Ours, too. No creature should ever have to live like that, inside a lie."

"If you free them," Will cried, "Malabron will be free, too. He'll take over everything."

"He can't, Will. Don't you see? The truth has been right in front of us all this time: there is no Night King. There is no Malabron."

"What are you talking about?" Will said. "He came after me. After you. I saw his eyes in the mirror shard. He sent those armies to the Bourne—"

Rowen lifted her arms. "All of this," she said, "is Malabron. This place is the heart of the Shadow Realm. When I was asleep, I became part of the nightmare, Will, and I *saw*. Now I've woken up and I have to wake others, too. The *Night King* is a story, Will. We're inside that story. We've become part of it, and we can't end it with hatred and killing because that only makes it stronger. All those armies fighting over Fable now were drawn there by the power of this story. We've all been telling it, and we're being told by it. A story that turns everything into *this*. Into more nightmare."

Will shook his head slowly.

"What about the Stewards?" he said, struggling to understand. "They fought Malabron a long time ago. Your people were there, Morrigan. The Night King was real then, wasn't he?"

"We do not forget the destruction of our city, Rowen," Morrigan said, her eyes burning. "We do not forget the one who drove us onto a road of pain and sorrow."

"This story is older than anyone knows, Morrigan," Rowen said. "Who can say how it began? I think the story we call Malabron has had many names, in many realms. This—all of this horror and hate—is a story woven from fear. The Stewards first helped it to grow. They didn't mean to. I think they loved all the stories so much they were afraid to lose them. They wanted to keep the Realm whole and perfect for all time, and their fear became another story, a story they hadn't meant to weave. And the harder they tried to unweave it, the stronger it grew. The story became like a living thing with one purpose: to go on living. To be the only story, forever."

"What about the fetches?" Will asked. "And the harrowers? If there's no Night King, then who's telling them what to do?"

"No one is, Will," Rowen said. "They're like . . . characters in a book who always do the same thing, no matter how many times you read it. The fetches are marching on Fable because that's how it *must be* in the story."

"Then my people . . ." Morrigan said, and for the first time Will saw tears in the Shee woman's eyes. "If the story can end, they may return someday. They need not remain fetches forever."

"No, they need not. You may see them again one day."

"But what happened to the First Ones?" the Shee woman asked. "Why did they fail against something they themselves created?"

"The Stewards tried to contain the story of fear," Rowen said. "They made the black river to seal it off from everything else, but it kept growing and weaving itself back into the Realm. Soon there was fear everywhere. Folk who fled from it gave it names. Malabron. Master of Fetches. The Night King. The Story-eater. And those names only made it stronger. The story wove itself into the tales and legends of the Fair Folk, and the Night King became your great enemy. You believed in him, even though you'd never seen him. The story was now so deeply woven into everything that the war to destroy it tore the Realm apart. That was the Great Unweaving. The Stewards gave up their bodies then. They became water and tree and stone, to hold the weave together from within."

"And the story of the Night King didn't die," Will said.

"Its threads were torn and scattered, like so much was in those days, but it was never completely forgotten. The threads were still there and they were added to, and slowly the story regained its power. We all kept it alive and helped it to grow. All of us."

"We all wove it, like the images in my tapestries," Morrigan breathed. "We told it to ourselves, time and again, and now it is telling us."

Then you cannot end us, the voices roared even louder than before. *We are one with you and you cannot end us without destroying yourselves.*

"No, we can't," Rowen said. "No one can. The battle for Fable will end one way or another, but even if the Nightbane are defeated, the knot of darkness in the Weaving will keep growing. There are Storyfolk and Nightbane still coming to the Bourne, from stories so far away and so strange we can hardly imagine them. Some who will join the fight haven't been born yet. The war will grow beyond the borders of the Bourne, and into your world, too, Will, if it hasn't already."

"Then what can you do?" Will asked. "What can anyone do?"

"We have to wake up," Rowen said. "All of us. We have the power to leave this story and make a new one. Together. It will take time, but it's the only way. We're all storyweavers, Will. The fathomless fire is in all of us. I'm going to help people see that."

While they had been speaking, the roar of the cloud of darkness had slowly fallen silent. Now they looked up and saw that the cloud had shrunk into a manlike shape that reflected no light at all but instead seemed to swallow it, as if it were not so much a presence as a hole into absolute darkness.

What will happen to us? cried a hollow voice that was emptiness and fear given speech. *If you leave there will be nothing for us. We will be hungry forever in the darkness. We will be alone.*

"You will not be alone," Rowen said, "because I will stay with you."

"Rowen, no!" Will cried. "What are you saying?"

"Will, so much is going to change. The black river will dry up and the walls of the Shadow Realm will fall. Not tomorrow and maybe not for a long time, but when that happens, folk will no longer fear this place. Some will come to help heal, to rebuild, but many will come for vengeance, and they will hunt these beings and kill them. That mustn't happen, or the nightmare will only grow stronger again. I have to stay and protect them."

"Protect things like Dirge and Gibbet?" Will said. "They're monsters, Rowen. They're evil. Think of what they've done."

"I can't forget it. When I first woke up I wanted to use the golden thread to seal this place up forever and let its creatures devour one another until none was left. I wanted to hurt them the way they hurt me. But if I did that, I would only be like Lotan or Dama. In time I'd become the new Master of the Fetches, and the war would go on. Then one day I would be hunting down my own friends. Even you. The beings that live here need someone to watch over them—to keep them from causing more harm and to keep others from harming them—until the day we've all learned what fear and hate make us become. Then there will be no need for walls. That's why I have to stay."

"No, not you, Rowen," Morrigan said. "When the shrowde and I came to this realm, we already knew we would never leave it, because we have nothing to return to. We will stay and watch over the Shadow Realm."

"I can't let you do that, Morrigan," Rowen said, shaking her head. "I'm the one who started this. I have to see it through."

"Rowen, this is no place for you. You are still young and your life is just beginning. You are right that this nightmare

around us will not change in a single day . . . it will be a realm
of shadow and terror for a long time to come. I do not have
your vision, but I can see that much. This place would sap the
life and hope from you in time. You know that. And you have
many duties now, too, not just to this place but to all the Realm."

Rowen was about to speak again, but her voice faltered.
She wiped away tears.

"They will call you the Shadow Queen," she said to
Morrigan at last. "They'll fear you at first. But you'll learn
the names of all these beings and walk with them. You'll
share their fear and pain. One day you will lead them out of
the nightmare."

The lightless shape spoke again from the hollow's rim.
We will accept this, it said. *We will have Morrigan of the Tain
Shee to rule here and protect us.*

The hole in the shape of a man began to contract further,
drawing the dust around it into itself as it did so. In another
moment it had closed over and vanished.

Rowen stepped away from Will and Morrigan, and again
she held the golden thread up in her palm. Then she knelt
and, with great care and tenderness, let the ball slide off her
palm and onto the grass. As it rolled away from her the
thread began to unravel. A golden filament so narrow it was
almost invisible started to wind out from the ball, like the finest of spider's silk. And at almost the same time it appeared,
it began to branch into many threads, each as fine and brilliant as the first. The branching, multiplying threads wound
and wove and darted through the grass. Soon the ball itself
had unrolled completely and there was only this growing,
multiplying network of threads spreading out across the entire hollow and beyond.

And then, as swiftly as they had appeared, the threads
began to vanish, sinking into the grass or drawing out so fine

that they seemed at last to thin into nothing at all. But somehow Will knew that they weren't truly disappearing; they were merging with everything. He could feel the threads all around him, under him, and then within him. He put a hand to his heart and gasped as awareness flooded through him, a seeing that was strange and yet utterly familiar, as if it had always been there, waiting for him to discover it. For one moment there was nothing between him and everything else. There was no beginning and no ending to what he was. What they all were.

Then he came back.

He was himself again, though something had changed. He felt that he was standing before a door that led to a new and unknown world. But the door was also himself.

"What did you do?" he asked Rowen.

"Grandmother's gift was not meant to bind anything," she said. "It was meant to unbind. You showed me that, Will, when you freed Shade, but I didn't understand then. I had to become the nightmare in order to see the truth. I couldn't destroy Malabron's story by sealing it away forever, because I'm inside it. I had to find a path out of it. A path for everyone."

Then he became aware that the light in the hollow had grown warmer, and he looked up and saw that the tree was no longer dead. Great sprays of yellow-green leaves had burst from its branches on one side of the trunk and had spread over their heads like a canopy. The other side of the tree was still ashen and bare.

"What happens now?" Will asked Rowen. "Will the war end?"

She did not answer him right away, but rose from where she'd been kneeling and gazed up at the cloven tree. Its pale leaves stirred and shimmered in the sunlight that now filled the hollow through the widening gap in the vault of dust.

"We must return home," Rowen said. "The battle . . . it's like a boulder rolling downhill. It won't stop because of what I've done here. Fable is still in danger."

"How will you get there in time?" Morrigan asked. "The border of the Shadow Realm is days away."

"By the way we came, yes. But there's another path now."

"What's going to stop the harrowers from taking it and invading the Perilous Realm?" Will asked.

"The path is everywhere, Will. For anyone to take, not just for some. The harrowers will be afraid to take it. Many people will be. They'll want to stay in the story they've always known. But it's there now and can't ever be forgotten again. That's what I did with Grandmother's thread. I wove a way out of any story."

25

BALOR SPENT MOST OF the second day of the siege in a cell at Appleyard. It occurred to him this might well be the same cell from which he'd rescued Edweth.

In this windowless room he couldn't be certain how much time was passing, but he reckoned it was past midnight when the sergeant who'd arrested him, Hutch Kenning, arrived with four troopers. They all had the same cold, lethal look in their eyes as Kenning when he'd arrested him. As if someone had blown out the flame of human warmth in them.

"Do you mind telling me where you're taking me, Sergeant?" Balor asked as they led him out of the cell.

"You're going to the archmage's citadel."

"You mean Master Pendrake's toyshop," Balor said.

"You're going to the citadel," Kenning repeated, "at the mage's command."

And I won't be coming back, Balor thought.

They escorted him from Appleyard and out into the streets, which were now as featureless and narrow as those he had seen yesterday surrounding Pluvius Lane. He noticed that none of his escort carried a lantern, as if they wished not to be observed. More evidence, he thought, that this was a journey from which he was not meant to return, with no trace of what had happened to him. He wondered how many others had been taken through the streets this way in the last few days. Then he looked beyond the streets to the sky, which was still dark. There should be birds already chirping in the trees on Appleyard Hill, he thought, but there was only silence.

"Have you heard how the battle is going?" Balor asked his escort. No one answered.

They reached a crossroads between the street they were on and two other narrow lanes, and Kenning raised a hand and brought the party to a halt. On all sides, figures emerged from the shadows.

A voice spoke quietly in the dark.

"You'd better lay down your arms, lads. You're outnumbered."

"Let us pass," Kenning said, and for the first time there was a catch of hesitation in his voice. "Hindering officers of the Errantry is an act of treason. This man is a traitor who must answer for his crimes."

"Well, he's also my friend," the voice said, and Balor recognized it then. "And he's probably the best hope your Errantry's got right now. So we're going to hinder you, I'm afraid."

Kenning shared a quick glance with his troops, and without a word they lowered their weapons to the ground. A moment later matches flared and lanterns glowed on every side. One of them lit the broad, beaming face of Miles Plunkett.

* * *

Fewer than a hundred were gathered in the square. A handful of his fellow Errantry knights, Balor was cheered to see, along with troopers, scouts, apprentices, many of those not much more than boys. A few, like Miles Plunkett, were ordinary folk who'd defied the curfew and were determined to help save their city. Hutch Kenning and his troopers had joined them, too. Whatever influence Brax had over their minds they'd shrugged off quickly when they found themselves in the midst of friends.

No one spoke as Balor made his way through the crowd and climbed onto the rim of the fountain. They had been waiting for him, he realized. Waiting for the most experienced officer in this little insurrection to speak the words that would lead them into battle. He liked to talk well enough, to tell a joke and sing a song, but he'd never had to make a speech like this.

Balor cleared his throat.

"From what I'm told we may find the gates held against us," he said. "We can try to persuade the sentries to let us pass, but if that fails we will have to force our way through. Let us remember that these are our comrades. They're carrying out their duty as they see it. If we can help it, let us shed no blood until we face our real enemy on the battlefield."

"Those armoured things out there," someone in the crowd shouted, "I heard that they don't have any blood to shed. That nothing can kill them."

"Perhaps not, but they can be broken," Balor said. "They can be stopped. I've seen it done. Our allies have come from every corner of the Realm to defend us while the Errantry cowers behind what's left of our walls. That isn't right. We may be breaking the martial law imposed on this city. We may be branded as traitors for what we do this day. I say so be it, as long as we hold true to the oath we took when we joined the Errantry: to protect the weak and the innocent—if need be with our lives. Let us do that now."

There was silence when he had finished. No drawing of swords, no voices raised in cheer. *We're rebels, after all*, Balor thought. *We have to go quietly.* But he felt what was stirring in those gathered around him, and he saw it in their eyes. They would stand with him, whatever they met on the other side of those gates.

Freya saw with the eyes of the dragon.

She was with her friends from Skald, she knew, in the midst of the thousands upon thousands of knights and warriors and soldiers who had come to Fable from the four corners of the Realm and perhaps beyond.

She stood among them but apart from them and looked down the valley. She saw with utter clarity the long, snakelike column of fetches coming up the Course, marching without pause or hesitation to their goal. And then she seemed to see that column running backward in time, through the days and nights of its ceaseless march, to the place where this armour had been forged, a land of fire and ice that her own people had once called home. She was seeing with the dragon's eyes, but also with the long memory of her people, the Skaldings, who had been driven from this northern land in ages past. She saw the ringed city of Adamant and the forges in its smoky depths where the fetches had been trapped and sealed into this armour of enchanted metal. She saw the Ironwise as they had been, the Eldersmiths in the time of their greatness and prosperity. Her own people had known them and traded with them. And she saw them as they were now, walled off in their deep chambers and tunnels, frantically scrabbling with picks and hammers at what was left of the precious, deadly ore. But there was almost none for them to find. The great vein of fever iron beneath the city had been nearly exhausted by those who had forged the fetch armour. The dwarf city would never be what it once was. The Ironwise had doomed themselves to a slow death in that barren waste.

Without warning her icy vision showed a great wooden ship with tall masts and white sails, a ship filled with grim, warlike men, but the ship was not sailing on the sea. It was soaring through dark clouds, through sheets of rain. The warriors inside it were coming to the Bourne, but as conquerors or friends she could not say.

Then she saw the face of someone she knew. A young man on board the ship. He was wearing black armour and his lank, dust-matted hair fell over a face that was haggard and bloodless.

Finn Madoc.

Beneath the ice that had sealed off her heart, she felt fear clutch at her. She called Finn's name, and then her sight faltered and the ship vanished, and she felt as if she were rushing back herself over the long miles, to the battlefield.

The Nightbane had parted to let the fetch host pass, but they themselves were holding back now. Their battle fury had been cooled by the blizzard that had ravaged their lines and might return at any time, for all they knew. They were content to let these mindless instruments accomplish what they had so far failed to do.

If they were not stopped, the fetches would plow through the hastily assembling defenders and then through the walls and lay waste to everyone and everything within the city. But Freya's vision of the dwarf city had shown her the one weakness in their enemy: if their armour was broken open, the fetches within would be released and drift away harmlessly, without purpose. The armour would become an empty shell.

"Freya." A voice was calling her. She blinked and turned slowly. Eymund Spearbreaker's hand was on her shoulder.

"Freya," he said. "Are you all right?"

She gazed at her friends in turn, at the former Errantry knight Brannon Yates, shivering with the pain of his craving for the *gaal* but with his sword at the ready. In her own hand was the sword of blue ice, all that was left of Whitewing Stonegrinder. She had thought, when she first took it in her hand, that it would shatter easily, like the icicles she used to break off the eaves of her father's smithy when she was a child. But when she had struck this sword against the ground, it had not shattered, and she'd felt the strength and power in it. The dragon had left her the sword for *this*, for Fable's last stand against the fetches.

She looked now at the wall of armoured death on its way toward her, bristling with terrible, cruel weapons. She was no warrior; she had never fought in a battle before. She would likely die here and never see her home and her family again.

Why am I not afraid? she thought. And then the answer came. *This sword in my hand is the dragon's heart. His blood still runs in my veins.*

"Follow me, Eymund," she said. "Follow me, all of you."

She held the heart of Whitewing Stonegrinder aloft and started forward, toward the enemy. Her friends followed, and the knights and soldiers of a hundred lands marched with them.

The Duke saw the slender gleam of Freya's sword from where he sat on his warhorse at the edge of the woods. It was too soon, he thought. He had given no order. But there was nothing to be done. Battle was about to be joined and his troops were needed. He brought his silver mace down, and a great thundering mass of horsemen poured from the trees. On the other side of the Course, King Shakya saw the mace fall, and with a great cry his warriors charged down the slope.

By this time the head of the fetch host had plunged across the stream and were coming up the other side, where they were met by the vanguard of the allied army. As before, the two sides met with a crash of steel, but the result this time was very different. The fetches came on inexorably, an unstoppable tide, and although many of them carried great clubs and spiked iron staves in their gauntleted fists, they hardly bothered to wield them but simply mowed through the defenders as if through a field of tall grass. The defenders, for their part, drove at the fetches with swords and spears, but most of the blows they landed glanced off the armour harmlessly. Then they would be shouldered aside or fall beneath the iron feet of the host.

Those who were driven or fled back toward Fable expected to see the gates closed against them, as they had been since the siege began. To their surprise, the gates were opened and troopers were marching out, led by a small band of knights on horseback.

The Errantry had come at last.

* * *

Freya and her companions reached the front lines. Freya gave a cry and swung the ice sword with all her strength at the fetch that made for her. The blade cleaved through the faceless helmet and the fetch shuddered to a halt. Freya drew out the blade and staggered back. A wispy grey shadow slid from the rent in the helmet like thick smoke. It curled and flowed toward the defenders so that some cried out and dropped to the ground in fear. But the shadow had no force or will, and only drifted away into the dust and smoke.

"Don't be afraid of them," Freya cried to those around her. "Once the armour is broken they're harmless."

The next rank of fetches was upon her, and she swung the sword and shattered the shoulder guard of the nearest one. It came to a sudden halt like the first one and the same unearthly grey shadow poured out and vanished.

The defenders who had seen this rallied and charged forward once more, and some hacked again and again at the fetches until they succeeded in cracking the armour, as well. Some were not so lucky and they fell before their enemy and were trampled by the surging mass of iron feet.

At that moment the cavalry slammed into the column of fetches from both sides and drove into it like two spearpoints. Some of the fetches staggered and fell as they were knocked into one another, and the column was breached and broken in places. Metal rang on metal. The mace of the Duke split open the breastplate of one. The King's great spear pierced another. But most simply bludgeoned their way through, so that the horsemen seemed to be floundering through a churning river of iron.

Freya and the other Skaldings were in the midst of the column, too, holding their ground as well as they could as the fetches came at them. Yet each of them could only face one fetch at a time, and many flowed around them and rejoined the column, and it continued its unstoppable advance toward the gates of Fable. Here they were met by Balor Gruff's small force, swelled now by the troops that had turned and run but had rallied at the arrival of unexpected aid from the Errantry.

Balor had spread his troops in a line across the field, to make a final wall between the enemy and the gates of Fable. But Balor himself and the few fellow knight-errants who had joined him spurred their mounts and, with a great cry, drove into the midst of the fetches.

Then for an instant it seemed as if the sun had sheared through the clouds. A white bolt of lightning lanced down into the churning mass of the fetch host, with a crack of thunder that shook the ground. Shattered pieces of armour flew through the air, and then all was dim and smoky again. Moments later another bolt tore open the sky, striking close to the Viceroy's carriage. A third blasted into the woods at the edge of the Course, and soon trees were burning and adding a thicker pall of smoke to the gloom. The defenders gazed up, searching for the source of the lightning, and they saw something they could not understand: the hull of a ship descending out of the clouds.

Only Freya knew where this ship had come from and whom it carried.

The ship had its sails furled and it descended swiftly. Men shouted warnings to one another and scattered, as the shuddering hull struck the advancing column and plowed across it, sending armoured fetches flying through the air along with a great plume of stones and earth and dust. Freya dropped to the ground with her friends and shielded her eyes as the dust cloud swept across them.

The earth shook. With a cracking and groaning of timbers, the ship came to rest.

The iron worm had not been stopped, but it had been broken in two.

The defenders watched in stunned amazement as gangplanks slid out from the sides of the ship, and men and mordog and other Storyfolk of unknown kind hurried down to join the battle.

There were so many of them that some climbed over the sides and jumped to the ground. Those who witnessed this gave a cry of joy, for they understood now that these newcomers were on their side and there was a chance the tide of the battle could be turned. As the last of the new arrivals leaped from the side of the ship, a deep rumbling could be heard, and the hull was torn open by fire and black smoke.

As the ship burned and its timbers collapsed, another figure stepped out of the wreckage, a towering man of clay. He did not join his companions in the battle, however, but walked calmly to the aft of the ship, bent to its flat keel and dug his arms down underneath it into the churned, blackened earth.

There was another groan of stressed timbers, and the ship rose slowly and ponderously from the ground. The clay man lifted the burning wreck over his head, paused for a moment in which everyone who witnessed this feat held their breath, and then hurtled the ship through the air at the oncoming fetches. It plummeted on them like a castle falling out of the sky, burying dozens in a shattering, blazing mass of wood and metal.

The clay man did not stop then but marched into the midst of the host himself. He picked up one of the armoured fetches, cracked it open in his mighty arms, then swung the lifeless, broken armour into its fellows, scattering fetches in every direction.

The main body of the defending army had stood in silent wonder as these marvels unfolded. Now they rallied and came up at a near-run to meet the thousands of fetches that had made it past the ship and were still advancing on the city. And then warnings were shouted because there was another threat. The Nightbane had taken advantage of the tumult and confusion and were now pouring across the stream to join the fetch host.

Freya picked herself up from where she had fallen when the ship had descended. She didn't know who these new defenders were, but she knew that Finn Madoc had been on board the ship and that he was close to death. Her only thought now was to find him and help him get away from the battle before it swept over him.

She plunged into the heat and smoke that billowed from the burning ship, her eyes stung to tears, and men rushed past her, eyeing her and her pale, gleaming sword in wonder.

Then she saw him. He was stumbling away from the ship, being helped by a tall mordog whose savage-looking head was streaming with blood. She shouted his name and he glanced up, straining to see who had called to him out of the noise and smoke. But then the fetches were there, and they swept between her and Finn and she could no longer see him.

She lunged, cutting through the legs of the nearest fetch, and it toppled before her with a clang. But another was in her way, and another, a wall of them, and for each that she split open, more appeared and blocked her way. She fought without anger or fear. Her blood was still cold with the dragon's touch. She would not lose another of her friends. Not if she had the power to save him.

She was surrounded now, hacking and slashing with the icy blade, but the iron shapes were pummelling her, shouldering past her, and soon she was stumbling back and losing her balance. She would fall and be crushed beneath them.

Then the world went still. Her arm was raised, the sword ready to strike one last time, but there was nothing to strike at.

All around her the fetches had drawn to a halt. There was no sound. The light had dimmed, as if evening had suddenly fallen.

She looked down and saw that a fine, delicate thread of gold was winding over the dark, trampled earth. And whatever the thread touched—stone or blade, the iron feet of the fetches, even herself—was illuminated from within so that other threads could be seen, uncountable threads, dark and light and every shade in between.

In that instant Freya understood what she was seeing. These were the threads of all their stories. Of friend and foe, of everyone who had been drawn here into the madness of war. The vision lasted only a moment. The golden light faded and the threads vanished. But Freya knew that everyone on the battlefield had shared her vision. They had seen what she had: that their many stories had been woven into one, an ancient tale that held them spellbound. They were as much its puppets as were these mindless fetches. But they had seen a new path that was open to them now. A way to freedom.

But would they take it? In the next instant the world was plunged again into noise and chaos. There were shouts and screams and the clash of arms all around her. . . .

The vision lasted only a moment, and then the golden light dimmed and vanished. The threads were nowhere to be seen, but Freya was certain they were still there, still everywhere, and that somehow, because she knew this, nothing would ever be the same.

Then Freya looked up and saw that the armoured fetches had turned about. They were marching now toward the Nightbane host, which was retreating in stunned disorder.

Freya looked down at the ice sword in her hand. It was melting now, the water trickling over her arm and spilling onto the earth. The dragon's heart was leaving her.

It was as if every last shred of her strength was gone, too. She dropped to the ground. The last thing she saw was the fetch host surrounding the Nightbane like a swiftly closing ring of dark metal.

26

PENDRAKE STEPPED FROM THE raincabinet and halted, leaning on his staff to catch his breath.

He was back in his own house. And yet it was no longer his own.

He struggled to collect his thoughts, to remember how he'd gotten here. The harrowers had taken him from the hollow, from Rowen. They'd brought him swiftly over the bleak miles of the Shadow Realm, and then he found himself alone in a bare, rocky place under a clouded sky. Whether he was back in his own realm or not he had no idea. He'd wandered then, for three days and nights, drinking from the thin rivulets of water that trickled down from the rocks. Within the staff he felt a faint power that sustained him, and guessed that Rowen had somehow placed it there.

And then there was a path under his feet. Just a faint

track in the dirt, but he understood that it was meant for him, and that Rowen had done this as well. And so he followed the path and time had fallen away, and then he was here, in the toyshop. He had been gone only a few days but it seemed a lifetime.

He faltered then at the thought of his granddaughter left behind in that terrible place. He would return. He would find her, and Will and Morrigan. But he knew Rowen had remained behind to give him this chance to end what should never have begun.

At the far end of the hallway was where his own workshop had stood, but there was no workshop anymore. The stone walls came to an end at a gaping hole ringed with green fire.

He walked softly down the corridor, peering in each doorway and finding the rooms vacant and the walls blackened, as if they had been emptied by a great burning. He reached the hole in the wall and passed through it into what remained of his workshop, a jagged semicircle of stone floor, a few of his books scattered on it, his worktable chair fallen on its side, needles of glass lying everywhere. Beyond the edge of the broken floor there was nothing to be seen but a boiling churn of werefire, rising into hideous, grotesque shapes and faces that darted toward him then fell away again and were replaced by others just as ghastly.

Beyond the edge, a huge stone chair hung in space, anchored there by no visible means. In the chair sat Ammon Brax. He wore long robes of gleaming white, like a sage of ancient time. The green fire played about his long dark hair and his shoulders.

"The real Nicholas Pendrake has found his way home," Brax said.

"Someone else found the way for me," Pendrake said sadly.

"Where is your clever granddaughter, Nicholas? And her friends?"

"Someplace no one should ever have to go. I will be returning there when I have finished what must be done here. Fable is not yours to rule, Ammon."

"This city needs me," Brax said. "The Realm needs me. My power sustains us all now. If I fall, everything falls."

"The threat to Fable is no more. I know you can sense that as well as I can. It is time to use what power we have to heal and restore, not to destroy or take what isn't ours. Just let it go, Ammon. Before it consumes you. Let the fire return to where it belongs."

"Like you, old man? You hid the power away, refused to share it with anyone. You hoarded it here all this time, and what good did it bring you? Think of what you could have accomplished . . . Now it's up to me to do what you would not dare. Those armies waiting out there for another chance to hack and maim and kill will be mine. I will command, where you hid and let others fight for you. I will lead my host to the gates of *his* realm, and he will kneel and set his crown at my feet." He raised a trembling hand. "All I have to do is reach out this hand and it will be mine."

"Then do it, Ammon," Pendrake said. "Use the fire to take those armies for yourself. Take them and crush anyone who dares oppose you."

Brax faltered. He gazed at his hand, at the pale flames rippling over it, then at the Loremaster.

"Why are you hesitating, Ammon?" Pendrake said softly. "You have the power now. All the power you ever hoped for. Stretch out your hand and finish what you've begun."

A spasm of fear mingled with rage flickered across Brax's face.

"You know what will happen, don't you?" Pendrake said.

"The werefire takes from the one who wields it. If you do harm with it, it harms you. It's already taking your mind, and before long it will take everything that you are."

"All I wanted was to serve you and learn from you," Brax said, his voice hoarse with reproach and pain. "You could have invited me into your confidence, old man. You could have shared what you knew. If you had trusted me, warned me about the fire, showed me patiently how to tame it, I could have followed in your footsteps. But you turned your back on me. You left me with nothing." He rose from the chair and stood in empty space, the werefire blazing over his head like a poisonous halo. "Everything I've ever gained I had to tear from someone else's grasp, including this. *You* did this to me."

"I failed you, Ammon, and I am sorry for that," Pendrake said, putting out a hand. "But now you know the truth of the fire, and that is the beginning of wisdom. It's not too late—for either of us. There is another way. Let me help you find it."

The mage stood motionless with his arms at his sides. Then slowly he began to descend, as if he were walking down an invisible flight of steps. And now Pendrake could see the faint ribbons of flame under the mage's feet, shaping themselves into ghostly steps and bearing him as he descended.

"Help me, Master Nicholas," he said in a hollow voice. "I . . . cannot control it anymore. Don't let it take me."

When he was only a few steps above Pendrake, the mage's fear-stricken face suddenly changed. A cold gleam came into his eyes as they flicked to something behind the Loremaster.

Pendrake caught the movement and turned, but too late. A huge dark shape sprang from the shadows and struck him violently to the ground. The staff clattered to the stones.

Flitch stood over the Loremaster, his rotting fangs bared like a beast's. He seemed to have grown even larger and more malevolent, as if the fire had gone on changing him along with everything else in the toyshop.

Hodge had followed his brother. He stood apart from him, his hands knotted together. He looked sick and afraid.

Pendrake raised his head and struggled to rise. Flitch's booted foot pushed him back down onto the floor.

"You can do this for yourself, Ammon," Pendrake said, his words coming slowly and heavily. "You can kill me with a thought, can't you? You have the power, after all. You don't need any help."

The hogmen glanced up at the mage in surprise, as if the same notion was only now occurring to them.

"Use the fire, Ammon," Pendrake said. "Show the Marrowbone brothers that you still command it. They won't fear you otherwise."

Flitch and Hodge kept their eyes on the mage.

"Kill him," Brax said.

Flitch clutched Pendrake's cloak in his huge fist and began to drag him toward the edge of the stone lip and the werefire below. Sputter darted in front of him and bobbed in the hogman's huge face like an insect. Flitch swatted at him with a curse and kept on. He was about to throw Pendrake over when Hodge put a hand on his shoulder.

"I won't let you do this, brother," Hodge said. His voice was shaking, but his eyes held his brother's and did not flinch. "I won't let you hurt the old man."

"You simpering idiot," Flitch snarled. "Let go of me."

"No, Flitch, I won't. You've been telling me what to do all along. And it always turns bad. You never listen. The girl showed me we don't have to kill and hate. We could go back to the way things were before all of this."

"And you believed her," Flitch sneered. "Your stupidity has finally reached its pinnacle. I tell you what, I think I'll kill you next, brother, and make you into a travelling case or a throw rug. Then maybe you'll finally be of some use to someone."

"Let him go, Flitch," Hodge said warningly.

Flitch turned with a snarl and heaved Pendrake toward the edge, but at the last moment Hodge caught the Loremaster and pulled him away.

"Kill him!" Brax roared.

Flitch ignored the mage and threw himself at his brother. They grappled with each other at the edge of the drop, jaws snapping and claws tearing. Flitch had grown under the power of the werefire, but Hodge had always been the larger and heavier of the two brothers, and his greater bulk won out now. One of his immense hands caught Flitch by the neck, and slowly, grunting and growling, he bore him to the edge of the lip. As his boots slid backward on the stone, Flitch struggled to speak, but Hodge's grip choked off his voice, and all he could bring out were weak gasps of terror.

With one last mighty heave, Hodge drove Flitch over the edge and followed after. They fell in each other's clutches and the werefire swallowed them.

Pendrake crawled away from the edge. His head was bleeding and his limbs shook as he groped for his staff. But Brax was there now and he laid his hand on the staff and lifted it away from Pendrake's reach.

"Well, Ammon," he said. "It looks like you'll have to finish me yourself after all."

The green fire was in the mage's eyes now. He gazed at the staff in his hand. Then he gave a cry of rage, and the fire flared from the staff and struck Pendrake, throwing him back violently into the corridor. But even as the Loremaster fell, the fire roared back along the staff and enveloped Brax himself.

As Pendrake lifted his head and watched, the mage was

engulfed in raging flames that took up his cry of terror with many voices screaming in agony and madness. He staggered back and the staff slipped from his hands and fell into the abyss. He clawed at himself now, frantic to push or tear the flames from his face and his arms. But now the fire was shooting out of his mouth and eyes.

And then there was only the fire, and in it many faces and shapes writhing and struggling as if for command. The roar of voices rose to a wail and then died away. The fire dimmed and sank. A few last scraps of it fluttered on the stones and then went out.

The stone chair fell with an echoing crash. The walls shook and great cracks appeared in the stone.

Pendrake climbed unsteadily to his feet. He looked over the edge and saw the fire subsiding, bleeding away into the dark corners of what remained of the toyshop below.

He turned and gazed at the remains of his workshop. Stooping with a groan of effort, he righted his chair and sat down heavily.

"I just need to rest a moment, Rowen," he murmured between laboured breaths. "Just a moment. Then I'll come and find you, I promise. I'll bring you home."

When the fetch host had turned against it, the Nightbane army had been thrown into upheaval. A surging sea of metal-clad figures flowed around the viceroy's great iron carriage, trampling one another in their haste to escape the wall of metal they had suddenly found closing around them, and causing the beasts who drew the carriage to panic and run mad. The carriage was battered and rocked off balance until it crashed onto its side. Nightbane continued to mill and thrash against the barrier of the fetches, but as it became clear that the fetches were not going to attack, but merely contain them, the remnant of the invading army lowered their weapons and stayed where they were.

Then a single arrow whizzed out from among the Nightbane; it arced through the smoke-filled sky and landed near the vanguard of the allied forces. There appeared to be a paper tied around the shaft. An Errantry trooper ran out, snatched up the arrow and brought it back to the allied commanders.

It wasn't long before word spread that the invading army was asking for a truce and a laying down of arms.

But no one was rejoicing yet. There was a reek of blood and a stench of burning in the air. Ash floated down like grey snow. Stunned by the same vision Freya had seen, and by the unexpected victory that had followed, the defenders were slow to stir. Then the allied army began to come apart again as fighters from different lands found their country-men and began the work of tending to their wounded and carrying away their dead. The dwarven folk of Stonesthrow Mine marched in a slow procession up the field, weeping as they carried the bodies of Mimling Hammersong and two of his brothers from the stream, where they had fallen in the first assault of the fetches.

While all of this was going on a strange rumour spread among the troops who had come with Balor from Fable. The boy Will Lightfoot had been seen on the hill at the edge of the battlefield. The boy everyone called the Pathfinder, who had come from the Untold to destroy the Night King and save them all.

"He travelled to a dark land to bring back some great magic," exclaimed a trooper with utter certainty. "It was he who turned those fetches, not the mage, there's no doubt of it."

A girl was with the Pathfinder, some said, a girl with red hair whom few recognized. But the rumour came to Balor as well, and when he heard it, he halted what he was doing and wiped tears from his eyes.

"You did it, lad," he murmured. "You kept her safe and brought her home."

Amid the wreckage of the skyship stood the golem, as still and unmoving as stone. Around him men were slowly gathering from various places on the field, their armour covered in dust and blood. Some were wounded and being helped by their companions. There were mordog among them; they glanced warily at the soldiers of the allied forces who were now approaching. When the Errantry troopers among them caught sight of the mordog, they drew their swords or gripped their spears and staves in readiness.

Balor shouldered his way through the crowd.

"Lower your weapons," he said quietly.

Most obeyed him but not all.

Last to join the Stormriders were Finn and Corr Madoc. Corr gazed at the faces around him. He had his sword in his hand as well but tossed it to the ground and stood waiting. Finn, helped along by Grath, still wore the battered, cracked *gaal* armour. His sword arm was in a sling and he looked barely able to stand.

"Finn Madoc," Balor said as he approached. "I thought I'd never see you again."

Finn's eyes met the wildman's. He appeared to be struggling to speak, and then his knees buckled and Grath lowered him to the earth.

"What's happened to him?" Balor cried.

"Are there any healers here?" Corr asked. "My brother doesn't have long."

"What about Doctor Alazar?" Balor asked. "Isn't he with you?"

"The doctor is dead," Corr said.

Balor stared.

"Dead? Alazar? No, that can't be." His face darkened. "Sky Lord, if you had anything to do with this—"

"I did, wildman," Corr said. "The doctor died because of me. And I am sorry for it."

The rage left Balor's face as suddenly as it had appeared. His shoulders sank.

"Alazar," he muttered, his eyes welling with tears. "Not you."

The crowd parted again and Freya appeared. She was still carrying the ice blade, but there was much less of it now, so that it was more a long slender knife than a sword. Everyone stared as she approached Finn and knelt beside him.

"Finn," she said. "Do you remember me?"

He glanced up, blinking, then his eyes widened.

"Freya," he said. "How can you be here?"

"It doesn't matter," she said. "I can help you. Take the blade."

Finn could no longer move his swollen arm. Freya had to place the sword in his hand. Slowly his stiffened fingers closed around the hilt. He looked at Freya with a puzzled expression, and then he gasped. His eyes filled with wonder.

"The pain is gone," he said.

The sword was melting away more quickly now, but where its substance was going no one could say. They saw no water dripping onto the grass, but swiftly and steadily the ice diminished until it was nothing but a gleaming sliver in Finn's palm. Then even this last tiny splinter seemed to sink into his flesh and was gone.

Finn tore away the sling and stretched out his arm.

"There's feeling again in my fingers," he said. "Freya, what was that? What did you give me?"

She placed her hand on his. Her hand was no longer cold and the warm light had come back into her eyes.

"That was the last of the dragon," she said. "The last of Whitewing Stonegrinder."

The troopers and knights of the Errantry had slowly gathered around the Stormriders. On Balor's command weapons had been lowered, but still no one spoke. The only sound was the wind snapping banners and tugging at cloaks.

Then a young man stepped out from among the Errantry ranks. His head was bandaged and one eye was swollen shut. "Father," he said. "It's me."

One of the older Stormriders moved forward. "Caleb," he said. "My son."

The Stormrider and the wounded Errantry soldier met in the space between the two armies and embraced. Soon many of the other Stormriders had found friends and relations among the Errantry ranks, and there were many tears and much laughter.

To Balor's astonishment, Corr approached him, unbuckled his sword belt and let sword and scabbard fall to the earth. Then he bowed his head and knelt before the wildman.

"I have done terrible things," he said in a strained voice. "Take my life now, for the life of your friend. For all the lives lost because of me. I only ask that you pardon my men and let all my Stormriders who are not Bournefolk—the mordog and those from other lands—leave in peace to return to their homes."

Balor stared down at Corr, then glanced up at the crowd of Stormriders, most of who were now laying down their own weapons. He swallowed hard and cleared his throat.

"It's not for me to decide any of that," Balor said. "I'm like you now, Corr. I broke my oath and I'm no longer an officer of the Errantry."

"You are, Balor Gruff," a voice cried. "One of its finest."

All heads turned. The Marshal, Lord Caliburn, was coming toward them, walking slowly with the support of two knight-apprentices. Captain Thorne followed behind, his head lowered as if in shame, though he darted anxious glances at the troops around him.

"I submit to your justice, my lord," Corr said as Caliburn halted before him. "Take my life in payment for your son's."

"There will be justice, yes," the Marshal said. "But not vengeance."

He gestured to one of the knight-apprentices, a young woman, who handed him something bundled in grey cloth. The Marshal unwrapped the cloth, which they all saw now was a stained and faded apprentice's cloak. Inside the cloak lay a sword belt, a short knife and an Errantry brooch, a white five-petaled flower. The Marshal drew out the knife.

"Rise, Corr Madoc," he said.

Corr climbed to his feet. His eyes met the Marshal's.

"This was my son's knife," the Marshal said. "He was wearing it the day he was taken from me. He was wearing this cloak, too, with this Errantry pin."

Corr lowered his head. "I know I cannot be forgiven," he said. "I have never forgiven myself. Do as you will."

The Marshal took the knife by its blade and held it hilt-first toward Corr.

"No one can bring my son back to me," the Marshal said. "But you are a son, as well, Corr Madoc. You had a father who was taken from you long before he should have been."

Corr looked up, surprise and confusion in his face.

"You are a son without a father, and I am a father without a son. You will live in my house," he said. "You will be my son."

"My lord," Captain Thorne said. "Are you certain you're recovered from your illness? This man has caused much harm to the Errantry."

Caliburn turned. "We all have much to answer for, Captain," he said.

Thorne lowered his head.

"Take my son's knife and his cloak, Corr Madoc," Caliburn said. "Serve the Bourne and the Errantry with all your strength and heart."

Corr stared at the Marshal. His eyes filled with tears and he fell to his knees before the old man, kissed his hand and began to tremble as sobs shook him. The Marshal placed his hand on Corr's head, and after a while his shaking stopped. Then Corr rose again and took the knife and bowed.

"I have no right to call you Father," he said. "But I will live in your house, and I will serve the people of the Bourne as your son did."

The Marshal stayed to help direct the stretcher-bearers who had arrived to carry away the wounded, and a mount was brought to him and he rode to meet the allied commanders at the Duke's pavilion. Captain Thorne returned to Fable with most of Balor's Errantry troops. A few of the Stormriders went with them, to search for friends and family. Corr remained with his men for the time being, and Balor Gruff stayed as well, with Finn and Freya, as they had much to talk about.

Brannon Yates came to see them, to say goodbye.

"I'm going to find my mother and my sister," he said. "If they still live."

"You haven't been in the city yet?" Corr asked, surprised. "You were here days before us."

"I had to remember who I was first, like you, Corr," Yates said. He turned to go and then paused. "Balor, I almost forgot. During the fighting I thought I saw you."

"You did see me, Brannon," the wildman said with a puzzled look. "I was there."

"Yes, but the Balor I saw was older. With a grey beard. And there were others with him, like you."

Balor climbed to his feet.

"You mean . . ." he breathed. "Where did you last see them?"

Yates pointed across the Course, and Balor took off at a near-run in that direction. He hadn't gone far before he caught sight of a tall figure looking over the battlefield as if searching for someone. The figure was manlike, but when he turned in Balor's direction his face could be described as resembling a cross between a lion and an angry pug dog. His long beard was iron grey, as were his bushy eyebrows. His dark eyes widened when they caught sight of Balor.

The wildman halted and then came forward more slowly.

"I was told there was another like us on this field today," the older wildman said. "I didn't believe it. There are so few of us left. I was just about to give up searching and take my people home."

"I thought I was the last one," Balor said with a catch in his voice. "I thought I was alone."

"My brother and his wife had a boy child," the older wildman said. "When our people fled the plague that came into our valley from the ghostlands, they died on the journey. The child was lost. In the forest, near—"

"The Fell of Thraws?"

"Yes. Twenty-seven summers ago."

"That's where the Errantry found me. They named me Balor Gruff."

The older wildman nodded.

"Your name was Baikul," he said in a strained voice, his eyes glittering. "I am your father's older brother, Haggai. I never thought we would see you again. But our wisewoman said that if the wildfolk fought for this city, if we helped defend it, a great treasure would be restored to us. She spoke truly. You are alone no longer, Balor Gruff."

The Stormriders had begun salvaging what they could from the ships to set up their own encampment on the Course. Finn approached the golem, standing patiently at Corr's side.

"What will you do with Ord now?" Corr asked.

"He's not mine to command," Finn said.

"Perhaps not, but it's better he stays in your keeping. I imagine he could be of great help rebuilding this city."

Finn gazed up into the stony grey face of the golem, a face that had never blinked or smiled or changed in all that they had gone through together. He remembered how they had first found him, relentlessly piling stone upon stone to build a tower doomed to sinking into the mire. If they freed him, would he simply return to that futile task? Not even a creature like Ord deserved such a fate. Finn had often wondered where this powerful being had really come from, and now the answer was clear to him.

"Ord has done enough for us already," Finn said.

He reached up, and as he plucked the green stone from the golem's forehead, he said, "Sleep." He backed away.

At first it seemed that this command was one the golem could not or would not obey. Then the grey stone eyes closed for the first time and the giant body of the golem began to sag and collapse in on itself. Ord's face dissolved into a featureless mass. His hands became rough clubs. His legs fused. At last he toppled over, and there was nothing left of him but a lifeless mound of clay.

27

LATE THAT AFTERNOON LORD Caliburn rode out to the stream with the Duke and King Shakya.

A curtained litter appeared in the Nightbane camp, carried by four bearers and flanked by four riders in armour. The fetches parted long enough for the litter to pass through. It carried the same black standard that had flown above the viceroy's carriage. As the procession came slowly up the Course, many wondered what sort of terrible being was hidden behind those black curtains, but when they were drawn back and the viceroy emerged, supported by two of the litter-bearers, those with keen eyesight or spyglasses saw that the viceroy was only a man like them. He walked haltingly, as if he might have been injured in the overturning of his carriage.

The conference ended more quickly than anyone expected.

The two parties soon went their separate ways, and those who watched from a distance feared that the negotiations had not gone well and that the fighting would begin again. But the Nightbane host began to take down their tents and fortifications, and the order sounded for the allies to do likewise.

The siege and the battle were over. Many from both sides eyed the fetches apprehensively, but they stood motionless and seemingly dead, like cut stalks of wheat. What was left of the enemy forces began to trickle away in small companies, leaving most of their weapons and gear behind.

King Shakya rode back to his men, and as he dismounted before his pavilion, a young man in an Errantry cloak approached.

"I would speak with you, Sire," the young man said. He was carrying a leather-bound book in one hand.

"Who are you?" the king asked. Through his golden mask his voice seemed to come from far away.

"I am Finn Madoc of the Errantry," he said. "I'm here to keep a promise."

By sunset Brax's labyrinth of walls and narrow, twisted streets had almost completely crumbled away. A few people were brought alive out of the rubble, while many others had died and some who had disappeared days before were never found.

Rowen and Will found Pendrake in the ruins of the toyshop. He was still sitting in the chair, in what was left of his workshop. When Rowen knelt beside him, speaking his name softly through her tears, the old man lifted his head and opened his eyes.

"My child," he said, touching her wet face in wonder, as if he doubted what he was seeing. "How can this be? Where are we?"

"We're home, Grandfather. In the toyshop. I found a way home."

Pendrake rose with Will's help and they took him downstairs to the library. It was still strewn with the books Ammon Brax had been searching through, but this was one of the few rooms the hogmen had not defiled, and the walls and roof beams were still intact. The old man sank into one of the armchairs and Rowen knelt beside him and held his hand. Will gathered the broken pieces of a shelf from the hall outside and got a small blaze going in the fireplace.

"I turned the fetches back, Grandfather," Rowen explained. "I turned them against the Nightbane. They obey me now, but I'll release them from their armour once the enemy's gone. The fetches will be free to return to the Weaving."

Pendrake was staring into the fire and didn't seem to hear her.

"No one understands what you've done," Will said to Rowen. "Did you hear what people were whispering as we passed by in the streets? They think I did this. The Pathfinder. They don't know it was you who saved them."

"Every story needs a hero, Will," Rowen said with a smile, then she grew serious again. "It's better this way. Most people aren't ready yet to hear the truth. It will take time for the vision of the thread to sink in. For folk to understand we all created this story and we don't have to believe in it anymore."

"So you don't want me telling anyone what you've done?"

"Not now. Someday you'll tell the whole story. When the time is right."

Will glanced around uneasily.

"What happened to Brax?"

At the mention of the mage's name, Pendrake stirred and looked up.

"He's gone," the old man said. "The fire took him."

The Loremaster seemed to have recovered his presence

of mind. He asked Rowen what had happened to her after he left the Shadow Realm. She began to tell the story in more detail, but there was much she had trouble finding words for. When she spoke of the Night King and what she had discovered, a light came into the old man's eyes.

"You would think," he said with a bitter smile, "that a man who has told stories all his life might have understood."

Will asked about the Marrowbone brothers, and Pendrake related what had happened to them.

"I'm sorry for them," Rowen said. "Especially Hodge. It all could have turned out so differently."

"The story you saved us from, Rowen, has destroyed many lives," Pendrake said. "There are many who can still be helped, many stories that need mending, but I do not have the strength anymore for the task."

Rowen stroked the old man's hand.

"All you need to mend is yourself, Grandfather."

"What will happen now?" Will asked. "If we're beginning a new story, how will it end?"

"It won't," Rowen said. "Or I can't see an ending. I think the thread will allow us a way out of all endings, Will, so that no story can do what Malabron's did. No story can make us believe it is the *only* story ever again."

They heard a noise at the door and hurrying feet, and Edweth entered, followed by Balor Gruff. The housekeeper threw herself at each of them in turn, holding them tight and weeping and stroking their hair. Everyone's story was shared again, and when Edweth had listened and told her own tale, she insisted that the very next order of business was to make them all something to eat. She wept anew when she saw what had become of her beloved kitchen, but she didn't weep long. Soon she had tied her apron on and was preparing a meal with her usual determined bustle.

Balor put a hand on Will's shoulder. "You've done all that a knight could expect of his apprentice and more," he said. "I'm proud of you."

"We all are," Pendrake said.

While they were eating the meal Edweth had prepared, Finn and Freya arrived. Finn's arm was no longer in its sling and the colour had returned to his face. Balor embraced him, and they spoke again of Doctor Alazar. Freya joined Rowen at Pendrake's side and took the old man's hand in hers and kissed it.

"I had hoped you were safely on your way home to your family, my dear," Pendrake said to her.

"I will go home someday," Freya said, and then glanced at Finn. "Not yet. I'm good with tools, Father Nicholas. I learned much from my father. I want to stay and help you rebuild the toyshop."

"It should be rebuilt," Pendrake said with a nod. "But it won't have a toymaker, at least not for a while. Perhaps, Freya, if you stay in Fable, you could take up my trade and make toys for the children. They will need toys as much as anything after all this."

"What do you mean, Father Nicholas? Are you leaving?" Freya said, and then understanding came into her face, and she leaned her head on Pendrake's arm and wept.

Rowen understood, too. But she had thought of an answer.

"Grandfather," she said softly. "Grandmother told me she had . . . become the past. She said she had woven herself into it, and that's why she had to remain in the Weaving. I think that where she is, time doesn't pass like it does here. Or maybe time doesn't even happen there. I think that if you went there, if you found Grandmother, you could stay with her. You would be together again."

Pendrake nodded sadly. "I promised Maya that I would

never leave you," he said. "I can't keep my promise, as it turns out. The werefire has made that a certainty."

"But you can be with Grandmother," Rowen said through her tears. "She lives in a cottage like the one at Blue Hill. It's peaceful there. And maybe someday, when I'm finished what I have to do, I can visit you. I know the way now."

"I will hold you to that," Pendrake said softly. "And now, Will, help me up. It's time."

Will took the old man's arm, and they helped him climb the stairs to the raincabinet. Edweth had come out of the kitchen and joined them, and when she understood what was happening, she struggled with her grief and embraced the Loremaster and wished him well.

"If you're with her, as you should be, Nicholas, then all will be well."

"What about you, Edweth?" Pendrake said, holding her hand. "I'm afraid I've left you without a house to look after."

"Don't concern yourself about me, Nicholas," Edweth said. "Believe it or not, there's a man in this city whose things are maintained in a worse shambles than yours ever were. I've already had a go at cleaning up after him, being cooped up and having nothing else to do, and I can see it's a job that will keep me busy for much time to come."

They gathered in front of the open door of the raincabinet. Only a few drops were falling softly in the darkness.

"If I understand what you've done, Rowen," Pendrake said, "this isn't the only doorway in and out of the Weaving anymore."

"Maybe it never was, Grandfather," Rowen said. "I think the Weaving isn't really a place. It's more like a way of seeing. Seeing how things really are."

Balor grunted in surprise and they all turned to the cabinet doorway, where a tiger stood watching them. It had come out of the rain without a sound.

"Riddle will guide you to Grandmother," Rowen said.

The Loremaster said his farewells to everyone. He held Rowen for a long while before he let her go. But at last he turned to the raincabinet door and stepped under the falling rain with the tiger at his side, and they were gone.

Everyone was quiet when they went back to the study. Without anyone having to speak, they all began the work of putting things to order as much as was possible: picking up books and returning them to their places, righting fallen shelves, sweeping the rooms and the halls of trash and broken furnishings. It seemed foolish to Will whenever he glanced up and saw daylight falling through the cracks and holes in the walls. The building itself was a ruin. But he understood. They were doing this for the Loremaster, and for themselves.

Freya was startled when she ventured into the rubble at the back of the toyshop, where the upper floor had fallen away. Something gave a squeal of terror and darted past her into the front hall. They all ran over to see what it was, and there, cowering in a corner, was a fat brown and pink-spotted pig, with the shreds of what might have once been a fine velvet coat still hanging around his neck.

"It's Hodge!" Rowen said.

"You're right," Will said. "Look at his face. I guess the werefire didn't destroy him."

Rowen approached the terrified animal, speaking to it in a soft, soothing voice. Just as she was about to place a hand on it, the pig sprang out of its corner, bolted down the hall and was caught, squealing and snorting, in Balor's arms.

"What do we do with him?" the wildman asked, struggling to hang on to the frantic, thrashing animal. "If I let him go someone else will catch him and he'll have an apple in his mouth by day's end. Probably what he deserves."

Rowen shook her head firmly. "No, we won't let that happen. Look after him, Balor, will you? For my grandfather's sake. Don't let anyone eat him."

"So now I'm the keeper of a pet pig," Balor muttered. "I'm not sure I like the way this story of yours turned out, Rowen of Blue Hill."

Balor found some twine and made a leash to keep the pig from running off. They all returned to work, and the day passed quickly, so that to their surprise it was soon time for dinner. Edweth outdid herself, given what she had to work with, and they ate and talked, and candles were lit at the table as the day faded.

As they were finishing their meal, Miles Plunkett arrived from the Golden Goose. When he saw to his relief that everyone was all right, he insisted that they spend the night not in the wreckage of the toyshop but at his inn, where he insisted there would be rooms for them all. Reluctantly they agreed, and followed him back to the inn. On the way, Will and Rowen saw to their surprise and delight how closely Edweth walked beside the innkeeper. When they reached the bridge where the Golden Goose stood, Finn and Balor took their leave, saying that they had to return to Appleyard to carry out their duties there. The wildman had Hodge with him on his leash, but Balor seemed to have warmed to him, and for his part the pig trotted alongside Balor as if they belonged together.

After the innkeeper had shown them to their rooms and made sure they had whatever they might need to be comfortable for the night, they all came down to the common room, which was full to bursting with Bournefolk and guests from many other lands, all talking of the battle and its aftermath. Will was relieved to discover that no one there recognized

him as the Pathfinder, the boy so many were praising and telling their own wild tales about. Others put forward the names
of various supernatural beings to explain the miraculous
turnabout of the fetches, and a loud, high-spirited debate got
under way.

Before long Rowen and Will grew tired of the noise and
light. They went outside together and leaned over the parapet
and watched the water flow quietly beneath them in the dusk.

"I heard you, Will," Rowen said after a long silence.
"Under the tree, after Dama struck me and I was in the nightmare and couldn't get out. I heard you talking to me."

"I didn't know what else to do," he said. "I knew you
hadn't given up, so I couldn't either."

"You saved me. I didn't want you to stay with me, but if
you hadn't, I would've been lost. I heard you, and I knew I
wasn't alone. That kept me fighting."

"I've been thinking about Shade," Will said. "Do you
know where he is now, or if he's still alive? I hate to think of
him as that . . . that monster."

To his surprise, Rowen's face lit with a mischievous smile.

"I fixed a few things," she said. "You and Shade will meet
again. I just don't know when or where."

Will nodded and swallowed the lump that had formed in
his throat.

"When you were talking to your grandfather," he went
on, "you said there was more you had to do. That you
weren't finished."

"I'm not," Rowen said, turning to look at him. "Or it's not.
The work, I mean. It's only beginning. There are still so many
places where people are lost and without hope, like the camp
of the Fair Folk. The stories they lived by are broken—they
don't work anymore—and they're frightened. And some are
angry, too, because everything is changing and they don't

want it to. We're all walking into the unknown now, but I can show people they don't have to be afraid."

"You mean that you have to go," Will said. "You can't stay here with me."

"I have to help where I can. I'm still a loremaster. But you can't stay, either, Will. Your father and your sister need you. The shadow also touched your world. There are people there who are lost in the same nightmare of hate and fear and trying to wake up from it. You can help them."

Will frowned, then nodded. "I do have to go home," he said. "I promised my dad I'd come back. But I don't want to leave you. It seems we keep having to say goodbye."

Rowen moved closer to him, and he put his arms around her and held her.

"I don't want to leave you, either," she said. "But it doesn't have to be forever. It won't be."

"You know that we'll see each other again? You're sure?"

"I'm not sure of very much anymore," Rowen said. "And perhaps that's how it should be. But I think, because of the golden thread, there won't be any more happy endings. Not because good things will no longer happen—they will, and maybe even more than they used to. People will still find what they've lost, and fall in love, and work to save what's good in this world. But we won't need things to *end* happily when we know that nothing will ever really end. Then maybe we can live as if every moment is the beginning of something new."

"I'll come back as often as I can," Will said. "I'll come to Fable, and if you're not here, I'll look for you."

"I'll look for you, too. And I'll need your help. What's happened here, to Fable, to all of us, mustn't be forgotten. The truth was lost once and so much was destroyed because of it. I can't forget poor Mimling Hammersong. And your friend the doctor. Even Ammon Brax. I have to tell the story. Share it with others. You can help me do that."

"I'm no storyteller," Will said.

"You will be," Rowen said, and Will heard sadness in her voice. "I don't think you and I have a choice about that. It's what we'll do to keep from getting lost."

Rowen and Will stayed in Fable the next day and the day after that. They couldn't bring themselves to leave each other or their friends just yet.

The army of the defenders was disbanding now; the tents were coming down and Storyfolk were leaving for their own lands. The fetches still remained standing, but it wasn't clear whether there was any spark of life within them. Finn and Balor went to find out. Cautiously they approached one of the motionless figures, and after much inspection and debate about what to do, Balor growled impatiently and gave the armour a shove. The fetch toppled over onto the grass and cracked open. Several others fell over on their own during the course of the day, and this seemed to confirm that the spirits had vacated their iron shells.

The question then became what to do with all the fever iron from which the abandoned armour was forged. Enough of it could be salvaged to power a hundred skyships, the Stormriders said, but in the end it was Corr Madoc who argued loudest that the armour should be buried as it was and left to rust in the earth until its power had seeped away and it could no longer tempt anyone to use it again.

The last of the allies to leave the field was the first who had arrived, the company of the Red Duke. On the third evening after the battle Balor Gruff brought Jodo Flyte, the Red Duke's captain of bowmen, to the Golden Goose. Flyte played his battered lute and the two of them sang together. They did not

sing about the battle or the strange way it had ended. They sang
about those who had fallen, a sad song that made many weep.
When they had finished that song, they began others, old songs
of friends meeting and parting, of happier times and good cheer.

At dawn the next day the Red Duke rode away with his
company, and the sun rose over the quiet, empty Course and
warmed the broken walls of the city.

Will and Rowen walked together from the gates. The
grass along the roadsides glittered with dew, and from some
farmyard nearby a dog barked. They climbed out of the valley and found the path that had brought them from Blue Hill
not very long ago. They looked back once at the city. The sun
was burning the mists away from the low places. Appleyard
Hill shimmered green and gold in the sun.

They walked on through the morning, taking their time,
neither wanting to reach their destination, but all too soon
they reached the familiar hilltop, and there was the cottage,
nestled in the tall grass at the bottom of the slope.

They descended to the cottage and found things just as
they had left them. The chimney leaned and the nettles and
dandelions were still growing thick around the walls.

"I've got a long way to go, but I think I'll start here,"
Rowen said. "This place needs some looking after. The cottage could still make a good home one day."

They embraced and said their goodbyes through tears,
swearing that they would find each other again. Then Will
turned away from Rowen standing at the door of the cottage
and kept on.

He was on his way home again. He had no idea how to get
there, but from experience he understood that all he could
do was keep walking, until the right path became clear.
He took a narrow cart track that led away from the cottage

toward the northern hills called the Braids. The sky was blue
and clear, and after so long in the grey dimness of the Shadow Realm, he felt a desire for sunlight and air. So whenever
his road branched he followed the path that looked as if it
might take him to higher ground. Eventually he found himself on a windswept ridge, the highest spot for miles around.

He stopped here to rest for a while and looked out over
the way he had come. He thought he could just make out the
green prominence that was Appleyard Hill. It was then,
while he was eating the bread and cheese that Edweth had
packed for him, that he had the feeling he was being watched.

When he was finished his meal he rose, looked all around,
then kept along the ridge. If he was being followed, this was
the best place to be for now. The wind strengthened and grew
colder, and eventually the chill forced him off the ridge and
along a path that wound down the far side, away from the
Bourne. As he was coming down the path he stopped suddenly and gazed around. He had come to a wide, sloping
meadow dotted with flowers and alive with butterflies and
the hum of bees. The ridge rose like a wall on his left, and before him emerged height after height of steep forested hills he
was sure he had never seen before. He was close to the border,
he knew, and out there were the wild lands beyond the Bourne.

He looked back the way he had come and saw shapes on
the crest of the ridge. Wolves. A line of them, dark against
the sky.

His heart leaped.

They had been flanking him, observing him, he suddenly
knew. But he also knew that they were not hunting him. If
that had been the case, he doubted he would have seen them
until it was too late.

The wolf at the head of the line broke away from the others
and bounded down the ridge toward him. When it was only

a few paces distant, the wolf pulled up short and regarded him with its bright amber eyes.

"Shade?" Will said softly.

It was his friend—and yet it wasn't. The pack that this wolf led had once belonged to Corr Madoc, but they had been released and now followed a new leader. They would not hunt him, he was certain of that, but neither would this wolf speak to him. Will understood now that Rowen had given their friend what he most desired. The life of Shade the Speaking Creature was over. The wolf was free again.

Will stepped closer and held out his hand.

The wolf came toward him and lowered its head so that Will could reach out and lay his hand on the fur between its ears. Only for a moment. Then the wolf turned and bounded back up the hill to rejoin its pack.

"Thank you, Shade," Will said. "I'll never forget you."

The wolves trotted along the top of the ridge, away from him, until their path took them among the trees on the far slopes, where they slipped one by one from his sight and vanished into the wild.

"THAT'S THE END?" THE older girl asked.

The young man looked up. He's almost forgotten he wasn't alone. The whole family was gathered around him now. The children's father had left his repairs on the truck and had come to sit beside the woman, the little boy and girl cradled in his lap. The older girl was perched on the tailgate of the truck, her arms around her knees, still keeping her distance, but from her question he knew she'd been listening. The grandmother was snoring quietly, her chin on her chest. *You can't please everyone,* the young man thought.

"That's all I have to tell," he said. "So far."

"What about Will and Rowen?" the girl asked. "Do they find each other again?"

"Well, if you remember, I warned you before I started that the story wasn't over."

The old woman's head shot up.

"Of course they find each other," she snapped, with a glare that defied anyone to accuse her of sleeping. "It couldn't end any other way. That wouldn't be right."

"I wish we knew for sure," the girl said.

"So do I," the young man agreed.

"I want Will and Shade to fight more monsters!" the little boy shouted, swinging an imaginary sword.

"*More* monsters?" the young man said, and he laughed. "There are always more monsters, I suppose."

"True enough," the man said, "but they'll have to keep for another day. We have a long road still to go, and that's all the time we have for make-believe."

He lifted the children from his lap and they groaned and said it wasn't fair, but the woman gave them a stern look that abruptly ended the complaints.

The man slammed the truck's hood shut and nodded to his wife. The family began to load their belongings into the back. The young man helped, and when they were nearly finished packing and making everything secure, the older girl moved close to him.

"What Rowen did with the thread . . ." she began in a hushed voice, as if she was afraid someone else might overhear. "How she gave everyone a way out of the nightmare . . ."

"Yes?"

"You told us you were there. You didn't make it all up, then. You knew them. You knew Will and Rowen."

"As well as anyone, I suppose."

"We had to move because of me," the girl said quickly. "I was getting into trouble. Into fights. I didn't start them. Well, most of them I didn't. But that's how it goes for me. When the others find out I'm not like them—when they find out I'm . . ." She gave the young man a sharp, distrusting glance.

"I wish things were different, that's all," she said, her eyes burning. "Sometimes I think I must be in a story, too, but it's the wrong one and I don't know how to get out."

"I was in a place like that, too—a long time ago. I'd say you're off to a good start if you're already looking for a door."

"Those paths Rowen made, do you think they're real?"

"I know they are. It's just that they can be hard to see sometimes. When you find the right one, you'll know."

The woman called the girl's name and she turned away and climbed into the back of the truck. The children's father stepped onto the running board and then paused.

"You need a lift?" he asked the young man. "Where we're going is a big place. Lots of folks who might trade a meal for a good yarn."

"I've been to that town," the young man said. "There are good people in it and I'm sure you'll be welcome. But I'm not headed that way."

"Suit yourself."

The man climbed in and shut the door. The truck coughed and sputtered to life, then trundled off down the road. The little children waved from the windows and the young man waved back. The older girl was half-hidden amid the family's belongings. She didn't wave but her eyes were on him until the truck went around a bend and out of sight. Then he turned away and walked on, until the rumble of the engine faded to silence and he was alone again.

For the rest of that day he met no one on the road. The night brought a biting wind, and he took shelter in a stand of old wind-bent pines.

He'd told the girl's family that the story wasn't over, that it was still going on and they were all part of it. Drawing his coat tighter against the cold he asked himself if he still believed that. He'd searched for so long and told the story so often that he found himself wondering the same thing his listeners always wanted to know.

Did it really happen?

At times like this, he would tell himself the rest of it. Everything that followed his last meeting with Shade. He needed to reassure himself that it was still there—the invisible thread between that other world and his own, between the story and his life after. He would recall the road he'd taken to get home. And then the back porch light gleaming in the dark like a star, just as it had the night he'd left. Returning to his old life with Dad and Jess, and then the days and years that came and went so quickly. He'd finished school and worked for a while at different jobs, none of which he stayed with for long. His dad had married again and moved with Jess and his new wife to another town. He hadn't gone with them. Instead he'd sold most of his things and set out on the road. Whenever he met someone who seemed to need a story, he would tell his own as if it were someone else's. And maybe it was. Maybe that's what he was doing: trying to tell his way back into the story.

Making his way into the Perilous Realm again hadn't been difficult. The two worlds seemed to have drawn closer to each other in many places, so that sometimes he would slip from one to the other without realizing it. Even so, very little in that other world was as he remembered it. He would glimpse a familiar line of hills in the distance or find himself crossing a bridge over a stream that he thought he'd crossed once before, but these hints and suggestions never came to anything. He couldn't find the Bourne, and almost no one he encountered had ever heard of a city called Fable. Some had heard stories, though. Tales of the Errantry. They said the knights had a new marshal, a young man named Finn Madoc. They'd heard of his wife, too—the famous toymaker.

And there was an ogre in some of these tales. Well, ogre or wildman, no one was certain which. The wildman lived in the woods with his own folk, but sometimes he emerged, when the marshal needed his help.

The young man listened eagerly to these tales. But when he asked those who told them if they knew the way to Fable, they would shrug or shake their heads, and confess that they weren't really sure how to get there from here.

In the morning he passed through farmlands where people were hard at work sowing the bare fields and no one stopped to talk to him. By late afternoon he came to a marsh where a lone blackbird called from a cattail stalk. He camped there on a dry hummock, under a willow, with a chorus of frogs for company.

He started awake that night from a deep and dreamless sleep. A sound had roused him. He thought it might have been the howl of a wolf. He listened and heard only the wind moving through the tall grass. Even the frogs had gone silent.

For the next two days he made his slow, weaving way through the marshland. It wasn't until night had nearly fallen on the second day that he found a good, solid road under his feet again. A road that soon brought him to a town. He lingered in the square, beside the dried-up fountain, and the few townsfolk who passed him on their way home for the evening stared at him without speaking or ignored him completely. As the sun was going down, a stern-looking older man approached and asked him who he was and what he was doing there. He said he was only passing through, but if anyone wished, he would be happy to tell a story in exchange for some supper or a place to sleep. The man frowned and strode away, but a short time later a few children gathered around him, some with their mothers and fathers in tow. He told some brief, funny tales to begin, and was asked for more, and as he started his own story the crowd grew in size. More people came out of their houses to see what was going on. Someone brought out lanterns and strung them in the trees, and when the story was done someone else called for a song, and soon there was music and dancing and good food to eat.

On the evening of the following day, he was camped on the shore of a lake. A fire of dry juniper branches cracked and snapped and sent embers shooting among the stars. Much later the blackened wood sank in on itself and glowed softly from within, as if it had fallen asleep and was dreaming fiery dreams.

But he could not sleep. He was waiting for something, although he didn't know what. Then out of the night a grey shape came gliding. A heron, he thought. It touched the surface of the water with its long bill and then rose again and vanished into the dark.

It was just a bird, he told himself. It wasn't a sign. He wanted everything to speak to him, to show him the way. But he was lost. He had to admit it.

Maybe he was trying too hard. Getting in his own way again. Or maybe he'd waited too long to return and his memories were no longer to be trusted. He watched the ripples spread out across the dark water. The bird had come and gone so quickly, like a fleeting thought, leaving only this brief trace of its passing. In a moment there would be no evidence at all that it had been there.

He recalled how they'd all been trapped inside a story, he and his friends. But if the golden thread had done its work, then that story must have come apart over the years, unravelling like a worn-out tapestry. Which meant there might be only a few traces of it left, scattered shreds he was stumbling across by chance. So why should he expect to find things as he remembered them? What he had come back to was a different story. It might still be called *The Perilous Realm*, but it was something entirely new. And what if this new story no longer had a place for him?

In the next town he came to three brightly painted caravans in the middle of the square, a happy, boisterous crowd gathered around them. One side of the middle caravan had been unfolded to make a stage, and on it a play was in performance. He stood and watched, as spellbound as the crowd. It was a very old play, with a knight, a lady, a magician and a devil.

Then he looked more closely at one of the players, at the familiar face under the wig and the thick greasepaint. The man wasn't wearing his straggly little beard or cardboard armour, but it was the Scholar. He was sure of it.

When the play had finished, there was much applause and some shouts for more, and then two men came onstage and he knew them, too. It was Arn and his brother, Vardo. A girl he didn't recognize followed them, carrying an armful of knives and swords. Arn sprang onto Vardo's shoulders, then Vardo lifted his brother by his ankles until he was balanced on one foot on Vardo's head. The girl tossed Arn the knives and swords one by one, and he juggled them—one, two, three, four, five, six, seven. Then he caught them all and tossed them back to the girl, one by one, and somersaulted to the stage. And the crowd applauded and cheered.

The brothers and the girl bowed and hurried offstage, to where an older woman stood in the wings, watching anxiously. He knew her, too: the woman from the camp who had wanted Rowen to stay. The girl slid her arm around the woman and kissed her on the cheek. Right away another act came onstage, a troupe of dancers and musicians, but he didn't stay to watch. What he had seen made him glad, but he thought that if the family saw him, it would only remind them of a dark time they might rather forget. *Still*, he thought, *I'm getting closer. I must be.*

The days passed and he left that town far behind. Early one morning he was walking along another lonely road in the rain, listening to the soft patter of the drops on the leaves. He thought of Shade, who loved that sound and taught him to love it, too. *You've been looking for something that used to be,* he told himself. *Time to look and see what's really here. It might be something you never expected.*

The rain drew off, and in the woods and fields around him the mist was lifting away. He walked on, but more slowly now, watching and listening with care. In the low places in the road, water had collected in pools, each as still and bright as a mirror. A raven croaked once, flew up from a hazel thicket and flapped away. Somewhere not far off a dog barked. There might be a town nearby, he thought, or a farm. It had been a long time since he'd spoken to anyone.

The sun found its way through the parting clouds and burnished the wet road so that it gleamed like a sheet of gold. He caught the scent of clover. A bee droned past. He walked a little farther, and then he stepped away from the road. He plunged into a leafy hollow alive with butterflies and pollen falling like snow, then climbed up the far side. When he came out of the trees, there it was: a cottage at the foot of a grassy hill, under a sky of fathomless blue. The stones of the front walk had been recently swept and the shutters looked freshly painted. A thread of smoke unwound from the leaning brick chimney. The door was slightly ajar, as if he was expected.

There are no more happy endings, he told his aching heart. But sometimes you find what you have lost.

GLOSSARY OF TERMS

FROM NICHOLAS PENDRAKE'S NOTEBOOKS

APPLEYARD
The citadel of the Errantry in Fable, at the foot of Appleyard Hill, and the highest point in the city. The Errantry's school for knight-apprentices is found here.

THE BOURNE
A small, little-known land somewhere in the Perilous Realm, inhabited mostly by the descendants of travellers from the Untold who found their way to the Realm and stayed. Fable is the Bourne's largest city.

THE ERRANTRY
The Bourne's defensive force, made up of knights-errant, troopers, scouts, and knight-apprentices. The knights of the Errantry take an oath to right wrongs and defend the weak.

THE FATHOMLESS FIRE

Also known as *innumith*, or "storystuff." A mysterious, intangible spirit or power out of which everything in the Perilous Realm is made. Loremasters can draw this secret fire out of the Weaving to shape and heal stories.

FETCHES

Spirits of those whose stories have been devoured by Malabron.

GAAL

Also known as fever iron. A rare ore with marvellous properties that some say is really concentrated *innumith*. Those who ingest this ore gain strength and fearlessness in battle, but in time their craving for the *gaal* becomes a madness.

THE GATHERING HOUSE

The main hall of the Errantry at Appleyard.

THE GREAT UNWEAVING

A dark time after the first war against Malabron, when the Perilous Realm was torn apart and much knowledge was lost.

LOREMASTER

To most people, a mere collector and teller of tales. Loremasters have kept their true vocation —to serve and protect the Realm through the power of the fathomless fire—hidden from all but a few.

MAGE

A wizard or sorcerer who attributes his powers to some vaguely defined "magic." Few mages know of the fathomless fire or understand where it comes from, and as a consequence, they can misuse this power and do great harm to themselves and others.

MORDOG
A race of powerful, warlike beings who serve Malabron and have long been at war with the Fair Folk and other free peoples of the Perilous Realm.

NIGHTBANE
The collective name for the many races that have banded together in the name of Malabron to spread war and terror throughout the Realm.

THE PERILOUS REALM
The world (or worlds) of Story. As vast and never-ending as all the tales that have been told or might be told, the Realm is made up of countless storylands. A traveller cannot always get to one storyland from another by way of a direct road or path, and maps are never very reliable.

THE SHADOW REALM
A region of nightmare set apart from the Perilous Realm, where fetches wander without hope and bloodthirsty harrowers prowl in search of living things to devour. The Shadow Realm continually grows as more stories are swallowed up by the Night King.

THE SPEAKING CREATURES
Birds and beasts given the power of speech by the Stewards. They were scattered and many were lost during the Great Unweaving.

STORYSIGHT
A loremaster's power to see into both the past and the future of Story. Even if a story is lost and forgotten, a gifted loremaster can find traces of it.

THE UNTOLD

A name for the world beyond the Perilous Realm. Many who
live there call the Untold the "real world" and believe that
the realm of Story is only imaginary.

THE WEAVING

Something like the world we visit in our dreams, the Weaving is a hidden "realm within" from which all things arise
and to which they must return, to be woven again into new
stories. The Weaving contains the past and the future, as well
as everything that might have been or never was. Apprentice
loremasters are initiated into the craft by venturing alone
into the Weaving and finding their way back—a difficult and
dangerous journey.

WEREFIRE

A name for *innumith* when it runs out of control and becomes
a destructive force. Power-hungry mages in Skald unleashed
a plague of werefire that nearly destroyed the city.

READ THE EXHILARATING FIRST TWO BOOKS IN THE PERILOUS REALM TRILOGY:

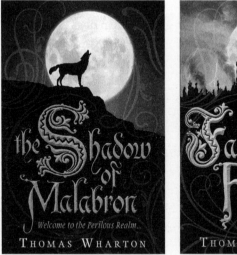

ACKNOWLEDGEMENTS

THIS TRILOGY BEGAN a long time ago with the first story-teller I ever met, my father, Tom Wharton Sr, who introduced me to the spell of a well-told tale.

Thank you to all those who gave encouragement, support, guidance and inspiration over the long haul of three books. To my agent, Lynn Bennett; to my editors: Lara Hinchberger, Amy Black, Chris Kloet, and Janice Weaver; to Nicola Makoway, Merle Jones, Gail and Laurie Greenwood, Susan Toy, and to the late Ralph Vicinanza. Thanks to Linda Quirk, Matt Schneider, Betsy Sargent, and Richard Harrison and family. Thanks to Tim Jessell, Ciruelo Cabral, Chris Hill, and Mary Wharton, the artists. A great big thank you to the students of Malmo School, who wanted to be in the book. Bows to Reverend Masters Mugo White and Koten Benson, and to my sangha, the Edmonton Buddhist Meditation Group.

Many thanks to Bill Thompson for long walks and talks in the realms of Story. Thank you to my family for love and support. Lastly, I am grateful beyond words for Sharon and for our children, Mary, Conor and Ronan, who provided the first spark of the fathomless fire.

For more about the characters, creatures and places of
the Perilous Realm, visit the author's website at
www.thomaswharton.ca